KATHERINE

THE
AZANTIAN
TRILOGY

THE

Girl

WHO

BELONGED

TO THE

SEA

THE GIRL WHO BELONGED TO THE SEA

KATHERINE QUINN

CITY OWL
PRESS

THE GIRL WHO BELONGED TO THE SEA
The Azantian Trilogy, Book 1

CITY OWL PRESS
www.cityowlpress.com

Cover Design by MiblArt. All stock photos licensed appropriately.

Edited by Charissa Weaks.

For information on subsidiary rights, please contact the publisher at info@cityowlpress.com.

Hardback Edition ISBN: 978-1-64898-156-2
Paperback Edition ISBN: 978-1-64898-072-5
Digital Edition ISBN: 978-1-64898-071-8

Printed in the United States of America

To my husband Joshua, who fell in love with the darkest parts of me and painted my world with stars.

THE EXILE

F<small>OR THE FIRST TIME IN A THOUSAND YEARS, THE MAN CRAFTED OF</small> neither flesh nor bone heard a voice—a prayer cast to the seas.

It carried on an impatient breeze, muffled yet brimming with urgency, the speaker's sweet timbre awakening a heart that had long since ceased to beat. The plea was so passionate that it jolted the man from bed, his silk coverlet pooling at his waist in a puddle of ivory.

A prayer.

The man couldn't remember the last time he'd been gifted with such a delicate thing, not since...

Well, not since he'd been stripped of all that he was.

The man had endured countless solitary years hiding behind the faces of others, and now he hardly remembered what his true face looked like.

His brother was to blame for that.

It wasn't the man's fault he wanted the sea for himself, that he desired to be its only ruler. He wanted *his* name whispered on sailors' lips, their lovers murmuring *his* name as they prayed for their husbands and wives to return to them safe and whole.

He hadn't wished to share the throne, and his greed had been his downfall. His punishment? For his memory to be wiped from the earth.

That was no matter now. The man—the *god* who'd been imprisoned in the body of a mortal—felt the stirrings of hope. If *this* prayer had reached him, then that would mean the person he'd waited patiently for had finally come. That, soon, he'd be released from his captivity.

Please, the voice whispered, *I cannot bear the thought of staying with my father any longer. Cannot fathom being under his cruel thumb for another moment.*

A wicked smile quirked the man's lips. He shut his eyes, indulging in the desperate melody of her voice.

I want so much more than this life.

As the woman spoke, her voice soft and full of dulcet lilts, an image began to form behind his closed lids. He glimpsed a rocky cliff shrouded in haze. A towering keep of impenetrable stone. An island of bronze and industry.

And amidst the distorted vision, the man saw *her.*

The woman who had reached him when no others had been able. A woman who was so much more than she seemed behind that innocent beauty.

He could see what she hid beneath her flesh, what was invisible to any who did not know what to look for. What he saw set fire to his blood.

So the man got to work, turning the knob of his lantern and fumbling for the red tome scattered amidst the chaos of papers and crudely drawn sketches, years of ideas and failed plans.

Flipping through the worn and stained pages of the ancient text, he landed upon an image of the island that had haunted him for centuries. An island that, up until a couple decades ago, protected a dangerous relic that could turn the tide in the man's favor.

And fate had just shown him the mortal woman who would help him find it.

I long to be free, the voice begged in the distance, and the man's smile flourished, a plan forming in his mind. All he had to do was align the right pieces and play the pawns already on the board.

And then he would have not only his vengeance but a fierce weapon to command. A weapon his brother would never see coming.

He would finish what he started over a thousand years ago. Though, this time, it would end with him sitting on the one true throne, his brother's blood spilled at his feet.

Oh, I hear your prayers, little one. And soon you will get your wish.

CHAPTER ONE

MARGRETE

MARGRETE WOOD HAD BEEN LOCKED INSIDE HER FATHER'S IRON contraption so many times that she *should* have been used to its rusted spikes, pungent rot, and the absence of light once he shut the door. It was her *penance* for misbehaving, he claimed. A way to cleanse her soul. But it was no more than a coffin. A vicious device he used for control.

When her father slammed the door, trapping her where dreams went to die, Margrete prayed to all the gods she could think of. Arios, the God of Spring and New Beginnings, and Delia, Goddess of Wisdom and Protector of the Pure of Heart. She even prayed to the wrathful God of War and Vengeance, Charion.

Yet only when she envisioned the sea, wild and unapologetically savage, did she receive any kind of answer at all. Trapped in the dark with nothing but her sinking hope, she chased after the elusive sound of the waves. It was soft at first, nothing but the gentle thrum of the waters meeting the shore.

Margrete closed her eyes and held on to that melody like a lifeline. Soon her body trembled and her heartbeat slowed, and then the song swelled.

The moment the waves became a roar in her ears, she released her prayers with a heart-wrenching hope. She wished to be far from her father. Begged for a life that was not her own. Pleaded to be *free*.

When the door to her box opened hours later, her father's wicked face staring back at her, the ethereal song came to an abrupt end. While he'd done his best to weaken her, to rob her of her courage, Margrete left that day clinging to a scrap of hope her father couldn't touch.

The sea had whispered a reply, a single, haunting word.

Soon.

It had been five days since Margrete emerged from the box and left her father's study. Five long days and *still* her body buzzed with apprehension and promise.

Almost as if the God of the Sea had truly heeded her prayers.

Now, she was being called back to the study, urged on by Adina, her lady's maid, who snapped at her heels like an anxious hound. And hurry she did, for every wrong Margrete committed, each act of rebellion, would not only be *her* punishment to bear. Not since her father turned his attention to her younger sister, Bridget, or Birdie, as Margrete fondly nicknamed her.

A thin layer of perspiration dampened her skin by the time she arrived. Lifting a closed fist, she knocked on the heavy wooden door, biting her lower lip as she awaited a reply.

"Come."

Margrete flinched, her father's voice unusually light. Pushing inside, she found the notorious sea captain of Prias lounging in his chair, his booted feet propped against the mahogany desk littered with maps and trade records. His short, flaxen hair and matching beard were sprinkled with age, white streaks interwoven throughout the strands, his square jaw prominent and masculine.

But it was the cutting edge of his gaze that could fell a man with one look.

"Daughter, sit." He waved her over to one of two plush blue seats before him. A devilish smile curled his thin lips, a malicious twinkle sparkling in his steel-gray eyes that promised nothing but torment.

Margrete had always been told that her hazel eyes and golden skin came from her mother. If only she could have met her.

Hesitantly, she slid onto the cushion, her muscles tensing as her father's gaze swept across her body from behind his desk, his forefinger and thumb pinching his graying beard in thought. Uneasy moments ticked by before he spoke, but when he did, she had to grab hold of her chair to keep from falling over.

"You're to be married here, at the keep, in two months' time."

Margrete couldn't help it when a small gasp left her lips, her mouth parting as though a silent scream wished to escape. It was her only reaction, the obedient words she usually reserved for the captain dissipating like dust in a windstorm.

"I see you're quite thrilled with the news, then?" He leaned back in his seat, pulling his muscled legs from the polished wood. "I'll give you a moment to process."

Tiny beads of sweat formed along her brow, the air in the room suddenly too hot, too stuffy. Her heartbeat thundered in her ears, a tumultuous staccato that sounded like angry raindrops during a squall.

"W-who?" she managed to ask, fearful of the answer. Knowing her father, her marriage was to procure some elusive business deal. She would be used for his purposes, however vile they may be, and her opinion on the matter was irrelevant.

"Count Casbian," he said.

"Of Cartus?"

"One and the same." The captain grinned, enjoying the obvious discomfort playing across her features. "Cartus is Marionette's greatest asset for defense, and the count's military position will do well for us. I'm told he's also a favorite amongst the king and queen."

This was about influence. As if conquering the seas wasn't enough, the captain now wished to gain the favor of Marionette's rulers through the count.

"And he *is* quite young," he added, "which is lucky for you. Meaning you won't soon be made a widow."

She didn't allow her bewilderment to show, but the truth was that she'd believed her reputation suffered too great a blow for any man to look her way after what happened two years ago. Then again, her substantial dowry might persuade suitors to overlook her past indiscretions.

She swallowed down the tears at the memory of her father's young guard, Jacob, who'd been foolish enough to fall in love with her. They'd been caught in the act by the captain himself, and to her horror, her father had thrust his dagger into the very heart that had once belonged to her. She was to remain pure until the captain found a match for his daughter that suited his needs, but thanks to Jacob, any purity vanished.

And yet now, none of that seemed to matter.

Pulling herself together, forcing her chin to lift, Margrete addressed the man who relished in misery with an icy calm. "I see," she began, sitting up straighter in her chair. "And this has already been decided? The count has agreed to this as well?"

"Yes." He didn't hesitate.

"And you didn't consult me." The words were out before she had a chance to rein them in.

Storm clouds brewed in his eyes. "*Consult* you?" He let out a mirthless laugh, his eyes drifting to the corner of the study where his sick contraption hid behind a silk screen. The unspoken threat was obvious. "You should consider yourself lucky I've given you this opportunity." He seethed. "I was never awarded such a thing."

The captain didn't speak of his past, of his parents, except for once, five years ago. Margrete woke in the middle of the night and crept down the stairs, only to overhear him arguing with a man. She hadn't recognized the voice, but before he kicked the stranger out of the keep, her father had told him, 'You can slither back into your hovel and tell our *dearest* parents I'm merely showing them the same kindness they did me.'

The captain caught Margrete that night, and without a word, dragged her to the box and shoved her inside. Only when dawn came did he open the door.

They never spoke of the man again.

"Don't make this hard on yourself, daughter," her father said, shaking the memory from her thoughts. "I'd hate for you to receive another lesson so soon after the last."

Margrete shut her eyes, and just like that, she was back inside the confines of the box. Its metal spikes poked at her skin, the smell of her blood fresh in the air. Her breaths quickened as shadows closed in on all sides. Sometimes he'd leave her in there for hours. After Jacob, she'd been trapped for a full day.

What would he do if she refused him now?

Margrete cleared her throat and opened her eyes, willing away the images that haunted her every waking moment. So many thoughts rushed into her mind that she couldn't think clearly, but one stood out amongst the rest.

Perhaps she didn't need to refuse her father. Marriage to the Count of Cartus would change her life, change *everything*. For better or worse, she couldn't say, but it was a way out of this keep and a way to flee her father's control.

There was just one problem.

"If I'm to marry Casbian, who will watch over Birdie? You're frequently gone, and the keep is no place for a young lady to live alone."

Birdie's mother, Margrete's stepmother, had died four years past, and the poor girl still suffered the loss. She needed her older sister now more than ever. Birdie's sweet disposition would never endure under their father's merciless thumb.

"Bridget will remain here," he said. "Under her governess's supervision."

Where she would be his latest victim.

Margrete's stomach clenched, a nauseating ache forming. She couldn't let that happen. She had to be brave now, had to find a way to shift this situation to one of advantage.

And she knew precisely how.

"I never ask much of you, Father," she said, nearly choking on the word, "but I will ask this of you now. One final gift you can give me as a farewell."

He cocked his head, eyes narrowing as he awaited her proposition.

"I would like Birdie, and her governess, to come to Cartus when the count and I set sail for his home. I cannot bear for her to be isolated and far from family." She paused for a single heartbeat. "And surely it would benefit you to have her stationed in Cartus."

Many influential men and their families settled there, and while Birdie was only seven, her early presence might be advantageous for a power-hungry sea captain—though Margrete had no plans to ever allow her little sister to be used in such a way. Her father highly underestimated her if he believed otherwise.

The captain considered, stroking his trimmed beard as he let time stretch thin. She waited, unmoving in her chair. This was a fear tactic he enjoyed using on his adversaries—silence—but she wasn't in the mood to play his games.

"You actually make quite a good point," he said, relenting, though his jaw ticked. "I will strike a bargain with you then. Marry the count without delay and without any of your *theatrics*, and Bridget will be allowed to leave with you to Cartus."

Margrete nodded, though she hardly felt herself move. The fact that her father conceded to her request so easily had her wondering what else was up his sleeve, what other little secret he kept close to his charred heart.

"Thank you," she said, hating the words. "If that is all, then I will leave you to your work." Margrete knew better than to leave the study without his permission, and she waited for him to wave his hand in dismissal, that malicious smile still twisting his mouth.

"Oh, and daughter," he interrupted before she was halfway to the door. She stopped, glancing over her shoulder. "You'd do well to remember the teachings of last week, because if you disappoint me..." He paused as her heart thundered madly.

Teachings. It was what he called his punishments.

"Oh, I never forget, Father," she said, gathering her long skirts and abandoning the captain to his plans.

I will never forget. And one day, I hope to make you pay.

CHAPTER TWO

MARGRETE

MARGRETE FOUND BIRDIE BY THE SEA. IT WAS A LOVELY SPRING DAY in Prias, the typically humid air graced with a refreshing breeze, one that lifted Margrete's skirts as she padded barefoot across the heated sands. Waves crashed against the shoreline as tiny white birds skipped out of the way before the spray could wet their wings. And the skies... They were the loveliest shade of blue—a blended hue of lapis and sapphire.

On days like this one, Margrete wished she'd learned how to swim. Her father forbade her from venturing too close to the waters, and his face would turn a deep shade of purple when she'd argue. She stopped asking years ago—his *teachings* would've only worsened.

A gull screeched overhead, swooping down to graze the tops of the Morning Burst flowers she passed. As she had little else to do when confined to her chambers, Margrete was afforded ample time to read, though she often sought books pertaining to plants, flowers, and the healing properties found within nature. She'd grown rather adept at identifying flora and fauna and wondered if she might have made a decent healer in another life.

But it was the origin of the bloom, with its bright golden center and delicate violet petals, that intrigued her. Legend held that fortunate sailors brought the flower back from the lost island of Azantian. Margrete had heard the tales of the mythical island more times than she could count, the sailors in her father's employ eager to fill the time spent on dry land with stories of the sea.

The story of Azantian was a favorite amongst the men, an island created by the sea god, where the sands were fashioned from the purest gold and the waters gleamed aquamarine. It was a realm of ethereal beings of immense beauty, entrusted with guarding the gates imprisoning the sea's nefarious children—monsters born from the depths. But much like the gruesome sea serpent in her childhood lore, Azantian was a myth crafted for the naïve and the youthful.

Margrete was neither.

Tilting her face to the sun, she took in a quiet moment, soaking up the day's warmth and its fearless light. With the rushing waves in the background and the sounds of the gulls overhead, she willed away thoughts of her father and his decree, pretending that, just for one moment, she was someone else entirely.

Seconds later, that fragile peace shattered like broken glass.

Someone was watching her.

She could all but feel the eyes upon her skin. A rush of awareness caused the hairs on the back of her neck to rise in alarm. She scanned the beach, the uneasy sensation growing stronger with each new breath.

The beach was empty, and the only other person she sighted was Peter, one of her father's most trusted guards. He stood watch beneath the fronds of a palm, his attention solely on the sands just ahead where Birdie played. Still, Margrete couldn't shake what she'd so plainly felt.

"Margrete!" Birdie jumped up from her blanket and rushed across the beach, her blonde curls tossing in the sea wind. With a radiant smile, she crashed into Margrete, wrapping two thin arms around her waist.

All thoughts of danger fled Margrete's mind the moment she enfolded Birdie in her embrace. The small sprite had the gift of chasing all worries away.

"Hello, little bird." Margrete wound her fingers through those unruly blonde strands. "I missed you this morning."

Birdie grumbled a reply, voice muffled by the thick fabric of Margrete's gown. She caught only two words: *pancakes* and *strawberries*. Adina must've prepared her favorite treats for breakfast.

Withdrawing, Birdie clutched Margrete's hand, dragging her across the dunes to a coarse blanket laid out on the sands, a wind-tossed umbrella providing the sanctuary of shade.

"Come sit with me!" Birdie's voice played in harmony with the crashing waves, the sweet timbre as lively as the playful breeze.

Margrete's smile felt genuine for the first time that day as she took her place on the blanket. Birdie instantly crawled into her lap.

"What did Father wish to speak to you about?" Birdie asked. "Adina told me not to pester you, but she was extra sour today." She wrinkled her upturned nose.

Adina was often in a foul mood. Gods, Margrete couldn't recall a time when she wasn't.

Brushing her sister's hair from her piercing blue eyes, she asked, "How would you feel about coming with me to Cartus?"

Birdie squinted up at her. "Cartus? Why would we go there?"

Margrete sighed, tightening her arms around Birdie's middle. "I'm to marry Count Casbian in two months' time. And you, my little one, are to come to his island with me. That is, if you wish."

Birdie paused to consider, her mouth twisting in thought. "Are the beaches in Cartus as pretty as the ones here?"

Margrete nodded. Though she'd only ever seen drawings of Cartus in books, she'd heard about the island's beauty from the lips of others.

"And I would get to be with you? Father will allow it?"

Birdie might be young, but she sensed the darkness in their father, how he could be joyous one moment and a storm of ruinous rage in the next.

Birdie was right to be guarded.

Margrete tilted Birdie's chin. "I will always be beside you. No matter what happens, or where our journey in this life leads," Margrete vowed. "And yes, I have father's permission."

A glorious grin brightened Birdie's face, rosy lips stretching wide.

"Then I can't wait for our new adventures! And hopefully, I'll get a new governess. Mistress Sophia has breath a dragon would reel away from."

She chuckled as Birdie stretched across the blanket and rested her head on Margrete's lap, her eyelids shutting against the blinding sun. It didn't take long before her chest rose and fell in steady breaths, worn from her earlier adventures frolicking along Prias's coast.

Taking in the wild sea, wishing she could, for once, have adventures of her own choosing, Margrete's calm began to dissipate. That same sensation of being watched returned, although this time, her body flooded with ice, even in the rising heat of the day.

Careful not to wake Birdie, Margrete craned her neck, scanning the sloping dunes and bent palms. Nothing but swaying grasses and skittering birds.

She was being paranoid. No one would dare follow the captain's daughter, not if they valued their life.

Margrete shook her head, feeling foolish. Soon she would be free of Prias. Free of the captain. She only had to survive long enough to marry the count and lead her sister to a new life.

A better one.

CHAPTER THREE

MARGRETE

Perched on the tips of her toes, Margrete peered over the ledge of her father's keep, the movement sending an errant pebble tumbling to the rocks a hundred feet below. Her life of unwedded bliss would meet its end today. She and Birdie would sail away for Cartus, and Margrete would have a husband.

She grimaced at the thought and squeezed her eyes closed, instead focusing on the way the waters sang to her from below. The winds shifted, their tangy scent wafting away, replaced by the sweet smell of Morning Bursts.

Margrete gazed out over the city one last time, her stomach in knots for the journey ahead. She'd always felt so conflicted about Prias, now even more so that she was meant to leave. The renowned trading hub was a world of bronze and copper and the rich chestnut wood of the Marionette Forest. Rosy pinks, divine cobalts, and sweet lavenders dyed the buildings, each one assembled atop the other, stacked like sea stones at twilight. For most everyone but her, the city was an enchanting realm of sea spray and untarnished dreams, a glimmering coastal port that led to the stunning continent beyond, a place where people lived and thrived.

"Margrete!" Adina's shrill voice snaked up the steps, severing

Margrete's connection to the sea. The reality of the day crashed against the stone of her heart, eroding the last of her dwindling resolve. "Margrete! Where are you, child?"

After saying goodbye to the waves one last time, Margrete turned for the stairs, silently praying for a miracle, for the God of the Sea to whisk her and her sister far away from here. She was nearly to the steps when a piercing horn shattered the calm, the waves below turning violent as they crashed against the rocks.

She halted, twisting to skim the wild waters. There was nothing but the vast blue ocean. She took in a sharp breath, hoping to ease her fluttering pulse.

Adina shouted again, this time much louder and significantly *less* patient.

"Coming, Adina!" Margrete hurried down the narrow staircase. The handrail, worn from years of use, slid like silk beneath her palm. How many times had she raced to this tower to hide away from the world—and from her father?

Countless.

Margrete nearly collided with a stern-faced Adina on the final step. The older woman's lips stretched into a thin line, eyes pointed and hard.

"Where have you been, girl?" Adina didn't wait for an answer. She grasped Margrete's arm and yanked her down the corridor toward her chambers.

Margrete resisted the urge to wrench away. Her blood boiled—she was no *girl*—but she willed her temper to cool, a task she found more difficult as of late.

"Everything is prepared." Adina motioned to the pressed crimson dress laid out neatly on Margrete's four-poster bed.

She felt confident that the entire city—and perhaps the surrounding ones—heard the cracking of her heart as it transformed to ice. The garment's high neckline had fallen out of fashion, and it promised to suffocate once wrapped around her throat. The flowing sleeves were pretty, though. Lacy and delicate.

Adina shoved Margrete closer to the bed. "Come on, then. Let's begin."

Margrete groaned when the maid retrieved the required underthings and a tight corset with too many laces from her dresser. The thought of the count seeing her wearing such intimate garments made bile rise in her throat.

"Oh, hush," Adina chided. "It won't be that bad. You want to look your best on your wedding night, don't you?"

While answering with a curt "no" was remarkably appealing, it wouldn't do Margrete any favors. This wedding was going to happen whether she wished it to or not. She supposed she needed to find a way to be happy. Marrying the count surely wouldn't be as awful as Margrete and Birdie staying with the captain forever.

Forcing a nod, she allowed Adina to help her dress, wincing when the woman tugged at the corset's strings.

"Hold still!" Adina scolded when she jerked during one particularly harsh pull.

Although Adina was callous and austere, Margrete had to remind herself that the woman had practically raised her. The captain had been too busy conquering the wild sea and capturing trade deals to assume the role of a proper father. Not that he'd ever been in danger of toeing that particular line.

"There." Adina stepped back to admire her careful work of torture. "Now to the final piece."

The dress. Margrete had just stepped into the puddle of red lace when a distant screech rang out from beyond the arched window of her chamber. "What on earth was that?"

Adina frowned. "What was what?"

It didn't sound like a bird, and it was too high-pitched to be a horn aboard one of the ships in the bay. It sounded familiar in ways Margrete didn't understand, but she ignored it.

"Nothing. Let's just get this over with."

Adina worked quickly and soon fastened the final button on the high neck, its ugly ruffles rising to kiss Margrete's cheeks.

"There," the maid said. "Now you look beautiful."

The floor-length mirror depicted the perfect bride—chocolate and caramel strands curled dreamily down her back, wide hazel eyes bright and vibrant, her sharp cheekbones highlighted with a shimmering pink rouge. What the mirror couldn't reflect was the screaming wraith trapped behind her practiced smile. How she mourned her unfulfilled dreams as they turned to ash at her feet.

"Come on, then." Adina headed for the door. "No time to dally."

When she hesitated, Adina huffed in frustration, twisting on a booted heel and waving at her to follow. Margrete scowled but begrudgingly marched toward her fate, but it was the tiny hairs on her arms—all standing at alarming attention—that froze her heavy steps. The horn sounded again, considerably louder. Urgent, almost.

Tilting her head, she closed her eyes and listened for it, only nothing came but a gentle shushing from the sea.

Just as she had months ago in the box, Margrete rolled her head, savoring the reassuring music of the waves. Her own personal lullaby, sung by the God of the Sea, a methodical—

Hello, little one...

Her eyes shot open.

Was she hearing things? No. There *had* been a voice. Albeit an eerie and peculiar one, but—

"Hurry, child!" Adina's shouts disrupted Margrete's concentration, and she shuddered back to reality.

Nerves. It had to be nerves driving her to madness.

Gathering her skirts, she chased down the stairs with a foreign grace. Not known for her poise, Margrete struggled in her new heeled shoes, her ankles wobbling on each rugged step. *Maybe I'll tumble to my death before this damned wedding can even begin.*

But alas, she didn't meet her end by means of too-high shoes. Instead, she landed on the bottom floor of the keep's main hall with a grimace.

Broad arches of polished silver and gold framed the lofty space, a sitting room filled with dazzling portraits, extravagant furniture, and colorful carpets of varying designs bringing wealth and opulence to a home that lacked heart. Waiting for Margrete, seated in a high-backed chair of obsidian velvet, was her father.

His gaze narrowed, the weathered skin around his eyes crinkling with sick joy and unmistakable triumph. He scanned her from the top of her head to her heeled feet. "You look...acceptable. Although, a bit pallid."

Rising from his seat, the captain smoothed the linen of his onyx trousers, squaring his broad shoulders as he towered above her. He was a fit man for his age, the years having done nothing to rob him of his threatening stature.

"I'm sorry, Father," Margrete made herself say, the tips of her ears heating with anger.

She'd noticed the dark circles under her eyes and the lifelessness of her skin in the mirror earlier. As she'd slept little as of late, the sight wasn't a surprise, but she despised having to apologize for something beyond her control.

Sleep shouldn't have been a problem. In truth, she *should* consider herself lucky. Her father had the opportunity to wed her off to a decrepit man with wrinkled skin and missing teeth, yet he chose a suitor of similar age. A *handsome* man, if the rumors she'd heard over the last two months were correct.

Since the announcement, she'd exchanged five letters with Count Casbian of Cartus, his elegant script filled with tender promises. His correspondence painted him as compassionate and kind, but Margrete surmised people differed from what they appeared to be behind the guise of words. She had to remind herself that no matter what his letters portrayed him as, the count was a stranger, using her for the same reasons as her father.

A muffled giggle floated from behind the captain, snagging Margrete's attention. She'd know that wonderful sound anywhere, and it forced her lips to quiver into a semblance of a smile.

"You look beautiful." Birdie hopped out from behind Father's chair, her blonde curls intricately braided into a golden crown.

Margrete scooped Birdie up in a spin. "You're the beautiful one, sister." She gave Birdie's rosy cheek a quick peck before setting her down gently.

Tying herself to a man she didn't know would all be worth it if she could save her sister from her father's wrath.

"Ready?" Birdie clutched Margrete's hand with a fierce grip, her tiny fingers warm and reassuring. She nodded, fearing that any more words might come out shaky or trembling, exposing her mounting anxiety. She fought this fear, though, for the sight of her sister gave her strength.

"Well." Captain Wood interrupted the moment. "Let's not keep Count Casbian waiting." The corners of his eyes lifted as if this was the happiest of days. He took her arm, aiming her toward the double doors leading to the courtyard.

As though summoned, two uniformed guards stalked down the main hall. After a curt nod from her father, the men pushed open the doors, revealing Margrete's inevitable future in the near distance.

Ignoring the pounding within her chest, she lifted her eyes as her father walked her into the sunlight. Overlooking the bay and bustling docks, the spacious courtyard had been transformed into a seaside spectacle of flowing green vines and blooming violet buds. The aisle parted a sea of wooden chairs, each tied with satin bows of shimmering cherry red. Seated were the nobility and those of importance from Prias and the island of Cartus—men and women with whom her father consorted. They all twisted to catch a first glimpse of the bride, their calculating eyes squinting through the golden rays.

Margrete looked beyond the guests, finding the towering figure of her soon-to-be husband across a sweeping courtyard of wildflowers and seashells. Count Casbian stood beside a holy man at the end of the aisle, the bright swirls of pink and tangerine clouds framing him like a pretty picture. And he *was* pretty. She could see his handsome face now as her steps brought her closer to the man to whom she was to vow forever.

He lifted his square jaw, a thin coating of stubble shadowing his features in the dwindling afternoon light. He rolled his broad shoulders, and his muscular arms flexed beneath the fitted fabric of his tunic—arms any girl would swoon over.

And if his impressive stature wasn't enough to sway a hesitant bride, his face completed the masterpiece—cerulean eyes sparkling with mischief, a dazzling, flawless smile of sincerity, and deftly combed blue-black hair that resembled raven's feathers.

He was a dream.

He *should* have been Margrete's dream.

Yet even though he was painfully attractive and all of his letters indicated that he was kind, dense dread settled in her stomach like an iron anchor. It grew heavier the closer she came to her betrothed, her feet dragging.

The captain played the part of the proud and fawning parent, ever the gentleman and loving father. Only those in attendance couldn't see how his grip bruised her, his hold more punishing than affectionate. He led her with grace and poise down the aisle, past those scorching gazes, precisely to where her groom awaited.

"You look stunning, Margrete." Casbian bowed and reached for her hand, placing a chaste kiss upon her knuckles. His lips looked as soft as pillows, and Margrete wondered what it would be like to kiss them. She supposed she would find out soon enough.

Swallowing the lump in her throat, she steeled her gaze on the man bowed low before her. "A-as do you," she sputtered, her voice ragged and breathless.

The count smiled wide, his teeth blinding her with their pearly brilliance. Everything about him was *too* perfect. He was beautifully unsettling, much like a red-ringed moon on a cloudless night.

The holy man cleared his throat, drawing Margrete's gaze. He was young given his station, and his eyes were the purest shade of turquoise she'd ever seen. Although he assessed her with a note of pity, he was likely another of her father's sycophants planted in the church. She'd lost track of how many "righteous" were under his thumb.

He opened his book to the proper place. "Let us begin."

Margrete turned from the holy man and his unusual eyes, daring to meet those of her intended.

Suddenly, she couldn't breathe. It was happening. Margrete Wood was about to be married. Destined to follow the whims of this stranger and bear his children.

Little black dots flashed across her vision, her hands instinctively going to her neck, fingers digging at the fabric around her throat. It was so hot, the thick air lacking its typical salty breeze.

Was everyone else hot?

She stole a quick peek to her right, eyeing the nobles in all of their finery. They appeared content. Why wouldn't they be? They were at the wedding of the year, their smug faces morphing into one sea of ugly superiority.

Her father pulled her wandering hand to her side, his eyes reproachful.

"On this fateful day, we bind two souls—" The holy man continued, but Margrete ignored the rest of his memorized speech. She was too distracted by something else she'd heard.

Again.

That shrill noise returned, the one that had followed her all day. Yet this time, it came in short blasts of three.

Scanning the crowd, Margrete found not one person reacting to the jarring sirens, their eyes trained dutifully on the bride. Oblivious, all of them.

Something's wrong.

Sweat dripped down her back, making the lace itchy. Her fingers longed to scratch, yank, and pull at her skin, but the lace wasn't the only thing making her skin prickle.

Ignoring the pointed glare from her father, Margrete's hand went to her neck again, tugging the tight fabric from her throat. She was suffocating, sheer panic igniting in her core.

The holy man kept talking, clearly unaware of her growing discomfort, and her intended smiled, as if the world were being gifted to him on a silver platter.

Internally, Margrete cursed them both.

But again came the screeching, same as before—three sharp pangs of warning.

Why is no one else hearing that?

Margrete looked over Casbian's shoulder, gazing at the waves, searching for the source of the sound.

"...it is important for a wife to abide by her husband..."

Nothing was out of the ordinary. The same colossal ships filled the aquamarine cove below the keep. Many of them bore her father's sigil of a gilded hawk, its wings outstretched across shades of red and onyx.

"...to carry out his wishes and wants..."

Margrete scanned the ships for anything out of place until her eyes finally landed on a brilliant blue vessel that hadn't been there an hour before.

"...she mustn't raise her voice or question..."

Captivated by the unfamiliar craft, Margrete stared at its lustrous sails, noting how the early evening light cast eerie shadows on the canvases. Amber flecks glistened like tiny starbursts against the cobalt hull, a polished silverhead reaching into the sky like a sharpened spear in flight. Fixed to the bow, a spindly octopus figurehead kept watch, two black gems vigilant in the light of the dying sun.

Margrete had never seen a ship like it.

It was magnificent in the way a gale could be devastating.

"...this will ensure a happy union, one that will last the test of time..."

There. A glint of silver caught her eye. Painted on one of the sails was a shining crescent moon, a golden star pinned to its center. Freckles of gold dotted the cloth, framing a sigil that looked so very familiar. It reminded her of a mystical symbol she'd only seen drawn in books—in childhood fairy tales, to be exact. It was a symbol of death. Rebirth.

One of myth.

"Margrete!" Her father's hushed voice shook her out of her daze. "The man asked you a question," he hissed between his teeth.

The count shifted, avoiding his bride's eyes. She was meant to say I do, or yes, or whatever words would tie her forever to a man she did not love.

"I—"

The sun had nearly set, her dreams for a future all her own setting with it. *Something's wrong, something's wrong—*

"Margrete!" Her father hissed again, louder. "Say it," he ordered, no longer hiding his irritation.

And then another set of shrill sirens split the air. Margrete covered her ears and cried out.

Count Casbian, to his credit, embraced her as the stinging of the alarm wormed its way into the deepest recesses of her spirit.

On the third and concluding ring, the sirens ceased, leaving the air still and haunting. Nothing. Not even a wayward bird sang or a breeze dared bluster.

Casbian's soft hands helped her rise. The guests sat stunned, mouths agape in speechless disdain. Her father would surely punish her for—

The sound returned. Louder than before and wholly penetrating.

This time, everyone noticed.

CHAPTER FOUR

MARGRETE

In half of a timid heartbeat, the world as Margrete knew it twisted and tore like fragile silk. A surge of strange men in leather tunics stormed the courtyard walls, a dozen more raiders in matching leathers advancing from inside the keep, their weapons slick with fresh blood. They aimed for her father's guards, raising their shining swords high in the air as bloodlust shadowed their eyes.

The guests screamed, shoving one another as they pushed their way to safety, sending satin-wrapped chairs and decorative vases crashing onto the courtyard's ivory stones. It was madness, and it all happened in the space of a single breath.

At her side, Margrete's father roared, commanding his men to action, spittle flying from his lips. He clenched his jaw and freed his sword from its scabbard.

"Push them back! Form a perimeter around the guests! Move!" His enraged cries drifted seamlessly into the howling chorus of answering soldiers, those sworn to protect the captain and his family at the cost of their own lives.

Margrete glanced behind her, expecting to see the holy man cowering in fear, but he was gone, missing somewhere amongst the screeching guests.

Her heart thrummed. Her sister.

A cold sweat trickled down Margrete's back as she remained rooted in place, scouring the crowd for a familiar head of blonde curls. From far away, muffled as though the world had been dipped underwater, a voice she'd recognize anywhere wafted to her ears. Her gaze followed the sound.

Birdie stood across the courtyard, a mess of curls and tear-stained cheeks. She let out an ear-piercing wail as her governess flung her over a shoulder, and a pair of guards ushered them inside the keep. Margrete prayed that her sister was well on her way to safety in the cellars where she'd be protected by guards and steel walls.

She couldn't let herself believe otherwise.

A muscular body slammed into Margrete, causing her to lurch forward into the bustling crowd of flailing limbs. A sharp elbow struck her in the ribs just as a boot connected with her calf, pain lancing up and down her leg. Her knees gave out, but two strong arms wrapped around her midsection, yanking her back from the fray.

"Careful, darling."

The voice whispered into her hair, the sound sending a bolt of electricity shooting down her arms. For the briefest moment, she saw crashing waves and lightning racing across open skies, tumultuous winds laced with salt and fury. Felt the sway of the sea beneath her feet.

She blinked.

The arms around her waist tightened, and the stranger's breath warmed her cheek.

A flash caught her eye, a golden sigil ring on the man's long pointer finger with two intertwined circles etched into the gleaming metal. It looked old. Valuable.

Before she could turn her head, a rush of air replaced the hands that had gripped her so reverently. She spun around—

Only to come face to face with a bewildered Casbian.

"There you are!" His eyes were wild, searching her for injuries.

Her hands flew to his chest as she caught herself, fists gripping his wrinkled shirt now stained with blood. Thoughts of the strange man and his peculiar ring were forgotten.

"My sister—" She spoke in a rushed panic, but Casbian cut her off.

"Your sister is safe, but we're not. We need to find another route. They're overrunning the courtyard!"

More attackers dove into the mayhem, descending upon guards and fleeing guests, blocking all exits, and crushing any hope of escaping through the main keep. The only option for getting out alive was to make it to the courtyard's edge, where a hidden stairway led to the shore below.

"The stairs," she blurted, the words coming out in short pants. "There are stairs hidden at the far side. Concealed behind a trellis."

"Then we must go. Now!" The count snatched Margrete's hand and held it tight, dragging her into the melee and toward the stairs.

Margrete and the count narrowly avoided the pointed end of a blade as they pushed toward the courtyard's perimeter. The sword, belonging to a bronzed giant, sliced a guard's skull clean open.

The guard didn't even have the chance to scream.

With a yank on her hand, Casbian pulled Margrete beneath the cover of an overturned reception table. The pair caught their breath as they assessed the distance they had to travel to avoid a similar fate as the guard.

When an opening presented itself, Casbian yelled, "Now!"

Once again, he yanked Margrete to her feet, and then they were jumping over fallen bodies. Her muscles screamed, but she didn't stop, not even when a leather-clad woman, strapped with daggers, appeared from within the sea of men.

Her thick blonde hair was intricately braided into her scalp, blood and dirt streaking her face as she raised her sword, effortlessly parrying with those who were brave enough to meet her rapid blows. Blood spattered Margrete's dress, her hair, her cheeks.

Still, they ran, Casbian's fingers gripping hers painfully. They sprinted along the curvature of the courtyard's stone walls, the keep and the ruined altar at their backs. Another twenty feet would bring them to the stairs, where an overflowing trellis hid the entrance.

Margrete glanced over the stone edge down to the beach and caught sight of a dozen metal grappling hooks digging into the courtyard's high walls. Thick coils of rope dangled down the sides of the keep, leading to unadorned rafts tied with rough-spun twine rocking against the perilous bluffs. The intruders must have paid the patrol to access such an advantageous position, and she couldn't fathom how much blood they had spilled to ensure the alarm bells weren't sounded.

She didn't see much more before the count hauled her toward the trellis, and then down the steep flight of steps camouflaged by the rocks, an escape route invisible to the naked eye unless one knew where to look.

At the bottom, a small fishing boat sat tied to a single wooden post, a modest vessel that hardly looked big enough for two. Safety was so close, but every time Margrete blinked, she saw empty, lifeless eyes and the red-painted stones of the courtyard.

They were halfway down the stairs when instinct urged Margrete to pause and glance over her shoulder once more. Maybe it was her friend, the sea, whispering a secret in her ear, or perhaps it was sheer intuition that had her taking in the most roguish pirate she'd ever glimpsed.

He stood atop the steps, hands clutching a thick rope with an iron hook on the end, his deep auburn hair dancing across his forehead. He squinted at the light of the setting sun, and while the distance between him and Margrete was great, the disdain he wore on his sharp features was unmistakable.

A burning chill chased the length of her spine. This man was violence and promised ruin all wrapped into one wicked present.

Margrete's breath caught in her throat. Surely he wouldn't follow them down these treacherous stairs, not unless the count was his target. Casbian was just as much a prize as her father.

She shook her head at the man, praying he would turn away and abandon them to their flight, but no, the bastard set his eyes on Margrete and Count Casbian as if they were *all* that he sought, as if everything in his life depended on cornering them.

"Margrete!" Casbian grabbed her hand. "Come!"

She let him guide her, but two steps later she lost her footing on a worn step. A pebble scattered from beneath her heel, plunging to the spiked rocks below.

That would be her if she weren't careful.

Gripping the count's hand tighter, she didn't look back until a thundering roar demanded her to turn. She almost wished she hadn't.

The man flashed a nefarious smile before raising his arm, swinging the hooked end of his rope round and round.

Margrete froze. "Casbian. Look!"

The count stumbled at her abrupt stop, but he too turned to stare.

The rogue slung the rope into the air, the metal hook catching purchase on a jagged ledge. He tugged it twice, and then, without a trace of hesitation, stepped off the side of the keep, his rope unfurling until it went slack.

"Gods!" Casbian peered along the side of the cliff. "We need to hurry!"

He jerked Margrete down the steps, but she couldn't take her eyes off the pirate and how he arced through the air with the grace of a hawk, his coppery hair catching the gold of the dying sunset. He flew toward them on a furious breeze until his shiny black boots collided with effortless ease on solid rock mere steps away.

He closed the gap between himself and Margrete *and* her count, who clutched her arm hard enough to bruise. She shuffled down one step, but the pirate only followed, his muscular frame eclipsing the sun, casting her in his conquering shadow.

The rogue leaned close, close enough that Margrete could make out the glint of emerald shining in his shrewd eyes, the hint of gold flecking his irises. She could practically taste the brine clinging to his clothes, his hair, his lips.

And here she'd wished for a miracle from the God of the Sea, a savior —something this man most certainly was not.

Fumbling behind her, Casbian grabbed at a jeweled dagger in his belt, a weapon more for show than a fair fight.

"Stay back!" Holding out the gilded blade, the count protectively shoved Margrete against the cliff wall. He made a few feeble jabbing motions at their attacker, but the pirate blocked Casbian's every attempt. Finally, he smirked and twisted the dagger from the count's grasp with such ease that Margrete almost missed it.

On a shaky breath, she said, "Who *are* you?"

The pirate's grin widened, indicating that he'd indeed heard her query, but he didn't speak. Instead, with a single motion—one that was too quick and precise for the count to anticipate—the man kicked her betrothed in the gut.

Casbian let out a choked cry as his limp frame tumbled down the steep flight of stairs. He landed in a messy heap of silk sleeves and raven hair on the stone banks.

"Casbian!" She prayed for a sign that he was still breathing. Thankfully, she glimpsed the rise and fall of his chest even as he succumbed to unconsciousness.

Stationed between her helpless groom and a man with murder in his eyes, the weight of the moment struck her. It was such an abhorrent and selfish thought given the carnage above her, but...

This was it. Her chance to escape not only the count and an unwanted marriage, but also her father. This was Margrete's moment to risk it all and taste the elusiveness of freedom.

Unfortunately, she had to deal with this damned pirate first.

It was with this scrap of daring that she turned toward her attacker and lunged up the steps, wrapping her hands around the silver hilt of the sword dangling from the rogue's hip.

He was taken aback by her unexpected move, and that wolfish grin fell from his face for the ticking of a second as she tightened her grip on his weapon. His large, calloused hands covered hers around the hilt, warm and firm.

She yanked, a growl vibrating in her throat, but the pirate—nor his sword—budged an inch. This man was solid, his hold unyielding, a giant in the land of mortals. Margrete might as well have been fighting a stone wall.

"You're going to hurt yourself, princess." Amusement brightened his severe features, his eyes drinking in her struggle. One that was shamefully futile.

"Then *leave*," she ground out between her teeth, sweat coating her brow. "I don't take too kindly to armed men who wish to kill me. And, believe me, I'm no princess."

The pirate cocked his head, the glint in his eyes almost admiring. "I'm afraid I cannot leave. Not without you, anyway."

"Me?" She refused to give up just yet, not that she had much remaining hope of robbing him of his weapon. "I'm nobody." She wasn't, not in the grand scheme of things. "Just let me go, and I won't be in your way."

The stranger's lips twitched, but he didn't respond, only smiled that coy grin of his, one that dripped of wicked promises.

She wouldn't make it to that boat, not if he had anything to do with it.

Margrete loosened her grasp, her palms slick with sweat and nerves. She itched to run, but the pirate held fast to her hands.

She thought of all the times she'd asked her father to let her train with his men. To learn how to defend herself should the need arise. Of course, he would never allow such a scandalous thing. After today, she supposed he might live to regret not conceding to her request.

Before the sun and its light abandoned this wretched day of ruin, Margrete made one final attempt. With the last of her strength, she jerked her knee up and landed a blow.

Directly between her attacker's legs.

He doubled over, a crude curse flying from his full lips. The hands that had enfolded hers dropped to clutch at himself, causing Margrete to stumble backward at the sudden release, the heavy sword coming with her.

Margrete's balance was all but lost as she grappled for the safety of the cliffside. She hoped to steady herself, to regain some scrap of control, but her head collided into a crag jutting from the rocks, and her vision swam.

With her world tilting on its axis and black dots prickling her sight, she teetered forward on unsteady feet, darkness blooming behind her eyes and blotting out the setting sun. The weapon slid from her grasp and clattered to the stones.

And then, she fell.

CHAPTER FIVE

MARGRETE

Death was not at all how Margrete pictured it.

Billowing amber curtains played with shards of moonlight, and briny sea air blustered through a rounded window. The wind made a *whooshing* sound as it passed through—the sea exhaling nice and deep. It was soothing, much like a thick wool blanket on a frosty winter morning. Margrete's body also rocked back and forth as if she were in a giant cradle, the motion both calming and nauseating.

Death wasn't meant to be nauseating.

With a groan, she shifted onto her elbows and the room swirled. Everything morphed into a blur of wood, linen, and night.

"Easy there, princess."

She jerked to attention and scanned the poorly lit room—or what she now realized was a ship cabin—searching for the source of that deep, full voice. Her sight sharpened as it landed on a dark figure standing in the far corner. Only the flickering light of a single oil lamp illuminated his rugged face, one that, while handsome, held the tension of a man twice his age.

He was dressed in different clothing than what he'd worn during the attack. During her *wedding*. Still, he was unmistakable.

The pirate.

She shot up, her back ramrod straight against the narrow headboard. The swift movement didn't bode well with her dizziness, and her stomach churned.

The pirate held up placating hands. "Whoa, whoa. Take it easy." He pushed off from the wall, straightening his spine as he stood to his full height—well over six-and-a-half feet.

Instead of leather and armor and weapons clinging to his body like a second skin, he sported a simple white tunic, a loose-fitting jacket, and dark trousers. His unassuming attire did nothing to disguise the predator lurking within.

This close, Margrete could make out the swirling tattoos of onyx strands weaving across his tanned skin. Deep gashes and whirls of crashing waves, anchors, and sea stars. A dolphin—frozen in midair—decorated his right forearm, while the left featured a shark with jagged teeth. More tattoos poked out from beneath his rolled-up shirt sleeves, and she wondered what other creatures painted his flesh.

"You," she grumbled, the remnants of sleep coating her voice. Her fingers twisted in the sheets. "What am I doing here?"

The rogue took another step into the light, the lamp's meager flames highlighting the strands of russet mingling with the deep red of his hair. That ray of light flickered briefly, as if winking, and illuminated an old scar running through his right eyebrow.

"What happened?" Margrete asked, her memory foggy.

"Ah," he scoffed, the corners of his mouth rising into a shrewd grin. "You kneed me, quite hard I might add, right before nearly tumbling off the cliff and to your death. You're welcome, by the way."

"*Welcome?*" she snarled. "You kidnapped me!"

There was no way she would've gone anywhere with him willingly.

Margrete flinched when the pirate sauntered to the chair situated before a decrepit vanity and dragged it across the planks to the bed. Taking a seat, he kicked up both legs on the thin mattress, his scuffed boots speckled with dried blood.

"See, I don't really like that word. *Kidnapped* is rather...harsh. From the looks of things, I saved you, princess. Hell, if anything, you should thank me for rescuing you from a life with that pompous ass from Cartus." He shrugged, full lips drawn into a thin line.

Margrete couldn't tell if he was joking or not. Her nostrils flared in response.

"Thank you? You slaughtered my people. Cut down innocent lives to further whatever agenda you have, one likely driven by your own barbaric greed. The day I'll thank you is the day you're buried ten leagues under the sea." Each word was lined with tangible disgust, and Margrete was proud her voice held firm. She raised her chin defiantly.

The pirate cocked his head and reached into his jacket to pull out a simple dagger. He laid it on his lap, his eyes never leaving hers. "Someone has a sharp tongue." He *tsked*. "I'd be careful if I were you, in case I have the sudden urge to cut it out."

A vicious shiver raced down her spine. Something told her that he would never—*could* never—do such a thing. Then again, he'd killed her fellow men, hadn't he?

As if sensing her discomfort, he smirked and reached into his pocket, this time to retrieve a shiny red apple. "Care for a bite? Or have you quelled your hunger by imagining my death?"

"What I'd care for is an explanation." Venom sharpened her tongue, though she surmised coming close enough to kiss death aided in her daring.

His smirk fell. "If you deserved an explanation, I'd readily give you one, but you're entitled to nothing from me."

"What does that even mean? Has my father cheated you in some way?" Gods, it wouldn't surprise her that this nightmare had been birthed from a deal gone wrong. Perhaps this rogue sought to ransom her. What other reason could there be?

A light dimmed inside the pirate's eyes, the fire within settling to smoke.

Just as quickly as the shadows formed, they dispersed, replaced with a mocking gleam that was somehow even more unsettling. At least the virulent glare had been real.

This was simply a mask.

"So it *is* my father." It wasn't a question. "Tell me what he's done. Why did you take me? On my wedding day of all days? How did you manage to get through to the docks? To evade the guards?" She was breathless by the time the final word fell from her lips.

Across from her, his hand curled around the apple, bruising the fruit. "It was simple, really. We walked right through the front doors. It didn't take much to bribe the dockmaster, and the soldiers less than loyal to your father were smart enough to accept our gold. The rest, we…"

The rest he slaughtered.

Margrete gripped the thin sheets. She didn't share much love for her father's men, but needless death set her blood on fire.

"It wasn't as if the guests at your little ceremony were all that innocent," he continued. "According to my spies, most were despicable enough to partner with your father in his lucrative slave trade. The women were spared, but they were likely implicit."

Her fists unfurled, rage morphing into horror. She hadn't known her father dealt with slaves. Or perhaps she'd chosen to ignore the signs. The knowledge might've broken her entirely.

"I didn't know," she uttered, not as convincingly as she hoped.

"Of course, you didn't," he sneered. "Are you that ignorant? Or are you merely content to turn a blind eye to the atrocities committed beneath your own roof?"

She swallowed hard. How dare he make assumptions about her? He knew nothing.

"Perhaps there were more atrocities under that roof than you can fathom," she replied. This man had no idea what she'd been through in that keep. What horrors she'd suffered. If he knew, then she doubted he'd speak to her as if she were some spoiled princess.

He stared at her, long and hard, almost as if trying to see a lie, but then his gaze softened, just slightly, and he looked away.

"The sirens," she said, needing to break the awkward silence. "Those were yours?"

He looked at her again, eyes narrowing in a way that wasn't cruel or malicious. He took her in as if attempting to solve a puzzle with missing pieces.

That curiosity shifted to something else, something that made her feel weighed and measured. It wasn't how the men of Prias stared at her during chaperoned visits through the market. Those men were always mindful of who she was and only glanced her way from the corners of their eyes. They were careful. This man was not, but then again, he had no reason to be.

"You heard the sirens?" he asked.

"Yes. I've never heard anything quite like it, and I've lived by the sea my entire life." Gods, at the altar she'd doubled over from the sound.

"Hmmm." He sat back, rubbing his scruffy chin. "Interesting."

"Interesting how?"

He ignored her question, swallowing a bite of his apple and licking his lips, instantly drawing her attention to his mouth. It was viciously sly, a devastating weapon all its own. His lips twitched, smugly aware of where she stared.

"Eyes up here, Margrete." His tongue flicked the tops of his teeth mockingly, and she hated that she blushed.

"I suppose I shouldn't be surprised you know my name."

"Oh, I know a lot about you," he said cryptically, giving her a tight-lipped smile.

He crossed his arms over his muscled chest, the only tell that he might have been uncomfortable, out of his element. The rest of him didn't betray uncertainty or anything but a heavy dose of cockiness.

"As much as I love you dancing around my questions, I've had an eventful day. How about we get to the point. If only so I don't have to hear the grating sound of your voice." The last words were meant to harm, but they had the opposite effect. The bastard's grin grew, and this time, it appeared genuine.

"You're here because you're useful to me," he replied. "Because your father is a clever man. But more importantly, because he is a thief."

So it *was* about money. Utterly predictable. But...

"A thief? My father doesn't have to steal anything. He's the wealthiest man in Prias besides the king."

"That's where you're wrong." Tossing his apple core to the floor, he abruptly stood, nearly knocking the chair to the ground.

Margrete eyed him up and down as if he were an opponent she'd fight. Maybe she *would* have to fight him at some point, if she was ever going to get away from him.

But then he turned and aimed for the door. He was going to leave her alone—which wasn't a bad thing.

"And what do I call the man who may or may not be extorting my *thief* of a father?" she called, unable to help herself.

His hands closed into loose fists. She was sure he wasn't going to reply at all, but then he looked over his shoulder. "Bash," he said, his steps frozen on the planks.

Bash. She inadvertently mouthed the name, her lips tingling.

As though battling some inner demon, he reluctantly turned around. The lantern light casting ghoulish shadows beneath his striking eyes. "There's a change of clothing in that trunk." He jerked his head toward the corner of the cabin where a faded green chest beckoned. "Your current...attire"—his gaze fell to the delicate lace of her gown—"is hardly appropriate for a ship."

Margrete was still in her wedding dress, the pristine crimson now stained and streaked with mud and speckled with blood. She could smell it, the blood, the subtle tang of copper wafting to her nostrils. And yet, when she reached to touch her cheeks—which had been painted in red and sweat back at the keep—she felt nothing but smoothness, the scent of fresh soap nearly masked by the fragrance of death.

Briefly, she noticed Bash's eyes drifting to another corner of the cabin, the one nearest her bed, before he hastily glanced away. Something akin to guilt flashed across his proud features. She traced back to where he'd looked. A bowl of water had been shoved into the shadows, a stained cloth draped over its rim.

He'd cleaned her face. Wiped away the grit and blood. She didn't know what to make of the thoughtful act.

She returned her gaze to the man who held her fate in his hands, refusing to believe he possessed an ounce of decency. How could he when the blood in that bowl contained the remnants of men he slaughtered?

Her thoughts raced as he watched her intently. He seemed to stare right through her, past the skin and bone, beyond the forced bravado and cutting words. She cursed how her heart thundered in reply.

"You looked relieved on the rocks. Still do," he observed, breaking the peculiar moment. "You didn't want to wed him."

"Relieved? Far from it."

"Well, you hardly seemed concerned when your soon-to-be husband was left unconscious and bleeding on the dock. You called his name, but barely gave him a second glance."

Of course, she'd been concerned, worried for the count's wellbeing. At least, she *thought* she had been...or maybe it was only the type of concern one expressed for a stranger, which, truthfully, he was.

"I hardly knew him." The words stunned her as they fell from her lips.

No. She knew him from his letters. He was kind, considerate, and thoughtful. Yes, Count Casbian was going to deliver her from her father and...

And what? Offer her the freedom she so craved? Doubtful.

Margrete hurried to correct herself, her slip filling the space with a weighted silence. "What I meant was that—"

"I believe I understood you the first time." Bash cocked his head to the side, appraising her, almost as if seeing her for the first time. "Your eyes tell me the truth all by themselves."

"And what do they say, pray tell?" She meant to sound derisive and scornful, but her words were soft and uncertain instead. No one had ever cared to read her before, to look into her eyes and wonder what secrets she kept close to her heart. That had to be the reason she held her breath and awaited the pirate's response. This man, whose burning gaze lingered in a way that should've been uncomfortable.

Gods, she was being an idiot. Why should she care what a—

"My people believe the eyes carry the truths of the soul. And yours, princess, are the saddest eyes I have ever beheld."

Margrete's breath caught, a steel band wrapping around her chest. Before she could deny the claim, Bash spoke.

"Sleep," he said, his deep voice turning gravelly and rough. "Tomorrow's a big day."

Again, he turned to leave.

Anxiety gripped Margrete. She shot to her feet, knees wobbling as she adjusted to the sway of the vessel. "What's happening tomorrow? Where are you taking me?"

He stopped and turned to face her. She suspected he wouldn't divulge their destination, but she had to try. To do or say *something* now that reality was setting in.

The corner of his mouth curved, and his gaze slowly washed over her body, lingering until he met her eyes again. His slow perusal caused heat to flood her cheeks, and at the sight of her reaction, his eyes turned a shade darker.

She crossed her arms over her chest, but the damage had already been done.

Bash grinned, though his smile was anything but warm. "What happens tomorrow is that we sail to my home. A place very, very far from here." He opened the door and stepped into the shadows beyond, but with one last look said, "If I were you, I'd get some rest, Miss Wood. "You're going to need it."

CHAPTER SIX

BASH

Bᴀsʜ ʜᴀᴅ ʙᴇᴇɴ sɪᴛᴛɪɴɢ ᴀᴛ ʜɪs ᴅᴇsᴋ ғᴏʀ ᴛʜᴇ ᴘᴀsᴛ ᴛᴡᴏ ʜᴏᴜʀs, patiently listening while Adrian, his commander and oldest friend, argued with one of his top soldiers. Atlas, young and stubborn, refused to back down, even before her superior.

"All I'm saying is we should've tried to hunt him down." She sat back in her chair and swung her golden, braided hair over her shoulder. Blood from the attack still speckled her face, though she wore it proudly. "His daughter was never our mission. We only chose this day because we assumed his guard would be down, but the bastard got away."

"I've told you, Atlas," Adrian began, "it was a last-second call." He glanced at Bash. "Even with all our men, we lost sight of Wood. We were lucky enough to get his daughter."

"I still don't understand *how* he got away," she grumbled. "We had all eyes on him, and then he was just...gone." She snapped her fingers. "Like that."

The two began to argue, but Bash was silently thinking of everything they had done wrong. All of his warriors had been directed to capture Captain Wood, and they were familiar with the exit points of the keep. The few spies he'd smuggled into the city weeks ago managed to create blueprints so that nothing was left to chance. Even still, the bastard had slipped between his fingers. When he'd seen Margrete fleeing with her groom, she became an opportunity.

One he hoped he didn't regret taking.

"We stick to the new plan," Bash said, interrupting their squabbling. Atlas instantly shut her mouth. "We use his daughter. Trade her. It was decided the second she was taken aboard this ship."

Atlas muttered something under her breath. Adrian shot her a look of warning.

"If that's all, then we're finished here." Bash pushed off from his desk, the top of which was covered with maps of Prias and the surrounding islands. "You should both get some rest." It was well past the time for sleep, and he could see the exhaustion weighing their eyes.

Adrian nodded in agreement. He was a man of few words, but his loyalty and devotion to their cause surpassed any other.

"Goodnight." Atlas bowed her head before retreating, leaving Adrian and Bash alone.

"Everything all right?" Adrian asked, taking a step closer to place a reassuring hand on his shoulder.

"Yes," Bash lied. "Though I'm not a fan of this change of plans." He sidled away from his friend's affection, choosing instead the solitude that often cleared his mind. He couldn't afford to be distracted by foolish emotions. People relied on him, and if he unraveled, then he wouldn't be of any use to them.

"I'll leave you to it then," Adrian murmured after a moment's hesitation. "Goodnight, old friend." He shut the door softly on his way out.

Bash sighed and turned to the porthole, where the moon's light glinted on the waves. He prayed to all the gods that his plan would work. That he was right to take Wood's daughter.

Knowing he should attempt to sleep, he settled on the thin cot in the corner of the office and rested his head on his folded arms. The ship rocked and swayed; the waves crashing against the hull should've been enough to calm his thoughts.

But they weren't.

His mind was restless with all the things that could go wrong. With the consequences that would ensue should they fail. If Captain Wood didn't make the trade, then he would all but condemn the world to needless bloodshed. Bash suspected that even if he did know of the danger, the man would hardly care. That was why the bastard deserved to be gutted. By Bash's hand, preferably. If anyone had earned the honor of ending Captain Wood, it was Bash.

But images of slicing the captain's throat weren't lulling him to sleep tonight. Bash itched to move, to do anything but lay there and wait.

He sat up with a groan, resting his elbows on his knees. Today wasn't a complete loss. He *should* be happy enough for now, but there was a sense of dread that wouldn't leave him, like something dire was transpiring right under his nose.

Instantly, he thought of her—the woman currently aboard his ship, the daughter of his greatest enemy. She certainly wasn't what he expected. Not that he'd spent all that much time thinking about her in the first place.

Now, he couldn't stop.

Before he could think better of it, Bash was on his feet, opening his door, and striding down the narrow corridor. He didn't knock before he unlocked her door and slid inside, his feet silent as he took in her slumbering form lying in the dim moonlight.

Margrete Wood. Age twenty-three. Oldest daughter of Captain Wood. Known to spend her days within the keep doing gods knew what.

He dared another step, his pulse racing.

She appeared so soft in her sleep, so unlike the fiery woman who challenged him hours before. He almost laughed at the memory of her kneeing him in the groin, her small hands encircling his sword as if she'd drive it through him.

Maybe she would have.

Seeming to sense the eyes upon her, Margrete shifted, a faint sigh escaping her full lips. Lips he'd washed blood from when he first brought her to this room. He let his gaze travel down her petite body to where the coverlet lay bunched around her narrow waist, her fingers fisted in the fabric as though she were fighting something even now.

She'd changed out of the red gown into his day tunic, a garment of thin, white linen. He imagined that if she knew it belonged to him, she'd throw the shirt overboard. The neck remained untied. Spread wide, the opening revealed the delicate lines of her throat, the curve of her shoulder, the swell of her breast. She was beautiful. Alluring.

That was without question.

Bash hovered over her bed, feeling both intrigued and furious with himself. He didn't know why her room was the first place he'd gone. Maybe the need to check on his prisoner drove him to such madness. She was invaluable, after all. Yes, *that* was why he was looming over her like death's shadow.

He was about to turn around and leave—go back to tossing and turning in his own bed—when her voice pierced the silence.

"No," she murmured, eyes still closed tight. Her brow furrowed, and her lips grew pinched as her head lolled from side to side. "Not again."

Bash flinched. She was having a nightmare; her breathing came out in anguished gasps. He was familiar with the affliction, and often spent his nights pacing instead of sleeping, avoiding the demons that haunted his dreams.

Bash muttered a curse before he sat on the bed next to her, his hand trembling as he brought it to her brow. He wasn't sure why he was trying to soothe her or why the pain twisting her features upset him, but he cupped her cheek, using his thumb to rub soothing circles on skin that felt like pure silk.

"Shhh," he whispered, watching as his touch instantly calmed her thrashing. Bash preferred the anger in her eyes to...*this*. He would recognize fear anywhere, and for some reason, he decided he despised the look of it on her face.

Bash's hand lingered even after she relaxed, her chest rising and falling evenly. It was then that he realized his own pulse had settled, his mind beautifully blank.

He snatched his hand back as though she'd burned him.

Rising from the bed, careful not to disturb her, he slipped through her door and locked it behind him.

"Shit," he hissed, his back pressed against the thin wood.

He had to squash whatever this was churning inside him every time he looked at her. He didn't know her, and he couldn't try to change that. What kind of king would he be if he trusted the enemy's spawn? If he were so easily blinded by a stunning face?

Bash spent the rest of the night in bed, thinking of all the ways he would end the captain's life.

His dreams were ones of blood.

CHAPTER SEVEN

MARGRETE

Margrete jolted awake, clutching the tangled sheets in her fists. They were still slightly damp from her nightmare. As she often did, Margrete dreamt of her father, of the box, of screaming for air, but this time, trapped within the box, she heard a voice, one that whispered a single word over and over again.

Soon.

But it was only a dream.

Margrete glanced around the cabin. While the visions of her father and the box were not real, she was still in another prison. She surmised it was better to be trapped in the cage she knew—one controlled by a master she'd encountered before—than here, where she didn't know what to expect. The unknowns were what terrified her most.

With a curse, she flung aside the coverlet and yanked on the boots she'd discovered the night before, a wool sock rolled into the head of each tip. Thankfully, she'd been able to rid herself of the bloodied gown after Bash left her cabin, and the loose linen shirt and too-large trousers she found in the trunk were mercifully clean.

Margrete brought the flowing sleeve to her nose, inhaling the scent of salt and dried ocean water. The fabric held another smell she couldn't name, something dark and earthy that reminded her of clear skies and summer nights.

Dropping her hand, she turned to the porthole. As if mocking her fear, the sun painted the morning clouds in shades of orange and blush, a beautiful sunrise after a wretched day.

Sunrise.

The ship swayed as it crested waves, though Margrete's feet were steady as she went to the porthole for a better look, expecting to see nothing but open waters and sinking hope. She blinked away the sleep from her eyes and took in the island ahead. The exquisite city that rose up from beyond the coast stole her breath.

She stumbled until the backs of her thighs hitting the cot. They were no longer anywhere near Prias. She wasn't certain they were even in the right *world*.

Majestic ambers, mighty blues, vibrant emeralds, and dreamy silvers filled her sight, captivating colors from a foreign land of magic. Swaying palms and distant mountains rose high into the sky, a city of sea glass buildings nestled below. Surrounding the vast island were golden sands, each grain a glittering gem in the early light. Margrete had never seen anything like it, and its beauty struck a chord deep inside her chest, a note that the sea had never sung before. She'd imagined ending up on some sinful island of pirates and brutes, a place of petty savagery, rotting ships, and rusted iron.

Instead, she was in paradise.

"Where am I?"

As if answering her question, the door to her cabin unlocked and opened, swinging on its hinges. Bash stood there, his presence making the room seem even smaller.

"Beautiful, isn't it?" He rested against the frame, arms crossed and eyes glinting with admiration for what must be his homeland.

"Where are we?" she asked.

"Azantian." He spoke almost reverently.

Margrete's heart skipped several beats. "Azantian? But that's not—"

"A real place?" Bash shoved off the threshold and closed the gap between them. He eyed her borrowed clothing as he approached, lingering where her curves tugged at the fabric.

Margrete's breathing sped up as he neared. The scent of feral sea winds and masculinity clung to him like perfume. It smelled like the clothes she was wearing, and she wondered if they were his.

"Azantian has always been real. *Your* people simply haven't been welcome. That's why it stays hidden. The savages from your world would surely destroy something they couldn't control. Humans and their weak greed."

Margrete let out an indignant scoff. "You speak as though you're not flesh and blood yourself."

His lips twisted into a mischievous grin. One she was beginning to associate with him.

"I'm flesh and blood, princess. Prick me, and I bleed. Kiss me, and my skin grows hot." He leaned close, his voice a dangerous whisper. "But just because something bleeds and wants doesn't mean it's human."

She swallowed hard, her mind racing with thoughts—no, *myths*—of Azantian and the race of beings rumored to rule over its shores. Stories, that's all they were. But as she studied Bash, *truly* gazed upon the sharp planes of his face, her conviction began to falter. She couldn't deny the island she'd seen. How it beamed from within. Just as she couldn't deny how different Bash was from every other person she'd ever known. If it wasn't for the scar running across his brow, he'd be almost unnervingly perfect.

Still, her pride was not something she was eager to sacrifice. "Not all humans are alike." Her mind drifted to her father. "You can't condemn an entire species simply because evil men live amongst them. There's beauty out there. People who deserve all the good the world has to offer." She thought of her sister. "Those who carry love in their hearts rather than greed."

The sneer vanished from his face. "Maybe you're right." He dipped his chin, catching her gaze, so close she could taste the mint lingering on his breath. "Or maybe you've been safe in your gilded prison and haven't seen what your kind is capable of. Because if you knew, princess, I doubt you would defend them so easily."

She let out a mirthless laugh. "I've walked beside evil all my life. Endured when others have perished. Yet I still see the good in the deserving and believe that the sins of some do not eclipse the decency in others. And that, pirate, is a skill I don't think you possess."

Bash stilled, his retort seemingly trapped in his throat. When he finally summoned the words, they were not what she expected. "I find that I'm rarely wrong." His voice softened, full of reluctant amusement. "Although I do enjoy it when someone is brave enough to question me."

He was so close. She should push him away, shove the bastard off his feet, do anything to rid herself of the unwanted sensations fluttering through her chest thanks to his nearness.

She began to take a step back—

A crashing wave rolled under the ship and the vessel lurched, sending Margrete careening forward into Bash's solid frame. His arms surrounded her like a vise. Gasping, she looked up to find his haughty mouth and self-righteous eyes mere inches away.

He tightened his hold as another wave struck the hull. With her breasts pressed firmly against his body, Margrete's thoughts grew muddled. She could only smell the salt and wildness of the open seas upon Bash's skin, could only think of how his hands were strong yet gentle around her. How...secure she felt.

Which was entirely absurd.

Before she succumbed to whatever madness had befallen her, Margrete placed her hands on his torso and pushed, stumbling away from his heat. She stabbed a finger into his chest. "Don't...don't touch me."

The corners of Bash's mouth turned up wickedly. He was enjoying this.

"What?" She refused to lower her accusatory finger. Not that she was at all threatening, but she was making a stand.

"Nothing," he mocked, eyes sinking to where she prodded his chest. "You're just not what I expected."

Margrete returned his penetrating stare and poked him again. "You shouldn't have expected *anything* from me. You're nothing but a low-life, despicable scoundrel, dirty pirate, bastard—" She searched for another wounding slur, her lids fluttering wildly as she wracked her brain for anything that might cause him offense.

"You done?" he asked, grinning.

Margrete flustered and snapped, "No, I most certainly am not!" Then, she added, "And a vile rogue!"

"Oh, Miss Wood, you disappoint me. I know you can do better than that," he said, winking. "But while I'd love to stay and hear what other *insults* you conjure up, we really should be on our way." He dipped his chin and his eyes sparkled, seeming to look forward to her ill-conceived taunts.

Margrete sealed her lips, not giving him the satisfaction. Bash looked almost disappointed as he wrapped a firm but gentle hand around her elbow and guided her from the cabin and down a narrow hall, one barely wide enough to accommodate his broad frame. He paused only when she bumped her shoulder as she came upon a slight bend, but his attention remained ahead, the muscles in his neck impossibly taut.

Margrete kept quiet and took in her surroundings, noting the smallest of details, if only to glean information that might assist in an escape. She wanted nothing more than to raise her knee between Bash's legs again and run, but she was on a ship and had to bide her time.

Gods knew patience was a lesson she'd well learned.

Bronze starfish and polished shells decorated the rails leading to the deck, and Margrete trailed her fingers over the intricate designs as they ascended. Whatever else could be said about Bash, the vessel he sailed was still one of beauty.

Margrete knew a beautiful ship when she saw one. With a chamber overlooking Prias's bay, she'd spent her short lifetime staring longingly at more fine vessels than she could count. Though being *onboard* a ship when she didn't know how to swim was an entirely different thing.

Bash's grip tightened as he led her quietly up the stairs and into the sun. A few sailors on deck stopped their work to stare, but most ignored her completely, carrying on about their duties.

Unlike Bash, they all wore the same deep blue tunic, the one she recognized from the attack, a moon and sun symbol brushed in gold on every chest. Booming demands rang out as men and a few women bustled to fulfill orders.

The presence of women was new for Margrete, as most captains were superstitious about having them onboard, as if the lack of manhood somehow attracted unfortunate weather. Margrete studied each face, noticing similar features in many of those she passed—the same sharp angles, luminescent skin, and haunting eyes of varying hues.

Bash steered her toward the vessel's starboard, and, with a prod to her shoulder, he pointed across the thundering waves. Silently, she followed his gaze.

Azantian came closer with every rocking swell. A thick band of smooth stone ringed the island, held aloft on beams of burnished silver. Ships sat moored at various posts along the outer band—grand vessels worthy of a king. Connecting the surrounding docks to Azantian's beaches were four bridges constructed of the sheerest blue glass, their strategic locations reminding Margrete of the points on a compass.

"How did we get here so quickly?" she asked.

"Another thing that doesn't concern you," he replied without emotion.

"Of course, it doesn't. Why ever would it?" She gestured around them and then back at herself. "Apparently none of this is my concern, even though it seems to have *everything* to do with me."

"Just because you're involved doesn't mean you have a right to know. You are, after all, *his* daughter."

"And that means what, exactly?"

Bash ground his teeth, his lips a thin line. "It means...I don't trust you."

"And I don't trust you, so it appears that we have one thing in common."

He didn't respond, not that she expected him to, but she glimpsed the subtle way his mouth twitched at one corner, as though repressing a smile.

Ignoring the mercurial pirate, Margrete turned to the dock where men in crisp amber uniforms—with the same moon and star symbol—stood patiently at the ready, waiting to catch the coiled ropes set to be tossed overboard by the sailors on approach. But it was what laid just beyond the scurrying men and their shouts that stole her attention. Every sea glass building gleamed like a colored mirror, as alive as the waters dancing just out of reach. Margrete's heart ached at the sight. Prias was dull and dreary in comparison—a copper penny set against a glittering diamond.

"It's the most breathtaking thing I've ever seen." She thought of Birdie, who would, for once, be speechless had she seen such a place.

Bash responded with a satisfied smirk. His hand, while still clasping her elbow, loosened as the vessel's gangway lowered.

Bash eyed her with interest before releasing her elbow, only to slip his arm through hers and link them together. He motioned to the gangway, where sailors bustled down the planks, carrying heavy trunks and barrels. "Let's go."

Avoiding the swerving and dodging sailors and workers storming up and down the planks, Margrete descended, only to pause before the final step. The dock glimmered with an unnatural glow, silver and gold flakes mixed in with the deep wood. Bash led her through throngs of people who watched her with hauntingly vivid eyes. At her side, Bash motioned in the direction of a sheer blue bridge, one of the four that crossed to the city's towering center.

"Hope you're in the mood for a short hike," he said, seeming to enjoy how her eyes widened at the sight of the bridge. It was longer than she'd believed.

"Of course," she replied, but that was a lie. She was in the mood for a hot bath. One taken as far away from the pirate and his band of rogues as possible.

Margrete's boots thudded across the glass, the material clear enough to see to the waters below. A dolphin frolicked in the depths, chasing playfully after a wave. It reminded her of one of Bash's tattoos, and she turned to him then, hoping to get a better look.

It was no longer there. The shark was missing as well.

Margrete squinted in the bright sun as strands of ink morphed and took shape below Bash's right elbow. The shark returned, but it was far from immobile. The magnificent predator of the deep swam gracefully up and down his arm, settling back into place when he reached Bash's wrist.

"Incredible."

Bash glanced at his arm, shrugged, and then ignored her stares as if it wasn't out of the ordinary for living ink to swim across his body.

"They didn't move before," she pointed out.

"Let's just say they come alive on these shores," Bash replied, taking in her obvious wonder.

"Well, that certainly answered all of my questions, thank you."

"Always eager to be of assistance," Bash said. "Now, if you're done staring, I have a schedule I need to keep."

Turning his back on her, he marched ahead, the guards at her heels prodding her to follow. "I'm going," she muttered.

As the city, with its many domed glass buildings and lush, green vege-tation, grew sharper with every step, Margrete considered the other legends swirling around Azantian. Namely, those that spoke of the monsters locked below the island itself. The sea's wicked children. The depths had been free of them for centuries, though sailors still recalled harrowing stories of men braving the seas when the waters ran red with blood. She prayed it was just that—another myth—but she shuddered at the thought.

When they reached the sandy shores on the other side, Margrete's muscles were screaming, the sun's brutal rays heating her every inch. Of course, Bash wasn't even sweating.

With the sun beating down on them, their small group abandoned the beach and started down a curving pathway of indigo stones. Not far from the shore stood a gleaming tower with a domed roof, the tallest structure in the city that she could see from this viewpoint. It was wide and circular, made of cerulean glass. Bright yellow and blue flowers overflowed from vine-covered balconies that extended from every level, the tightly-woven tapestries tied to the railings fluttering in the wind.

Beyond the imposing tower, Margrete could only glimpse a hint of the colorful rooftops in the distance, the tips of the pastel dwellings encased in burnished silver. It was almost too much to take in all at once, and her eyes fell back to the trail where she let out an involuntary gasp.

Solanthiums lined the pathway, bulbous honey-colored flowers she'd only read about in one of her books. They were said to have been eradicated ages ago. Unable to help herself, Margrete bent down and brought a bud to her nose. It smelled of fresh apricots.

"I'd make a quip about stopping to smell the flowers, but I'm not sure you'd appreciate it."

Straightening, she turned to Bash with a furrowed brow. "I thought Solanthiums were extinct?"

He gave her a quizzical look. "They can only be found on the island now. This was where they originated, after all." With narrowed eyes, he added, "I wouldn't have taken Captain Wood's daughter for a naturalist."

She arched a brow. "Perhaps you don't have me as figured out as you believed."

Wordlessly, he beckoned to one of the guards at her back, his eyes fixed solely on her as he whispered into the man's ear. A moment later, the guard rushed ahead of them, scurrying for the tower.

"Let's continue on," Bash commanded without further explanation, though his eyes lingered on her for a second longer than necessary.

She wondered what he told the guard, but she wasn't about to ask.

Margrete turned her attention back to the nearing tower as a set of arched doors opened. The most fetching woman she'd ever beheld stepped through. Her skin glistened as if it encased its own personal sun, her vibrant red tresses falling to the flare of her hips. An intricate sea star tattooed her shoulder, frozen in a careless spin below her sharp collarbone.

Her physical beauty was breathtaking, and her eyes were as blue as sapphires—depthless and brilliant and all sorts of sly. Opening her elegant arms, she trained her eyes on Bash.

He leaned into the woman's embrace, his arms encircling her tiny waist. Margrete wasn't sure why a sudden pang of annoyance sprang up inside her, but it was there, igniting like a sparked ember in a hearth.

"Shade." Bash dropped his act of teasing indifference like a discarded cloak. Scooping her up, he spun the woman around three times before placing her back on solid ground. She withdrew but only just enough to peer into his eyes.

"Miss me?" she asked.

"Of course," he offered, though his smile dipped at the edges. "I needed you here, though. What would we do without your brilliant mind?"

Shade cast her gaze to Margrete. "Bash, please tell me you haven't frightened the poor girl!" she scolded. Without waiting for his response, she came to Margrete. "Shoo." Shade waved the guard away, and he surprisingly complied. With a smile that lit up her face, Shade wrapped her hands around Margrete's. "My name is Shade. Welcome to Azant-ian's palace. I'm the court treasurer, though I have many roles here." Lowering her voice so that only Margrete could hear, she said, "And if any of these men give you trouble, come to me. I'm sure all of this has been alarming but know you will not be harmed." She dropped Margrete's hands, stepping back to Bash's side. "Well, shall we?" Shade asked the group.

Margrete caught Bash stealing a questioning glance her way before offering Shade his arm, and the rest of the guards fell into place. She wasn't sure what to make of Shade or her offer of protection. Either way, the woman was more welcoming than Bash had ever been.

The guard nudged Margrete forward, but she hesitated, debating how much of a fuss she should make. Bash must have felt her heavy glow-ering on his neck. He twisted back to face her, a silent warning trapped in his eyes.

Fine. She would play nice. For now.

Shade and Bash passed through the stunning archway, inches apart as they conversed in hushed tones. Margrete knew they were likely talking about her.

With her chin lifted, she entered the palace, her boots scuffing the polished marble floors. It was beneath the domed ceiling of silver and speckled pearl that the weight of where she was came crashing into her. *She was on Azantian.* A whole new world no story from her childhood could have ever prepared her for.

She couldn't shake the feeling that she'd never leave its shores again.

CHAPTER EIGHT

MARGRETE

THEY ENTERED AN EXPANSIVE THRONE ROOM WHERE A CHAIR OF woven sea kelp and netting cast out of polished metal sat raised on a marble dais. Tiny gems littered the throne's arms, a delicate vine of sapphire and opal stones. They spiraled up and around the arms to encircle an empty bezel of silver and gold.

Margrete's skin buzzed. She felt compelled to close the distance, to take a closer look at the otherworldly throne. To *touch* it.

She took an involuntary step forward, driven by some foreign need she didn't understand. It was the sound of Bash's deep voice that stilled her movements.

"This way," Bash commanded, forcing her gaze toward him. When she twisted away from the throne, everything quieted, and an unsettling numbness replaced the hum vibrating on her skin.

Bash ushered her past the dais with a lazy wave over his shoulder. She hurried after as he entered a winding corridor, leaving the strange room behind. Even still, the sense of unease didn't dissipate.

She shivered in the warm air, the prickling sensation of being watched constricting her throat. It was a feeling she couldn't shake, not even when the corridor finally came to an end.

Sunshine chased away the darkness of the hall, and Margrete let out an involuntary gasp of relief. The warm rays filtered through colored glass windows, designs of mighty sea beasts and crippling waves cast upon the stones.

Up ahead, a silver staircase spun, the metal fashioned to resemble coils of rope. Margrete paused at its bottom step, though Bash was already climbing the stairs. She placed a hand on the railing only to flinch, the metal icy beneath her palm.

It felt alive. As if the metal moved at her touch.

She began the ascent, telling herself to keep calm, but the farther they journeyed, the more her knees trembled, and the steps beneath her feet swayed as if she were aboard a ship. Soft hisses seemed to echo all around the stairwell, raising the hairs on the back of her arms.

Margrete was thankful when Bash exited on their desired floor, some four levels up. The moment she stepped into the dimly lit hallway, the voices vanished, though goosebumps still pimpled her flesh, and she couldn't shake the feeling that the walls themselves watched her every wavering inhale.

At the end of the hall stood a single door with silver and gold whorls etched into its metal casing, a guard posted just outside. They were undoubtedly bringing her to her cell. The place she would be kept until they understood her father would never trade anything of value for her. What would they do with her then?

About ten feet from the door, Margrete realized her door was moving.

No. The closer they ventured, the more she grasped it wasn't a door at all. It was a dark cloud. A cloud trapped within an ornate sterling frame. She halted a few feet behind Bash and Shade, not sure her eyes could be trusted.

She took a step back, hands fisting at her sides, uncertain of what she could possibly do to avoid this. A guard stood behind her, and even if she somehow made it past him and ran back down the stairs, he would be on her in an instant.

"I'm...I'm not going in there." It was all she could think to say.

Bash stiffened, and an annoyed sigh left his lips. "Ah, but you see, you are." The shark tattoo on his arm twitched its tail as if in warning, and then clamped its deadly jaw shut. Bash peered down at the inked beast with a raised brow, then brought his eyes back to Margrete. "You're invited to dinner of course," he added, his voice less severe. "I'll send for you tonight."

Bash lifted his hand, pressing his palm against the barrier, and the smoke scattered at his touch.

Margrete opened her mouth to argue one last time but was unceremoniously shoved from behind and thrust into the unknown.

THIS WASN'T THE CELL SHE'D BEEN EXPECTING.

Much like *nothing* so far had been what Margrete could have ever imagined, the room she was brusquely pushed into didn't appear at all like a cage.

Curtains of sheer blue fluttered around a massive bed cloaked in tones of gray and silver, the mattress raised on a platform of steel. An onyx armoire was the only other piece of furniture in the room, flecked with pearls and adorned with silver handles. But it was the walls that stole Margrete's attention. They'd been carved with depictions of the sea's mighty children—all the monstrous beings that would make even the heartiest sailor tremble. She trailed a finger across an image of what appeared to be a half-woman, half-fish. Long claws poked from blackened fingers, and her eyes were a shade darker than a cloudless night.

A nymera.

Margrete knew from stories that nymeras were the most feared of all the sea's spawn. They were cunning and deceptive and sucked the soul from their victims with a single inhale.

She dropped her hand and walked back to the door—or, no, the *portal.* She breathed in sharply before reaching out to the swirling smoke, her skin tingling with anticipation. Rather than a fine mist tickling her hand, her fingers collided with a chilled barrier of glass.

Margrete let loose a frustrated huff and lowered her arm. That exit certainly wasn't a viable escape route. She'd just have to find another. Every palace or keep had them—the servant's entrance at her father's keep was the least protected.

As there wasn't much to explore in her barren chambers, Margrete walked to the set of double doors leading to a covered balcony. She pushed down on the mother-of-pearl handle.

Unlocked.

What a pleasant surprise.

The breeze picked up as she grasped the railing and peered over the side of the palace to the jagged cliffs below. That wouldn't be an agreeable fall.

"Everything meeting your needs?"

She spun around. A broad-shouldered man with golden brown skin and hair the color of midnight stood at attention near the doorway. She held his eyes, which were a striking shade of jade, a color that was soft and gentle and altogether soothing. He wore glossy trousers dyed kelp green and a linen shirt with pearl buttons tucked loosely into the waistband. A shark's tooth tattoo marked his lower forearm, the creature it came from poking out beneath his rolled-up sleeves. All she glimpsed were two pectoral fins and an open jaw full of sharp teeth.

The man was beautiful, as everyone here appeared to be.

"I'm Adrian, Bash's commander," he said. "He sent me to check on you."

"I see," she replied coolly.

Check up on her. Of course. What was unexpected was that he assigned a high-ranking official to do so.

Margrete assessed her latest warden, hoping to find something displeasing about him, but his smile was genuine, and his stance, while at attention, was unthreatening and effortlessly serene.

"I'm Margrete, but I'm sure you already knew that." She lifted her chin. "What will happen now?" She wasn't in the mood to play games.

Adrian sauntered to the railing, his movements unhurried and easy. "Now, we wait."

"I'm assuming we're *waiting* on my father?" For him to return whatever precious gem or treasure he stole?"

It had to be something of immense value for Bash to go to such lengths.

Adrian scrunched his brow. "Bash didn't say anything else to you?" he asked, as if surprised.

"Was he supposed to?" she retorted. "He was probably too busy smirking at his own reflection."

Adrian choked down a chuckle, clearing his throat while his eyes laughed instead. "That sounds like him all right." He shook his head, a smile blooming. "I'll speak to him tonight."

His jaw ticked, a slight tell that something was amiss. "Perhaps tomorrow I could take you for a tour about town. I'm sure Bash won't have a problem with you getting some fresh air."

Margrete nodded, but she hoped that by the time the sun came up tomorrow morning, she would be long gone.

Adrian bowed. "I'll be right outside if you need anything. And..." He glanced from side to side as if making sure no one was in earshot. "Don't let Bash give you too hard of a time. He's not as awful as he lets on."

With that, Adrian drifted to the portal, lifted his palm, and sent the mist scattering to the edges. He stepped through, and the clouds swirled chaotically before settling back in place. Margrete wondered how that worked—the door. How it could tell one person apart from another. It was but one more mystery on an island full of secrets.

With a defeated sigh, she took in the titles of the books stacked neatly on top of the dresser.

Weaponry and Defense

Enemies of Azantian

Mortals and Humans: A Guide to a Fragile Species

A fourth book caught her eye. One that was noticeably out of place resting amongst the others.

Flora of the Western Islands

She traced the delicate spine, her mind going back to Bash and their conversation beside the Solanthiums. Bash had murmured to a guard and sent him running ahead to the palace. Had he procured this book for her after she'd expressed her interest? It was too much of a coincidence to overlook, but Margrete couldn't imagine that the pirate cared enough to acquire such a thing for her enjoyment.

Here she was, trapped on an island that shouldn't exist, stuck dealing with an insufferable man who alleged he wasn't human, and she'd just witnessed magic with her own eyes—even if that magic was fashioned to imprison her within these very chambers.

Myths. Immortals. Azantian.

The leatherbound books in her father's study claimed there had been a time when humans had been blessed with otherworldly gifts. Some had visions of what was to come, and others could delve into minds or manipulate small objects.

Of course, there were other stories, too, ones where humans participated in the banned arts of dark magic. The kind that required death and sacrifice and blood.

But those stories had been dated centuries back, and no reports of magic had been written in recent history. All Margrete had heard of such things were rumors, nothing more than petty gossip. People loved a good story in Prias and the surrounding islands. It added spice to an otherwise dull existence. Even so, Margrete found it hard to ignore the proof of magic right before her very eyes. A whole island full of myths. An island full of a beautiful and mysterious people.

Abandoning the heavy tomes, Margrete scanned the foreign surroundings with a keen eye. She needed to find a weapon, anything with a pointy end that she could use if she were caught escaping. She certainly wasn't going to stick around and find out what would happen to her when her father didn't pay.

Her first task consisted of rifling through the armoire and digging amongst the piles of folded shirts and trousers. Nothing. Even the bathing suite was devoid of mirrors and glass bottles storing soaps and lotions. Bash clearly predicted that she might use a shard of glass as a weapon. He would've been right.

Margrete grew excited when she discovered a floor-length mirror tucked away in the corner, but when she kicked at the glass, even going so far as to smash it to the stone floor, the damned thing didn't shatter.

She hefted it back into place with a grunt. Whatever it was made of, it was not natural glass. Or at least, a kind that wasn't easily breakable.

She'd explored every crevice by the time the sun lowered in the sky, the twilight casting the room in an ominous haze. There was nothing here she could use, and the portal was out of the question. That only left her one other option, one she didn't much like.

The balcony.

The waters were calm directly below, but beyond the outer beaches of gold, past the arched bridges, the waves were roiling and anxious. Closing her eyes, she allowed her spirit to drift, only momentarily, and imagined herself diving off the balcony and gliding on a breeze. She pictured herself as a bird, wings outstretched, feathers flinching as she curved down to the waters.

The sea was luring her closer, urging Margrete to explore.

I am here, little one, the ocean called. *Do not fear.* The aquamarine crests reached out as if to grab her, whispering a name over and over again. *Shana,* it sang, breathing the name reverently. *Shana.*

Her eyes shot open, and her body jerked as if she'd been falling. The tranquil moment passed, only a brief reprieve from reality, but those whispers still lingered in her heart. Even if she were unable to hear them with her ears.

Perhaps she'd hit her head harder than she'd believed back in Prias.

Margrete lifted onto the tips of her toes, peering over the railing. Another balcony, nearly identical to her own, lay directly beneath her feet. Twisting further, she found that a thick ledge separated it from an expansive terrace that wrapped around the palace.

A ledge that was wide enough to climb across.

If she could make it to the ledge below, to the balcony, and then through its double doors, she might have a chance at getting out of here. If they were locked...Well, she'd deal with that when the time came.

She would find out tonight, she supposed, memorizing every line and curve of the ledge. The trouble would be lowering herself to the balcony below while hanging in midair hundreds of feet above the cliffs. While she'd prayed for a more exciting life back in Prias, scaling buildings wasn't what she had in mind.

Margrete passed the time exploring her suite. There wasn't much else to do until she could execute her plan, and instead of wallowing in self-pity, she focused on the living legends decorating the walls of her beautiful cage. She studied them for hours, tracing her fingers over the smooth grooves, memorizing the eerie images with her hands.

When the sun began to lower leisurely into the sea, she moved back to the balcony. While the waters typically soothed her nerves, the sight of them brought her little comfort now. Dinner was nearing, and Bash had told her he'd send for her when the time came. Though she hardly wanted to spend time with these strangers, she was impossibly hungry, and her stomach growled in agreement.

As Margrete retreated into the room, her eyes landed on the finely crafted dresser with palm trees and mangroves detailed on the edges. With a sigh, she peeled off her borrowed pants and flowing shirt and folded them neatly on a white ottoman. Instead of the fine dresses hanging in the armoire, she chose another pair of trousers and a billowing silk blouse.

Spinning to the floor-length mirror, she took in her reflection for the second time in two days. The first time, she'd been an anxious and chaste angel, all lace and false purity, but the high neck of her wedding dress had made her feel trapped, constricted. Suffocated.

Now she hardly recognized herself—not that it was necessarily a bad thing.

Margrete took in a steadying breath, only to release a choked scream.

Behind her reflection was a man.

One with several sharp blades secured to his belt.

CHAPTER NINE

MARGRETE

"I would've knocked but, well, there isn't a door."

Margrete spun around. A lithe blonde stood at attention, and while shorter in stature, he was all lean muscle, suggesting he was more deadly than he appeared.

"Who are you?" she asked, heart pounding.

The man approached with slow steps. He lifted his hands in a show of peace. "Bash is...detained at the moment," he said. "So I'm here to escort you to dinner." His voice had a calming lilt to it, light and full of warmth. "Sorry if I startled you."

"And you are?" She found her breath again as she eyed his many weapons.

"Of course, how rude of me." He let out a sharp exhale, his lips twisting into a coy grin. "My name is Bay. I'm the one who trains the sorry lot they send to the guard before I make them into soldiers." He gave a slight bow. "And you might have met my boyfriend earlier. Tall, dark, handsome. A bit serious."

The guard with the kind smile. "Adrian?"

"That's the one." He winked. "Now, come on. I'm starving, and you look like you could use a meal yourself."

She *was* starving, and Bay appeared friendly enough. So when he offered his arm, she accepted, if only to get some food in her belly. When was the last time she ate?

Bay gave her hand what she assumed to be a reassuring squeeze as they walked through the portal and out into the corridor. "I have to admit, I was rather excited to meet you," he said. "Not that I envy your predicament, but any new face on our island is a rarity."

Margrete didn't know how to respond, so she didn't. Bay kept talking, undeterred.

"You're a quiet one, aren't you? Bash spoke of you like you were some kind of hellion."

That made her lips quirk up. The thought that she might've unsettled the pirate brought her a small amount of satisfaction.

"Then again," Bay continued, "Bash is not the easiest of people to get along with, and first impressions are not his strong suit."

Well, they could agree on that.

"However, he has a way of growing on you. Much like mold." Bay chuckled, pleased by his own joke.

Margrete couldn't hide her smile as they took to the stairs, her companion chatting about what would be served at dinner. The staircase spiraled, and on the second descending curve, Margrete's blood rushed to her ears, her skin growing slick and clammy. The feeling struck her like a wave, and she would've stumbled if not for Bay's grip on her arm.

Find me, a voice hissed from nowhere and everywhere at once. A voice that dripped like honey. Full and seductive and sickly sweet. It sounded familiar, and she recalled the nightmare she'd had onboard the *Phaedra*, a voice whispering '*Soon*' into the shell of her ear.

She shuddered.

"You all right?" Bay asked. They had reached the ground floor where a sweeping chandelier lit with hundreds of candles illuminated the palace's grand entrance.

"Fine. I'm fine." The lie came easily, but her skin prickled, and her chest constricted, and her thoughts wove around the sinister timbre of that new voice.

"Are you sure? You look quite pale."

"Is there somewhere—" She searched around the hall as bile rose in her throat. She was going to be sick.

"Ah, yes, of course!" Bay seemed to understand her predicament. Guiding her down a corridor off the main entry, he directed her into a small privy. "I'll...I'll just be right outside." His cheeks were red, his face pinched in concern, but he mercifully closed the door and allowed her some privacy.

Margrete made it to the basin before she dry-heaved, her empty stomach protesting as she panted for air. Gripping the basin's cool porcelain, she willed her breathing to calm.

Closer, the unnatural voice whispered, and she weakly lifted her head to stare into the mottled mirror. Her skin was still sallow and clammy, but the nausea was subsiding. She turned around, her gaze instantly drawn to what she'd missed while rushing into the room.

A damned window.

Margrete smiled, wiping at the sweat coating her forehead. Bay had brought her to a room, alone, where an unlocked window dangled freedom before her eyes.

She didn't hesitate.

Shoving open the shutters, she inhaled the fresh night air, eagerly slipping one booted leg over the sill, followed by the other. She landed on her feet. Reeds licked at her calves and scratched the tips of her fingers as she ran through a garden of untamed shrubbery. The moon cast the world in an ivory glow, highlighting the abundance of colorful flowers and lush green trees. A small fountain trickled somewhere in the distance.

Her heart was a pounding mess, but adrenaline fueled her limbs.

The garden wound around the palace, blocks of ashen stones surrounding the verdant enclosure. Had she not been running for her life, she'd have taken the time to study the many foreign plants and flowers she'd never glimpsed in nature. But she didn't slow her pace for a second, swerving around overflowing pots and dodging vines that dangled from overhead tree branches. As she rounded the bend of the palace, she saw a gate, its edges carved with extravagant whorls and twists.

So close.

Peering beyond the gate and the cover it provided, Margrete noted two guards milling about with their backs turned. One of the men was in conversation with a woman who ran her hands up the length of his arm, a demure smile on her lips. When the man leaned down to whisper into her ear, Margrete made her move.

She slipped through the gate and turned in the opposite direction of the guards and their female companion, sliding into the darkness on silent feet. It wasn't bright enough to fully admire the island's sea glass buildings or to imagine what the empty marketplace would look like bustling with noise, but even in the quiet dim, it was striking.

Although muted, color was everywhere, woven linens and dyed ribbons of every hue were tied to posts, waving with each gust of wind. There was a whimsical quality about this area—from the arched windows of the homes to the eccentrically painted pots lining the street, all overflowing with wildflowers.

Margrete's heart thumped in her chest as she slowed her pace, trying to appear unassuming should more guards approach. But with her sweat-soaked skin and nervous feet, she surmised she'd be easy to spot.

The winding path abruptly curved to the left, and while she should've been stealthier, her nerves had gotten the best of her. It took everything in her not to run.

Margrete turned down the street—

Only to crash into a figure cloaked in shadows.

She stumbled to a halt, instinctively clenching her hands into tight fists.

"You shouldn't be out here all on your own." The man stepped into the light, the moonlight flowing across the planes of his rounded face. With a graying beard and laugh lines crinkling his eyes, he almost came off as welcoming.

"I-I don't know what you mean." She tried to step around his massive frame, but he mirrored her every movement.

The street was much narrower here, the walls closing in on both sides. The stranger stood directly in her path.

"I know exactly who you are, and I know you shouldn't be out here on your own." He let out a heavy sigh, rubbing his temple. "You don't know the island, and there are people here who are not what they seem. People who hate your father and would wish for nothing more than to see his daughter dead."

His words seemed sincere—worried, even—but Margrete still eyed the dimly lit street, searching fruitlessly for something to free herself of this man's attention. Just as she garnered the courage to make a run for it, his meaty hand wrapped around her wrist.

"We have so much to talk about, Margrete." He lowered his mouth to whisper into her ear. "If I'm right about you, then you have much more to worry about than Bash. Or your father, for that matter." His fingers pressed into her wrist almost painfully.

"What are you talking about? What more do I have to fear?" Her father was enough of a concern to plague her, and Bash...Well, he was keen on using her for his own purposes.

The man clucked his tongue and shook his head as though he pitied her. "You haven't the faintest idea of what awaits you. Though you'll soon find out," he warned, eyeing her with fierce interest. Margrete's skin burned beneath his inquisitive stare, his eyes a breathtaking shade of coral.

She wanted to demand what he'd expected of a woman he'd never met, but instead, she asked, "Who are you?" The more she looked into his astonishing eyes, the more she felt like she was falling, slipping into a memory that wasn't hers to own.

"I've never cared for names or titles, as they are often irrelevant in the grand scheme of things, but I suppose you might call me—"

"Ortum!"

The shout came from behind them. Margrete spun around, the man's fingers still biting into her wrist. Storming through the garden was a very angry Bash and the blue-eyed soldier she duped trailing at his heels. Bay's head hung low as he hurried to keep up, and she nearly felt guilty for deceiving him.

"You found her." Bash approached the man—Ortum, he had called him. The pirate's eyes were narrowed into slits, his unruly hair appearing as though he'd run his hand through it one too many times.

"Yes, my king." Ortum gave a deep bow.

My king.

Margrete's eyes flickered to Bash in surprise, Ortum's words repeating on a twisting loop in her thoughts.

King. Bash was the *king*.

Of Azantian.

She'd assumed he was some high lord or influential captain like her father, but instead, the man who kidnapped her was the ruler of an island of ancient magic. Of legend. And he was looking at her now as though he wished to strangle her.

"You seem skilled at surprising me," he said, his voice lower than she'd ever heard it before. Deadly. Dangerous.

"I told you not to assume anything about me." The words flew from her lips before she could stop them. Not that she would have. Margrete certainly didn't regret taking her chance to run tonight. Hell, she'd do it all over again. Rolling over and accepting defeat had never been something she was good at.

Bash drank in her glower, seeming to savor it like a fine wine. She was challenging him and judging from the fascinated look on his face, it was something he wasn't used to.

"You're more brazen than I gave you credit for." He took her from Ortum's hold and wrapped his fingers around her wrist, the calloused pads of his fingers rough. "That is a mistake I won't be making again, princess."

Margrete tilted her head and met his stare, silently relaying all the words she kept trapped. Bash had underestimated her, and he would do it again. Margrete was sure of it.

"Take her back to her chambers," he barked, his eyes never leaving hers. Men stepped around him, easing from the shadows to stand on either side of her. "Make sure two guards are posted outside her rooms. Apparently, Miss Wood is wilier than she appears."

He let go of her, then clenched and loosened his hand into a fist, shaking it as if to rid himself of the feel of her. With one final glare, one threatening her to defy him, he twisted on a heel and walked back through the garden.

The guards grasped her upper arms and dragged her away from Ortum, who stood nearly forgotten in the dark. The man had remained quiet throughout the encounter, but just before Margrete was led away, he spoke.

"We'll meet again...Soon," he promised.

She peered over her shoulder, his vow raising the hairs on the back of her neck, but Ortum was gone. In his absence, she felt a heavy sense of dread creep into her chest.

She needed to get the hell off this island.

CHAPTER TEN

MARGRETE

Margrete wasn't retrieved for breakfast the following morning, though she couldn't say she was surprised. Two guards had been posted outside her door the night before, a reminder that breaking out was futile.

After last night, she'd been too exhausted to consider the balcony and its chance at escape. Instead, she climbed into bed and didn't leave it until shortly after sunrise when a servant delivered a platter of fruits and cheeses. The boy set the tray on Margrete's bed, then handed her a small, folded piece of parchment before leaving her alone again.

She opened the note, only to be met with a few lines of elegant scrawl.

> *Let me know if you need anything.*
> *Shade*

Margrete studied the note, half wanting to crumple it and half thrilled that at least one person seemed to care about the prisoner locked away in the tower. But how was she supposed to let Shade know if she needed help?

When she finished eating, she paced her room, praying someone would come for her, give her answers. *Anything*, really. She needed *out*. An hour passed, then another, and another, driving Margrete mad.

She went to the portal and peered through the dense mist in hopes of making out the sentries she knew to be flanking her door. "How long is he going to keep me here?" she shouted, her voice harsh, but no answer came.

Frustrated, Margrete groaned and collapsed on her bed, holding back tears that constricted her throat. She missed Birdie, worried for her. If only they'd made it to Cartus, they'd be together now. Gods, she couldn't believe she actually *wished* she'd been married off to the handsome count. Instead, she was stolen by a pirate king.

She sat up, her attention wandering to the stack of books that had been left for her. There had to be something in those pages she could use.

Margrete crawled out of bed, scooped the books beneath her arm, and carried them to the balcony. Sitting in the lone chair, she picked up the first book.

Enemies of Azantian.

It was thick, weighing heavily in her lap, the leather cover worn from age. She opened it to the first page.

A map of the island stared back. While half of the illustration was covered in splatters of what appeared to be spilled ink, enough of the map was visible for her to glean just how large Azantian was. A delirious chuckle bubbled up from her throat. Bash didn't trust her, and leaving this for her to find was a mistake he might regret.

She planted her finger on what had to be the palace. Azantian's sigil, a crescent moon and star, had been drawn right above the towering building. It was located on the southern side of the island, and most of the homes and markets were concentrated around the fortress. She scanned the page, noting a few scattered settlements farther inland surrounded by dense trees, at least a day's journey away.

She found nothing helpful when she flipped through the rest of the book, as the majority of the text was dedicated to the art of war and combat. Before setting it aside, she tore out the map, folded it neatly into a square, and tucked it into her pocket. She might find a use for it later.

The next book was a compiled history of the mortal realms, and while she remembered her studies well enough, she thumbed through the pages until she came across one of her favorite stories.

The legendary story of Madius and the Gates of Haldion.

A city located across the sea and nestled on the coast of Vlesa, Haldion was often a stop for traders dealing in goods and spices, its lively markets brimming with travelers and wealthy merchants. According to the tale, a ship bearing hundreds of lost souls—refugees fleeing war in search of a better life—landed at the gates of Haldion. The ignorant king turned the ship away, claiming his city hadn't the room to house so many. In truth, the king didn't want the impoverished refugees polluting his lands, and he certainly didn't wish to waste supplies and efforts on what he deemed a hopeless people.

So, on the second night, the wayward vessel was moored, and a holy man traveling amongst the refugees greeted the king. He was described as a giant, otherworldly, and cruelly beautiful.

He gave the king two options. He could either open the gates and let them in, or he could refuse. However, if he refused, a great plight would overcome Madius and his people—a disease spread by greed.

The king had scoffed, disbelieving of such a grand threat made by a seemingly lowly and desperate man. So, the gates were closed and bolted.

When the second day turned into the third, the sun rose upon a crimson tide. Just as the holy man had warned, death came to the king's home. It spread through the exchange of coins and valuables. It jumped from hand to hand, the jangle of silver the tolling bells of loss.

Death by greed.

The legend goes on to say that when the city was wiped out, and once every woman and man and child lay still and cold in their beds, the people aboard that ship opened those gates. They settled in the land of Haldion, making their home upon the bodies of the fallen. It is *not* said where the infamous holy man went, but he disappeared soon after, vanishing into the waves.

On the next page was an elaborately drawn picture of the open gates of Haldion, refugees spilling inside. Standing before them was a man cloaked in black, his face obscured and hands lifted to the skies. Margrete squinted at his depiction and noted the glint of a gold band on his right hand. A twinge of familiarity struck her at the sight of it, but she shut the book with a groan. It was only a myth, though, she could certainly use the holy man's aid right about now.

With sinking hope, she moved on to the next book, the collection of various plants and herbs of the western islands. She recalled the stunned look on Bash's face when she told him she was interested in botany. The pirate probably thought she didn't have a thought in her head. She grinned at the prospect of catching him off guard.

She spent the remainder of the day flipping through the pages, committing to memory the many plants she wasn't familiar with. There were quite a few that stood out, though she'd yet to see them in person. When she could no longer concentrate on the words, she lost herself to the view of the sea and the endless horizon always just out of reach.

Tonight, under the cover of darkness, she'd make another attempt to leave this place.

She set her book aside and walked to the railing to peer over the side of the palace. The balcony below, the one connected to the terrace and its double doors, beckoned. She noted that the room had been quiet all day. Maybe it was an unused study or library.

Margrete was gauging the distance between her balcony and the ledge when a familiar voice cleared the air.

"Preparing to jump?"

Margrete startled as the deep voice wafted from her chambers and out into the balmy heat. She faced the King of Azantian, her cheeks heating at being caught.

"I'm daring, but I'm not mad." Margrete straightened her spine and formed her hands into loose fists. She was grateful her voice never wavered.

Bash sauntered closer, the twilight painting his face a rosy blush.

Dressed in fine onyx trousers and a matching shirt with the top buttons carelessly undone, he was the picture of a rakish king and rogue.

"I'm not sure what to expect from you anymore, so excuse my assumptions."

"Assumptions are dangerous things. You remember last night clearly enough?"

He took a step closer, and her pulse quickened.

"I'd be impressed if the world wasn't at stake," he said.

The breeze picked up, blowing his coppery locks across his forehead. This close, she could see the thin scar running through his right eyebrow, the light casting it in a nearly pearlescent shimmer.

"How about you tell me what it is you seek, and maybe, *maybe,* I will be inclined to stay put."

His masculine scent of smoke and sea wrapped around her like a cloak, her every inhale filled with him. She made to step back, but she only pressed further into the railing.

"I'm surprised your father never told you," he said, an accusation evident in his tone.

Margrete kept from rolling her eyes. "We must have skipped the topic over our many heart-to-heart conversations," she snapped.

She expected him to reply with a cutting remark of his own, but instead, his lips dipped into a frown. "In any case, at the insistence of my advisor, I've come to fetch you for dinner. Are you hungry? Or would you prefer I let you starve?" He extended an elbow. "Your choice, princess."

She released a frustrated sigh and, after a long moment of deliberation, linked her arm with his and let him lead her from the room in silence. She had to eat. She needed all her strength for the hours to come. Besides, having lived with her father, she recognized that dull edge lacing the king's tone, the danger lurking behind every syllable. In his eyes, she was an enemy.

If only he knew they shared a common foe.

The silence was deafening during their march down—only the crunching of boots on stone filling the uneasy gaps. The lack of idle chit-chat wasn't necessarily a bad thing, as she and Bash weren't exactly *friendly*, but Margrete couldn't stop from asking him what she'd wanted to know since the moment she woke on his ship.

"*How* did my father come into contact with something so precious that you would ransom his daughter? Isn't Azantian supposed to be hidden from the mortal realm?" At least, that's what lore claimed. "And if it's hidden, how did he manage to find it and evade your forces?"

It didn't make sense. Margrete knew she was missing a larger piece of the puzzle.

This gave Bash pause, one boot hovering over a step.

He let out a heavy sigh before turning around, rubbing at the nape of his neck. "Your father stole something vital to the island, something that he *shouldn't* have been able to get his hands on but did. All I will say is that he used his cunning to fool a very powerful man." He gripped the banister, knuckles turning white. "Now, we just want it back. We want what is rightfully ours. What he lied and killed to take." A new tattoo slithered across the back of his hand, a squid with spindly tentacles. It spun in a tight circle before a plume of ink spread across Bash's skin.

Margrete chewed her lip in thought, doing her best to ignore the impossible creatures that thrived upon his body, the works of art she secretly desired to explore.

"But *what* did he steal?" She hoped he might answer her question now that he'd opened up, if only slightly.

Money? The captain had plenty of that. *Ships?* There were hundreds in his fleet. *Maps?* While rare and precious, an abundance of detailed maps littered his study at home.

"It's not something that could ever be replicated or replaced," he answered. "It's not something from *your* world." Shadows danced across his face, the flames from the sconces illuminating all the dark secrets of his eyes. Secrets, and all the shades of honesty as well.

Captain Wood had truly wronged this man. People tended to reveal a great deal about themselves when love or vengeance was the root of their pain.

"I'm sorry," Margrete said, meaning the words. Bash's eyes flitted to hers in surprise. "He's not a kind man," she added.

Bash frowned. "You truly speak as if you do not like your own father."

While it wasn't a question, she answered, truthful and without her usual restraint.

"I thought I made it quite clear that I do not."

Bash loosened his grip on the banister. The squid glided away, the inky stain swept along with it. "What has he done for you to hate him so?" he asked reluctantly.

Margrete could almost mistake his voice as caring. Maybe it was the rawness in his tone, or how he appeared to hold his breath in anticipation of her reply, but her lips parted on their own accord.

"He—"

"There you are!" Shade appeared around the next curve in the staircase, gliding up the steps in a deep emerald dress that matched Bash's eyes. "I was wondering what took you so long, so I decided to come up and check on you. Make sure Bash wasn't giving you too hard a time."

The moment Bash released Margrete's gaze, she experienced a hint of regret. She wasn't sure why.

"Thank you, Shade, but we're fine. Margrete just had a few...questions." His eyes flickered to her before lowering. "But let's not keep everyone waiting. I know how testy they get when they're hungry. Especially Adrian." The smile he forced was strained, but Shade didn't seem to notice. She merely dipped her head and began the descent, shooting Margrete a timid smile over her shoulder as if to say, 'I'm here for you.'

Margrete gripped the railing and craned her neck, eyeing Bash with interest. He stood immobile, watching Shade as she took the stairs slowly. She could sense an inner battle brewing just beneath his surface, and a part of her longed to understand the tumultuous thoughts that had him scrunching his brow.

At that moment, she heard more whispers, a chorus of hisses that spun around the spiral staircase in a hollow echo.

"We should go." Bash cleared his throat and shook his head slightly. She noted how he scanned the stairwell, his jaw ticking.

Had he heard the whispers, too?

If he did, he made no mention of it, walking past Margrete as he led the way down. Occasionally he'd peek over his shoulder to assure himself she followed, though he never lingered for long. She found she was thankful for the silence. Telling her secrets would have done nothing but pain her. Whatever compulsion she'd felt to trust him had to have been borne from exhaustion. This was what she told herself, at least.

With the last step taken, Bash delivered her to an opulent dining hall. Golden beams met with sea glass walls, and arched windows reached for the top of the cathedral ceiling. Seashells of varying color and design lined the massive table of polished wood, and six place settings were set out before high-backed chairs of winding metal. Four courtiers were already seated, and the three she recognized—Shade, Adrian, and Ortum—eyed her with curiosity.

She held Ortum's stare as they glided into the room. The man's lips tugged up at the sides, clearly glad for her presence. In the light of the dining hall, he appeared older and more rugged, but she still felt the power—the *danger*—lurking beneath his thin skin. She glanced away quickly.

The other courtier, a lithe woman with pallid skin and straight, jet-black hair, kept her eyes on her lap, though she briefly brought her gaze to Margrete, taking her in with a quiet appraisal. The two open spaces were at the head of the table and a spot beside Adrian.

Bash situated himself at the head of the table, leaving her to sit next to Adrian. The commander offered her a timid smile.

"Good evening, my king," Adrian greeted.

Those assembled tilted their heads to Bash in a sign of respect. One he returned.

"Well, don't wait on my account." He motioned to the food laid out on plates of gold—a delectable dish of pan-seared snapper on a vibrant citrus salad.

A cautious chatter picked up around her, everyone seemingly content to ignore the prisoner at the table. The entire situation was peculiar.

As Margrete pretended to pick at her salad, she listened to a conversation taking place between Shade and the dark-haired woman to her right.

"Anything today, Nerissa?" Shade asked beneath her breath.

The girl lifted her head and a fringe of black hair fell over her dark eyes. "The gates are weakening."

Shade cast a subtle glance to Ortum who nodded his head sadly in return, the pair sharing an unspoken conversation.

"Do you know how much longer he can hold them?" Shade asked, her eyes once more wandering to the advisor.

Margrete hadn't the faintest idea what they were talking about.

"No," Nerissa replied, using her fork to poke at her full plate of food. "But everything is what it should be. At least that is how it appeared to me, but I will alert you if another vision strikes." Her eyes flashed to Margrete, as if those cryptic words had been meant for her.

That was when Margrete realized with startling clarity what Nerissa was.

A seer.

There'd been rumors of those gifted with the Sight, but just as Azantian was painted as a myth, seers were dismissed as remnants of the past. She pondered what abilities this young woman, who looked like she would be knocked over in a gust of wind, possessed.

Ortum cast his eyes to his plate, a contemplative expression marring his weathered face. Margrete could've sworn she glimpsed a flash of anger twist his lips, but it was gone before she could fully register it.

"He hasn't been much for talking these last few weeks," Adrian whispered against her hair, startling her. As if he sensed them speaking about him, Ortum turned his head in their direction. "He was the late king's most trusted advisor, and now he's Bash's. But Ortum has had a lot on his plate over the years, so he can come off as...peculiar at times. Though I suspect his responsibilities are finally taking their toll."

So Ortum was the advisor who'd insisted Bash include her tonight? Was that why he appeared so satisfied when she'd entered the room? Although, what she truly wished to know was *why* he wanted her there at all.

Margrete watched as Ortum turned a knowing gaze to Bash. The king nodded at him with a curt show of respect. What made this man so special as to receive the admiration of the king? But even if she asked, she doubted Bash would give her an answer.

"I might be able to convince Bash to allow me to escort you around the markets tomorrow."

Margrete abandoned the king and his advisor, looking to Adrian. "I doubt he would. Not after yesterday."

"Eh." He waved a hand. "He knows I won't let you out of my sight. Bay got into enough trouble last night for me to be on my guard." Adrian's words weren't malicious. If anything, he was teasing her. Margrete wasn't sure what to make of it, but she could use this conversation to her advantage.

"I suppose fresh air would do me good," she said, even though she didn't plan on being around long enough to take a tour with him. Her eyes flickered to the knife resting beside her plate. The silver glinted in the quivering light of the sconces.

"Is it a large island?" She angled her body so it concealed her hand as she reached for the cutlery. "My view faces the sea, so I'm unable to take in the city," she added.

Guilt lay heavy in her chest as she distracted Adrian, engaging him in conversation while she made her hasty grab. In different circumstances, she could imagine them getting along quite nicely.

She gripped the cool metal and dragged the knife below the tablecloth, slowly sliding the blade up her fitted sleeve.

It wasn't extraordinarily sharp, but it was something with a pointed tip, and if she put enough force behind it, damage could be done. At this rate, it was better than nothing.

"Azantian is larger than it looks." Pride brightened Adrian's features. "I think you'll be surprised by what you see. Our markets are like none in the world."

"I look forward to it then," she said, thankful when Adrian's focus was directed to Shade a moment later.

She may have lost Adrian's attention, but she'd gained another's.

Lifting her gaze, Margrete locked eyes with the King of Azantian. Bash boldly drank her in as he lounged in his seat, the sharpness of his stare unnerving. Her pulse raced. She felt the chill of her stolen knife acutely, fearful that the cunning king had caught her in the act. But his fingers only idly tapped the arms of his chair, and his gaze lay solely on her eyes. It might as well have been only the two of them in that room.

Just as he so brazenly inspected her, Margrete decided to delve beyond the mask *he* wore, past the facade of cunning pirate and stoic king. It might've been the first time she *really* looked at him, and what she saw sent shivers down her spine. She'd recognize that look anywhere—it was what her mirror reflected every morning.

Sorrow. The kind that rooted deep within your bones.

Bash was the first to glance away, and a part of her felt like she'd won.

Margrete smiled, her grin flourishing as the knife pressed against her skin. She almost regretted that she wouldn't be there to see Bash's face when he discovered her missing the following morning.

CHAPTER ELEVEN

MARGRETE

Bash escorted Margrete back to her room. He'd remained in silence for most of the dinner, allowing the others to fill the void with their own noise. She'd done much the same, occasionally conversing with Adrian, who was clueless to what was concealed beneath her flowing sleeve.

Margrete rushed up the remaining steps. The hallway leading to her room seemed longer than she remembered. Eyeing it wearily, she continued her punishing pace, forcing the pirate to keep up with her long strides. Even if he were these people's leader, he would continue to be a rogue pirate in her mind. That title suited him more than *king*.

The misty entryway neared, and Margrete halted inches from the churning haze. She kept her back to the king as she waited for him to open the portal and allow her access. The seconds ticked by painfully, but Bash never raised his hand.

"Are you just going to stand there?" she barked, keeping her face forward. All she wanted was to retreat to the privacy of her chambers and prepare for the night ahead. The more she thought about scaling the damned palace, the more her pulse raced. "Open it," she commanded, spinning on her heels and finally giving him her attention. The bastard was leaning against the wall, a devilish smirk lifting his lips as though he found her amusing.

She wanted to smack him.

He shoved off the wall, his long limbs carrying him forward until he was inches away, his head tilted down to look into her eyes. That cursed smirk never left his lips. Lips that she found herself staring at.

"I seem to have found myself distracted. You're rather quick for someone so small." He raised a mocking brow. "My sincerest apologies."

Something told her he was far from sorry. "Fine. Just do..."—she waved her hand in the air—"whatever it is you do and open the damned door. I find myself preferring solitude to your company." She shot him a saccharine smile.

He crossed his arms against his chest, and his sea star tattoo slid into view from beneath his sleeve. "I've been told I'm quite charming. Though I must say, I don't often find myself in such a position."

"Where women are eager to run from you, that is?" she asked sweetly.

"They're usually eager for other things, princess." Bash leaned down to whisper into her ear. She shivered as his breath caressed her skin. "Perhaps I could show you."

For a moment, she froze, lost to the sensations running up and down her spine. The flutters in her belly. How her heart thumped savagely in her chest.

She regained her senses quickly.

"As if I'd ever be with a man like you. You son of a—" She released a string of colorful curses at him, each more vivid than the last. Her words would've made even the hardiest of sailors blush.

"Ah, that mouth is so very wicked," he taunted, retreating a few steps back when she raised her hand. He missed her slap by a mere inch.

Undeterred, Margrete reached out for him again, craving nothing more than to wipe that arrogant smile off his handsome face. *Just one blow*, she prayed, knowing full-well how satisfied she would be if her strike landed.

"My *mouth* is not what you should be worried about, pirate." She thought of the knife hidden in her sleeve. If she used it now, when Bash was on his guard, she'd end up weaponless and back where she started.

Bash grabbed her wrist before her palm struck his face. His fingers curled around the delicate bone, heat blossoming in her chest at the contact.

His gaze turned dark. "Believe me, I'm more worried about what's in here"—he tapped her forehead before she could swat him away—"than what comes from those beautiful lips of yours."

She stilled, the compliment searing her cheeks.

His grip around her wrist tightened, and Margrete's heart thudded as cold metal pressed against her skin. The knife had slipped in the struggle, the blade held in place only by the cuff of her sleeve. As if only now realizing what he'd said, Bash unfurled his fingers and took a generous step back.

Margrete released a relieved sigh, the sting of the blade still fresh in her mind. Thankfully, it wasn't sharp enough to inflict much damage where it rested, though she hoped it would be enough to drive through an enemy if need be.

"You know," he said, gaze lingering on her form, "you can actually learn how to fight while you're here if you'd like to not be so...defenseless."

Margrete surmised he was going to use a different word but decided that 'defenseless' was less insulting. She might have hated him at this moment, but she found her heart pumping faster at his unexpected offer.

"You want me to learn how to...fight?" Gods, how many times had she begged her father for training? Bash's proposal felt too good to not be a trap.

"Of course." He snorted, like it was obvious.

"And why exactly would you teach your prisoner how to defend herself?" She narrowed her eyes, feeling wicked. "Not a very clever king, are you?"

Bash leaned against the doorway, those stupidly full lips lifting at one corner. "It's not you I fear, Margrete Wood. I also don't fear you escaping. You're surrounded by punishing seas and waiting guards who have

instructions on what to do if you set even one foot outside this palace. But
—" He held up a long finger. "I've a feeling you have battles of your own
back in Prias, and if I don't get the chance to kill your father, I'd like to
know that perhaps I gave his daughter the ability to do it for me."

All the air left Margrete's lungs.

"Does that shock you?" Bash pushed off the wall and sauntered
closer. "I'd very much like to see the man dead by *any* means, and, from
what I've gathered, you wouldn't mind if you were free of him yourself."

A world without the captain. How many times had she envisioned
that? When the nights were long and bruises painted her skin, she'd think
of what would happen if he were to drink too much, if he were to acci-
dentally fall to his death from the top of the keep. When he'd lock her
inside the box, she would picture one of his enemies swooping into the
keep and slicing his throat. Or that maybe he would simply choke on his
dinner.

Yes, Margrete had conceived every grisly scenario in which her father
could die, but even after everything he'd put her through, she still felt
wrong for thinking such things.

"I'll take that as a yes." Bash cocked his head to the side, auburn hair
falling into his eyes. Eyes that were shrewd and calculating, devouring
the emotions she was sure danced openly across her face.

When she went to protest such an accusation, the argument died on
her tongue. Her silence said more than any words ever could.

"You shouldn't feel guilty for wanting to be free of a man like him,"
Bash said, his tone softening. "Believe me, I've witnessed his cruelty firsthand as a boy, when I was unable to defend myself. Too weak to fight
back." His gaze flickered to his boots. "Since that day, I've worked hard
never to be defenseless again. Especially if the moment comes when I can
redeem myself."

Pressure weighed upon her chest, increasing with every exhale. "I
don't know if I'm capable of...killing," she finally said, her voice a whisper
of a thing.

Bash once again grabbed her hand, his grip firm. "You may not *want*
to kill, Margrete, but believe me, in this world, you should know *how*."

Ignoring the way her hand tingled in his grasp, Margrete met his stare. "You said you saw his cruelty firsthand as a boy." The fingers wrapped around hers tightened. "When was this?"

Bash's jaw tensed. "Now is not the time to discuss that," he bit out, though Margrete knew full well he was only deflecting. Again. She imagined whatever Bash had endured at her father's hand must've scarred him deeply.

She understood his pain all too well.

"I'm sorry for what he did. That he...hurt you." *Hurt* seemed like such a small word.

Her eyes fell to where Bash was still gripping her hand, which was turning a shade of purple. Following her gaze, Bash let out a curse and released her, apologizing beneath his breath.

"I'll send Adrian by tomorrow. He's highly skilled and a good teacher. The best." Bash straightened before running a hand through his hair. She noticed how his fingers trembled.

He was sending someone to *train* her, to teach her how to fight back, a skill she could certainly use when it came time to take Birdie from the keep. The offer made it tempting to stay at least one more night, but Margrete couldn't be swayed by promises, not when she'd known only empty ones in the past.

"Thank you," she said, dipping her chin.

The tension in Bash's jaw eased and his sly smirk reappeared. This was the smile he fashioned when he was out of sorts.

She wondered how he would feel if he knew just how easily she read him.

"It will be me thanking you, if you somehow manage to kill the bastard before I get my hands on him. Even if you don't, no one should be rendered defenseless. Only small men fear a woman who knows her own mind and wields a sword. Who fights back. Because those women...Well, they have the power to send men to their knees."

Warmth spread through her chest. He truly meant those words.

"Goodnight, princess." Bash tilted his head toward the portal just as a guard approached from the end of the hall. Tall and muscular, the guard strode down the corridor, situating himself outside her door. But his presence wouldn't be of concern, not when she'd already set her mind on a far more precarious exit.

"Goodnight, pirate," Margrete replied, hoping this was goodbye. Narrowing her eyes, she watched as Bash raised his hand and opened the portal, the mist clearing.

She could feel Bash's smirk as she walked through the swirling haze, and for some reason, she smiled, too.

But her smile didn't last for long. Not when she had work to do, and death to cheat.

CHAPTER TWELVE

MARGRETE

THE MOMENT SHE WAS THROUGH THE PORTAL, THE CHURNING MISTS settling into a solid shade of ash, Margrete considered her mission. The cool metal of the dinner knife she swiped from the table pressed against her forearm, hidden by the flowing sleeves of her tunic.

Margrete waited another hour—just to be certain she was left alone for the evening—before she carried out the next step. With her weapon secure, she went to the armoire and yanked a midnight-colored cloak from its hanger. She wrapped it about her shoulders, tied the strings into a knot, and drew the hood over her head.

She wasn't thrilled about scaling a building, as the last thing she'd climbed was a tree when she was twelve. But she had to try. Waiting around for Bash to hand her back to her father was simply not an option.

The balcony doors creaked on their hinges, and the night air tickled her skin and ruffled the hair beneath her hood. It was heavenly outside— the stars twinkling against an onyx canvas, the moon sitting high in the clouds. Margrete took this as a good omen.

Inching to the railing, Margrete peered down, and down...and down. The palace had to be as high as her father's keep, if not more so.

Ice shot through her veins. One slip and—

No. Don't you dare think like that.

She *would* make it down to the landing and then across to the balcony. After that, she would steal away in the shadows and venture down to the shore where she'd procure—well, *steal*—a small fishing vessel, then sail as far away from Azantian and her father as possible.

With determined breaths, Margrete squeezed the railing. She hoisted herself up and perched atop the banister, the sea at her feet.

Don't look down, don't look down—

She looked down.

A wave of nausea sent the night violently spinning, the stars a blur of white. Swallowing her rising bile, she lowered herself to the other side of the railing, then crouched and grabbed hold of the bottom posts, slowly easing her right leg to drop. Her arms protested, as did her resolve, but she forced herself to let her left leg fall. Now she was hanging in the air, only her sweat-slicked hands keeping her from plummeting to her death.

You can do this. The words played in her head, a mantra. The balcony directly below hers was within reach. All she had to do was lower her legs a little bit farther, and she'd be standing on the banister.

Just as she was about to drop deeper into the abyss, her heart racing and her palms growing increasingly sweaty, reverberating thunder shook the palace walls. *Lovely,* she seethed, her feet thrashing wildly. She let out a growl of frustration, flailing as she angled herself to where she knew the balcony's ledge to be.

The first crystal droplet splashed across her cheek, followed by a second on the tip of her nose.

Don't you start now, she threatened, knowing her chances of scaling to the terrace would be impossible if it rained.

Her chest tightened with unbridled panic. *No.* That wasn't a possibility she could face, not when she didn't have the strength to pull herself back up to her rooms. The only way out of this mess was down. Rain or no rain.

As more taunting droplets fell, soaking her hands and trickling down her forearms, Margrete's already weak grip loosened. She would have to swing down *now*.

Tilting her head to the rain, Margrete cursed herself for such an idiotic plan. Fresh tears welled in her eyes as the rain battered her relentlessly, a flood of hopelessness easing her grip on the railing above her head.

With a hasty glance over her shoulder, one that sent her heart pummeling into her stomach, Margrete noted that the balcony's ledge was close, tauntingly so, and all she had to do was make it another foot or so before she would be able to stand firmly on the rail.

A bolt of lightning pierced the deep charcoal skies, electricity coursing through the air. As the ensuing thunder rattled the palace walls, Margrete let out a howl, her right hand slipping free.

She screamed as she floundered, her left hand losing its hold as the rain came down harder. It drenched her clothing and plastered her hair to her temples and cheeks, making it difficult to see. The blade she concealed sliced at her forearm, sending pain lancing across her skin.

When the next bolt of lightning illuminated the night, a streak of fire and silver, Margrete's left hand slipped—

She was falling, a trapped scream on her open lips.

Just as her feet collided with the wood of the ledge below, just as she felt her body bend and lean backward, away from the safety of solid ground, a hand wrapped around her ankle while another hand fisted the material of her damp shirt.

This time, her scream released into the storm, a shrill cry of desperation. Yet those same phantom hands held her upright while her right foot still swung wildly for purchase.

Then she was falling again, tumbling forward and onto the balcony below...directly into a solid wall of muscle.

Powerful arms enfolded her quivering frame, strong and reassuring, crushing her firmly against a hammering heart. The rain lost its biting edge, the lightning dimming to muted flickers, the deafening thunder a distant, vibrating growl.

No.

That wasn't the thunder.

The rumble came from the chest pressed against her—a very bare, tattooed chest.

CHAPTER THIRTEEN

MARGRETE

BASH GRABBED MARGRETE'S WRIST, HAULING HER INSIDE AND OUT of the rain. He spun to face her, his wet, auburn hair framing his gratingly handsome face.

"Fancy seeing you here," he said, dragging her against him as he stared down into her eyes. His voice was deep and seductive, yet his irritation was clear. "If you wanted to come to my chambers, Miss Wood, believe me, all you had to do was ask."

Shivering, she pushed against the solidness of his chest, only getting far enough away to peer into those emerald eyes once again. Somewhere behind her, candle flames danced, casting a seductive darkness across the rigid planes of his half-naked body and damp face, the wavering shadows unable to resist the temptation to kiss those full lips.

"Bash," Margrete whispered, hating how raspy she sounded, how breathless. "I—I wasn't—"

"Trying to escape? *Again?*" Bash offered, his brow raised as a hint of anger flashed across his irises. The scar that ran through that brow gleamed white when it caught the light. "Or were you just trying to kill yourself?"

Not one of her wisest decisions, granted, but what choice did she have?

Bash's fingers played on the small of her back, his arms made of steel. His impenetrable hold thoroughly imprisoned her, his frame towering nearly two feet above the top of her head.

It was then that Margrete remembered what her sleeve concealed.

Before his easy smirk could dip, Margrete pulled out the dinner knife and pressed the blade against the hollow of his throat.

She would've been proud of herself if his sly smile didn't flourish, a twisted sort of excitement playing across his face.

"A dinner knife?" His eyes flickered down, noting the thin silver hilt of the blade. "I would've thought I'd meet my end by a grander weapon. Certainly not one I used to cut my fish with earlier."

Margrete thrust it deeper. "Maybe we can see how well it cuts an Azantian man?"

Bash let out a deep rumble of laughter. "I don't mean this as an insult, but I don't think you will. You told me yourself that you couldn't kill a man."

Margrete's hand trembled. He was right. She couldn't kill, even with her own freedom on the line. And kill *him*? For some reason, the thought of Bash, lifeless and bloodied, sent tremors down her spine.

Bash tipped his head back, exposing his throat. "Go on, then. Do it."

The hand holding the knife shook, but her voice stayed strong. "I *should* kill you, right here and now. You kidnapped me, took me away from my little sister." She pushed on the handle, and a thin line of blood formed at the edge of the blade. "Birdie was innocent in all of this, and now you've left her alone. With him." Wetness lined her lower lid, but she swallowed back her tears.

Bash's playful grin dropped.

"The way I see it," she continued, "you're in my way, and I fight for those I love. So please, just let me go so I don't do something I regret."

"You fight for everyone...except yourself." Bash spoke on a breath, sympathy creasing his eyes.

Margrete resented that look, one she took as pity.

"I do what I have to." She dug the blade deeper now, and more blood rose. "I'd gladly take the brunt of his attention so she doesn't have to."

"That's almost admirable." Bash swallowed hard, the blade shifting with the movement. "But there are other ways to fight back. Ways that don't involve you rolling over and accepting your fate."

"That's why there's currently a knife to your throat. Unless you haven't noticed that little detail yet."

"And here I thought we were getting along." Bash heaved a sigh. "You wound me. Quite literally apparently," he added, one brow arching.

He was unfazed, finding Margrete's threat amusing. That just pissed her off more.

"Don't push me—"

One moment she was pressing the blade to his neck, and the next, she was spinning. A rush of air replaced the knife she'd been clutching as Bash drew her against him, her back flush with his chest.

Kicking the dinner knife with the toe of his boot, he sent the useless weapon flying across the room, well out of reach. She could *feel* the smirk playing across his lips as he lowered his head, his hot breath tickling the shell of her ear. "You were saying?"

Well, that wasn't how she hoped the moment would play out.

"That was just my first attempt." She struggled in his hold. "What do they always say? Try until you succeed?"

Bash *tsked*, his nose nuzzling her hair. "I'll have to make sure we count the cutlery after each meal."

"So I'm supposed to sit back, enjoy the wine and conversation, and wait for you to either kill me or return me to my father?"

The room whirled once more. Her hands shot up on instinct, her fingers digging into the rigid muscles of his chest.

The sting of her nails biting into his flesh elicited a hiss, though the sound wasn't one borne of pain.

"You're more courageous than I believed." A wicked smirk teased his lips, and his hooded eyes lowered to where her nails undoubtedly marked him.

"I told you that you didn't know me." Margrete stiffened in his embrace, her body enveloped in his addicting warmth.

She shouldn't find his touch comforting. It *should* disgust her. Minutes ago, she'd held a knife to his throat, and yet...

"It seems you wish to remedy that." Bash's gaze blazed down her body.

She glanced down, too. The front of her cloak lay open, revealing her white blouse and much more. The fabric had been ripped low, likely when he'd yanked her from falling to her death. The tops of her breasts spilled out of her undergarment, her skin still glistening with raindrops. Margrete didn't move or speak, thoroughly caught in the snare of his gaze. Bash's throat bobbed, and he lifted his eyes, his breaths coming out sharp and fast.

Margrete's mind went to Jacob, the only man who'd ever held her in such an intimate way, and the only one who'd ever seen so much of her laid bare. He'd been kind and gentle, reverent whenever she was in his arms.

Bash's touch was harsh, demanding...*and not entirely unpleasant.*

"You can release me." She shifted in his embrace, but Bash made no move to yield. Instead, dimples popped up on either cheek, his sharp features devilish.

"And have you try and kill yourself again? I think not." One hand moved to her cheek, the other securely positioned at the small of her back. His palm was calloused, the pads of his fingers rough against her skin.

Margrete swallowed her gasp as he ran his knuckles down her jaw, the tender contact sending warmth into her belly. Wherever he touched, the skin prickled, coming to life.

"See." His smile turned smug, infuriatingly so. "You don't want me to release you at all."

That was enough for Margrete to snap out of her trance and regain what was left of her dignity. With a shove that was neither graceful nor gentle, Margrete sent Bash stumbling back a full step. Knowing how strong he was, she surmised he allowed it.

"You're blushing, princess." That haughty grin flourished, the candle-light playing across his handsome face as he shoved his hands into the pockets of his trousers. *Wet* trousers that hung low on his hips, revealing a deep V of muscle that led to the last place she should be looking.

"I am *not* blushing." Clutching her blouse closed, she forced out the lie, the heat in her cheeks searing. She told herself her blush was due to mortification at how quickly her plan had failed. If she were being truth-ful, the way the soft light flashed across his bare chest—and the rest of him—was enough to cause such a shameful reaction.

Bash was all broad shoulders and lean muscle, chiseled by years of what was undoubtedly hard work. Dark ink covered the expanse of his chest, and sea creatures from the deep moved about his skin.

But it was the treacherous nymera depicted across his heart that had Margrete's eyes widening. The beast's sharpened claws and scaled fins sent a jolt of unease through her veins. Even still, her eyes wandered lower again, her pulse quickening.

No human should be that handsome.

Although, he had claimed he was *far* from human. She forced her gaze away.

Bash turned to a low table where a glass of liquor perched beside an open notebook full of illegible scribbles. His long fingers wrapped around the glass, lifting it to his lips and taking a hearty drink.

"Well, that explains it," she scoffed, eyeing the nearly empty bottle accompanying the notebook.

"Explains what?" Pausing the glass at his lips, he looked at her in question.

"You're drunk." That was why he was being...not friendly, per se, but not as harsh as he'd been before. It also explained why he wasn't as furious as she'd anticipated having just caught her scaling the palace walls. While she'd expected his temper to flare, for him to raise his voice and send her back to her chambers, Bash had done nothing of the sort. She would say he was even *pleased* by her presence.

"Can't a man enjoy a drink after a trying day?" Bash brought the glass to his mouth once more, the amber liquid sloshing against the rim.

She watched the column of his throat work with every swallow. Even that part of him was enticing.

The glass was empty when he lowered it, his hand already reaching for the bottle to pour some more. "Thirsty?" He raised the replenished tumbler in her direction, those impish dimples deepening.

Margrete shivered, her clothing soaked and her hair plastered to her face. She wasn't sure if she trembled from the cold or something else.

Surprising herself, she reached for the tumbler, much to Bash's amusement. It was still warm from where he'd grasped it. She tilted her head back and drained half of the contents before she thought too much about it.

The liquid went down easy. Smooth. Heat pooled in her belly, spurning the cold. With the drink in hand, Margrete warily scanned the room. *His* chambers. A king's chambers.

It was shockingly bare, devoid of any personal touches. A fine gilded bed took up the center of the room, a plain white desk situated in the corner, and two chairs and a table sat before an empty fireplace. Aside from a dresser, there was no other furniture decorating the room.

"Meet your approval?" Bash waved about the space, angling himself toward the two simple black velvet chairs sitting before the barren hearth.

"It's a little...sparse," Margrete admitted, taking another bold sip. The liquor eased the embarrassment of her disastrous escape attempt. She would have to think of another way to leave this island. Maybe Adrian would be her key out of here; he seemed sympathetic enough. Perhaps she could exploit his kindness.

"I don't like a lot of clutter." Bash fell into one of the chairs and rested his elbows leisurely on the wooden arms. "Sit," he commanded a moment later, not glancing back to see if she'd comply.

Her pride begged her to deny him, to instead ask if she could be escorted to her room in shame. But Margrete's feet moved on their own accord, deciding for her. She was exhausted, and rightfully so. Her arms would be sore tomorrow morning.

Margrete sank into the plush velvet and placed her glass in her lap. She cradled the drink as though it were a lifeline. Her body still shivered, even if it wasn't necessarily cold outside, and she pulled her damp cloak tighter around her shoulders.

"You're cold," Bash observed, lifting from his seat before she could deny the claim. "Can't have my bargaining chip freeze to death, now can I?"

"Your bargaining chip thanks you," she murmured when he returned to his seat minutes later, the beginnings of a fire blossoming. She could already feel its divine heat kiss her skin, chasing away the tremors.

"Although, you're going to be sorely disappointed when you discover I'm not of use," she said. "As I've told you before, my father and I aren't close. He wouldn't trade anything he prized for me. Daughter or not."

A look of worry crossed his face. "I don't believe that. You're his blood."

Flashes of the box and its unholy darkness flickered across her mind.

"Some men hold power and riches in higher esteem than kin," she said. "I can promise you now, he won't come for me. You're wasting your time."

"Tell me why, then. Help me understand why your father would abandon his daughter?"

She couldn't get into the complexities of their relationship. Not with Bash, anyway. Her father's hatred for her had been a confusing, awful part of her life since she was small. There was no explaining it, because no parent should despise their child the way her father despised her.

"It wouldn't change anything," she said, jaw clenching. Why should she open her heart to this stranger? Tell him of her darkest moments?

"If you refuse to tell me, then you're right, it doesn't change anything," he agreed when the seconds ticked by, and she'd yet to speak. "I still think he will come." He spoke forcibly, as if attempting to convince himself. "He's a prideful man, and even if you claim there is no love shared between you, his daughter being taken would make him appear weak to his enemies. His ego wouldn't stand for that."

Margrete thoroughly disagreed. He wouldn't come. He would leave her here to rot.

Instead of arguing a point Bash refused to acknowledge, she asked,

"Why haven't you sent me back to my chambers? I'd have expected some form of retaliation when your prisoner attempts to flee for a second time."

"Oh, sweet Margrete, my reasons are entirely selfish. I simply didn't wish to drink alone." He gestured with his glass then downed the contents. The bottle at his side held enough for one more pour.

"Why? What's driving you to drink tonight?" Margrete couldn't help but ask, a swell of curiosity making her brazen.

Bash kept his eyes trained on the hearth. "Many things will drive a man to drink." He gave a derisive scoff. "There are far fewer things that don't."

The liquor, in combination with the fire, was doing wonders for Margrete, her shoulders losing some of their tension.

She took another sip.

"Is it lonely?" She should've asked any other question, but the despondent look in his eyes coaxed the words from her lips.

"What? Being king?" Bash shook his head, shifting to meet her cautious stare. "The world is lonely regardless of whether or not one wears a crown."

A steel band wrapped around Margrete's chest. Loneliness was an emotion she knew all too well.

"That's true," she agreed before finishing off her drink.

His long, muscled arm snaked around his chair. After digging beneath a pile of notebooks and papers, he deftly produced a new bottle. With a flick of his thumb, he dislodged the cork and filled Margrete's tumbler again. She mumbled a thank you and took a long swig, enjoying how the liquor dulled the edge of her despair and the sting of her desperate thoughts.

"You know," Bash began, leaning his head back and kicking out his boots before the hearth. "You're nothing like him. Nothing like I imagined." He paused, seeming to gather his thoughts. "While Wood is a fire set on razing everything in its path, you hold a different kind of flame in your eyes. The kind that's warm but altogether blinding. I can't seem to explain it to myself, but I recognized it the very first time I saw you. When you nearly killed yourself—and me, for that matter—on that cliff."

Margrete's mouth opened to protest, but Bash cut her off.

"Gods, you must have a thing for dangerously high places." He shook his head as a genuine smile brightened his features, strands of auburn hair tumbling into his eyes. She hadn't seen him smile in such a way. He looked at her. "You're a reckless little thing, aren't you?"

He didn't mean it as an insult, and Margrete found her lips lifting, captivated by the drunken words spilling from his mouth. "If I was going to die, then I was planning on taking you with me."

"Good thing I have amazing reflexes." He shot her a roguish wink. "Again, I find myself deserving of a 'thank you' and receiving none. Your manners might need some work, princess."

Margrete scoffed. "Why would I thank you? You're merely protecting your *asset*. Without me, you have no leverage."

Dimples popped up on his cheeks at that. "I think I'm growing to like your bite." His gaze fell to her lips. "It makes me wonder what else hides beneath that pretty exterior."

Her cheeks burned at the compliment, but the drink was loosening her tongue. "And you," she began, her voice taking on a playful lilt. "Is there more to you than a man seeking revenge and hiding behind clever retorts?"

His smile dipped at the edges before he righted it. "I wouldn't ask questions you don't want the answers to."

Margrete's body buzzed, and not only from the drink. "And if I do? If I do want answers?"

Gods, the words were out of her mouth before her mind could keep up. She hadn't meant to speak the thought aloud.

She noted the bob of his throat, the rise and fall of his chest. He hadn't expected that, but Bash recovered quickly, just as he always did.

"You need to stay alive to receive such answers, and your little escape attempt almost resulted in your very unfortunate and painful death. I would've expected better from you."

"I would've been successful if not for the rain!" Margrete bristled, not sure if that was entirely true.

"Of course, you would've been." Bash gave a wry twist of his lips and rested his head idly on his open palm. "If it makes you feel better, I don't plan on killing you." He gave an indifferent shrug as though the words didn't carry any weight at all.

"I can't make that same promise," Margrete threatened, but her voice was light, airy.

A deep chuckle bubbled up from his chest, the sound like an easy hug. This wasn't the same person she'd met in Prias, not the same coarse and jeering pirate who'd taken her from her home. It was as if she was staring at an entirely new man.

"That's fair." Bash set down his glass. "Maybe it would be fun to see you try," he added as he rose from his seat.

Bash towered over her as he closed the distance, his movements surprisingly graceful given his inebriated state. His skin rippled across his taut abdomen, and her eyes wandered to where the dark dusting of hair disappeared beneath his trousers.

Suddenly, her mouth grew parched, and her tongue darted out to wet her lips. When she dragged her eyes away, she caught Bash fixated on her mouth.

"Yet another reason for you to train with Adrian," he said. "I do love a challenge."

Margrete clutched the glass as Bash leaned forward, placing both hands on the arms of her chair, caging her in. She sank deeper into the plush velvet, taking in the way his broad, rounded shoulders and curved, thick chest flexed with the movement.

"Don't tempt me," Margrete forced out, her voice cracking. "I learn quickly."

Bash lowered his gaze to her lips again, absentmindedly wetting his own. "I imagine you do."

Margrete's body warmed in a way that had nothing to do with the fire or liquor. He was inches away, eyes hooded, the firelight reflecting in his irises. She leaned in, drawn by whatever magnetic pull consumed them both in this trapped moment.

A moment where she'd forgotten why she was there to begin with.

The bitter smell of liquor wafted to her nostrils, but it mingled with

Bash's signature salt and smoke scent. She wished she hated it.

Bash edged closer, his breath tickling her mouth, their lips a hair's breadth from touching. *I do love a challenge*, he'd said. And this certainly felt like a challenge.

She was determined not to fold first.

Tingles raced up and down the curve of her spine, the sensation of floating and falling threatening to undo her sensibilities. She tried to remind herself that Bash was drunk and not himself, that this was the reason he gazed upon her lips as though he wished to kiss them. Yet Margrete couldn't speak, couldn't move, not even when her mind whispered that she should.

But the warmth spreading across her body was more intoxicating than the drink. Her eyes instinctively closed, and her breathing caught in her throat as—

Someone pounded on the door.

Margrete jerked away, and Bash uttered a soft curse.

He pushed back from the arms of her chair, though his eyes lingered on her for a heartbeat longer, an unreadable expression on his face.

"Who is it?" he called out, annoyance painting his every feature. With one brow raised, his mischievous smile transformed into a sneer.

"Adrian. We need to go over some things before tomorrow's council meeting, remember?"

Bash heaved a sigh and ran a hand through his tousled auburn strands.

"You better not be getting drunk in there!" Adrian scolded from behind the door. "Although, it does make you more bearable."

Margrete snorted, but Bash rolled his eyes, clearly not as amused.

"Hold on, I'm coming!" Bash muttered a few choice words and turned his attention back to Margrete. "It's been...interesting, princess." He offered her his hand.

Margrete swallowed the lump in her throat, choosing to stand without his assistance. Bash's grin grew wider.

She lifted her chin and made her way toward the door where a guard would undoubtedly escort her back to her chambers. But Bash's warm fingers stopped her, wrapping around her wrist, making her turn back one more time.

"I'm not going to hurt you." Bash's eyes were wide, sincere. This was most definitely not the same man who'd cornered her on the cliffs. "Everything will go back to how it was," he promised. "Your life will be the same as it was before I ever showed up."

Her stomach sank.

"Maybe that's the problem," she whispered, unable to meet his pene- trating eyes. She was finding it difficult to hate him when he stared at her in such a way.

Bash stood there for a long moment, an unspoken reply burning between them. She could feel the tension in his body—it wafted off him like a breeze.

He scrubbed long fingers through his hair and, with a frustrated sigh, stepped to the door. He was met by a startled Adrian, who wasn't sure who to look at first.

Bash signaled to the guard. "Please escort Miss Wood back to her chambers. Oh, and station two more guards on her balcony."

Margrete clutched her cloak between her breasts, hiding what Bash had so openly seen, and headed toward the door, watching the king closely. She caught the way he gazed at her, how he swallowed hard as though the simple act of sending her to her rooms was difficult.

Pausing at the threshold, she glanced at Bash, her eyes narrowing at his new decree. Bash merely shot her a crooked smile, but she saw how the facade wavered.

"Your fault, princess. Sleep tight."

Whatever moment they shared had passed. Margrete was *almost* sorry she hadn't injured him when she had the chance.

"Goodnight," she said, not allowing him to see the red tinge of anger burning her cheeks. Over her shoulder, she added, "And I'd cut off on the drink, your highness. It seems you've had enough this evening."

She could practically feel his smirk as the two guards escorted her back to her rooms.

Margrete hoped he had a headache tomorrow morning.

CHAPTER FOURTEEN

MARGRETE

As promised, Adrian arrived early the following morning. He didn't wear gossamer trousers or a crisp, starched shirt as he had at dinner. Rather, he wore thick leather from head to toe, resembling a beast more than a man.

The only visible ink today was the pointed shark's tooth, but it still didn't move like Bash's. Margrete had enough time on her hands to speculate as to why no one else had such enchantments, why their tattoos didn't dance in such bewitching ways. She eventually decided it was because Bash was their leader and perhaps possessed some sort of magic the others did not.

"Good morning," Adrian greeted from just beyond the door.

Margrete was already dressed and waiting, after having scoured the armoire in search of more clothes. The blouse she'd worn the night before was thoroughly ruined, her pants still damp and dirty, but she found four similar outfits magically laid out for her. She'd seen no servants entering her rooms, though, whenever she spotted one in the hallway, they bowed their heads and refused to meet her eye. Regardless, she was grateful for the clean clothes.

In Prias, Margrete wasn't permitted to wear pants. Apparently, it was deemed 'unseemly' for a woman to display so much of her body. But now, when she was no longer constricted and confined to certain movements, she had a sudden urge to run about like a child.

Adrian gave her a quick, assessing glance, bowing his head when she caught his eye. Margrete expected him to bring up last night, when he'd seen her coming out of Bash's chambers. She knew he wanted to, judging by how he eyed her curiously.

But no pestering questions followed, and Margrete found that she was incredibly thankful for his restraint.

Adrian's narrowed eyes halted on her flowing turquoise sleeves, and then he was rolling them up, his fingers nimble and quick. "Wouldn't want these to get in your way," he said, buttoning the sides so they would stay in place.

Margrete nodded as if she understood, but in truth, she had no idea what *would* and *wouldn't* get in her way. She never had a *way* before at all. Nonetheless, the earthy smell of leather and the calm way Adrian carried himself put her at ease. It was the kind of ease that shouldn't have existed in such a predicament, but it took up space anyway.

Adrian offered his arm, and she hesitantly slipped her own through the crook of his elbow. His skin was soft and warm, and she shuddered at the contact. It wasn't the same as when Bash touched her—it was more like how a kindred spirit finds solace in another like soul. Adrian was attractive and kind, but he didn't make her heart flutter and skip...and she didn't have the urge to punch him in the face. Adrian made her feel centered, at home.

The irony wasn't lost to Margrete.

Once they'd ventured up two flights of winding steps, Adrian brought her through an archway of gnarled wood and interwoven metal strands, the silver twisting and turning into delicate nautical designs. Beyond, a wide terrace wrapped around the palace. It floated above the city, luscious green plants and leaves lining the edges. It was a paradise of earthy tones that contrasted pleasantly with the sea it overlooked.

The walls facing the waves were stacked with various weapons she'd never been privy to *see*, let alone *use*. Her father certainly hadn't educated her on such matters, and while she should've been afraid, Margrete's fingers ached to touch the steel and polished wood. If Azantian's king wanted to make her even more of a fighter than she already was, so be it. Perhaps she might snag herself a weapon in the process. She doubted she would get as lucky as she had last night with the dinner knife, though. She was sure Bash informed Adrian of her theft. Ultimately, Margrete had to be smarter in order to get herself out of this mess.

"You can touch them." Adrian chuckled, motioning to the wall. "They're tempting, aren't they?"

Margrete nodded. Any one of the mounted weapons would be much better than a dulled dinner blade.

There were quite a few spears, so sharp that it stung to look at the points. Their polished handles had been carved with varying designs of war and sea, eerie wraiths of destruction, meeting with a rush of calming waves during low tide. Hung parallel was a gilded crossbow.

It lured her forward, the finely crafted weapon begging to be held.

"That's a beauty." Adrian waited behind her, observing her curious assessment. "Many of my men prefer this this to a traditional bow. It has a longer firing range with better accuracy." Adrian lifted the bow from its holdings and turned it over in his hands. Unlike the others, the only design carved onto the handle was a single white star. "But," he added as he drew back, taking the beguiling weapon along with him, "first we warm up. Then, we play with the toys."

Margrete wasn't sure what warming up entailed, but she quickly learned. Adrian had her running and jumping in place like a madman, and soon enough, Margrete was drenched in sweat. "Keep going!" he encouraged, after ordering her to complete a round of pushups.

"You're making me regret accepting this offer," she grumbled. Her arms were still sore from the previous night. Adrian forced one more set of ten on her, claiming that he was being generous. After a few more drills—all various forms of physical torture—Adrian said something that startled her.

"Try to land a punch." He bounced on his feet, clearly unaware of how his demand struck her. "I'd like to see what I'm starting with."

"Excuse me?" Margrete halted, hands lowering to her sides. "*Punch* you?"

Did her guard just ask her to assault him?

Adrian continued bouncing around, his breathing even where Margrete's was ragged. "Yes," he said. "If you wanted to learn how to fight, then throwing a decent punch is rather important. Next time we'll focus on defensive maneuvers."

This made sense, but Margrete was having a difficult time complying. Though, had she been asked to punch Bash, she might not have hesitated.

"You're not going to hurt me," Adrian promised, urging her on. "Close your hand into a tight fist, like this." He modeled it for her, and Margrete complied. "No." He jumped closer, removing her thumb from inside her fist. "If you keep your thumb there, then it will break when you hit your target. When you land your blow, you want to make sure you strike with these knuckles." He tapped on her index and middle finger. "Slightly twist your wrist down." Adrian adjusted her hand where he wanted it. "Better. Also—" He pushed her hips back and twisted her body in a way that reminded her of an archer's stance.

Hopping back in place, he instructed her to strike him in his chest.

"Think of someone you dislike," he offered. "Dig deep and find your knotted aggression, the side of you I'm sure you keep well hidden." He was attempting to be playful, but Margrete *did* have a part of herself she kept hidden. It was tangled and murky, and it twisted her gut whenever it rose too far from its prison.

Although, if she were honest, she'd allowed it to drift from its cage as of late. She told herself it was a defense mechanism, but that was also a lie.

The beast within was enjoying its newfound freedom.

"Come on!" Adrian urged, but Margrete wasn't angry enough yet. Or perhaps she wasn't determined enough.

"Think of the person you hate the most. Someone who's wronged you. Channel that rage and use it to your advantage." Adrian continued shouting words of violent encouragement, but Margrete didn't need any more. She already had a cruel, familiar face in mind.

She pictured him—those blue eyes of steel, his depraved grin, the way his jaw ticked whenever she said something that displeased him. Which she did quite often.

Margrete saw her father before her, not Adrian, bouncing around, taunting. In her mind, he was reaching out, ready to fling her inside the box. Shut the iron door and trap her in a realm of inescapable nightmares. Monsters that wrapped around her body and clawed at her insides.

He's going to put you in the box.

The words were on repeat now, flowing through her spirit like a flame that refused to be smothered. *He's going to put you in the box.*

Margrete narrowed her eyes and curled her lips, exposing her teeth. She wasn't going back in that box. Not now, not ever.

Her father jumped back and forth mockingly.

Margrete could hear him calling her worthless.

A disappointment.

A *waste.*

All of the punishing names she'd been called over a lifetime came roaring into her ears, and through the rumble of malicious memories, the box shone like a flare—a symbol of the life she'd always wished to leave.

I'm not going back.

When Margrete's fist collided with Adrian's chest, a surge of grati-fying aggression poured from her soul, her bones, and into her curled fist. That force—comprised of resentment and deep-seated rage—sprang forth like a thundering wave.

Adrian jolted upon impact, his easy smile now wiped from his face.

Stumbling back, he stilled, eyes wide. "You—" He coughed, the air knocked from his lungs. "You're stronger than you look."

While he endeavored to return to his previous nonchalant demeanor, he wasn't convincing. Margrete noted every concerned glance and twitch of his jaw, the way he rubbed his sternum.

"Maybe we should play with that crossbow now," she offered, lowering her fists. She suddenly didn't want to punch anything anymore, even if it bore the face of a monster. Having Adrian look at her like that left a sour taste in her mouth, and, in truth, her hand hurt.

He nodded, too quickly, and strolled to where the crossbow was proudly displayed.

"Can I ask you something?" she said, anxious to diffuse the tension that had grown.

Adrian rested the bow's cradle on his shoulder. "Of course."

"Are you not truly...human?"

He bit the inside of his cheek in thought, but she was grateful when his expression softened. "We are, in a way. But no, we are not entirely human. Think of it like this," he said. "Azantians are born *of* the sea. Our people were crafted from sea foam and the lost souls the ocean keeps. We may look and act as you do, but our veins flow with blood and saltwater."

"Are you immortal?" She hadn't really considered this but fighting her way off the island could be even more difficult than expected because of it. If she actually plunged a knife into an Azantian's heart, would they even die?

"We age at a slower rate and heal quite quickly," Adrian replied. "But no, we are not immortal. We will eventually die."

Margrete nodded, eyes downcast. "I see," she said, when in fact, she felt blinder than ever.

"I imagine it might be difficult to wrap your mind around, but you'll get there." Adrian tapped her shoulder and handed over the crossbow.

Shaking off the thoughts of mortal gods and the sea, Margrete clutched the weapon as he instructed. He adjusted it here and there and modeled how to place the bolts with his own bow.

Slipping her foot through the stirrup, Margrete reached down, placed her hands on either side of the stock, and pulled the bowstring with both hands. As she brought it to the cocking mechanism, an audible click sounded.

"Now the bolt." Adrian handed her one, and she placed it in the groove so that the end touched the string. "There you go." He adjusted her into a proper stance. "All set to pull the trigger."

She peered up at him. "You do realize you've given me a fully loaded weapon?"

Was she truly *that* unthreatening? All she had to do was aim and pull the trigger, and he'd be dead.

"If you wanted to kill me, you would've grabbed the spear when we first arrived and at least attempted to drive it through me. Even if you did somehow manage to strike me, Azantian bodies don't retain the same damage as those of humans. I'd likely be left with a scratch."

She glanced down to the arrow, thoughtful.

"And if I aimed for your head?" she asked, curious now that he'd given her more detail about Azantian mortality.

"Then I'd say your aim is exceptional, and I'd have a lovely funeral. But seeing as this is the first time you've ever held a bow, I'm going to gamble and say I'm safe. For now," he added with a wink.

"Azantians are truly the oddest people I've ever met," she murmured, focusing on the bow and the comforting weight of it in her hands. Her body trembled with power—the buzzing flowing through her arms and down to the tips of her fingers. It felt good to hold the bow, as if she were a force to be reckoned with. With her index finger on the trigger, Margrete inhaled and aimed for a yellow bullseye. She wanted nothing more than to pierce the painted wood.

"I wouldn't be handing her a weapon if I were you!"

Margrete's finger jerked on the trigger, releasing the bolt as she twisted toward the new voice. The bolt zipped past Bay's ear just as he emerged onto the terrace, the sharpened tip striking the sea glass with a jolting clang before dropping harmlessly to the stones.

"Oh," Margrete breathed, slack-jawed and apologetic. "I am *so* sorry."

Bay waved a hand as if that sort of thing happened all the time. "No worries, but if I didn't know better, I'd say you have it out for me. First, you get me in trouble with Bash, and now you're shooting arrows at my head. Seems like I have to watch myself around you." He waggled his brows before striding over to Adrian, throwing his arms about him in an endearing hug. "I missed you," he purred, leaning up to peck Adrian's lips.

"I missed you, too." Adrian bent over so that he no longer towered over the man he kissed back with tender affection. "I was just training Margrete here."

"She certainly is slippery. With enough training, she might surpass you." The sincerity in Bay's smile both warmed and surprised her, like she hadn't only recently caused him to be the target of his king's wrath. "Don't let him push you too hard," he warned, wagging his finger Adrian's way.

Adrian rolled his eyes and shook his head, but he was grinning from ear to ear. "You're ridiculous, Bay."

"I know this well," he replied on the coattails of a sigh, then looked at Margrete again. "Well, I'll be around for dinner tonight if you'd like better company. But I'm not escorting you anymore." He gave a mock shudder.

Margrete bit the inside of her lips to keep from smiling. "Probably a smart decision."

Bay pecked Adrian's lips one last time and gave a playful wave to Margrete. In a blur of smooth steps, he was gone.

"I like him," she decided out loud, much to Adrian's delight. He radiated the sort of happiness Margrete hadn't believed possible. She doubted she would ever find such joy or companionship in another. For her, it was as unobtainable as freedom appeared to be. "I'm surprised he isn't..."

"Upset that you duped him?" Adrian laughed. "Oh, he was impressed by you, though he'd never admit it. Bay admires those who don't back down when cornered, and he's particularly fascinated by the human female who knows how to get under the king's skin."

Margrete bristled. "Hardly," she retorted. If anything were true, it was the king who got under *her* skin.

Not that she would admit it.

Adrian's lips curled into a knowing smile, but he didn't argue. Instead, he said, "I'll bring you back for a bath, if you'd like. I'm sure your muscles would welcome it after today."

She nodded, eager to get out of her sweaty clothes and away from Adrian's perceptive eyes.

They were nearly to the doors when she caught movement from the corner of her eye. Slowing her steps, she scanned the palace windows until she halted on a handsome face framed by auburn strands.

Bash.

A heartbeat later, he was gone, the curtains falling back into place where he'd stood.

The King of Azantian had been watching her train, and Margrete didn't know how to feel about that. All she knew was that her pulse picked up the moment their eyes locked.

He'd given her the chance to train, telling her no woman—no *person* —should ever be defenseless. And because of him, Margrete realized she wanted to learn how to defend herself, if only so she'd never feel so helpless again.

For the first time, she didn't think of Bash as her enemy, and that was a frightening thought.

CHAPTER FIFTEEN

MARGRETE

MARGRETE DRIPPED WITH SWEAT ALL THE WAY BACK TO HER chambers. Adrian explained there were servants available should she need assistance with her bath. She assured him she did not. Margrete didn't need any more eyes on her, not with the extra guards already posted on her balcony. Bash should've known their presence was useless. She wouldn't make the same mistake twice.

Snatching up the first outfit she could find, she brought the folded clothing into the bathing suite with her. With delight, she found the copper tub already filled, steam rising from the water. Adrian must've sent someone to tend to it. After shutting the door from any prying eyes, she peeled off her sweat-soaked garments and flung them into the corner.

The water was the perfect temperature, right between scalding and warm. Her aching muscles sighed as she sank further, muscles she hadn't known she possessed.

An hour passed and Margrete still soaked, the waters long since turned cold. She thought of her sister and her father, and how much she'd seen in only three days. Margrete felt as if she'd endured a whole lifetime since her wedding, a day she wasn't keen on repeating...even without the deadly attack and kidnapping.

When her fingers were nothing but prunes, she rose from the tub, quickly drying herself and toweling her hair. She meant to change into fresh clothing, but the pieces she'd gathered were both too large. Thankfully, a silky robe hung near the door. She tugged it on and entered her bedroom.

A cough broke the silence. Margrete jumped at the sight of her unexpected visitor, leaning against her dresser with his arms crossed.

"Sorry to disturb you."

She tightened the sash at her waist. "I highly doubt it."

Bash shoved off from the dresser and strode closer.

Why did her breath seize up at his approach? And why did her traitorous eyes drink in the way his white shirt clung to his strong chest? Gods, even the way his damned trousers hugged his lower body caused tension to build low in her belly.

A wolfish grin spread across his full lips, one that indicated he was far from sorry for disturbing her. In fact, he made no attempt to hide his roving stare. She felt that green gaze everywhere. Drifting over her mouth. Lingering on her breasts. Dancing down to her bare feet and then back up her entire body in a long, lazy drag.

Heat warmed her cheeks—and other places—as his eyes grew stormy and hooded.

Breathing harder than she should've been, she said, "You know you can remove...*them*." She tilted her head toward the guards on her balcony. "I'm not stupid enough to try that again, and I'd prefer not to have an audience when I wish to undress." She didn't care for men's eyes on her all the time. Well. Not most men, anyway. She shoved that thought to the back of her mind. "It's also rather unnerving having someone watching over you whilst you sleep," she added.

Something dark flickered across his features. "Have they bothered you?"

"No, nothing like that." She understood exactly what he meant. "I'm just not comfortable with them right outside my chambers."

His gaze floated to the balcony, and then he was suddenly moving in long strides, swinging the doors open and hissing demands. Seconds later, the guards rushed past her, escaping through the portal and out of sight.

Bash returned, the clouds that had darkened his eyes dissipating. She was about to open her mouth and thank him before she remembered it was his fault the guards had been there to begin with.

"So." He cleared his throat. "I came here to tell you that we seem to be ahead of schedule."

"Meaning what?"

"Meaning, your father has consented to our terms. We set sail to the agreed-upon location in five days."

She was to leave. Already. Go back home and to her father. To the count, if he still lived and wanted to marry her.

She'd failed to escape. Failed at finding a way to liberate herself from her father's reach. She hadn't planned on going back to Prias, or even Cartus, but now there wasn't any choice. Her thoughts left her feeling as if she were stranded in between worlds, something she should've been used to at this point in her life.

Margrete wanted to tell Bash all of this, to ask for his help, but she didn't trust him not to betray her, and she was too prideful to seek aid when she surmised he'd only deny her. Bash had made his priorities very clear, and she was not one of them.

"Why not tomorrow then?" If her father agreed, why not set sail right away? The sooner she got it over with, the better. She couldn't afford to daydream any further.

Bash shifted on his feet. "That was what our scouts were told. That the captain requested time to prepare." His hands fisted at his sides, his jaw tense.

"I see." It made sense. Fitting a vessel was no easy task. "Well, great then." She swallowed, eyes drifting to the floor where she scrutinized Bash's scuffed boots. It was easier to silently berate his appearance than it was to deal with her emotions.

"In the meantime," Bash said, "I've agreed to allow Adrian to escort you through the city."

Her eyes lifted. Why in the world would he do that? She wanted to ask but thought better of it. This was an opportunity. Clear and simple.

"I'm trusting you to follow his orders," he added, seeing the smile that graced her lips. "I shouldn't permit such a thing," he said, as though reading her thoughts, "but perhaps I'm not the bastard pirate you believe me to be."

And just like that, his face morphed into stone, the reminder of what they were to one another weighing down the very air in the room. His eyes went dull, lacking their typical gleam, those playful sparks that flared whenever he took her in. Whenever he teased.

For some inane reason, she wished to coax that side out of him now, if only to destroy the apathetic façade he currently wore.

"I'll, uh, leave you to dress, then." The barest hint of regret laced his tone, turning it into a tentative whisper.

Margrete folded her arms beneath her breasts, unsure how to react. The sight of his throat bobbing caused her brows to furrow. There was something he wasn't saying, something he was hiding. Whatever it was, it was twisting him up inside.

"Fine," she said. She could ask what bothered him, but she had a good feeling that he wouldn't tell her what was on his mind. They didn't know one another that way, and they definitely didn't owe each other anything.

"Good," he said.

"Great," she added.

They seemed to be alternating different words with the same meaning. It didn't all seem *fine*, or *good*, and certainly not *great*.

"Anything else, Bash?" A slow smirk crept to her lips. *Come on, fight with me.*

"No," he barked, a little *too* forcefully. "Nothing else. Enjoy your time in the city. I'll see you at dinner."

Margrete shouldn't have been disappointed when Bash twisted on a heel and left—but not before glancing back at her one last time.

Something about that final look, the way his eyes searched hers, indicated it was so much more than a backward glance.

Once the swirling mist of the portal engulfed him, Margrete gripped the edges of the dresser, her knuckles turning white.

The idea of home was more paralyzing than the idea of kidnappings and ransoms. Home meant the iron box. Commitment. Marriage. An unwanted fate she couldn't outrun.

But Margrete no longer wished to play the role fate had chosen her.

She had to make her own magic. Carve her own destiny.

She would not be handed over like a prize.

There had to be a way off this island.

And she meant to find it.

ADRIAN EMERGED THROUGH THE PORTAL LATER THAT AFTERNOON, his eyes crinkled with excitement. "Ready?" he asked, seemingly eager to play tour guide.

Margrete imagined that Bay would argue he was the better choice; she could sense Adrian's spirited boyfriend owned a competitive nature. The corners of her mouth tugged up at the thought of Bay, who'd left quite the impression on her during training.

"Yes, all set." She took Adrian's offered arm. "Where to first?"

"That's a surprise," he whispered, adding to the suspense.

Margrete rolled her eyes but grinned back at the stunning Azantian. She hadn't imagined finding herself in such lovely company, given that she was a prisoner and all. But then again, nothing here was how she pictured it.

Azantian consisted of high sea glass buildings and, among them, lively markets thrived. The roads were crafted from the same material as the docks, and the gleaming metal flecks captured the sun's brilliance, their golden rays dancing up and down Margrete's frame with every step. At her side, Adrian escorted her into the chaos of an open market. The symphony of voices made her head swim with excitement.

She spotted the intricately woven tapestries and multi-colored ribbons that she'd seen the night she fled through the garden. In the light of day, the colors dazzled.

"Our people add a ribbon to the post to represent every loved one they've lost," Adrian said, in answer to her unspoken question. "But it's the color of the ribbon that's important. Each color represents the dominant trait of the individual. For example, red is for those who are full of passion and determination. Blue, those loyal and wise. Yellow—well, Bay would be yellow." Adrian's lips formed a carefree smile. "He's definitely spirited and too brave for his own good."

Margrete tilted her head back to look at the ribbons fluttering above the streets, all representing a person who'd left this world. She found it beautiful that, even in death, those souls still added light and color to the island.

"There are five distinct bazaars," Adrian continued, lowering his head to murmur into her ear above the roar of patrons. "One trades in fresh seafood, fruits, and vegetables. Another, one we've fondly named the Reef, specializes in colorful fabrics, gauzy linens, and luxurious clothing." Adrian grew animated as he described his home. "My favorite is Quill Row, though. You can find all sorts of inks, parchment, and leather-bound books. I get in trouble with Bay weekly for spending too much coin there."

He gave a mischievous grin, and Margrete wondered if he was as fond of books as she was.

"Oh, and the final two markets specialize in hearty land animals and handcrafted weapons. Azantian has the finest blades known in existence," he said with pride.

"I can't wait to visit all of them." It was the truth, even if this tour held the greater incentive of familiarizing herself with her surroundings. She paused. A thought had scratched at her mind ever since her time with Bash that morning. "Adrian, I have to ask..." She came to a halt, and the commander stilled at her side. "I can't understand why Bash is allowing this. I'm his ransom, and yet he's letting me walk Azantian's streets, even placing weapons in my hands and a fighter's skill in my bones. He hopes that if he fails, I'll kill my father for him, but he can't know what I might do once I'm returned to Captain Wood. It just all seems rather...foolish."

This was what she'd wanted to say to Bash earlier, but that would've been the wrong move. Adrian felt safer, like he would hear the inquiry as curiosity, not a threat.

Adrian laughed and pointed to a rugged man watching from a balcony above the streets. While the man's hands were hidden from sight, his steely gaze felt as heavy as a touch. Adrian motioned to the other end of the street, where another unassuming man leaned against one of the stalls, alert as he observed Margrete from the corner of his eye.

"Bash is anything but foolish," Adrian said. "I think a part of him desires for you to see how beautiful our island and our people are, so that if you do return to the outside, you might be inclined to protect our secret." He glanced at the man at the end of the stall again and back to Margrete. "But have no doubt, he's always watching. If you did *anything* stupid, his men would have you locked in your rooms before you could so much as curse our king."

Adrian moved forward, taking Margrete with him into the throng of bustling customers. She should've known that Bash would assign guards to trail them, and she took it as a challenge. He didn't trust her not to run.

And he shouldn't.

In the meantime, she'd get a better feel of the island's layout.

While she would soon leave, it was a sight she wouldn't forget, and being amongst the bedlam of the thriving markets heated her blood in the most thrilling of ways. The spirited people of Azantian matched the pastels of their homes—blues, greens, purples, and coral pinks the most prominent colors. Their clothing was billowing and loose and, often, more revealing than Margrete was accustomed. Women proudly wore dresses featuring deep necklines that went to their navels, and the men went about their business without shirts, the sun tanning their backs.

Margrete had to avert her wandering gaze, especially when a dashing vendor in the weapons market approached her and Adrian. "We have the finest spears! This one would be perfect for you!" he shouted at Adrian who waved him away. The shirtless man had rippling stomach muscles, a deep vee leading—

She looked at anything but the half-naked man who, thankfully, dashed off to another customer. Gods, why was she remembering the way Bash had looked the night before in his room? That curved, glistening chest. That hard body looming over her. His mouth so—

"I don't blame you," Adrian said, jolting her from her thoughts. "That vendor was exceptionally attractive." He began to continue, then he halted and whispered, "Don't tell Bay I said that."

Margrete chuckled, imagining the trouble he'd get into if she did mention it to Bay. Based on the fearful look in Adrian's eyes, she surmised his boyfriend might be the jealous type. "Your secret is safe with me," she promised, pausing a moment to take in the splendidly chaotic market around them.

This market was the closest to the palace, with all manner of weapons and defenses proudly displayed. The streets here were a deep amber color, and the doors of homes painted a luscious cream. As they neared the Reef, the avenues morphed into a divine peach tone, with the doors and shutters dyed bright turquoise.

A breeze rustled the palm trees that lined the avenues, making the coconuts hanging beneath the massive fronds sway. It wafted hints of citrus to her nostrils, an airy scent that reminded her of long summer days.

Adrian nudged her into a quaint shop selling brilliantly crafted gowns and fine apparel, where he pressured her into letting him purchase her a flowing cobalt dress, one with a daring neckline. Her father would thoroughly disapprove, and as tempted as she was to wear such a scandalous garment, she'd grown rather attached to trousers.

They'd just exited the shop and were passing a stall full of silver rings and other assorted jewelry when an icy hand gripped her wrist.

Margrete twisted. Blue eyes lined with smudged kohl stared back at her in wonder. The hand holding hers belonged to a woman with straight white hair, her weathered skin a beautiful shade of copper.

"Excuse me." Adrian made to intervene, but Margrete held up her free hand. There was something about this stranger that demanded her attention, and when she opened her mouth to speak, the frenzied sounds of the market lowered to a dull roar.

"For you. Free of charge," the woman said, thrusting something cold and metal into her hand. Margrete frowned. "It's not every day I meet a creature such as you."

The stranger still grasped her wrist, but Margrete opened her palm to find a stunning ring. Delicate and feminine, the ring bore intricate swirls and sea stars, all etched into the thin metal. They reminded her of Bash's tattoo.

"I—I can't accept this," she stuttered, attempting to free her hand and return the unusual gift. The woman shook her head and pushed the ring deeper into her palm.

"It was meant for you. I knew it as soon as I saw your face."

Margrete's heart thundered as the woman cocked her head, blue eyes examining Margrete's face with chilling interest.

"I see it in you, girl," the old woman said. "Something dark and old. Something I can almost remember feeling long ago."

Now Margrete *did* jerk her hand free. The ring felt oddly heavy in her palm.

"Let's go." Adrian ushered her to move along, but she couldn't stop staring at the woman. Couldn't cease replaying those eerie words over and over again in her mind.

"They're looking for you!" the stranger called as Adrian pulled Margrete away.

A rush of patrons pushed onto the street. Margrete peered over her shoulder, seeking out the woman, but she was nowhere to be seen.

"Who was that?" Margrete glanced at her hand, eyeing the thin band warily.

Adrian sighed. "Arabel. She's slightly crazed but completely harmless. Don't pay her any mind."

Easier said than done.

Margrete shuddered but slipped the ring onto her pointer finger. It was ice against her warmth, a pleasant weight that centered her.

"Come on." Adrian smiled, luring her out of her thoughts. "There's still more to see." And so Margrete followed, pushing the old woman and her cryptic words far from her mind.

By the time they'd journeyed to the last bazaar, it was getting late. The stands here teemed with impressive coconuts, tangy oranges, spiky pineapples, and colorful mangos. Vendors bragged to all who would listen that their fares were the best in a never-ending screaming match amongst neighboring stalls.

A merchant peddling skewered slices of pineapple advanced, and Adrian readily tossed him a silver coin. "Try this. It's heaven." He handed Margrete the wooden skewer.

Margrete strolled the coral streets, sampling the sweet fruit. Its juices dripped down her chin, which she wiped away with a sleeve. The sun was setting, its apricot and saffron rays striking against a clear sky. Margrete was about to suggest they head back to the palace when she spotted a familiar face across the way.

She swallowed hard. Bash. He strode through the streets, taking the time to pause and greet every islander who called his name. They shook his hand and some bowed. Small children dashed up to him, tugging on his shirt and offering smiles. Instead of shoving them off, Bash beamed, his sly grin turning into something radiant. When a girl stumbled and scraped her knee in an effort to get to him, Bash scooped her up into his arms, instantly ridding her of a frown.

"They love him," Adrian said at her side.

Something inside her chest squeezed. "I see that."

Indeed, the Azantian people appeared to favor their king, and Margrete was stunned that he freely strode about without guards or security. Her father employed four guards wherever he ventured, the people of Prias not so content with their unofficial leader.

Bash caught Margrete's eyes from across the way as the girl in his arms jumped down to race back to her mother. For a moment, Margrete stood transfixed, heart thundering, a rush of adrenaline pounding inside the confines of her chest.

He appeared to be under the same spell, his auburn hair flying wildly about his face in the descending sun, highlighting the scar on his brow. Margrete wondered how he'd received such a wicked wound.

Was he recalling last night? The moment they almost shared? Perhaps this morning?

Margrete wished her pulse didn't quicken and her breath didn't catch, but it was useless. Whether they were bantering or arguing or staring, Bash's presence had a way of setting her nerves on fire. It was exhilarating and altogether dangerous.

Bash's attention drifted momentarily to the ring on her hand before he broke contact. With a curt wave to Adrian, he turned down a side street, one that led in the opposite direction. She noted how his hands formed into loose fists at his sides, his strides growing more forceful.

Margrete composed herself and looked to Adrian, whose impassive expression gave nothing away. She would miss him when she left. Adrian. Not Bash. Had they the opportunity, Margrete imagined that she and the commander might have become the dearest of friends. She didn't have many of those.

But her new friend wasn't looking at her. Adrian was too busy gazing at Bash, sprinting away, a curious expression twisting his features.

"Hmmm," was all he said, a slight smile tugging at his lips. "Interesting."

CHAPTER SIXTEEN

MARGRETE

MARGRETE AND ADRIAN WERE ON THEIR WAY BACK TO THE PALACE when she glimpsed a line of islanders walking to the beaches. Young and old, they carried tiny wooden baskets in their hands. An abundance of bold orange and yellow flowers decorated the woven sides.

"Where are they going?" Margrete asked, grabbing at Adrian's arm and bringing him to a stop. The sun was nearly set, the moon rising to reign in the sky.

Adrian sighed, tilting his head toward the growing assembly. "They're preparing to honor their dead."

Margrete squinted into the dying light, watching as a young girl with blonde hair and bright blue eyes tugged on her mother's skirts, dried tears on her ruddy cheeks. She couldn't help but think of Birdie.

"When an Azantian finally passes," Adrian continued, "we weave baskets, place our loved ones' most treasured possession inside, and offer it to the God of the Sea. It's our way to say goodbye." He paused. "Our way of honoring the waters from where we came. We're born in the waves, and we die amongst them."

The little girl beamed up at her mother who must have whispered soothing words into her child's ear. They vanished down the path, replaced by more islanders and their brightly colored baskets.

Adrian followed when Margrete headed toward them, compelled by curiosity, perhaps. She didn't stop until her booted feet struck gilded sand.

Dozens of islanders wearing silks and jeweled finery littered the patch of beach, arms laden with treasures, their families at their sides. Some had tears in their eyes, and others wore sad smiles, but all reverently stared at the calming waters lapping at Azantian's shore, the endless horizon an untouchable line in the distance.

"What are they waiting for?" Margrete asked.

"They wait for night to come," Adrian answered. "Then they'll place their offerings in the sea and say their loved one's name."

Adrian slipped his arm through hers, although he remained captivated by the procession. Margrete leaned into his embrace, and the pair shared a silent moment of contemplation.

When full dark arrived, a chant, deep and reverent, filled the air and mingled with the salty breeze.

Margrete listened. She didn't recognize the words, but her heart understood them well enough. One by one, the small groupings wandered to the waves, their bare feet tickled by crystalline waters. Families gathered around the floral baskets as they prayed, the deceased's name murmured on their lips.

It was heartbreaking and beautiful, and Margrete found herself yanking off her boots, sighing when the grains touched her exposed skin. Respectful of the mourners, she didn't move closer to the waters. The beauty in which the families relinquished their love to the sea mesmerized her, melting her heart.

The chanting swelled until it triumphed over the whistling breeze, until all she could hear was the mourner's prayer. The little girl she'd watched earlier took her place next to her mother. It was their turn to say goodbye, and the mother choked on the tears that escaped.

Margrete startled when the woman stumbled, her feet as unsteady as her heart. She was about to tumble into the waves when a man dashed to her side and wrapped a secure arm around her waist.

His auburn hair glinted in the gentle moonlight, his green eyes doleful as he held the grieving woman upright. Margrete hadn't seen Bash arrive. Then again, she'd been too focused on the sorrowful procession to notice much else.

But now, the king was all she could see, and her chest constricted when he tightened his hold, enfolding the tearful woman into a hug. The child held the basket now, staring up at Bash with questioning eyes. He nodded, shushing into the mother's ears and soothing her flying blonde strands as they whipped at her cheeks.

The young girl waded into the waves and placed the basket on the swaying sea, a single tear dripping upon the woven offering. She stood there, watching as the waters accepted the basket, her skirts drenched and her hair a tangled mess from the merciless wind.

Bash stood his ground as the waves delivered the basket to the God of the Sea. His attention remained fixed on the woman he held close, rocking her back and forth in his arms as she cried, whispering words of comfort.

A rush of icy wind, so at odds with the humidity of the island, wafted across Margrete's cheeks. She shivered, goosebumps pimpling her arms. The oddness of the cool breeze left her mind as quickly as it arrived, however, because a spark of light flickered across the waves.

Her breath caught when that spark became a blaze.

The offered baskets had been ignited. Pale blue lights lit up the darkness, the souls of the deceased seeming to bid their final farewell.

The baskets swayed on gentle crests, their luminescent glow altogether unearthly, an enchantment Margrete couldn't tear her eyes from. Her lips parted as a *whoosh* of air left her lungs, the display of magic and somber splendor breathtaking. Beside her, Adrian let out an audible gasp. She'd forgotten he was there.

"That hasn't happened since..." The king lifted his head to find his commander. Their eyes met, and they exchanged a knowing look.

"Since when?" Margrete whispered, turning to Adrian. His jaw slackened, and his eyes widened. He swallowed hard before answering.

"It's been well over two decades since the sea showed its acceptance."

Margrete's brow furrowed when Bash lifted his head to her now, his eyes seeking and fierce. He gazed at her as though she were a question he couldn't answer, a riddle set before him to solve.

She was about to ask Adrian why it had been so long when a rumble shook the shore. What began as a quivering tremor quickly transformed into a great quake. Margrete's knees gave out as the world shuddered, the glowing baskets blurring into a distorted blue line on the horizon.

"Margrete!" Adrian wound his arms around her waist and yanked her to the ground. A chorus of shouts and screams echoed as the islanders rushed from the waters back to the beach, their baskets gripped in their trembling hands.

"What's happening? Margrete choked out. Adrian's giant frame blocked her sight as vibrations danced up her body and a foreign wind hummed in her ears.

Panic surged. She wrapped her hands tightly around her companion, though he remained silent.

There was another hand that grasped her arm now, the touch hot and searing. Bash hovered above them like a wrathful god, snaking his fingers around her arm while he scanned the island.

"Adrian." Bash narrowed his eyes. "Check on Ortum."

Margrete didn't have time to grasp what that meant, because Adrian jumped up, leaving her cowering beneath Bash.

The ground still trembled, but as the reverberations grew weaker, Bash hoisted her up against him, wrapping his warm arms around her like bands of steel.

"Are you all right?" Bash pulled her to his chest, holding her just as he had the grieving mother. Margrete didn't understand what was happening, but when she opened her mouth to claim that she was fine, the quaking world shuddered to a halt.

She lifted her head and surveyed the island. The screams that had filled the air were replaced with eerie silence. No sound filtered to her ears—none except Bash's heavy breathing.

"What happened?" she asked once more, gripping Bash's shirt, her hands at his back. She wasn't sure she wished to know, given how his face contorted in uncharacteristic fear.

"I plan to find out, for certain, but I cannot ignore what I know to be true," was all he said, hauling her closer to his chest. She could hear his heart beating wildly. What did he suspect?

As much as she wanted to ask him more, her lips remained frozen, her heart beating wildly from the island's initial assault. Bash's hold was as fierce as his heart, even though the apparent danger seemed to have passed. He moved his hands to the small of her back and rubbed absent, soothing circles there with his fingers.

"I'm fine, Bash," she said again, searching his wild face for answers. He turned his attention from the island and peered down to meet her eyes.

As if realizing he still held her, Bash loosened his grip but didn't let go entirely. "We need to get you back to your rooms. You'll be safe there."

Safe *there*? She felt safe *here*. With *him*.

She hated how secure she felt in his hold. He didn't have to send Adrian away. He could've let his commander deal with her instead of personally seeing to her wellbeing. He was a king, after all. And yet, he was here, wrapped up in her arms, guarding her in the only way he knew how.

Suddenly, the humid breeze felt too heavy. Suffocating.

"You can let go now," she whispered, even though she liked the feel of his weight.

Bash flinched at her words. His hands fell to his sides, and the king took a step back, his eyes never leaving hers. She took in the shark on his forearm, its beady eyes reproachful as he vanished to the underside of Bash's arm.

Something had happened tonight that frightened the king, and it wasn't just the offerings or the quake that shook the island.

Could it be...

Among the myths surrounding Azantian, one stood out in her mind, a story that claimed Azantian was a prison, and that the sea's nefarious children, the beasts of sailors' worst nightmares, were entombed below its shores.

Margrete shivered and looked up at Bash with wide eyes. She was ready to open her mouth and ask him if what she feared was true, but the rigid set of his jaw deterred her. The alarm twisting his features told her now wasn't the time to ask questions.

"Let's get you back," he murmured, lifting a hand for her to take. "I'm sure the danger has passed, but I'd rather you be safely inside the walls of the palace."

Margrete looked at his outstretched hand, contemplating. She noted the slight tremble.

When her fingers grazed his, surprise softened his sharp features as though he hadn't expected her to accept. Margrete was stunned that she did as well.

CHAPTER SEVENTEEN

MARGRETE

The morning after the quake, her breakfast arrived on a silver tray as usual. This time, however, something else accompanied her eggs and toast.

A book.

Before digging into her plate and devouring her tea, Margrete picked up the thick tome which looked to have been read numerous times. The pages were yellowed with age. *Tides of Revenge*, the title read, and a sword embossed the cover in gold.

She brought the cup of steaming tea to her lips and opened to the first page. There, she found a single word circled in black ink.

Pirate.

Her brows scrunched, but she kept reading...until the tenth page, when rogues attacked the protagonist's ship. In the scene, one of the rogues held a dagger to the hero's throat, but the assailant hesitated to make the killing blow, and the story's hero escaped his hold.

Scrawled in the bottom right corner of the page, with an arrow pointing to the skirmish, were five words.

This reminded me of you.

Margrete scoffed, knowing exactly who bestowed this gift. She flipped through the pages and found several other notes, most teasing. If she closed her eyes, she could imagine the laughter that laced Bash's every scribbled word.

That afternoon, Adrian fetched her for another training session, and she abandoned the novel, but when he brought her back to her chambers, she hastily grabbed it and resumed her reading. More often than not, she found herself smiling at the king's jokes. At the circled words meant for her eyes only.

At dinner that night, Bash didn't mention the book, but she caught him looking her way whenever she glanced up from her plate, a spark only a secret could ignite.

She bit back her smile.

The next day, after she stayed up well into the night to finish reading of the pirate and his high-seas adventure, another book arrived with breakfast, this one thin and blue.

She opened it, expecting another work of fiction, but she wasn't prepared for what she saw hidden between the pages.

Poetry.

Margrete flipped the book in her hands. It had to be some kind of mistake. A man like Bash wouldn't favor such heartfelt and flowery words.

There were no scratches of ink scribbled in the corners of this book, though she found the corners of several pages folded, as though the owner wished to be able to return to his favorite poems whenever he desired.

One particular earmarked page caught her interest—

The Lure

I float on the crests of your love
And drown when the tide has changed

I am a fool, pulled by the promise of the wild
That sweet surrender of being drawn under

A fool in love with a toxic beauty

I choose the wild and pray for the thrill
Jumping into a sweet oblivion of vicious waves
Realizing too late, my mistake

The sea never gives—it only takes

Margrete nearly dropped her tea, but before she could think too much on what she'd read, Adrian emerged through the mist of her portal, dressed in his training leathers. While she wished to read further, she was eager to learn more from the skilled warrior. Learning how to defend herself was entirely liberating.

Hours later, after she washed away the sweat and grime from practice, she curled up on the balcony and consumed the entire collection of poems. This time, when Bash lifted his head at dinner, his eyes sparkling with mischief, she didn't hold back her smile.

Margrete woke before dawn on the third morning, hating how much she anticipated what Bash's next book would be, what he'd picked out for her today, but it was another hour or so before her tray would be delivered, and she had no choice but to be patient.

"Good. You're up."

Margrete jumped at the voice, which possessed too much energy for the early hour.

"Good morning," she said to Bay, who bounded into her room and made himself comfortable on her bed. She was thankful she'd already dressed, her fingers working to tie the ribbon at the end of her braid. It made it easier to train when her hair wasn't flying in her eyes.

Bay's eyes strayed to her nightstand, the two books Bash had sent on display, though he didn't say a word of them.

Margrete cleared her throat, wishing to draw his attention away. "Have there been any more...tremors?" She hadn't felt anything since that night, and Adrian had been rather tight-lipped about the subject. Perhaps Bay would be more willing to open up.

Bay heaved a sigh, seeming to read the desperation in her gaze. "No. Not since the other night. It's only a matter of time before Ortum isn't able to hold them any longer."

"Wait. What does Ortum have to do with it?" Bash had asked Adrian to find the advisor the night of the quake, but Margrete had been too shocked to question anything.

"Shit." Bay grimaced. "I thought you knew already."

She eyed him, hands drifting to her hips. "Knew what?"

He let out another curse, this one fouler than the last. "Ortum has been...keeping the monsters secured since the captain stole from the island. He's the reason the barriers went up in the first place. It was the only way he could keep the sea's children imprisoned, but it keeps *us* imprisoned as well. It wasn't until recently that the barriers shielding our island wavered. That was why Bash decided to act when he did, why he sought out your father. Ortum is losing strength, and we *need* what Captain Wood took from us or all hell will break loose."

"So it's true...the legends." She took a seat beside him on the bed. "Since all the other myths have been accurate, I shouldn't be surprised that the monsters of the deep are locked below the island."

A deathly chill crept up Margrete's spine as she recalled how the island shook with fury. It was the sea's children testing the bars of their cage. No wonder Bash had held such fear in his eyes.

"I had no idea Ortum held that kind of magic." She turned to Bay. "What *is* he?"

Only a god, or something damn near like it, could possess such an ability.

"That, I will leave to Bash to tell you." A guilty look weighed Bay's face. "I shouldn't have even said anything at all. It's his place to tell you our island's secrets, not mine."

Margrete nodded, not wanting to get Bay into trouble.

"All I know is that the other night was a taste of what will come should we fail to make the trade with your father."

She suppressed an involuntary shudder. If that had simply been a taste of the beasts' increasing strength, then she'd hate to see what would happen if they broke free.

"Enough talk of monsters and the possible end of the world." Bay forced a smile, changing the subject. "Today, I thought it would be best to show you one of my favorite places on the island. I am, after all, a much better tour guide than Adrian."

Margrete smiled, thinking about what Adrian had said about Bash wanting her to see the beauty of Azantian. She still had to find a way to leave, but she had to admit that this place was growing on her. Not that it mattered. It wasn't home and never would be.

She didn't have a home. Not anymore.

"I thought you weren't risking escorting me anywhere after that first night?" she said, a teasing lilt in her tone.

Bay huffed. "What can I say? I'm a glutton for punishment."

Margrete's lips quirked at that. "After you, then." She tilted her head toward the portal.

The mist lightened when she and Bay stepped through, her companion's steps giddy. He was nearly skipping as they went down the staircase and through a narrow corridor on the ground floor. His lively energy was infectious, and she didn't even try to hold back her smile.

Thoughts of beasts and thieving captains were pushed to the back of her mind. For now.

Bay guided her to a new part of the palace where the glass walls were an obscure shade of dark gray. It smelled damp and salty, and reminded Margrete of the docks back in Prias.

"Is this where you murder me?" she quipped, poking Bay in his side none too gently.

He tilted his head and gripped his angular chin as if mulling the thought over. "No," he said. "If I were to kill you, it would be under the cloak of darkness, and certainly not in the palace. Harder to dispose of a body." Bay shrugged, one eye winking mischievously.

"That's good to know," she replied coolly, though her lips tugged up at the corners.

Bay beamed back before twisting to a lone door at the end of the hall.

It was the color of a lush palm frond, decorated with gilded dolphins along the edges.

"It's beautiful," she remarked, trailing a finger over the border.

"And that's only the door." Bay maintained his wicked smile as he pushed it open.

A strong breeze assaulted her as bright sunshine warmed her skin. Her hair whipped up and around her shoulders and danced in the briny flurry. She squinted her eyes against the light to make out her surroundings.

Bay had brought her to some sort of private beach behind the palace. There were three guards posted beyond the door, all of whom nodded and waved at Bay. It appeared as though soldiers manned every entrance and exit point. Bash must've added security after her little trip through the garden.

"Come on." Bay scooped up her hand to tug her forward.

They walked down a short flight of stone steps to where a wooden walkway twisted along the shore's golden sands. The lapping waves of aquamarine caressed the grains before receding back to their home.

The boardwalk creaked beneath their boots as the path steered around a slight bend. "It's just past this turn," Bay assured her.

When Margrete stepped onto the last plank of the boardwalk, her eyes widened with both fear and wonder. Before them stood the looming mouth of a vast cave, the opening stretching like a gaping maw.

"So *this* is where you kill me," she said, peering into the obscurity.

She was only half-joking. If Margrete had seen such a place etched into any storybook, she would've instantly turned the page to a less menacing venue. The cave resembled what she pictured the gateway to the underworld might look like.

Nothing could be seen through the gloom besides a single streak of wavering light. If she tilted her head just so, the light morphed into an iridescent rainbow.

"Oh hush," Bay chided, sliding his arm through hers. "Where's your sense of adventure, Miss Wood?"

"Possibly buried beneath my sense of self-preservation," she replied, holding her ground. "Seriously, this place is...unnerving."

That was putting it mildly.

Bay sighed. "I promise no harm will befall you here. Bash would kill me if anything happened to you."

While this served as a reminder that she was a prisoner, his words *did* manage to soothe her nerves. Bash wouldn't have permitted her anywhere near this place if there was the slightest chance of danger. She meant too much to his island.

Margrete allowed herself to be guided through the dim cave, her feet unsteady over the unknown terrain. The rock was slick, making every step treacherous. "It's just up here," Bay encouraged, gripping her arm.

"You keep saying that," she muttered, but she continued to clutch at him as she stumbled on a slippery patch of rock. So much for Bash not allowing her anywhere dangerous.

There was nothing but the patter of their boots and that single streak of light guiding their way. Margrete was about to question just *how much* further it would be when an ethereal glow lit up Bay's face, a result of the sun reflecting off a deep turquoise sea. The light bounced from the waters and into a sea cave, highlighting each and every otherworldly feature.

The rocky landing that they stood upon rounded against lapping waters, a trail of brilliant sea-green leading to the open sea. Overhead, the rock curved like a cathedral ceiling, the walls comprised of hundreds of hexagonal columns of basalt. The six-sided columns were nearly a hundred feet in height, an impossible triumph of nature.

"It's—it's gorgeous."

"That it is," Bay replied, his voice reverent. "I am silenced every time I see it. A very rare feat, I might add."

Margrete smiled, but her eyes didn't stray from the sea cave. It was so serene, the whistling wind playing an eerie melody that lifted the fine hairs on the back of her neck.

"What is this place?" she asked Bay, whose eyes were watching the open waters with uncharacteristic caution.

"It's called *Kardias* in the ancient tongue. Roughly translated to 'dawn.' It has been in our lore since the beginning of Azantian."

Her fingers trailed down a column, the geometric pillar a spectacle in itself.

"They say the walls were chiseled by the God of the Sea himself," Bay whispered. "It is also the entrance to the gates holding the sea's children. If you were to dive below, you'd find an opening beneath the rocks we stand upon."

"You brought me to the place where, at any moment, monsters could emerge?"

Bay only shrugged, unaffected. "Eh, I think we're safe today."

"You *think* we're *safe*?" she bit out, incredulous. But something else niggled the back of her mind. "Does Bash plan on feeding me to the beasts beyond?"

Bay laughed. "Of course not. I *may* have lied to Bash about where we were going. He thinks we're sticking to the shoreline, but once we return safe and sound, I doubt he'll be all that mad. I wouldn't let anything happen to you, Margrete. Know that."

She shook her head, impressed with the young soldier. "You certainly don't fear your king's wrath, do you?"

"I've known Bash for most of my life. He may have a temper from time to time, but he's like a brother, and brothers don't stay mad at one another for very long." His eyes danced with mischief. "Let me be the one to worry about the brooding king."

"You better," she threatened, though she was hardly angry. Not when she was standing in such a place. Even if it held monsters below the surface.

Something pricked Margrete's finger where it rested, some jagged rock perhaps, and she withdrew her hand. A bubble of blood formed on the tip of her finger, a perfect bead of crimson. She placed her finger between her lips and licked it away absently, her attention focused on the majesty of her surroundings, a sight she imagined very few mortals, if any, had ever witnessed. The longer she stood there, the more her pricked finger itched with a foreign buzzing, and an ensuing tingle began running up and down the length of her spine.

As if her spilled blood on such hallowed ground had awoken the waters, the pull she'd known her entire life grew taut, the chorus of the rushing waves roaring in her ears. With a shudder, she focused her gaze ahead, scanning the never-ending stretch of blue.

Margrete closed her eyes and pled for but a hint of the sea's ethereal song, the melody her soul knew by heart. In reply, a mighty breeze gusted, tangling her hair and filling her lungs with a wildness she longed to capture and keep forever.

One word, the same whispered name she'd heard since arriving on Azantian, rang true, the ethereal voice that uttered it a silken caress. *Shana.*

A name. A plea. A request.

Shana. You've come home.

CHAPTER EIGHTEEN

MARGRETE

After they explored the Kardias Cave, they wandered the beaches. Bay picked up a few shells claiming they were for Adrian, and while he talked, Margrete scanned their surroundings from the corner of her eyes. Bay began to rant about the newest recruits he had to deal with when Margrete spotted a few fishing vessels moored below the palace. They appeared out of use, likely older crafts no one had bothered to fix up, but they could float. Right now, that was all she could hope for. Although, getting ahold of one of them unnoticed would be damn near impossible.

"Seems like you've got your hands full," she remarked, once Bay finished venting. "But from what Adrian's told me, you're the most skilled warrior on the island."

Bay scoffed, but the barest hint of a blush washed over his cheeks. "He *has* to say that."

Margrete laughed and shook her head. "I don't think Adrian says what he doesn't mean."

As Bay's blush grew, her eyes drifted to the tall grasses ten or so yards ahead. She noticed a patch of the rare yellow flowers she discovered her first day on the island. The temptation to pluck one and bring it home with her to study struck, but it would die before she landed on Prias. She sighed, about to move away from the cluster of flowers, when a trace of blue caught her eye. She stilled.

Perhaps the God of the Sea had heard her prayers after all.

Liander Blooms. She recalled the flower from the book Bash had left in her room. Leaving her with such knowledge was a mistake he hadn't realized he'd made.

The purple flower was rare, its violet petals and brilliant silver center sought out for a single purpose in this part of the world: sedation.

"Look, Solanthiums," she said excitedly, gaining Bay's attention. She picked up the pace, knowing he'd be right on her heels. She had to get closer to those blooms. "They're supposed to be extinct."

Her enthusiasm was easy to feign, and Bay indulged her when she crouched next to the patch and ran her hands through the satiny petals.

"Bash wasn't lying when he said you were interested in plants." Bay settled beside her.

Margrete's hand stilled. Bash spoke about her to the others, and it had nothing to do with who she was to Azantian...or her father.

She wasn't sure how to feel about that.

Margrete let her hand drift to the left, out of Bay's view, as she grabbed the stems of the three Liander Blooms growing amongst the Solanthiums. There were only a few stems, another grouping farther down, but she didn't want to give away her plan before it even had a chance to form. She prayed the few petals she'd been able to pluck would be enough.

"Bash also seemed pleased to learn from Adrian that you throw a decent punch," Bay added with a grin that took up his whole face. He seemed pleased about that fact as well.

"If I'm honest, I'm surprised he speaks of me at all, especially if my father isn't involved in the conversation," she said, standing. Her palms grew clammy, and not just from what she held in her closed fist. She hastily tucked the petals inside her pocket and wiped the residual sap on her trousers.

Bay rose, one corner of his mouth quirking. "Oh, sweet Margrete.

Please don't tell me you're *that* naïve." He chuckled, ushering her back to the path.

"I don't know what you mean," she replied coolly. She knew what he was insinuating, and the very idea of it was preposterous.

"Of course, you don't." His grin grew even wider. "Now, let's head back because I hear the cook is serving something other than seafood for lunch. Thank the Gods," he muttered beneath his breath.

Margrete followed, her heart racing, and not at the mention of Bash having taken a liking to her.

She had a sedative and, if things went her way, she had a boat, too.

Now all she needed was the right timing.

Back in her rooms, Margrete immediately opened the book of flora and fauna. Flipping through the pages, she spotted the telltale petals of the Liander Bloom. According to the description, a paste could be made using the crushed petals and a teaspoon of water.

Using the bathing suite's marble countertop as a makeshift workstation, Margarete cupped the two ingredients in her palm and used the rounded handle of her hairbrush to grind the petals into the water. After some time, a paste formed.

Margrete wasn't sure how much she would need to knock out a fully grown man—let alone a fully grown *Azantian* man—but she prayed she had enough.

She wrapped the thick paste in a silken scarf and hid it in her pocket.

It wasn't until Bay showed up to escort her to dinner that Margrete realized she'd neglected to check for a new book from Bash. With a sidelong glance at her untouched breakfast tray, she glimpsed the edge of a red cover peeking out from beneath a folded napkin.

"Forget something?" Bay asked, hesitating by the portal.

Margrete turned on her heel, abandoning the book and the secrets within its pages.

"No," she said. "I have everything I need."

CHAPTER NINETEEN

MARGRETE

AN UNBEARABLY HUSHED DINNER TOOK PLACE THAT EVENING. Before taking their seats, Adrian and Bash exchanged peculiar glances Margrete couldn't help but catch, and even Shade was noticeably quiet. A contemplative look graced the woman's stunning face from the moment she entered the room.

Once everyone settled around the table, servants rushed to fill goblets with wine and plates with fresh seafood. But unlike the nights before, everyone dove for their drinks and swallowed the rich red wine with fervor.

Margrete drank as well, aiming to calm her nerves. The paste was tucked securely in her trouser pocket, the silk scarf barely masking the floral scent.

"We should go to the market early tomorrow morning," Bay whispered in her ear, startling her. "I also was thinking we could run through a few drills afterward. I won't be needed until late afternoon."

"That sounds lovely," Margrete murmured, feeling eyes on her. Glancing up from her untouched meal, she found Bash watching her from the head of the table, a curious look on his face. His smirk was noticeably absent tonight.

"Bay," Bash broke his silence. "I hear you brought our guest to the Kardias Cave today. I can't say I'm too pleased."

Beside her, Bay stilled. "I did," he admitted. "It is Azantian's treasure, after all."

Bay had rightfully predicted his king's disapproval of her visiting the cave, but she was surprised when Bash merely gave a grunt of indignation in reply.

"See, I told you it would be fine," Bay murmured. "The key is to never get caught in the act."

Margrete shook her head at Bay as cautious chatter picked up around them. But when she glanced from her plate, two green eyes held her fast, the king watching from her above the rim of his glass. She swallowed hard.

The folded scarf in her pocket seemed to burn against her thigh, but there was no way Bash was aware of what Margrete had stolen from the beach. It was paranoia that caused her legs to jostle beneath the table. She hadn't even been this nervous when she slipped the knife up her sleeve, probably because she hadn't felt the ticking clock of her impending journey back to Prias so acutely.

"Bay." She turned in her seat, knowing her time to strike was approaching. As much as she hated it, down to her very marrow, Bay was her best chance. "Can we go for a walk after dinner?"

Bay pushed his empty plate aside and tossed his napkin onto the table with a grin. He leaned over to whisper conspiratorially in her ear. "Only if that one over there allows it." He tilted his head to the king, who had yet to turn away. "He's all eyes tonight."

"What's the harm in a walk?" she asked demurely, forcing her tone to lilt in innocence.

"I'll take you." Bash spoke just above a whisper, but the command in his voice didn't go unnoticed. The rest of the table fell silent.

Margrete's palms were damp with sweat. "But I was hoping Bay—"

"*I* will escort you, Margrete." Bash lifted from his seat, and every eye in the room raised in his direction. "I could use some fresh air myself."

Margrete's heart fell into her stomach. Fooling Bay had been her plan, but Bash? The spark in his eyes only burned brighter as he neared her seat, gently pulling out her chair to allow her to stand.

The silk scarf felt heavier in her pocket with every step she took away from the dining hall, the king trailing behind her at a leisurely pace. She bit the inside of her lip until she tasted blood. She *could* still do this, right? Somehow?

"We're making a stop at the kitchens first," Bash said, picking up his pace until he was leading the way. Margrete followed nervously.

Her hands were clammy and sweat began pooling down her back, but Bash seemed unaware of her anxiety.

He brought her into the bustling kitchens, ignoring the startled faces of the servants he passed. After grabbing the neck of a bottle of wine and two crystal glasses, he turned to face her, his eyes dancing.

"What's a good walk without wine?" The dimple on his right cheek popped up. She found it hard to focus when that happened.

Instead of answering, she snatched the bottle from his hands with a nod and clutched it to her chest. He had no idea that he'd just handed her the ingredients she'd need to make her escape possible.

"You're awfully quiet tonight," Bash observed once they were beyond the kitchens and through the palace doors. He'd waved off his guards when they stepped outside into the night, the air mercifully cool. Sweat was beginning to line her brow, and the breeze was welcome.

"I would have thought you preferred me this way," she answered. They walked side by side onto the soft sands of the beach, and she had to tilt her head to glimpse his reaction.

His teasing smile merely widened. "I prefer to be able to read people." He paused before they reached the shoreline, his gaze cast out to the waters. "I certainly didn't expect you to be some knife-wielding botanist with a penchant for scaling buildings." His eyes flickered to hers. "You're full of secrets, Margrete Wood."

Her breath caught in her throat as her name rolled off his tongue, and heat blossomed across her cheeks. She was thankful for the cover of night, because he had no idea what secrets she happened to be hiding tonight.

"And you, pirate, are one to talk."

He gave a light scoff. "A king without secrets is not a king." He climbed up the sands, forcing Margrete to follow. "Now, tell me, princess." He took a seat, staring up at her, the moon caressing his rugged face. "Are you sure you wish to know all of my secrets?"

Something dark flickered across his features, something borne from the rawness of truth.

"A man can only bear the torment of his secrets for so long before he has one of two choices." She turned toward the waves and slid her hand into the pocket of her trousers. With nimble fingers, she undid the wrapped bundle and dipped a finger inside to scoop out the sedative.

"And what might those be?"

Margrete shifted to face him before dropping to the sands at his side, careful of the sedative on her left index finger. Their thighs brushed against one another, but neither of them made a move.

"Either he succumbs to the weight he refuses to share..." She uncorked the wine and secured the bottle between her legs, then motioned for him to hand over the glasses. She took them both and hastily wiped the paste below the rim of his glass before pouring the wine. The liquid washed the sedative down to the bottom.

"Or?" he asked, barely a whisper. He didn't look anywhere but her face, seemingly captivated by whatever words might leave her lips next. When he looked at her like that, she almost regretted what she was about to do.

Without breaking eye contact, she handed him his wine. When he accepted his drink and brought it to his lips, she had to stop herself from smacking it out of his hands. Why did it feel like a betrayal? Bash was going to use her. Return her to her father. She *shouldn't* feel guilty, but she did. Gods, how she did.

"Or he finds the courage to allow another to shoulder the burden with him."

Bash took a long drink, his throat working as he swallowed. She watched the movement as she sipped from her own glass, intending only to steady her nerves.

Long moments passed before he spoke, but when he did, the very waves seemed to calm, eager to listen.

"Your father killed my father when I was a child."

The words rang into the night, his crushing gift of truth causing Margrete's wildly thumping heart to still. Bash continued to stare straight ahead, the glass of wine clutched tightly in his grasp. Deep grief lived within this man, the kind that would always steal his air. She was familiar with this pain and had the sudden urge to reach out. To take his hand in hers. To do anything to wipe that desolate look off his face. But her hand remained at her side.

"Captain Wood's trading ship went down one day, a grand vessel carrying over one hundred men. He was the sole survivor, clinging to the wreckage. My father was coming home from a sacred hunt when he spotted a man floating amongst pieces of the splintered hull and sheared sails. My father was kind—too kind for his own good—and he took pity on Wood, scooping him from the waters and bringing him back home to Azantian."

Margrete tried to envision a young captain, a man rescued by a mythical people. What she couldn't imagine was his ship wrecking at all. For as long as she could remember, he'd been one of the luckiest captains in the realm. His fleets never suffered from the wrath of storms or pirate attacks. Her ears perked up as Bash continued.

"Wood stayed in Azantian for three years, and my father, the king at the time, took a liking to him. He bestowed favors and riches and lavished him with whatever he desired. Your father wanted for nothing. He even married one of our women, although she was lost to us after..." Now Bash's tone grew glacial, and his eyes darkened. "His new wife stood by his side as he betrayed us, and we never saw her again."

Margrete's blood ran cold. She had no idea that her father had been married before meeting her mother. Adina always told her that her mother was a noblewoman from Marionette, that her father was lucky to have wed such a beauty.

"After he murdered my father, he took the only thing that can reinforce the gates imprisoning the sea's children, which left Ortum to..." He paused, looking at her as if debating whether to continue.

"I know Ortum is the reason the beasts haven't escaped," she said, "and that he was the cause of the barriers. I just don't know how or why." She left out the mention of Bay's name, not wanting to get her new friend in trouble. He said it was Bash's story to tell, and she would honor his request.

"I see," Bash said. "I won't ask how you know, though I do suspect whose lips were loose, but Ortum is a story for another day." He brought his drink to his mouth. Margrete grimaced as it went down his throat. "In any case, Ortum can't keep the monsters back any longer. He already lost control over the barriers, and if the gates fall, too..."

Then the sea's children will have nothing to stand in their way of escape.

"Gods, this wine is hitting me tonight." Bash peered at her from beneath his lashes, his heavy lids fluttering. The nearly empty glass in his hand trembled.

The sedative. She'd been so captivated by his story, so lost in the rawness of his voice, that she hadn't realized how much time had passed.

"When I look at you, I see the water," he said. "The wild waves that refuse to be tamed." His voice took on a dreamy tone, the words growing slurred. "I hate that you make me feel like this." Her brows furrowed, and he let out a delirious chuckle. "Don't *frown*." He raised his hand to wipe at her forehead, his movements sloppy. "Am I that awful at compliments?"

He tucked her wayward curls behind her ear, then brushed his fingers along her cheek. Barely there, a hint of a caress. It nearly undid her altogether.

"Bash—" she said his name as he swayed, as his hand dropped to the sands to steady himself. He was struggling to keep his eyes open, and the sight of him, weakened and dazed, had her reaching out to grasp him, her fingers digging into his muscled bicep.

He'd just reopened an old wound. The agony of reliving that night was painful in itself, but he'd still shared it with her, the daughter of his greatest enemy.

And she had drugged him out of his wits.

Bash tilted his head, struggling to keep himself upright. A look of hurt crossed his face. "Margrete, what did you do—"

He barely got the words out before he collapsed, his face turned to the moon and the clear skies above. Margrete froze, stunned at how well the Liander Blooms actually worked.

She leaned over his body. His chest rose and fell steadily, and she placed a finger to his throat to feel the rhythm of his pulse. She might have lingered there, her hand on his warm skin, for longer than necessary. She might have gazed down on him and wished she'd heard the rest of whatever secrets he'd been willing to share. But that time had passed, and regret was not an option.

Still, her heart fell as she cupped his cheek, the stubble rough against her smooth palm. "Sorry, pirate, but I can't let you decide my fate."

She stood, hovering above the sleeping king. *You need to do this,* she reminded herself. *Now, move!*

The wine bottle lay upon the sands, the red liquid soaking into the sand. With no other weapon at her disposal, Margrete grasped the neck and swung the bottle against a piece of driftwood. It shattered soundlessly, the green glass glinting in the moon's light.

Using the scarf she'd smuggled the sedative in, Margrete carefully wrapped the broken bottle neck and tucked it in her pocket. She felt better knowing she had something with which to defend herself. Who knew what she might encounter?

Taking off on unsteady limbs, Margrete raced across the packed sands and along the coastline to where she'd glimpsed the tethered boats earlier. No guards had followed them to the beach, but she stayed close to the tall reeds just to be safe.

A rickety dock jutted into the waves, the vessels she aimed for a welcome sight. Margrete thanked the moon goddess, Selene, for hiding behind the cover of the clouds. Even if a guard found himself close enough, they wouldn't see her easily under the heavy shroud of gray.

Her boots thudded against the mildewed planks as she sprinted across the deck and got to work untying the knots securing the small craft. Tossing aside the rope, Margrete hurled herself onto the fishing vessel, where she attended to the lone sail and readied herself for her journey. Adrenaline coursed through her as an image of falling overboard stole her thoughts, but she refused to allow herself to think about her inability to swim. Not when she was so close to succeeding.

As if to torment her, a band of lightning streaked across the sky as she shoved off from the dock, gray clouds forming to blot out the gleaming stars. *Surely not again,* she thought, but then rain started to fall. Gods. This damn island seemed to have it out for her.

Without another thought, desperate to craft her own fate, Margrete ignored the jagged lightning and booming thunder, pretending her skin wasn't being soaked through by the rain that ensued. She had battled storms before, and she would do so again.

It was a minute later, when a vicious wave crashed over the side of the skiff, that she realized she was in over her head.

CHAPTER TWENTY

MARGRETE

Seasoned sailors claimed to know when the sea was at its angriest. They could take one look at the waters and sense when conquering the waves would be futile. Margrete gleaned now would be such a time.

As soon as she made her way from the dock, away from the golden shore of Azantian, the sea grew angry. It had come about so suddenly, this storm, just as it had the first night she'd tried to leave. Whatever forces were working against her, Margrete cursed her luck, but she was too invested and too determined to turn back.

Her movements were uncertain as she adjusted the sail and struggled to hold tight to the till. She'd learned everything she knew about boats from books and watching others sail from atop her tower or, on the few occasions she was allowed, on the docks. On top of the riotous waters, her lack of experience wouldn't bode well.

Margrete grimaced as another mighty swell splashed over the hull. She wanted to shout into the night. Ask why the sea, the very entity that she knew spoke to her, was keen on hindering her plans for freedom. Wave after wave assaulted the small boat, and it took everything in her not to plummet overboard to certain death.

Yet even as she fought, she was being pushed back by the waves. Back to shore.

Away from *freedom*.

The waters hissed at her as though in reproach, great waves soaking her clothing and hair, weighing her down further. She could sense the anger, the saturated ire in the air, as the wind whipped at her cheeks.

She gripped the sides of the vessel, hands shaking while she prayed she had the strength to keep from being tossed overboard.

The damned storm had appeared out of thin air. Even the lightning blazing across the sky was strange, the jagged bolts an uncanny shade of white. It would almost be beautiful if she wasn't hanging on for dear life.

I'm not going to make it, she thought just as a flash of silver blinded her, the night alight with fire and surging electricity. She would either die on these waves or she would have to return and face Bash. Face what she'd done to him.

With sinking hope, Margrete knew her only way out of this mess alive was to turn around. Abandon the last chance she would likely have to forge her own path.

With a foul curse, she roared into the pounding rain, pushing on the till, forcing the vessel around. Margrete couldn't tell if it was only rain wetting her cheeks or if tears of frustration had joined the fallen drops. At this point, she didn't care.

She'd failed. Again. Nature had worked against her, *twice*. She was either extremely unlucky or the gods were simply cruel, toying with her for reasons she didn't understand.

Her hands trembled as she maneuvered the ship closer to the shore, the wild waves driving her to land. As though the sea knew it had won, the roaring wind and pelting rain eased, the drops falling in a steady rhythm. It was too late to turn back around and try again, not when all of her strength had been drained merely keeping herself afloat.

The swaying waters pushed her to the shore, and when the boat struck sand, Margrete fumbled overboard, the waves rising up to her thighs. Struggling through the water, she pressed on, tumbling into a heap when she made it to the shoreline.

In a moment of weakness, Margrete thought she heard whispers of her name being called. It sounded again, and this time, she lifted her head, not expecting to see the dark silhouette of a man in the near distance.

"Shit," she gasped, sputtering as a wave crashed around her.

Climbing to her feet, completely drenched from head to toe, Margrete reached into her pocket for the shard of glass she'd salvaged, but a jagged edge dug into her palm instead. A sharp pain lanced up her arm. She'd cut herself.

But the sting it brought about was the furthest thing from her mind as the man came closer. Swaying unsteadily on his feet, a bolt of lightning illuminated his face.

Pure, unadulterated *fury* painted Bash's features as he staggered toward her, his lips curled upward in rage. The sedative wasn't strong enough to knock him out for long, but it had certainly slowed him down, which almost made the anticipation worse.

Margrete realized, for the first time, that she was afraid, and not because Bash was angry, but because of *why* he was angry. Beneath the simmering ire, she glimpsed a fierce panic that could only be concern.

Concern for *her*. Not his bargaining chip.

"Are you *completely* insane, woman?" he roared, towering above her as he reached out for her wrist. He dragged her to him until her chest pressed against his. She shivered in her wet clothes as the rain picked up once more, seeming to match Bash's wrath. "You could've killed yourself!" His grip tightened, and he gave her a slight shake. "You could've drowned. *Fuck!*"

She could feel his hold loosen, the drug still making him weak. But even as he swayed and fought to remain standing, he held firm, demanding an answer.

"I had to try!" she said, unflinching. "You have no idea what it's like to live your life beneath the thumb of another. To have others decide every aspect of your existence. To not be in control. I can't do it anymore!" She was outright screaming now, the rain pelting her skin.

His eyes lightened ever so slightly as he swallowed her words. When he spoke, it was a soothing balm to her heated skin. Soft and gentle and so unlike the man who held her.

"You asked for my secrets." He swiped his free hand through his hair, brushing the wet strands out of his eyes. "You want to share the burden? I will tell you. Come dawn, I'll show you why I lay awake every night, unable to sleep because I'm worried that I will fail my people. That I won't measure up to my father. That I will be the king who destroys Azantian."

Margrete's arms moved on their own accord, snaking around his torso. Adrenaline flowed through her like a fresh breeze, his poignant confession warming the last of the ice barricading her heart.

"I'm nothing like the great man my father was," Bash murmured, eyes downcast. "And my people know it well. But that doesn't mean I will ever stop trying to do the right thing. If not to prove to Azantian that I can be the man it needs, then at least to myself."

Margrete gripped the back of his shirt and twisted the damp fabric in her fists. Bash lived beneath the shadow of his father, a leader who wasn't able to teach his son how to rule. That loss became a phantom that haunted his every decision.

"It is *because* you worry of such things that you are a good king," she finally said, holding his stare even as she sensed he longed to glance away.

She knew bad men—was raised by one—and bad men didn't lose sleep worrying about the welfare of others. They didn't struggle to keep a mask of control in place, if only to soothe the fears of those who looked to them for guidance.

Bash had finally lowered his mask, and what Margrete saw in its place had her heart racing in the most savage of ways.

Lightning spiderwebbed across the sky, and they both flinched. Bash dipped his head closer, glancing at the dark horizon before turning his attention solely to Margrete.

He stared into her eyes, gaze dancing, and suddenly she was too aware of his hard body pressed against hers. Perhaps they were *both* too aware, because she felt Bash's body begin to respond.

Her breath stilled, and though her mind said *RUN*, the rest of her had other ideas.

She arched against him, just slightly, but it was enough.

His breathing increased, and he pressed his forehead against hers. "Don't ask for something you don't want, princess."

Bash's voice came out on a raspy breath, his mouth so close. She wanted him to kiss her. Wanted to taste the rain on his lips, to feel his teeth drag down her throat. She should want anything but that, and yet...

"You have no idea what I want," she said.

And then she kissed him.

CHAPTER TWENTY-ONE

MARGRETE

The King of Azantian tasted of wine, want, and open seas.

Margrete couldn't seem to remember a time when her lips hadn't been on his or her body wrapped in a steel embrace of muscled arms and desire. She pressed into him, rising on the tips of her toes as he groaned, and the sound went straight to her core.

The kiss wasn't gentle or sweet. It was a vicious tangle of tongues and clashing teeth. Wild and full of life. Margrete couldn't imagine kissing him any other way.

"Margrete." He pulled away only long enough to murmur her name. His hand roamed to her breast, and she bowed into his touch, her body burning, her heart racing. She needed to feel him, to feel his skin on hers.

She'd lost all sense of who she was. What she *should* be doing. There was him and the sensation of freefalling. That was all.

Her fingers threaded through the wet curls at the back of his neck, pulling him closer, his stubbled jaw deliciously coarse against her cheeks. She could feel his excitement press into her stomach, his hunger driving her mad with need. His hand moved to the nape of her neck and slipped into her hair. He gave it a tug, exposing her to him, his lips a hot brand as he kissed up and down the length of her throat.

Bash worshipped her heated skin, his lips tracing the delicate curve of her neck. He breathed her in as though he were a man starved, disbelieving that she would return his passion with a ravenous appetite of her own.

Her fingers curled in his hair, and she yanked on the strands to guide him back to where his lips belonged. Margrete could feel his smile through his kiss, but Bash obliged her, nipping at her bottom lip as his hands settled on her waist.

Gods. She wanted *more*, her insatiable greed both terrifying and thrilling.

A bolt of lightning ignited the skies behind her closed eyelids and thunder shattered the air, the force of it shaking the sands they stood upon. Her lids flickered open as Bash pulled away with a groan, his eyes hooded. He looked completely undone, and Margrete secretly smiled at the knowledge that it had been her to do that to him.

But her smile soon dipped at the corners when she realized what she'd just done—and with *whom*. Her chest constricted as Bash's own features morphed into one of shock, his eyes widening as his gaze fell to her lips. When he lifted his eyes back to her stare, they were guarded, the spark that had ignited them seconds before now smothered.

She could only surmise what he was thinking. That he'd kissed his enemy's daughter. The woman he needed for the trade. His bargaining chip.

Margrete was prepared to break the uneasy silence that had fallen, to say *anything* to rid his face of the shame he appeared to feel, but the words died on her tongue. Bash sniffed the air and his nose wrinkled slightly. Worry replaced the mixture of remorse and lust clouding his gaze, and in a move too quick to be human, he grasped her injured hand.

Margrete had forgotten about the wound. She barely felt her limbs at all.

"You cut yourself." It wasn't a question. "We need to clean this," he forced out, his voice strained.

"Did you just...*smell* my wound?" she asked, her voice hoarse.

"Heightened senses," Bash explained, adding no further clarification to the unusual claim. He was more focused on her palm, examining her bloodied flesh with care.

Margrete's mind immediately drifted to thoughts of *what else* he could smell.

Her chest blossomed with heat, but she managed to say, "It's fine. Really, I've had worse." The last part slipped out, and Bash's face morphed into one of displeasure.

"No," he ground out. "It's not fine. It looks deep."

"Bash, truly, I'm all right," she argued, but now that the haze was wearing off, heat radiated from the wound. It did hurt. The passion that had struck her so fiercely was suddenly replaced with a heaviness in the pit of her stomach. She'd just kissed the man who'd kidnapped her. Welcomed him into her arms and yearned for his touch.

Was she that starved for affection? No. She knew it was more than that, but she wasn't ready to admit what she'd felt ignite the moment she saw him atop the cliffs in Prias. What she told herself was merely a little curiosity and a lot of hatred.

"Don't be stubborn." Bash was avoiding her gaze now. "Please," he added, swallowing visibly before offering her his arm.

Maybe it was because of the pleading in his tone, but she slipped her hand through the crook of his elbow and allowed him to lead them up the beach and beyond the palace doors. He was silent as they passed the guards posted in the main hall, his face contorting back into the apathetic mask she had grown to despise.

She liked what was beneath it too much.

"There's really no need for all of this," she protested when they entered her chambers. Bash was already striding into the bathing suite, ignoring her entirely. Margrete grabbed a folded blanket to sit on. Her clothes were soaked through, and there was no sense in getting her bed wet.

She lifted her hand and turned her bloodied palm in the dim light. It had stopped bleeding, but the rain had washed the blood down her arm and left her skin splattered with red.

Bash emerged moments later, carting clean linens and a small bowl.

He set them gently on the floor beside her feet and stood to his full height, his hands going to the buttons of his drenched shirt.

"You should get out of your wet clothes," he suggested without looking up from his work.

"I-I'm fine," she managed to say. Her lips parted as she watched his nimble fingers move, the nearly transparent material giving way to bronzed skin and a gloriously muscled stomach.

"I hope you don't mind if I do." He caught her eye, pausing on the final button. She gave a jerky shake of her head, and he continued.

He crumpled the shirt in his hand and tossed it to the floor out of the way. Margrete drank in the many tattoos that decorated his arms and chest. An image of herself licking the remaining rain droplets that slid down his rippling abdomen flashed across her mind.

"Ready?" he asked.

Margrete lifted her gaze from his chiseled body. It was difficult to think, let alone speak, and against her will more sinful images flooded into her thoughts like a rushing wave.

"Y-yes," she managed to croak, brushing a strand of damp hair behind her ear. Bash let out a shaky exhale before taking a seat beside her on the bed, his thigh pressing into hers.

When he shifted to get a better look at her injury, she noted how his eyes traveled the length of her body, only pausing when he reached her blouse, which left little to the imagination. The top buttons had come undone, and the thin material clung to her like a second skin.

"Let me see your hand, Margrete," he rasped, his chest rising and falling unevenly.

With strained movements, he bent down to retrieve the rag, squeezing out the excess water. She held out her wounded palm when he straightened, and with a tenderness she hadn't thought him capable of, he began to clean the cut. He tended to her wound like she was fashioned from the most fragile glass, his eyes trained to his work.

Margrete was thankful when he broke the silence that had befallen them. If another hushed moment passed, she might've shattered entirely.

"You really could've hurt yourself." His face turned serious as he briefly glanced to the balcony, to the storm raging outside. "It came out of nowhere," he mused. "I've never seen anything like that in all my years."

She hadn't either. Then again, everything had seemed so much more intense upon the waves.

"You know, when I was a young boy, I made the foolish attempt to sail during a storm as well." She lifted her eyes from her hand. "I thought I was a skilled sailor simply because I was the son of the king. That, and Azantians were made to hold their breath underwater for long periods of time, so I assumed I would be safe. I always did love storms," he added with a shake of his head.

Margrete smiled softly. It appeared there would be no discussion about the fact that she'd drugged him—or their kiss. Not for now, at least, and she had to admit that it was probably best to simply act as though neither incident had happened at all. Acknowledging them could only lead to trouble.

Bash dipped the cloth into the bowl, which now had a red tinge. "The sea devoured me." He chuckled, eyes glazed as he worked. "When my sailboat wrecked, the current took me under, right by the reef. I managed to slice myself open, and I barely made it back to shore in one piece."

"Your scar." The one across his brow. Bash lifted his head and tossed the dirtied cloth to the side. He flinched when she raised her hand, thoughtlessly running her thumb over the long-ago healed wound. Realizing she was touching him, again, Margrete dropped her hand to her lap.

Bash swallowed hard. "Azantians may be able to heal, but we still scar. It wasn't my first, nor will it be my last." Clearing his throat, he turned his attention to wrapping her hand with fresh linen, tying the cloth in place. "Now you have your first scar."

Their eyes met and held.

"It's not my first either," she said, thinking of all the horrors her father had inflicted on her body. "And I also doubt that it will be my last," she added, her own voice a throaty whisper. Her hand sat cradled in his warm palm, and when his other hand lifted to her face, Margrete's lashes fluttered, hating how she anticipated his touch.

Reverently, he grazed her cheeks, tucking damp strands of hair behind her ear. His fingers slid down the side of her neck, her throat, traveling down to her collarbones, seeming to memorize the shape of her. Margrete inhaled a sharp breath, her skin tingling.

She would do well to remind herself of her predicament, but she was rendered utterly mindless as the calloused pads of his fingertips traced the smoothness of her skin. She wanted his hands everywhere.

Needed it.

The contact was stealing all rational thought, all the air from her lungs. She remembered how he felt pressed against her body, how his lips fit perfectly with hers.

Heat stole across her cheeks. He'd wanted her, too.

As if he, too, realized his actions, his thoughts, Bash's wandering hand jerked from her skin. Clearing his throat, he stood abruptly, the soiled linens and bowl in his grasp.

"It's late," he ground out, but she could hear how his voice wavered. "You should get out of those wet clothes."

Margrete rose to her feet, standing inches away from him with her heart hammering. She was tempted to ask him to stay, her body mourning the loss of his touch, but instead, she said, "Thank you for..." She angled her head toward her wrapped hand.

Bash nodded, his jaw tense. "No problem, princess," he replied, still not moving.

This close, she had to tilt her head to take him in. She could see the turmoil roiling in his eyes. The flashes of what she knew to be desire.

"Goodnight, pirate." Margrete boldly inched closer, relishing the way his breath caught and how his pulse thrummed wildly in his throat. It made her feel powerful.

"Goodnight," he said, and Margrete smiled at the warring emotions twisting his features. They were the same ones she knew to be darkening her gaze.

They shouldn't have blurred the lines. They both knew that. She was smarter than this, not some silly girl who believed in happy endings.

Bash gave her a nod before turning on his heel, as if he too didn't have the words, the strength, to say anything that would further wreck them both.

Margrete watched him open the portal and disappear into the hall, leaving only the memory of a stolen moment in the rain.

CHAPTER TWENTY-TWO

BASH

Bash stared at the ceiling as pre-dawn light filtered into his room, trying to do anything but think of her. He'd barely slept, his lips still tingling from her taste. Her touch. Margrete had branded him, right there on the beach. She had utterly destroyed him.

Never in his life had he felt so out of control. He *needed* control as much as he needed air. It helped him cope with the weight of his crown. It was the only way he could see clearly. Think clearly.

But now, that control was nonexistent.

He thought of that kiss. The way she crushed her lips to his, fearless and hungry. She'd pressed her soft body against him and gasped when she discovered him hard for her. But she'd only pushed against him more, her desire matching his own. He'd wanted to strip her bare and take her on the sands in the middle of the storm, and he was fairly certain she wouldn't have protested.

He slid his hand below the covers. So much for not thinking about her.

Gods, he ached. He didn't know if this blinding lust was from the remnants of the drug still flowing through his veins or if she'd simply affected him that severely. It didn't matter. What mattered was that he needed release before he died of want.

And certainly, before he saw her again this morning.

Bash closed his eyes, letting himself envision what might've been if he'd taken her right there on the sands. He would've stripped her of her clothing, allowing the rain to wet her golden skin. He'd have licked the raindrops from the hollow of her throat before moving on to explore the valley of her breasts, the curve of her hips, the apex of her thighs. Bash imagined tasting her there, and a groan escaped him at the thought of the sweet sounds she'd make when she released upon his tongue. How her head would roll back, and she'd call out his name.

His hand moved quickly beneath the covers as images of her writhing beneath him, eyes hooded in ecstasy, drove him closer to the edge.

He could almost feel the bite of her teeth as she nipped his lips, his throat, her hands pressing against his back in a demanding plea to move faster. Harder. She would match his every savage thrust, taking everything he gave her.

Pleasure ripped through him in a violent wave. He buried his face in his pillow to muffle the moan he couldn't hold back.

Gods. All he had managed to do was torture himself further. Because now he desperately needed the real thing.

"Fuck," he cursed, slipping out of bed to clean himself. After, he sat in his chair by the fire, resting his head in his hands. His breathing slowed, and his heartbeat gradually eased into a normal rhythm. Control was simply not possible when it came to her—and for some reason, Bash didn't fear the loss of restraint. Not when it felt so damn good.

Too good.

Abandoning the fire and his wicked thoughts, he dressed in a rush, yanking on his boots and sliding a trembling hand through his hair. He glanced to his nightstand, at the book of fables his father had gifted him on his sixth birthday. For the past few days, he'd sent Margrete his favorite books along with her breakfast. After he found the old adventure novel, he circled her favored word for him—pirate—and sent it to her in hopes he'd get a reaction, though he wasn't sure at the time why he craved such a thing.

But of course, when she ignored him at dinner that evening, he grew more determined.

So Bash delivered another the next morning, this one more...personal. When she smiled at him that night, he'd gone straight to the library after dinner to select more. And like a fool, he found he wanted nothing more than to see if a smile graced her full lips when she read the notes he scribbled on the pages. If they made her laugh.

Without another thought, Bash grabbed the book from the table, tucking it below his arm. He was restless, anxious to see her again, and when he walked into the hallway outside his room, the guards eyed him with curious expressions.

Of course, they quickly averted their stares when he shot them a look of warning. He was still a king, and he didn't want his men witnessing him acting like a schoolboy.

Steeling his spine, he climbed the stairs and marched down the corridor to her room. With a nod to the guard, he placed his palm on the portal and inhaled a sharp breath as it cleared.

Her scent was everywhere. Floral. Innocent. Wild. She smelled of a summer's day by the water, and he breathed her in as he arranged the book of fables on her dresser for her to discover later.

He turned toward the bed with a quickening pulse. Margrete was sound asleep, curled up on her side, her deep chocolate hair splayed across her pillow. He wanted to run his fingers through the strands, to feel the silken smoothness of them. He pictured her hair wrapped around his fist, her back arched—

Bash shook his head, cursing himself. He had to stop this madness before it consumed him.

Swallowing down his insatiable need for her, he took a seat beside her tiny frame, the mattress groaning beneath his weight. Gods, she was beautiful.

Focus, he chided, hesitantly raising his hand. It fell on her bare arm, the smooth skin warm beneath his calloused hand.

He gave her a gentle shake. Bash had come here for a reason. He told her he would share his secrets, and last night he decided that she should know what her father stole. What they were up against. Ultimately, he was starting to...trust her.

The thought sent his heart plummeting.

"Bash?" Margrete's lids fluttered open, and he quickly withdrew his hand. "What are you doing here?" She sat up, wearing nothing but a flimsy ivory nightgown. His eyes drifted to the clear outline of her body. The thin material did little to hide the most tender parts of her—curves he wanted to map with his hands, his mouth, his...

He clenched his fists and forced himself to meet her sleepy stare.

Margrete's cheeks flushed a pretty pink, which was almost humorous given what they'd done last night.

Yanking the sheet above her chest, she lifted her hazel eyes to his.

"I wanted to show you something today. Explain some things." He knew that was all she wanted—answers. "Dress, and I'll return for you in twenty minutes."

Bash stood and turned for the portal before she could utter a word in reply, not trusting himself around her when she looked like that, all soft and warm and inviting.

He cursed, marching past his guard, venturing to the open terrace below her chambers. It was the same one she nearly killed herself trying to get to. Gods, he wanted to wring her neck for her recklessness. He also hated how much it impressed him.

Bash let out a weary groan, propping his elbows on the railing. He listened to the song of the sea, trying and failing miserably to clear his mind. He must be under some sort of enchantment. That was the only explanation for this insanity. This hunger.

When twenty painstakingly slow minutes had come and gone, he pulled himself from the railing. His blood roared in his ears as he walked back to her chambers.

When he entered, she was dressed and sitting on her bed, cradling her injured palm as she looked to the balcony and the sea beyond. She was uncharacteristically quiet, and he found he missed the edge in her tone whenever she battled with him.

"Ready?" he asked, his voice coming out gruffer than he intended.

She turned to face him and nodded. Her steps were light as she walked to his side, following him through the portal and down the corridor to the stairs. Every now and then on their silent trek to the main floor, Bash stole glimpses of her, wondering if she was thinking about last night. If she'd lain awake in bed as he had.

"This is Azantian's library," he told her before pushing open a set of double doors off the main hall. Instantly, they were assaulted by a breeze of dust and the potent smell of old books. "And within these walls lay all the answers you've been searching for."

CHAPTER TWENTY-THREE

BASH

Bash turned to Margrete, watching her reaction as she took in the room with wide eyes.

"It's..."

"Creepy, eerie, sinister—take your pick." He scanned the shelves of overflowing books and scrolls.

The entire room was comprised of dark stone, and the wooden shelves teemed with thick tomes and scrolls. Grim statues lined the space, depictions of nymeras and sea beasts keeping watch over the knowledge that Azantian held sacred.

Margrete stood before him, and Bash couldn't stop himself from closing the gap, his mind ignoring all logic and sense. Her hair tickled his cheeks as he leaned in to whisper into her ear.

"Are you ready?" he asked, enjoying the way she shivered in response.

He slid by her and sauntered to a stack of books lining the western wall. Behind him, Margrete let out a trembling breath, but she followed.

"These are the oldest books on our island. Likely the oldest books in the world." He trailed a reverent finger across the bottom of the shelf. "Our history lies within these pages. The birth of the sea itself."

Margrete reached out, her delicate fingers brushing across the cracked leather. A smile curved her lips, and Bash surmised she could spend all day trapped in this room. She had a clever mind and a sharp tongue, and he couldn't decide which one he liked more.

"And this..."—Bash cleared his throat and lowered to a knee, grabbing hold of a dense green tome—"...is what may help you understand why I can't stop until the captain returns what he stole." He handed her the book, a cloud of dust fluttering in the air. "Sit." Bash pulled out a chair beside one of the mismatched tables littered with texts and parchment.

She took a seat, eyeing him warily. He'd give anything to know what she was thinking. Instead of asking, though, he opened the cover and flipped through the pages until he found the chapter he sought.

"Here." He angled the book and tapped his finger on the bold lettering marking the top of the page.

She lifted her gaze to his before turning her attention to the book, grasping the edges and bringing it closer. "Stratias," she read aloud.

"It means balance," he explained, and she read on.

> The sea was born from the Goddess of the Wind and Sky's tears. It was said that Surria let two tears fall, flooding the barren earth and creating the sea. Twin boys rose from the waters, gods destined to one day rule the home of their birth. But while brothers, the boys grew into men with different ambitions.
>
> Darius longed for power, to become the greatest god amongst the divine. To be worshipped and revered. Malum didn't possess the same desires, content to share the sea with the mortals and uphold the ideals of justice and neutrality.

Margrete paused, brows furrowed. "There were *two* gods of the sea?" Bash knew most humans only knew of one—Malum. "Yes," he answered. "But you're not at the important part yet." He dropped his eyes to the text, and she continued reading.

> After thousands of years, Darius, the god who longed for domi-

*nance, grew impatient and decided to take matters into his
own hands. Fashioning creatures of teeth and claws, night-
marish beasts born from the depths, he sicced his abominations
upon his unassuming brother, thirsting for total control over
the waters.*

*But his brother was no fool, and not without power himself.
Malum created his own beasts, ones larger and mightier than
those of his kin. These creatures tore apart Darius's horde,
forcing him to surrender to the mercy of his twin. But the
monsters who triumphed escaped, fleeing across the realm
where they wreaked havoc and ended the lives of many.*

*Their mother, watching from the heavens, had seen her two sons
cause enough bloodshed and decided to intervene. Before they
could ruin the waters she adored, Surria condemned both her
children to harsh fates. Darius, she imprisoned within the body
of a human. He would be stripped of his powers for a thousand
years, doomed to walk among the mortals he nearly destroyed.*

*But before Surria could cast her punishment on Malum, he set off
to slay his beasts himself. When the time came to make the
killing blows, however, Malum hesitated. Unable to kill his
children, he fashioned the island of Azantian, where his
monsters would remain secured behind gates he forged from
his own bone shards.*

*Malum entrusted the woman he loved, a mere mortal, to watch
over his creations. As a safeguard to protect his lover and their
descendants, Malum gifted them with a piece of his divinity—
his own beating heart. Removing it from his chest, he placed it
upon the throne of Azantian, gifting his offspring with enough
of his power to maintain the creatures should his forged gates
ever fail. At the time, Malum didn't consider the consequences
of cutting out his heart, how it might drain him as time
progressed. He, like most gods, was arrogant, though Malum
would soon come to realize the error of his ways.*

When Surria learned what her son had done, she doomed Malum

to a thousand-year sleep. His coffin would be the Axilya
mountain ravines, thirty-five-thousand leagues beneath the
seas.

Margrete glanced up from the pages, questions brightening her eyes. "Wait. So the first Azantians were children of Malum and his lover? Does that mean..."

"There is only one Azantian still living who is of Malum's original bloodline, and you've met him already, though he isn't one for many words."

"Ortum," she whispered.

Bash nodded. "Ortum is the last of Malum's descendants. The last of the original Azantians. Ortum realized that the barriers needed to rise in order to protect the world, that the gates Malum forged for his beasts were weakening, and that we no longer possessed the Heart to keep them confined. We were only recently able to leave these shores and hunt down Malum's essence because Ortum cannot maintain a tight hold on his magic. Keeping the beasts in place drains him with every passing day."

Her eyes drifted back to the text, her lashes fluttering against her cheeks as she processed it all. "If Malum wakes and returns after his thousand-year sentence has ended, then won't he simply guard his children? Protect the realm from them?"

This was where Bash stumbled. "Ortum told me two months ago that he no longer felt the same connection to the waters as he once did. Before, he could sense the slumbering god through the mystical blood in his veins, but now he feels...nothing. Malum didn't consider the consequences of removing his heart, and, in doing so, doomed himself. Even when a thousand years comes and goes, he will be too depleted to return and protect the island he adored. And his sentence is almost up."

Margrete let out a slow breath. "Has anyone heard of Darius throughout the years?"

"Of that, I don't know, though, there have always been rumors. Darius was a known trickster, and I wouldn't be surprised if he showed himself over the years." Bash didn't have proof, but there were too many stories of powerful men with unusual abilities—abilities that would be impossible for a mere human to possess.

"Gods. My father stole the only thing that could protect us should the monsters escape. He all but ensured his own demise." A humorless scoff escaped her full lips. "He needs to be found," she added under her breath. "Malum's *heart* needs to be found. And taken. Because even if you tried to tell my father the truth of what he's done, he'd never believe it."

Bash reached over and grasped her hand, needing to feel her warmth enfolded in his palm. He wanted her to know the truth. All of it.

"After the captain betrayed my father's trust, he returned to Azantian one night with a ship full of mercenaries. They stormed our beaches and slaughtered everyone. They killed our people. Butchered them in their beds. Women, children. Even babes nestled in their cribs. Nobody was safe."

His heart clenched when he saw her eyes fill with tears that she didn't let fall.

"He ravished our palace and took as much gold and riches as his ship would allow. I was a child, so my father confined me to our royal suite, but I heard the screams. I don't think I could forget them if I tried.

"It was the night my father died, and I became our leader. When I found him, after the captain and his men had abandoned the dead within the palace, his body was still warm. I escaped my guard and flung myself on my father's body. It took two guards to remove me."

Margrete opened her mouth, but Bash held up a lone finger, silencing her. He wouldn't be able to get through this if he stopped. That night was a wound that would never properly heal.

"Before my father was murdered—before the captain stormed the palace—he implored Ortum for help. Ortum knew only one way to prevent Wood from ever returning, and while it was a risk, he performed the ritual anyway, desperate to stop the madman we all had trusted.

"Using the sacred words of the ancients, Ortum attempted to steal the power within the Heart. He hoped to place it within another vessel so that at least Malum's protective power remained on the island, but something went wrong. When he performed the ritual, most of its divine essence vanished into thin air, and only a small portion of its power remained in the Heart itself. After Wood left, he lifted the barriers to surround the island, ensuring nothing could pass through to the mortal world...and that your father could never find us again.

"In any case," Bash added, "only Ortum has the power to call forth the missing essence once he has his hands on the original vessel." It killed him to watch Margrete's face fall.

"If anyone can help, it's Ortum, princess," he said, trying to reassure her. His heart fluttered in his chest when she gave him a hint of a smile.

Gods, he had told her everything. And yet, he didn't feel as worried as he thought he would. If anything, releasing this truth brought him a sense of peace, because now she might understand his actions, the reasons he couldn't fail. If she understood, then maybe she'd look at him differently. Like someone who was worthy of respect. He'd seen a glint of that in her eyes last night, and he needed more.

"Nothing I say can make it better," Margrete began, her other hand coming to rest atop his. "But please know, I'm aware of how evil my father is. We need to get the Heart back so Ortum can attempt to call back Malum's power." Her features turned to stone as she added, "And in the process, my father needs to be destroyed. If only so he cannot harm anyone else ever again."

Oh, Bash would destroy him. He'd take immense pleasure in the act.

Bash opened his mouth before he thought better of it, the words he didn't dare speak before now tumbling out in a rush. "You know, I cornered Ortum years ago, asking him for solutions should we never get the Heart back. He told me my prayers would be answered when the blood of our enemy arrived on our shores. Only then would I find the peace I craved." Bash stared at her intensely, his heart racing. "I used to think he meant the captain, but now, I imagine he was talking about you."

Margrete bit her bottom lip, and Bash's eyes fell to where she trapped the flesh between her teeth. It took great effort to look away.

"Bash, I—" She surprised him when her lean fingers threaded with his. "I hope I'm a part of the reason the Heart is returned. I want to do everything in my power to help. To help *you*."

Those eyes, so wide and full of breathtaking sincerity, stole his air, and, for just a moment, Bash imagined that nothing in the world could ever be wrong if he remained trapped in her gaze.

Just when he was about to do something he might regret—like lean over and press his lips to hers—she cleared her throat, withdrawing her hands from his. Bash watched as she moved away from him, her fingers trembling before she hid them in her lap.

He was amused when she glanced shyly to the stacks, her long hair shielding most of the blush that painted her cheeks. She scanned the rows and rows of books in calculating silence, and Bash curiously observed as her expression became shrewd.

All at once, she shoved from her seat and went to a stack of over-flowing texts. "Maybe there's another answer," she mused, her fingers whispering along the ancient leather spines.

"I've searched for everything. Spells, rituals, even blood sacrifice, which is forbidden in my kingdom."

Margrete crouched and pulled out a thin red book worn from age. She turned it over in her hands and saw the two interwoven circles adorning the cover, their edges shining in gold.

"What do you have?" he asked, not remembering ever having seen that book before.

"I'm not sure," she answered. "If I'm not mistaken, I'd say it was some sort of...journal." She flipped through the text but then held down a page, her eyes widening at whatever she saw there. "*I am forgotten. I am nothing when I should be all,*" she read aloud, her voice trembling.

Bash felt the hair on the back of his neck rise as his heightened senses picked up the scent of copper and rust.

"Shit," Margrete cursed, pulling her hand away. The bandage around her palm was red with blood.

"What happened?" Bash jumped to his feet.

"My wound must've opened up. I got a little blood—" Margrete let out a hiss of pain and dropped the book to the stone floor.

The ground beneath Bash's boots trembled, vibrations working their way up his legs. Margrete opened her mouth in horror as the floor tilted and books flew from their shelves and landed in a disorderly heap.

He was halfway to her when the very shelf she gripped began to wobble. Without a thought, Bash lunged forward and wrapped his arm around her waist, propelling them out of the way. The wooden bookcase crashed to the floor seconds later.

Bash cradled her head before it collided against stone, his chest pressing against her soft curves.

Her breaths came out ragged, her eyes creased with fear. He didn't move, not even as the earth settled, quieting, the beasts below them calming. If anything, he tightened his hold, her hot breath tickling his lips as he fought to regain control.

"Margrete." He spoke her name like a prayer as pages fluttered down all around them. "Are you all right?"

She was looking at him the same way she had last night, right before she leaned onto the tips of her toes and kissed him, setting his world on fire.

"I'm fine," she managed to reply, her words coming out on a rasp.

He tensed at the sensuous quality of her voice, a heat building within him.

Her lashes fluttered, hands moving to his chest. She lingered, her parted lips a temptation he wouldn't be able to resist if she didn't push him away. Margrete had the vexing gift of being enticing without even trying.

Slowly, she lifted a lone finger to trace the curve of his jaw, his cheek, before mapping out the column of his throat. Bash could feel nothing but her caress, the softness of her as she memorized him, her cunning eyes devouring every detail.

"I'm going to help you, Bash," she said. Heat pooled in his belly at the sound of his name on her sweet lips. He wanted to capture the sound for his own.

"You're going to make the trade with my father and get the Heart," she insisted, and his chest constricted at the thought of her in that monster's presence. "But if he manages to evade you, I will hunt him down myself."

She dropped her hand back to her side, her expression fierce and deadly, her mouth set in a determined line. Bash found her hard edges beautiful.

"Together," he said, forcing himself to his feet. He offered her his hand, and she readily accepted. Even when she stood, he didn't release his grip. Her hand belonged in his. "We'll take him down together."

CHAPTER TWENTY-FOUR

MARGRETE

THAT AFTERNOON, ADRIAN WAS KIND ENOUGH TO TAKE MARGRETE to the training terrace where a welcome breeze battled the scorching sun. Still, she found herself sweating by the time Adrian demonstrated how to get out of a chokehold. It didn't help that her mind drifted elsewhere—back to all the truths Bash had revealed in the library.

Truth he'd *trusted* her with.

There wasn't much time until dinner when she returned to her chambers. She found a cool bath waiting and was about to slip into the bathing suite when a flash of red caught her eye. She stopped in her tracks, zeroing in on a leather-bound book placed on the edge of her dresser.

Margrete moved closer to pick up the tome, its edges rounded and worn. Running a cautious hand across the faded cover, she brought it to her nose, shutting her eyes as she breathed in the familiar scent.

It smelled of him.

Margrete exhaled slowly before setting it back on the dresser. She turned to the bathing suite, forcing the book and the meaning behind it to the back of her thoughts.

But it was when she was sinking into the tub, her aching limbs seeming to sigh in relief, that she felt the crushing weight of reality rob her breath.

If her father didn't trade her for the Heart, and Ortum couldn't call forth the missing power—that divine essence bestowed to Azantian by the sea god himself—then what would happen to her world? A world she hadn't even begun to explore, with people she hadn't yet met and adventures she longed to be a part of.

Bash opened her eyes in the library, making her appreciate how vital his mission was to the realm. Margrete now understood that she couldn't hinder his endeavors any longer. She would willingly go back to her father—if he made the trade—and she would do so knowing what was at stake.

This acceptance helped her realize something else. Right now, at this very moment, she wasn't at the keep. Not under her father's thumb. No. She was *here*, in one of the most legendary and stunning places known only through books of lore. And maybe she just wanted to enjoy the time she had left, to indulge for *once* in her young life.

While shadows of doubt followed her as she dressed for dinner, there was also a lightness in her heart, a feeling of peace that came from letting all else go. She breathed in the wonder she'd previously denied herself, and the crushing weight of the things she couldn't control tumbled from her shoulders. Even as the sands of time flowed to the bottom of the hourglass, she felt...*liberated*.

It was minutes after she'd finished dressing and mere seconds after she'd put the last touches on her smoothed hair that a familiar voice startled her.

"I can genuinely say I'm impressed by you." Bay stood by the portal, his hands shoved into his fine blue trousers, a bored look on his face. "Adrian told me all about your little midnight sail. He saw Bash bring you back into the palace, your clothes all wet and your hand bloody."

Margrete flushed. She hoped Adrian hadn't seen what else had conspired on the beach.

"I seem rather terrible at escaping."

"You truly are," Bay said. "Possibly the worst displays I've ever seen, though one has to admire your determination."

If they were friends, *true* friends, she might've gently smacked his shoulder. Instead, she shook her head and tried not to roll her eyes.

"Well, shall we?" Bay asked. "I bet you want to eat before you try something else tonight. Bash really has his hands full with you."

She wanted to tell Bay that she wasn't a flight risk anymore, that she'd made up her mind to stay, but the words didn't find their way to her mouth. Instead, she smiled and walked beside him to dinner.

By the time they entered the dining hall, Ortum, Nerissa, and Shade were already present, Nerissa tapping her long nails impatiently on the glass tabletop. Margrete took her seat with Bay at her side. Not long after, Bash and Adrian arrived, the former wearing a scowl.

As he lowered himself into his seat, Bash met her gaze. Gradually, his eyes drifted to her wrapped hand. She saw a hint of concern flash across his stoic features, but then he twisted to Adrian, who sat on his left.

Ortum appeared noticeably drained, his shoulders drooping, coral eyes creased. He caught her stare more than once and held it, bestowing her with knowing smiles. The man was born from a god. He was the reason the gates remained strong after Malum's heart had been stolen. She'd been wrong to feel uneasy around him, though to be honest, her pulse still raced whenever she locked eyes with the ancient man. Margrete told herself it was merely because of *what* he was.

Surely that had to be why her stomach churned.

Dinner was served while the king and his commander caught up in deep conversation. Not that it mattered much to her. She endured in silence for most of the meal, occasionally sneaking peeks at the Azantian king. Only once did he catch her, and she quickly averted her eyes to Bay, who proceeded to ask how she liked her fish.

Her mood, the one she fashioned from hope that she was doing the right thing, diminished the longer she was in the king's presence. He was a living reminder that there were so many things she *hadn't* experienced. Whatever was happening between them—the teasing, the flirting, the stolen moments—would come to an end. A week ago, she would've laughed at such a thought, that she would possess any sort of remorse over leaving. Now, the idea of never seeing him again left her feeling hollow.

At her side, Bay tried his best to carry their conversation, but she found it too difficult for practiced niceties. While his attention momentarily brought a weak smile to her lips, it faded, replaced with a frown that wouldn't seem to leave.

Instead, she passed the time by fidgeting with the ring Arabel had given her at the market. The polished band glittered with every rotation, and she thought of the woman and her mysterious words. Maybe Arabel was simply mad, but the ring settled her roiling emotions, and for that, Margrete was thankful.

"I wish you didn't have to go," Bay confessed, his voice hushed so no one else could hear. It seemed he'd forgiven her earlier brusqueness and recognized that her silence signified a greater hopelessness.

Across the table, Bash lifted his head, ears perked as he listened. Shade was speaking animatedly about some new vessel being constructed, but Bash's focus remained steadily on the captain's daughter.

Margrete willed her thoughts away from the king and responded to Bay's declaration with a melancholy smile. "I find myself wishing to be anywhere but back at that keep. However, I do not plan on staying long."

"Bash doesn't have a choice."

In sending her home, he meant. In exchange for the Heart.

"I understand that now. Bash explained the importance of this trade, and while I do not look forward to it, I understand why he's worked so tirelessly to return order. Something I can't help but commend him for." She shot Bay a look and, attempting to lighten the mood, said, "But don't tell him that. Wouldn't wish to inflate his ego further."

Even though freely cooperating in the trade was the right thing to do, panic squeezed her lungs at the thought of returning to her father. The captain's presence always turned her into a helpless girl. No matter how old she was, he had a way of making her feel so small.

Margrete suddenly pushed up, her chair screeching against the polished marble floors. "I'm tired," she announced, suddenly the target of every eye in the room. "I'd like to retire for the evening."

All of those eyes shifted to Bash as if asking his permission *for* her. He nodded, and their heads dropped in response to refocus their wavering attentions to their full plates. Bash shoved out of his chair, hands smoothing the nonexistent wrinkles of his trousers. "I'll accompany you back."

Nerissa's fork clattered to the plate, the sound echoing.

"Adrian can always do that, Bash," she chimed, her sing-song voice laced with apprehension.

Bash stiffened. "There's no need." He gave Nerissa a nod of dismissal, but the seer wouldn't be silenced.

"Do you really think it's a good idea?" The room fell into an uneasy hush. "We all see what's happening here, and as I've told you before—"

"Enough, Nerissa," Shade said. Nerissa shut her mouth and averted her gaze.

Margrete swallowed hard, ready to flee the tension that had swarmed the room. She was thankful when Bay stood up, gave her a quick peck on her forehead, and wished her a good night. Adrian merely bestowed his usual gentle smile, but his eyes flickered to Nerissa.

"Let's go." Bash tilted his head, and she didn't hesitate to leave.

When they were safely in the main foyer, beyond the hearing of the others, Margrete asked, "What was that all about?"

Bash let out a groan. "Nerissa is very...protective of me. She seems to think that you and I are..." A hint of color entered his cheeks. "That we're getting closer than we should."

They *were* getting closer than they should.

Bash closed his eyes for a moment, the weight of the silence deafening.

"I know this isn't what you want. Tomorrow, I mean," Bash began, uncharacteristically tentative, "but I trust you will not let him win ever again." Bash took her hand in his, his warmth wrapping around her fingers. "You have no idea what I would do for my people and the waters I've been entrusted to protect. Without you, my legacy, my sacred duty..."

"You no longer have to convince me, Bash," she promised. He nodded, yet to release her hand.

A long moment passed between them. As if they couldn't help themselves, they drifted closer, pulled by that cursed invisible bond. Margrete's chest filled with heat.

"You didn't count the cutlery." The words tumbled from her lips without thought, but they had their desired effect.

Bash took a step back. His eyes slowly lit up, the gold flecks swirling with renewed mischief. "Ahh, yes. It must have slipped my mind." He squeezed her hand, and she could've sworn the smile he wore brightened the entire hall. "How very kind of you to remind me."

"Just giving you a heads up, is all." She shrugged, her chest loosening. With the moment shattered, she could breathe again.

"Hmm. Well, if you plan on trying to kill me tonight—again, I might add—then at least do me the kindness of allowing me to show you my favorite place on the island. Though, I might be the only one who holds that opinion."

Margrete's lips parted. She was torn. If she went with him now, she might find herself liking him even more. A part of her missed the days when it was easy to hate him.

"And if you could wait to murder me until *after* we get to our destination, I'd appreciate it. I'd hate for my blood to stain the marble floors. They were just polished."

"I'll consider your request." She smirked, shooting him a shrewd look. She nearly faltered when both dimples popped up on his cheeks.

Bash tugged on her hand, sending her feet into motion. "Come on, princess. Let's go before you get any more ideas about drugging me again."

As they walked, the quivering flames of the sconces danced upon the glass walls, highlighting the natural beauty of the palace. They passed countless gilded archways and intricate doors, and Margrete speculated silently as to what each one concealed. She was about to inquire what lay behind a forest-green door with intricate silver spikes when Bash abruptly halted. Margrete collided into his muscular back with a groan.

"Ouch." She rubbed at her forehead, and Bash twisted around to smirk. But he didn't apologize, and he didn't let go of her hand.

They'd just descended a flight of stone steps where a set of iron doors loomed at the end of a stretched hall. With a lightness in his step, Bash pulled her along, closing the gap between them and the approaching doors, each footstep echoing.

"Through here." Bash waved his hand over the lock. The tarnished metal felt out of place amongst the ethereal silver and delicate sea glass of Azantian.

The lock clicked, and a light flashed. The gates swung open a second later.

"I'd ask how you did that, but I have a feeling it's similar to the workings of my portal."

"You'd be correct," Bash replied, ushering her into the gloom and beyond the dim lighting of the corridor. "The magic responds to those who are granted access, but not many have access to this place."

"I can't make out a damn thing." She swore, stepping deeper into the void.

Bash chuckled, the rich sound of his laughter heightened in the dark. "Patience," he chided, and clutched her tighter.

After many long moments of silence and darkness, Margrete prepared to hassle him for an explanation, but her open mouth soon closed.

A flicker of purple light shined across the rocky walls. It lasted but a heartbeat.

"Almost there," Bash assured her, steering them farther into the tunnel's depths.

If she narrowed her eyes, she could just make out the walkway, but even so, it wasn't enough to move around without Bash's assistance. He seemed to know this tunnel as well as he knew himself.

Margrete heard the patter of dripping water, the sound growing louder as they approached. Above, the ceiling rose hundreds of feet high, stalactites pointing threateningly to where Bash and Margrete stood. Every now and again, the ephemeral purple sparks ignited, leaving the jagged walls buzzing with living color. When those playful lights faded, their world was once again cast into obscure darkness.

"Just wait for it." A beam of light illuminated Bash as he held up a lone finger. His eyes shifted to the center of the cavern's ceiling, a spiraling roof that escalated to a single apex—much like the inside of a tower.

"What am I waiting for?" she whispered, growing increasingly curious. Something about this place was both familiar and uncomfortably sinister.

"I promise...You won't regret it."

Another flicker of violet brightened his emerald eyes which held an unnatural quality. It made him appear wraithlike, a ghost of a soul with a human face.

When nothing happened, she said, "Still waiting, pirate."

"Patience certainly isn't one of your virtues, princess." Bash's face glowed with a boyish smile. Whatever this place was, it meant a lot to the king.

"What is it called?" she asked, her voice low. "It's...unreal." That was an understatement for what she was witnessing.

"This is the Adiria Cavern. Roughly translated to *the soul*," Bash replied reverently. "Malum stood on these hallowed grounds and forged the island with his lover. Even we Azantians don't know all the secrets that this place holds."

Her pulse quickened with anticipation.

"It happens once a day, always at the same time. Most watch it from above, but I like to watch it from down here. It's like being inside of a starflame." Bash chuckled. "Just don't ask Adrian about it. He has way too many theories about this place and will talk about it for hours."

Margrete smiled at the thought. She could picture Adrian doing just that.

"What's a starflame?" she asked.

Another flare lit up Bash's face, and she glimpsed the crookedness of his grin. "Oh, you'll see."

Caught up in his excitement, Bash inched behind her until his chest pressed flush against her back. Looming over her with his chin brushing the top of her curls, he trailed his finger against the underside of her jaw.

Tipping her head back, he whispered into the shell of her ear, "Look up." His breath came out ragged and hot.

She froze, icy adrenaline coiling through her chest. The kind that made her knees weak and her breaths short.

Her swirling thoughts came to an abrupt halt when Bash pushed more firmly into her back, the solidness of him pressing against her. Like a switch, the ability to care that he was touching her in this way vanished.

He dropped his hands to her waist and hooked his thumbs into the thin fabric of her trousers, gently digging them into her hips. Her responding exhale came out shaky and uneven, and Margrete had to bite her lip to contain her trembling.

She mouthed a silent curse.

"Right now," Bash whispered, "in the dark where it's only us, I want to pretend. There is no tomorrow. I'm not a king, and you're simply a woman who drives me insane." His raspy words tickled her skin. "For once, I don't want to hold myself back." He pressed his lips to the side of her neck and drifted down to her collarbone, his mouth warming her flesh. "I don't want to resist what you do to me. What you've been doing to me since the moment I saw you." His lips brushed the sensitive area below her ear. "Would you like to pretend with me, princess? Give in for just a night?"

She couldn't breathe properly. Not when he was touching her—kissing her—like this. Instantly, she was transported back to the beach, to the moment she leaned up and pressed her lips against his. How right it had felt. How oddly...natural.

In answer to his question, his plea to simply pretend, Margrete wrapped her hands around his muscled forearms. He let out a hiss when she trailed her fingers across his skin, his nose pressed into her hair.

She imagined it helped being here, secluded in a cavern of wonder, hidden from the eyes of the men and women he ruled. He could simply be...*Bash*. It had to be why he brought her here, so he didn't have to think about all the many reasons they shouldn't be doing this.

As the violet lightning struck the sides of the damp cavern and their combined breaths became their own kind of forbidden melody, Margrete felt drunk off his nearness. Bash was a rush, and she craved the high.

"Margrete." Bash's voice cracked with a desperateness that curled her toes. "What have you done to me—"

And then their world exploded.

Violent bursts of light and color erupted, breaking free from their rocky prison. It was startling, the sheer brilliance of it. Blinding and hypnotizing all at once.

Margrete gawked as the cavern danced with life, the violet-blue gems embedded in the walls igniting with life, a thousand flecks of burnished silver captured within their smooth facets. She stood in the center of an enchantment, gaping as resplendent waves of periwinkle and plum crested and fell against the rugged walls. Like an echo, those incandescent ripples pulsed across the stone ceiling, which became a spiked sky of delicate fairy stars.

Back in the center, the lights danced, tinsel sparks of purple frolicking up to the spiraling point. Pirouetting around and around, they erupted into an explosive finale, bolts of lilac and vibrant orchid shattering as they fought to escape through the pinprick of an opening. A single star could be seen from where they stood, and Margrete knew without a doubt it was the same star sailors followed when they lost their way home.

Bash tightened his grip on her waist, sending her jolting back from her dazed trance. The cavern's roof settled and shook, once again calming to darkness and then on to nothing.

They were left in the pitch black, alone. Without her sight—in this void where reality couldn't find them—Margrete swung around. Even in the dark, Bash found her face, and he cradled her cheeks in his hands. His touch was tender, and Margrete's eyes fluttered closed.

His breathing grew closer until she could feel his hot breath tickling her lips. She could do this. Pretend. Give in to the magic and give in to her desires.

"Bash—"

The force of his lips silenced her. He snaked his hand through her curls, fisting her hair at the nape of her neck. She groaned against his mouth, half in surprise and half in blissful relief. In his ironclad hold, there was nowhere to go, nowhere to run, and in the darkness, she could feed her hunger, the fierce longing she was helpless to fight now that she'd tasted him.

His kiss was soft, reverent. Bash took his time, exploring her mouth with his tongue and groaning when she slipped her own past his parted lips.

His hands roamed her body, cupping her backside, her hips. His skillful fingers teased as they grazed the undersides of her breasts. Everywhere he touched she *burned*. Her own hands explored the rippling muscles of his chest, and she cursed the thin layer of linen that contained his heat.

When his tongue traced along the seam of her lips once more, she began to ache, the throbbing need between her legs the sweetest form of torture. She moaned, pleading, and curved her hips toward him, unable to resist, needing so badly to feel him.

Bash ravished her with renewed hunger, commanding her lips as he teased her tongue in ways she hadn't thought possible. Even in a world of magic.

But this was an entirely different manner of enchantment.

She arched against him again, her mind lost to wanting, and a low groan rumbled in Bash's chest.

"Margrete." He pulled away, tracing her bottom lip with his thumb. There was an unspoken question held captive within her name, and when he slowly undid the buttons of her trousers, she understood his need to touch her. He was hesitant as he toyed with the band of her pants, waiting for her permission.

Margrete lifted to her toes and placed a gentle kiss on his lips.

"Yes," she whispered against his mouth. "Gods, yes."

He groaned as he slid his fingers between her legs, leisurely moving up and down her silken undergarments. He paused when he felt the evidence of her desire, his chest reverberating with approval.

"You're so very wet, princess," he murmured as he ruined her in the most sinful of ways. "Have you fantasized about this? My fingers on your skin, between your legs?" She may have nodded, but everything became a blur. "I know I have. Since the moment I met you, I haven't thought of anything else. My need only worsened the more you challenged me, the more you surprised me..." He let out a strained exhale. "You've thoroughly corrupted me."

She could feel the smile on his lips when he kissed her, his forehead pressed against hers as he worked his skillful fingers under the silk band separating their skin. She gasped at the contact.

"Tell me what you want, Margrete," he rasped, his hungry voice sending shivers down her spine. That delicious ache in her core only grew, turning her into a panting mess.

"Do you want me to touch you here?" He glided across her heat, his strokes purposely light as he teased her. "Do you want me inside you?"

She sucked in a breath, and all she could do in reply was nod her head, a sound between a gasp and a groan falling from her mouth.

Bash chuckled darkly. "I see," he said, and his touch *finally* drifted to the most sensitive part of her. He worked his thumb in gentle circles. "More?" he asked.

"Yes," she said, her voice airy and wanton as she thrust herself deeper into his palm, shamefully begging.

Another groan escaped him, and she shuddered at the sound.

He nipped at her ear. "I can't wait to feel you fall apart," he whispered, before he plunged a finger inside her.

Margrete arched, releasing a frantic cry.

"That's it," he coaxed when she began to move with him. A strangled whimper left her as her hips matched his lazy pace, but she needed more. So much more.

"Bash." His name was a prayer. "Please."

She had told herself she wouldn't beg, but she no longer cared. The throbbing ache was almost painful, that coiling heat inside of her tightening. Another finger joined the first, filling and stretching her so completely. She bit her bottom lip when he *truly* began to move, thrusting his fingers in and out as his thumb pleasured her in ways she had never known.

She clutched his shoulders, her nails biting into the hard muscle. She held on tight, feeling like she might explode, much like the lightning that had erupted in the cave. She was going to—

The world around them ceased to exist. She was plummeting, falling into agonizing bliss. Her body shuddered as Bash held her steady, as sparks flashed behind her closed eyelids.

His movements slowed, milking every ounce of pleasure from her body.

Margrete's head fell against his chest, her breathing uneven—as was his. "That was..."

She had no words.

"I know, princess." Bash slipped his hand from her trousers, and she instantly mourned the loss of him. "I only wish I could've seen your face."

A lone bolt of periwinkle sparked, and Margrete's lids fluttered open, catching a hazy glimpse of him. His hair was tousled, those full lips parted. He looked as undone as she felt.

Darkness filled the cavern once more, and with it, Margrete found the courage to reach for his trousers.

But Bash stopped her, placing a hand over hers.

"No. Tonight was about you." He brought her hand to his lips and kissed her knuckles sweetly. "I got my wish already, and I fear I've taken far more than I deserve."

"Bash—"

He silenced her with his mouth as his hands once more tangled in her hair. While Margrete's lips were occupied, her hands were not.

The clang of his belt echoed in the cavern, and before he could pull away and protest, Margrete cupped his hard length in the palm of her hand. Bash groaned into her mouth even as his body went rigid.

Margrete didn't cease kissing him until she'd freed his velvety smoothness. Cautiously, she began to move her hand. The noises that escaped Bash were the most beautiful sounds she'd ever heard.

"Margrete." He chanted her name, his hot breath fanning across her parted lips.

"You say you don't deserve anything in return," she said, her movements quickening. Bash's grip on her hair tightened, and she savored the slight sting. "But you didn't consider what *I* want, dear pirate." She could feel him swelling, throbbing in her palm. "And I want to touch you. Make *you* fall apart by *my* hand."

He was nearing release. She could tell by the way his breathing stuttered, the way he gripped her hair even tighter, the way his body trembled. His hips began to move with the rhythm of her touch, and soon, a moan ripped from his chest, echoing off the cavern walls.

Margrete smiled in the dark, relishing the way he lost control. Sucking in a sharp inhale, Bash stiffened, and she swallowed his next moan with a kiss. She devoured the sounds of his pleasure as though they were hers alone.

When he calmed, still pulsing in her palm, Margrete pulled back, allowing him room to breathe.

He let his hands fall from her hair to cup her cheeks and rested his forehead against hers, their noses touching. "That was...Gods." He sighed. "Never again shall I deny your wishes, princess." He smiled against her skin as he kissed up and down the column of her throat, only to return to her mouth once more. When he finally pulled away, her lips were swollen and bruised, and he reached for her hand again. Their fingers interlocked. "Thank you," he said.

Margrete's brow scrunched. "For what?"

"For pretending with me."

CHAPTER TWENTY-FIVE

MARGRETE

Dawn came too soon.

Margrete dressed in pants and a lightweight navy shirt, the sleeves rolled up and secured with pearl buttons. The linen trousers hung loosely on her hips, so she fastened them in place with a belt made of crushed opals.

If she wasn't set to meet her fate, she might've admired how she looked in the mirror—not like herself. Not the Margrete from Prias. This would have even brought a smile to her lips, but she knew better than to smile. She knew better than to hope or to wonder *what if*.

That hadn't worked out so well thus far.

Last night came back in a rush. She could still feel Bash inside of her, his lips against hers as she pressed against his body. Gods, she could still hear his groan as he came undone.

Margrete cursed, shutting her eyes and willing away thoughts of Bash and what they shared. She told herself they'd only been *pretending*, that it wasn't real.

But she also knew a lie when she heard one, even if she was only lying to herself.

"Good morning."

Margrete's lids jolted open, and the man she'd been fantasizing about stood before her like some chiseled god. The breeze from the balcony ruffled his hair, sending it flying into his piercing stare, the green in his irises vibrant in the rising sun.

"Bash," she greeted, trying to regain her composure. "I didn't hear you come in."

"I knocked," he replied, shoving his hands into his pockets.

Had she been *that* consumed by her carnal thoughts that she hadn't heard his approach? Apparently so.

He swallowed hard as he took a hesitant step closer. "I wanted you to know that...last night meant something to me," he began, staring at her lips. "I wish today didn't have to happen." His throat bobbed, the muscles in his jaw impossibly tight.

Margrete knew he was attempting to present a strong facade, but it took only one look into his eyes for her to feel the crushing weight of his regret.

"It's all right, Bash," she said, taking both of his hands from his pockets and squeezing them. He cursed beneath his breath, but she squeezed him even tighter.

Bash threaded his fingers through hers, holding her steady as her pulse fluttered.

She was physically unable to speak when he looked at her that way.

He freed one of his hands and placed it on her cheek. "I'd forgotten what it was like to *feel*, Margrete Wood." His thumb rubbed soothing circles into her skin. "But my heart has never beat as fast and sure as it has when I'm in your presence."

"Bash." Her voice trembled as she said his name.

She wanted him to close the gap between them, to kiss her and weave his fingers through her hair again, to hold her against his solid body. Margrete wanted all of him.

Instead, he rested his forehead against hers, his warm breath tickling her nose. She inhaled his air, tasting a life she would be a fool to believe she could have. She tasted freedom, adventure, and nights spent with a rogue who might steal her heart if she wasn't careful.

He laid his chin atop her curls, and she wound her arms around his torso without thought. For minutes they stood like this, a frozen portrait of remorse and farewell. Finally, Bash spoke into her hair, barely above a whisper.

"It's time, princess."

Margrete pulled back abruptly, leaving the warmth he offered, abandoning what was had never truly been hers to begin with.

Bash stiffened, a statue of a man conflicted. At his sides, his hands rose as if to cup her cheeks once more, only to lower and curl into fists instead.

"Let's go, then." She broke the silence that had descended. "We can't delay the inevitable much longer."

As Margrete walked across the glass bridge leading to the docks, she thought about how the waters appeared duller than when she'd arrived. The sky was overcast and dreary, and the bleakness of this new day matched her emotions.

Margrete tried not to think about the perilous journey ahead. Of what seeing her father would do to her. But her reality refused to be ignored.

In the distance, the wharf teemed with sailors bustling to finish fitting the vessel before the fateful voyage. A few smaller boats rocked on the waves, but the ship's cobalt beauty stole all the focus.

"It seems you've made quite the lasting impression," Bash murmured in her ear as they stepped onto the ever-changing planks leading to the *Phaedra*. Neither of them had spoken a word since they'd left her chambers.

Before she had time to wonder who he was talking about, a familiar voice drifted over her shoulder, deep and kind.

"Margrete," Adrian said.

She turned around to find him and Bay standing there, worry etching every line of their handsome faces. They each held out an arm, and she went to them, allowing them to fold her up in an embrace. She would miss these two unlikely friends more than she cared to admit.

"We had to say goodbye." Bay sighed, squeezing and then releasing her shoulders. Adrian stepped back, eyes downcast.

"You've brought more excitement to this island than I've seen in a long time." When she shot him a look, Bay added, "And I get attached rather quickly to cunning women who scale palaces and wield words like knives. Especially ones who can make our brooding king smile. Gods know he's been in a better mood since you arrived—"

"Bay." Adrian's lips stretched thin in warning.

"Fine, fine." Bay waved him off. "But you know it's true."

Margrete glanced at her boots as heat crept up her neck. "Well, I'll miss you both," she said, suddenly feeling vulnerable. It wasn't a feeling she relished. "Perhaps we might meet again. In this world or the next."

"Margrete," Bash said from behind her. "We need to leave before the winds change."

Both Bay and Adrian bowed their heads, almost as if in respect. It warmed her heart and filled her with the strength she would need for her journey.

"Goodbye, Adrian. Bay." She nodded at them both.

Adrian dipped his chin while Bay pulled her to his chest for one final hug.

"Be good, Margrete." He waved as he backed away. "Oh, and Bash?" Bay raised a brow. "Take care of her, will you? She deserves better."

Adrian's eyes widened, and then he dragged his boyfriend behind him and far away from their king.

"He's right," Bash said after a moment, attempting a smile that didn't reach his eyes. He held out his arm for her to grasp, and she noticed how that smile wavered. She moved to him without hesitation.

Bash gently guided her up the gangway and onto the expansive deck. Not once did his grip loosen, but his features transformed into stone with every step they took.

"Gius." Bash tilted his head in greeting to a stout man with graying blonde hair and deep blue eyes.

The older man gave a slight bow. "Everything is set to go, sir. On your command." Bash gave a brusque nod of approval, and Gius scrambled off toward his gathering men.

"He's the quartermaster," Bash murmured, answering Margrete's unspoken question.

"Why does he address you so casually?"

"I don't believe in titles when they aren't necessary. Especially out here." He jerked his head to the open waters. "No man is a king. There is only family."

An abundance of churning emotion swirled in his emerald eyes, and his jaw clenched as he avoided her gaze.

"You'll be safe on this vessel. It was built from the wood of the Soliana Forest." When she raised her brow, he explained. "It's where the first tree grew on our island and is considered a sacred site. Any ship constructed from its wood has known only safe passage and swift winds."

There was so much she didn't know about Azantian.

She wished she had more time.

"I'd still suggest you remain below deck in case of unpleasant weather," he added, "but I suspect you won't heed my wishes." She detected the tiniest bit of playfulness in his tone.

"You'd suspect correctly," she countered, enjoying how he fought not to smile. It seemed she had a talent for loosening his mask, even if only slightly.

"Go below with me anyway? If only to humor me."

She smiled and nodded as she slipped her arm through his; he knew her well.

Bash steered her around his busy men and below deck to the same cabin she'd arrived in. She wandered over to the cot and took a seat, her limbs suddenly as exhausted as her mind.

"Margrete?"

She stilled at the use of her full name. Bash so rarely ever called her anything other than princess, a term she was beginning to see as an endearment. He stood tall, an arm resting casually against the cabin's doorframe. It might have appeared a relaxed stance, but the sea star tattoo on his arm curled in on itself, hiding.

Margrete swallowed the lump in her throat when he crossed the short distance between them and went to his knees, hands splayed on either side of her on the cot.

"Maybe after all of this—" his hands drifted closer, grazing the sides of her thighs "—you can find a way out of there and make your own path." His fingers inched higher, causing her breath to catch. "If I didn't have faith that you could do that, then I might not be going through with this now."

Those wicked hands remained on her thighs, her skin boiling beneath the thin barrier of her trousers. She watched as Bash slowly, painstakingly so, slid his hands to her hips, his searing touch a brand.

"I will not stay there." The words were fire in her throat. "Do not worry about that."

He nodded and tilted his face to meet her eyes from where he kneeled.

A king on his knees.

The sight would've sent her reeling if she wasn't already teetering on the edge of reason.

"I have every confidence that you won't." He tucked a strand of hair behind her ear, his eyes never leaving hers. "Maybe we will even meet again one of these days, Miss Wood."

Margrete's heart thundered at the promise.

"If we do, then I can assure you that I will certainly be equipped with something far deadlier than a dinner knife."

Bash's stoic face morphed, his eyes crinkling as he fought a grin.

"And I look forward to that day, princess." He trailed a knuckle down her cheek.

Margrete's eyes fluttered shut. But then his hand fell from her face, and coldness replaced his warmth.

By the time Margrete opened her eyes, he was gone.

CHAPTER TWENTY-SIX

MARGRETE

MARGRETE LEANED OVER THE BOW, WATCHING AS THE SETTING SUN gilded the waves thrashing against the sides of the *Phaedra*.

Slow us down, she urged the waters. *Cease your blowing,* she asked of the wind.

Time was moving too quickly, when all she wanted was for it to stop altogether.

The thudding of boots sounded at Margrete's back. She cast a glance over her shoulder to find Bash leisurely wandering over to rest beside her. He propped his elbows on the railing and gazed into the distance.

"Tell me what he does to you."

She took in the way the sunlight limned his strong profile, his hair like burnished copper. He squinted at the sea and tightened his hands around the ship's rail. He didn't have to say more. The pained look twisting his features told her all she needed to know.

When he'd first asked her why she hated her father, she refused to answer. But now...

"He's—cruel." She'd been tempted to lie, as lying about the kindness of her father had been ingrained in her since she was a child, but she didn't feel as if she needed to with Bash.

Tears pricked the backs of her eyes, and her throat constricted. She folded her arms beneath her breasts, unable to look at him.

"I've already spent too many nights assuming the worst, and I might be a bastard for asking this of you, but I need to know *exactly* what he does or I'll lose myself to my own wicked imagination. Margrete, I'm asking you to trust me enough to let me in. *Please*."

That one word broke her.

"He locks me in an iron box," she said, her voice steely, and her resolve strong. "He takes delight in the pain of others. In *my* pain." Margrete's nails bit into her palms. "He threatens to put my little sister in my place should I fight him. She's the only reason I would allow him such control."

Margrete would never forget the first time she'd been shut away. She'd just turned eight and wandered into her father's study uninvited. She came across him at his desk, his eyes trained to some object concealed in his hands. She recalled how those eyes had gleamed, and the sinister way they shined should have been enough of a warning.

But then he'd lifted that maniacal gaze, and that spark flared, a twisted look crossing his features as his lips curled upward. That was the day he began his 'punishments.' Her first offence, coming into his study without permission.

"How many times?" Bash's voice freed her from the unsettling memory. Gone was the stoicism—his ire had turned to a new mark, and the fierce look that sharpened his eyes spoke of a protectiveness she'd not known before.

Margrete shivered, even in the warm breeze. "He's put me in there too many times to count."

They remained in an uneasy silence that ate away at her skin. Her flesh prickled and her bones itched to move. To run.

"You shouldn't have had to go through that," Bash remarked icily. "No one should. I may have thought him cruel but never like...*that*." He ran an uneasy hand through his hair, the muscles in his jaw tensing. "When we attacked the keep, I assumed I would encounter some spoiled woman, one who had lived in luxury as her father stole and pillaged.

That is why you surprised me, even on that first day. I suppose I've been denying the truth ever since, if only to ease my own conscience. It's why I didn't push you for answers."

"I knew," Margrete said, surprising herself. "I knew you were fighting to make me into a villain. But I was also aware that, somewhere along the way, you ceased to gaze upon me as such."

Bash took in a heavy breath, opening his mouth before promptly shutting it again. He couldn't seem to find the words, the response that might set them both free.

She placed a hand on his shoulder. He tensed.

"I don't hold it against you," she said. "Not anymore."

His throat bobbed with emotion, but he didn't seem to find relief from her admission. Instead, his eyes met hers, darkening with lethal promise. "Gods, if you don't kill him, then know that I will. Have faith in that."

The vow hung between them. An oath spoken before the waters the king revered.

"I believe you," she said.

Margrete had known many broken promises in her life, had collected lies like grains of sand, but she believed him. Bash once told her that the eyes held the truths of the soul, and his eyes spoke to her in ways words never could.

Bash shifted uncomfortably on his feet, and Margrete's hand fell from his shoulder.

"If only you *had* been some spoiled brat, everything would've been easier. Now, I just find myself in awe of you. Truly." His smile went tight. "It is *because* I find myself drawn to you that I curse you."

"I wish I still despised you too, pirate," she said, returning his grim smile. She wondered what truths he saw in her own eyes. If he might glimpse the soul that wept within.

She gripped his arm as he turned to go. He looked back and covered her hand with his.

"It's all right," he said. "I just need time to think."

"There's no other way, Bash. If my father cooperates and arrives with the Heart, you must let him have me. You cannot risk it falling into the wrong hands."

He shifted closer, looming over her in a way that made her remember being lost in his arms the night before.

"I know the risk, princess." His eyes drifted over her face as though memorizing every line and curve. "I also know that Captain Wood has taken enough from me already."

She swallowed the knot in her throat as he lifted her hand and kissed her palm, his sharp gaze holding her stare all the while. "I'm anything but foolish," he said. "Know that. Trust me."

"I do," she said without hesitation. The desire to trust him began the night she tumbled into his chambers, when she saw the man beneath the mask. It only grew more potent as the days progressed, and the morning he shared his island's secrets, he earned the trust she guarded.

All at once, Bash lowered himself to one knee, grasping her hand in his and forming a fist above his heart with the other.

"I've sworn fealty to two things in my lifetime," he began, his chin lifted so he could gaze into her eyes. "To my island, and to the Gods of the Sea."

Margrete's heart hammered as she awaited his next words, his hold anchoring her in place.

"Now, I vow to you, Margrete Wood of Prias, that my sword is yours. No man or god will stop me from keeping this promise to you. You shall know the freedom you crave. Even if I have to part the seas to find you. Battle beasts and ruthless men. I will even endure the wrath of the gods themselves."

Her hands trembled, and his oath nearly sent her to her knees. "I pray it will never come to that, Bash," she said, her voice cracking under the weight of his stare.

A muscle in Bash's jaw feathered, his eyes fierce. "Oh, Margrete. The gods are cruel and seldom kind. And fate? Fate laughs at us all."

CHAPTER TWENTY-SEVEN

MARGRETE

The storm came out of nowhere.

One moment the sky was clear and full of light, and the next, gray steel washed across the world as rain pelted the *Phaedra* and its crew.

Bash found Margrete on the quarterdeck just as a massive wave struck the hull, sending the vessel rocking precariously to the side. He took her hand in his and wordlessly guided them below, his hold the only thing keeping her from tumbling down the stairs. Once they were in the safety of her cabin, Bash turned to her, his face pinched.

"It's too dangerous for you to be up there," he said. "We'll get out of this, but it won't be easy." He ran a hand through his hair as he turned for the door. Pausing at the threshold, he glanced over his shoulder and met her stare. "I need you to stay here, please. I *need* you to be safe, princess." His voice was coated with glass, the desperation in his tone nearly tangible.

"I will," she promised. "But you better be safe as well." The ship gave a violent lurch and she stumbled into the vanity. The thought of him going up into that hellish nightmare made her nauseous.

Bash lingered for a heartbeat longer, his eyes locked on her face, almost as though he wanted to memorize every detail. She did the same.

Then he nodded and closed the door.

If the storm continued into the evening, then they might miss the time set for the exchange. Margrete told herself that this was why she was pacing the cabin and not because a small part of her worried for a certain rogue on deck.

After wearing a path into the planks, a bolt of lightning pierced the skies. She staggered to her cabin's porthole to peer into the gray pandemonium. This was no ordinary storm. Not the kind that many survived, at least.

Gazing at the thrashing waters, Margrete pleaded with the sea, a recent, pacifying habit. As if in response, she was sent hurtling backward, her back colliding painfully with the sharp edge of the vanity. Cursing, she lurched back into place and grabbed hold of the wooden chair for support.

Margrete pressed her hand to the porthole, her ring clinking against the glass. She twirled the ring on her finger, thoughts drifting. *I see it in you, girl, something dark and old.* That's what the madwoman had said, almost like she believed Margrete carried something ancient inside of her.

Gods, Margrete wished that were true. That she possessed some power that could persuade the waves to calm and the skies to clear, power that could get the *Phaedra* and her crew out of this thing alive. Bash promised that the ship could weather any storm, but now she wasn't so sure.

Please, she pleaded. *Please, please, please...*

The graying depths swirled and screamed its reply, and for a moment, all Margrete knew was defeat. She'd foolishly thought that the ocean might listen to her—

Stupid, stupid girl.

A shock raced from her finger and up her arm. Margrete glanced down to find her ring glowing in the dim lighting. Her skin burned icy hot where the metal rested, but she didn't dare take the ring off. A burst of heat coiled inside her chest and her vision sharpened on a cresting wave.

She gazed through the porthole as a chorus of ethereal voices and the pulsating heartbeat of every wave consumed all that she was. For a moment, she could hear what the waters urged her to hear—and she answered back. But not with words.

Narrowing in on the roiling violence beyond the portal, she fixated on a wave the height of ten men. As heat blossomed within her chest, and the eerie whispers of the sea came to a crescendo, the swell before her rose and crashed harmlessly, sucked back into the ocean that had birthed it.

Yes! More sparks pricked her insides with every frantic exhale. The heat within didn't come from nerves or simple human fear. No. Margrete could taste the electricity in the air, an ancient sort of enchantment woven with a fragile thread.

This inner fire—crafted from all things unseen and unknown—escalated like the waves beyond her portal. Margrete shut her eyes and focused on calming the waters within herself even as the music of the untamable sea whooshed in her ears.

Control, a gentle voice whispered. It was the one she'd heard in the Kardias Cave, welcoming her home. *Control them.*

There was no time to wonder why she heard the otherworldly voice or why it had chosen to call out to her now. Not when the *Phaedra* was near destruction.

Instead, she shut her eyes and allowed images of still waters and crystal-clear skies to crush all other thoughts. She glimpsed the world through the eyes of another, her view high above the sea like she was some bird gliding overhead.

Yes, the foreign voice urged. *Control them.*

Margrete opened her eyes as her vision of serene waters dissipated. Beyond the porthole, the sky was a shade brighter. The waves were still angry, but not bloodthirsty. Her heart pumped in her chest. She couldn't possibly have been the one to do that—

A piercing scream penetrated the air, the sound like a dagger to her calm.

She knew that scream, would recognize it anywhere. Bash was in trouble.

Stumbling with every rocking wave, Margrete hurried to the main deck. The rain had picked up, the drops violent in their descent. Within seconds, she was drenched.

Bash called out again. A groan of pain. A growl of frustration and distress.

Grasping the railing, Margrete scanned the deck. If the crew were fearful, none of them showed it. They were seasoned sailors, borne from the sea itself. She, on the other hand, was not. She couldn't even swim. There was no doubt that these waters would swallow her whole if she wasn't careful, but she had to know if Bash was safe.

A thunderclap was the only warning before lightning struck the mizzen sail, leaving the nearly translucent linen a mess of smoking shreds. Margrete lurched forward, narrowly missing the plummeting wood and burning sail as they crashed to the quarter deck.

The impact sent her sliding across the slick planks, barely holding to the starboard railing as a tumultuous wave crested, battering mercilessly against the hull.

The downpour pummeled the crew, savage raindrops flying from every direction, making it difficult to see more than ten feet ahead. Margrete wrapped both arms about the rail. The squall was relentless.

But it was *his* voice that was isolated amongst the many. His voice alone that wafted to her ears and took up residence in her tumultuous heart.

She spotted him across the deck. A cannon had gotten loose and pinned three men, Bash among them. His men worked to free him, but the turbulent waters made it challenging.

She had to get to him.

Margrete slipped and stumbled as she ran, the rain obscuring her vision. She was close, Bash's cries growing louder, drowning out the hissing wind and hail.

Lightning struck again.

This time, it hit its target.

The mast above Margrete cracked and splintered, the smell of burnt wood mixing with the overwhelming scent of despair. The wood creaked and groaned, and before she could react, it all came crashing down.

Bash screamed her name.

She swiveled toward him just before a fierce wind swept her up, sending her tumbling over the railing and into the churning waters. She plummeted like a rock, her body striking the waves with force, her scream cut off by the ruthless sea.

The current stole her strength and pulled at the loose threads of her will, but she refused to give up so easily.

Push! she screamed at herself. *Fight!*

But the current was strong, the sea chaotic.

Margrete *did* push, though. She *did* fight.

But her determination to live wasn't enough to guide her inexperienced limbs.

She was sinking. Fast.

The sea lit up briefly, a striking flash of lightning illuminating the waters that held her firm. Another bolt. And another. Deeper she sank, her arms growing heavy, her feet stilling.

Margrete had always imagined Death and the sea to be the closest of friends and the most bitter of enemies. The line between the two had long ago blurred, just as loathing and love tend to combine and combust, turning vengeful strangers into hesitant lovers.

The current was wild and, while vicious, it handled Margrete almost reverently. It swept her further down until the bottom of the wooden ship became nothing but a cobalt dream on a moonless night.

Falling, falling, falling.

A ripple of electricity pulsated, so fierce and sudden that it forced her eyes to open in the darkness. A violent energy surged, the waters seeming to tremble as a spark of light erupted.

She heard the voice. This time, it wasn't gentle, nor muffled. It sounded close, as if murmured into her ear.

Shana, the ocean sang.

The voice belonged to an entity she couldn't see, and it rose into a commanding echo, repeating the foreign name like a prayer. She felt the waves calming, like they were eager to hear what the voice had to say.

I sense you, even from my prison. You call to me from the dark.

Amidst the rushing waves, Margrete could just make out the sound of dripping water. The noise reminded her of the cavern beneath the palace.

Malum? she asked, her thoughts drifting to a place far away.

You call to me, as I call to you, he replied. *I will be free soon. My time is nearing. It is then that I will need you, my dear Shana. But danger looms on the horizon. It is closer than you think.*

What danger? she asked.

But Malum didn't answer.

Find my Heart. Keep the beasts contained. Don't let him win. Do not answer him when he calls out to you. I sense him in your mind already.

Him? But she knew. The knowledge was sudden and sweeping.

Darius.

The last bubbles of air left her, floating toward the surface where shadows of chaos reigned, and her heart pushed out a final, thundering beat. The last thing she heard was the enraged sea, whispering commands she wouldn't live to heed.

CHAPTER TWENTY-EIGHT

BASH

FEAR.

Bash believed he'd experienced it before. The night his father was murdered. The day he assumed the throne. The first time the island shook as the sea's children fought their prison.

But he realized that, all those times, he'd been consumed by anger and guilt.

Not fear.

Not the true kind of terror that he suffered watching Margrete tumble over the side of his ship, the tumultuous waters yanking her to certain death.

The men heaved and, thanks to a tilting swell, the cannon dislodged and went careening toward the opposite end of the ship until it crashed into the railing. Bash cradled his arm, the pain blinding. A jagged gash opened his flesh from elbow to shoulder, but the wound was already knitting itself back together, thanks to his Azantian blood. It would scar, but he would survive.

He struggled to his feet. Gius, who'd taken the brunt of the blow, screamed at him. "Go! Help her!"

Bash needn't be told twice.

He raced across the deck, the image of her falling into the storm still knife-sharp in his mind as he dove into the thunderous waves. He sliced through the water as the sea raged around him. The muffled screams of his bewildered crew reached him as he fought harder against the current. He knew they counted on him to save them all. If he died, then—

No. Dying wasn't an option.

And neither was losing Margrete.

The sea trembled as he pushed down, and a sense of foreboding filled his chest. It was almost as if there was *something* else down here with him, and Bash couldn't shake the sensation of foreign, yet familiar, power that surged through the waves.

Bubbles of air escaped through his lips, but he didn't lose his rhythm, not even as a vicious bolt of lightning struck the skies overhead. The blaze of light sank below the waters, illuminating a dark form and a flash of silver shining twenty or so feet away.

It had to be her.

He couldn't fathom otherwise.

With renewed strength, Bash propelled himself deeper to where he'd seen the glimmer of metallic light. There wasn't time to think about how far they'd drifted from the ship, or what they would do should the *Phaedra* go down. Bash had to get to her first, and whatever happened after would have to wait—if they even made it out of this alive.

The deeper he swam and the longer he held his breath, the more grateful he felt that he wasn't human. His body was made for this. His sight crafted to see through the enveloping gloom of the depths.

Finally, Bash drew near. He reached into the dim and grabbed hold of Margrete's hand, the one attached to the silver that had guided him— her ring. The one she'd taken to wearing after her trip to the market.

Bash yanked her lifeless body to his chest and wound his arm around her waist, the pressure encircling his heart contracting. He hated how helpless he felt. Her eyes were shut, and he wasn't sure she was alive, or if she'd taken a final breath of water into her lungs and surrendered.

She better not have.

Margrete's head bobbed as he kicked, her long chocolate curls floating around her wan face like a shadowy halo.

There wasn't much time left. Bash's lungs ached for air.

When they finally broke the surface, Bash gasped, filling his burning lungs. He whipped his head around, searching for his vessel, his crew. For a chance at survival.

He was terrified to look at Margrete, but he forced himself. She was so pale, so lifeless, her lips tinged blue.

Fuck. He tilted her head, praying to and cursing the gods all at once.

A giant wave crested and then fell, revealing the *Phaedra* no more than fifty yards away.

He shouted, waving his free arm, hoping his men were keeping their eyes peeled for their king.

Tugging Margrete with him, his grip firm around her small waist, he set off in the direction of salvation. Only when he heard his men's returning shouts did he feel the sudden weight of his exhaustion and the pain of his still-healing injury.

He held on as the ship veered toward them, the waves growing less frenzied and wild. A rope ladder was tossed over the deck, and the joyous cries of his crew wafted to his ears. Bash stole one more look at Margrete's still face. He knew, even then, with her limp body pressed against his chest, that he would have dove into the storm again and again if it meant seeing her face one more time.

The key to his people's safety or not, Bash suddenly couldn't fathom the idea of a world without her in it. Where she wasn't rolling her eyes at him when she thought he wasn't looking, or daintily wrinkling her nose when she was frustrated with him, which, apparently, was quite often.

She made him feel something other than anger for the first time in over a decade.

And gods be damned, he refused to let her get rid of him this easily.

CHAPTER TWENTY-NINE

MARGRETE

A CREAKING GROAN, LOW AND MUFFLED, CALLED TO MARGRETE. She opened her eyes to what seemed like a blurry dream.

"Princess."

She struggled to focus, searching for that familiar voice. The world swayed, and her body felt heavy as lead.

"Princess."

The voice sounded once more, and the fuzzy edges of her sight sharpened. A tired face stared down at her, concern carving every distinct feature.

Again, Bash spoke her name, but this time he said, "Gods help us, Margrete, I thought I was imagining it. Your eyes, love."

Her eyes?

She blinked, unsure what he meant. He looked...frightened. Or maybe confused.

He leaned closer, cautiously, and brushed her hair away as he studied her eyes. The rough feel of his touch and the smell of salt and sun and man enveloped her, his nearness more comforting—more intoxicating—than it had any right to be.

The entire world felt brighter, more intense, and her vision sharpened into something fierce.

Was this a dream? Or some middle-existence between life and death?

Images of spinning shadows and whooshing currents assaulted her, of how she'd struggled to push to the surface. And then there had been a voice—

Danger looms on the horizon. It is closer than you think.

The echo of the sea's warning—of *Malum's* warning—wafted to her ears, and for a second, she was back beneath the waves, fighting tooth and nail to remain alive. The only thing that confused her—well, not the only thing—was that she remembered taking that final precious breath, all of the life sucked from her body in a last push to fight.

Yet now, she inhaled the fresh sea breeze into her lungs and tasted salt on the tip of her tongue. She felt Bash's warmth, his calloused fingertips skimming back and forth along her arm, sending goosebumps rising across her body. She touched his face, and after a sigh, he pressed a gentle kiss to the inside of her wrist.

She was most certainly alive. But how?

"Your eyes..." Bash said again, cocking his head to the side, auburn hair falling into his face. "They really *are* blue."

She didn't have blue eyes. They were hazel and gold.

"They're not," she said, her voice sounding as though she'd swallowed sand.

A coughing fit struck, and it took several minutes for it to pass. Bash helped her ease into a more comfortable position against the pillows, and then he handed her a glass of water.

Margrete shook her head at the sight of the full cup. The water sloshed about inside, looking about as appealing as a mouthful of glass. She'd had enough water for one day.

Bash placed the drink on the stool beside him and propped his head on his hands as he took her in. "Remarkable," he breathed, transfixed by her eyes. He resembled an awestruck child.

Even still, Margrete didn't believe him just yet, and he must've sensed her doubt. He left the room and, a moment later, returned with a mirrored compact.

He offered Margrete the brass compact and she clutched it with trembling fingers. She snapped open the lid and took herself in.

Blue.

Her eyes were *blue*.

But not any old blue—varying shades of turquoise, aquamarine, and hints of the sky all swirled inside her irises. She tilted her chin, and the dim lighting captured the specks of silver that glinted like tiny stars battling for attention. Her lips parted in shock.

Bash had been right—and she'd never seen anything quite like them before.

"Oh my." She exhaled sharply and dropped the mirror to her lap. "What happened?" she finally asked, her throat still sore.

"You were knocked over the side." Bash bit the inside of his cheek and glanced at the shadows clinging to the corners of the cabin. He couldn't seem to look her in the eye. "You were down there for a long time. I dove in after you when my men were able to free me of that blasted cannon."

"Are you okay?" She reached up, hands skimming over his chest and shoulders, only to pause when she saw the shredded and bloodied fabric of his sleeve. An image of him, imprisoned and screaming, came to mind, and she recalled the sense of helplessness she'd felt when she couldn't get to him.

His hand covered hers, and he met her eyes with a glassy stare. "I'm fine. Another crew member took the brunt of the weight, and Azantians heal faster than mortals." He moved his arm just so, revealing an angry red wound zigzagging across his biceps. Angry, but not open. Healing. "It's you I'm concerned about," he added. Bash brushed the backs of his fingers along her cheek and swallowed hard, his face stark with memory. "I swear, you were dead."

Margrete recalled how the numbness greeted her, the overwhelming feeling of tranquil nothingness. Death had swum up to her from the depths. But then…here she was, breathing thick air and gazing at the most captivating man she'd ever seen.

She touched his face. "I should have told you," she began cautiously, "but I was ashamed to admit it."

"Admit what?" He scrunched his face.

"I never learned how to swim," she admitted. "My father always forbade me from going anywhere near the water."

Bash's hand flinched on her cheek, but he didn't remove it. "You can't *swim*? Yes, that's something you should've told me." His eyes were hard. "I would have made certain you were protected. I would've *never* left you alone had I known." He clenched his teeth. "And the fact that you put yourself in danger, for me—"

"I'm fine." She cut him off as he began to spiral, and placed her free hand over his. "I heard you scream, and I couldn't stop myself. Nothing could have stopped me."

Bash shook his head, his brow pinched. "But you almost *weren't* fine, Margrete. You were dead at the bottom of the sea. I'm Azantian. If I fell in, I would've survived, but *you*…You shouldn't have come for me at all."

His voice held a sharp tone, but beneath his ire, there was pain.

"If the roles were reversed, would you have come for me?" she asked.

Turmoil twisted his features for only a second before he ground out his reply. "I think you know the answer to that." Bash's nostrils flared as he glanced at his lap.

"I've never felt like that before. That crushing *fear*. Even when I pulled you out, you didn't have a damn heartbeat, princess. *Nothing*. It took me minutes to revive you, and still, you were so pale, so…"

His eyes lifted to her chest like he was making sure she was still breathing.

The guilt on his face was tangible. Bash tensed when she threaded her fingers through his, but he didn't pull away. A part of her wanted to tell him what she heard, of the voice she knew belonged to Malum, but she stopped herself. She'd only sound mad, and after what she'd endured, Bash might attribute the encounter to shock.

Instead of what she so desperately wanted to share, she asked, "And then what happened? After you pulled me on deck?"

"Then you finally opened your eyes." He scrubbed at his face with his free hand. "It was *half a second*, but I saw the blue, clear as day. It was as though I stared directly into the sea." He looked at her, jaw tensing. "I know your eyes. I'd know them anywhere. Even in that sliver of a moment. But they changed. It took my breath away."

A warm flush raced up her throat, and she couldn't help but squeeze his hand. Bash glanced back to the shadows, and Margrete wanted to do anything to ease his guilt. She could sense him drowning beneath it all.

"I've never... I've never felt so damn helpless." His admission was hardly above a whisper, and she wondered if he even meant to say the words out loud.

Bash absentmindedly rubbed small circles on her skin with his thumb, his touch grounding her when the world felt like it was still tilting.

"The ocean saved you. *Chose* you," Bash murmured, after some oppressing moments of silence. "You wouldn't be alive if it hadn't."

She frowned. "*Chose* me?"

"That's the only thing that can explain what happened." Bash gave a mirthless laugh. "I should've known you had some connection with the sea. Especially when you told me you heard our sirens. Only those blessed by the sea can hear them." His eyes held hers firmly. "Only *Azantians* should be able to hear them, I mean."

The day of her wedding. When she'd asked him, Bash had brushed it off like it meant nothing.

Reading her thoughts, he said, "It appears as though I lie to myself quite a bit where you're concerned. Everything about you seems impossible."

Margrete let his words hang in the air. Bash had been wrong about her, but his admission, although framed by a forced smile, lifted a weight from her shoulders. And yet she couldn't stop ruminating on the first half of what he'd said.

How she was connected to Azantian.

To the sea.

Margrete thought back to all the times the ocean sang to her, its sweet lullaby soothing her to sleep. The way it shushed and calmed after her father locked her inside the iron box. The day she was to marry Count Casbian—the day her life was forever altered—she had heard the sea's voice calling out to her as if in warning.

"How would you know if I...if I were connected?"

"I—" He hesitated, rubbing the back of his neck. "I don't know," he answered truthfully. "Margrete, are you sure about your mother? Where she came from?"

"Yes. Adina told me many times that my mother was a noblewoman my father met in the capital of Aelia. Why do you ask?"

Bash rubbed at his chin. "It seems...odd. Your father fled with an Azantian woman twenty-four years ago. You're how old?"

No. What he was insinuating couldn't possibly be true.

"I think I would know if I was half-Azantian, Bash," she said, though she'd often wondered why her father refused to speak of his late wife. Almost as if the very mention of her brought him pain. "Surely you of all people would've been able to tell."

He sighed. "Honestly, this is entirely new to me. I've known very little of the world outside of Azantian, and while you appear human, I could very well be wrong. There are just too many coincidences. Too many connections you share to the sea and my island."

The truth of his words sent a chill racing down her spine. When she shivered, Bash tucked the blanket up to her chin, his other hand resting above her throbbing heart.

"*Whatever* you are," he began, his eyes hardening in promise, "we will figure it out. Together."

Bash cupped her cheek and she leaned into his palm, closing her eyes as the rough pads of his fingers grazed her heated skin. Her pulse fluttered from his heartfelt pledge.

She wordlessly lifted the blanket, a silent offer. A plea to *pretend*. To *feel* rather than think of what her connection to his world meant.

Without a word, Bash took off his boots, his eyes never leaving hers.

He slid below the covers and settled on his back, his muscled arm slipping beneath her waist before he tugged her closer.

With her ear pressed above his heart, she listened to its erratic rhythm. When she wrapped her arm around his torso and tangled her leg with his, his breath caught, and her lips curled into a hesitant smile. She affected him just as much as he did her, regardless of where they'd started. From enemies to two people who understood the words between the silence.

The gods truly did have a dark sense of humor.

Just before sleep took her under its heady spell, Margrete felt the press of lips on the top of her curls, a hoarse promise whispered in her ear.

"Before the sun sets tomorrow," Bash said, "I will reclaim the Heart, and when it is finally in my possession, I will lay the captain at your feet, regardless of how many he brings to defend him. By the time I'm done with him, he will beg you to end his suffering."

His vow sent her pulse soaring with a twisted kind of hope, though she knew Bash would have no other choice than to put his kingdom first when it came down to it. She couldn't fault him for that. If he couldn't end her father tomorrow *and* retrieve the Heart, she understood what he would need to.

"But if you can't," she began, his shirt crumpled in her fist, "then I won't hesitate to do it myself."

Margrete would rather be a killer than a coward. No longer could she allow evil to walk the earth and do nothing to stop it. She'd hidden her whole life, trembling in her father's presence and accepting his perverse punishments as if she deserved them.

But now, enveloped in Bash's arms, the waves gently rocking the storm-torn *Phaedra*, Margrete felt fire blossom in her chest.

Fire, and a rage so sweet it breathed life back into a woman who'd forgotten how strong she truly was.

She'd lost enough. It was time to take something for herself.

CHAPTER THIRTY

MARGRETE

MARGRETE WOKE TO AN EMPTY BED.

The sheets were cool beneath her palm, and Bash's warmth no longer enveloped her body as it had throughout the night. Despite the trauma she endured the day before, she found she'd slept well, and without a doubt, it was a credit to the man who held her in his arms, never once loosening his comforting hold. It was the first time she hadn't dreamt of her father.

"Morning, Margrete."

Margrete. Not *princess*.

She lifted her heavy eyes to where Bash stood across the cabin, his golden torso on full display. Her gaze dropped to where his trousers hugged his hips, a fine dusting of hair leading the way down.

She was tempted to call him back to bed, if only to feel the hardness of him against her one more time, but he grabbed his shirt from where it draped across the chair and slipped his muscled arms through the sleeves.

"Morning," she replied, silently observing as he finished buttoning his shirt. His movements were mesmerizing, and, for a moment, she imagined herself watching him dress every day.

"We'll be there shortly," he said, his Adam's apple bobbing. His gaze darted to the side, the way it always did when he couldn't face her.

"I'll get dressed," she said. The air was rife with tension.

Bash released a heavy sigh and took one step closer to her, then paused. "Before we left, we sent scouts to make sure he's coming alone. That he didn't bring an entire fleet with him. We've no word yet, but Wood knows how to find us. But if I somehow can't get my hands on him today—"

"Bash, I know what needs to be done. We can worry about the rest once you have what you need."

Her words did nothing to soothe the creases in his brow. She couldn't stand seeing him look at her like that, but she knew by the time they journeyed above deck, he would once again be the ruthless king his people needed. That was the Bash she could handle today, if only to get through this ordeal.

"I'll meet you on deck, Bash." She wanted to be alone, to collect her thoughts before she met with her father. Her mind was already made up. Once she sailed home, she would get her sister and find her own way to freedom—without anyone's help.

It was time for her head to return from the clouds. If the fates were kind, they would find their way back to one another, but Margrete couldn't afford to think in what ifs. If she allowed herself to hope, to dream, then it might very well destroy her if they failed.

Bash gave her a jerky nod, exhaling sharply. He dug into his pockets and tossed something on the vanity that she couldn't make out from her position on the bed.

"I'll see you above," he added. The door closed behind him with a resounding bang that rattled her chest.

She slipped from the bed and walked to the desk. The compact mirror Bash had brought the day before was left atop the small vanity. Only now, a violet-blue gem strung on a silver chain rested beside it.

She knew before she picked it up where it came from, recognized the way the gem captured the light of the sun beyond the porthole, its smooth facets glimmering with stars. Bash had given her a piece of the Adiria cavern. A piece of Azantian's soul.

Her fingers trembled as she fastened the clasp at the back of her neck. The pear-shaped stone settled against her chest, its smooth facets icy on her skin. It was beyond beautiful, for it represented far more than the magic of the cavern. Of Azantian itself.

It represented *them*.

And wherever today led her, Margrete would forever carry a piece of that night in the Adiria Cavern with her.

Her hands kept drifting to her neck as she dressed and left her cabin. The weight of the gem comforted her even as she willed one foot in front of the other up the steps.

On deck, her lungs immediately swelled with fresh sea air, and a savage gust of wind played with the strands of her hair. Her chest was still sore from nearly drowning, her limbs aching and weak, but she would heal, and as the ocean breeze kissed her skin, her steps grew steady.

The crew avoided her entirely as she walked to the stern where she found Bash gazing upon the horizon with an unreadable expression marring his handsome features.

Bash nodded as she approached. "We're almost ready," he murmured, once more looking just beyond Margrete instead of *at* her. "Our scouts returned. Your father has kept his word, and only one vessel sails to meet us."

A seagull screeched overhead, indicating they were closer to land than she'd thought.

"Thank you," she said, ignoring his words as her hand lingered on his gift. "It's beautiful."

A muscle in his jaw flickered, and when he spoke, his voice sounded strained. "It was the first time in years I felt alive again. Like I wasn't a king or the damned protector of the seas. I was just a man." He turned to face her, green eyes fierce. "And that night, the only magic I saw was you."

Heat rose to her cheeks and blossomed across the expanse of her neck. His penetrating stare relayed so many things—all the words they'd spoken and the truths they'd yet to confess. She wrapped her fingers around the gem.

"I was never pretending, Bash."

It felt as though they were saying goodbye. And in truth, they were.

"Oh, princess." Bash smiled, though it was grim. "Being with you is the only time I don't have to pretend."

She wanted to grab his hand and pull him close, to rid herself of the walls surrounding her heart, but she would crumble if she did. She couldn't afford to fall apart when she needed her shields up, if only to survive what was coming.

"They're approaching!" The cry pierced the air, putting an end to their somber goodbye.

The crew reacted to the warning from the crow's nest, scurrying about to ready for the captain's arrival. Every member of the *Phaedra* moved with grace and poise, as if they'd been born on the decks of such a ship and knew nothing of land. They were Azantians, and the sea sang to them as it did Bash. As it seemed to do with her.

But Margrete was unwilling to face the harsh truths of her own encounters—at least at this moment—for a heart brimming with sorrow tends to drown out the logic of the mind.

A grand vessel with bright silver sails appeared on the horizon. It was a fast ship, slicing through the waters with ease. Bash shot her one final look, one filled with unspoken words, before he strode away to deliver orders to his men.

The ship carrying her father grew close. The time had come.

Margrete watched from the railing, gazing at the vessel that would bring her back home.

THE CAPTAIN'S SHIP SAT SECURED AND PARALLEL TO THE *PHAEDRA*. The waters were calm on their advance, as if the ocean quieted in order to watch it all unfold. Men lowered a thick wooden board across the decks. It dropped to the planks of the Azantian ship, a bridge between the world of men and that of the gods.

Margrete didn't recognize any of the sailors on the opposing vessel. It wasn't one in her father's fleet. She'd wrongfully assumed that he would command the *Iron Mast*, his fastest boat. It was odd, but she didn't have long to question why, because the man who strode across the wooden plank was not her father.

He didn't wear a cruel smile or possess steel eyes that scorched her spirit. He had a square jaw with dark stubble and wind-blown hair that resembled raven's feathers.

Count Casbian.

His blue eyes found her almost immediately, the facade of calm he wore faltering. Even from far away, the man was striking.

Margrete's breath caught, and a lump took up residence in her throat. *Why was he here?*

When Bash told her the captain was willing to make the trade, she'd been rightfully skeptical, but here instead was the man she'd almost married, a man she'd almost entirely forgotten about.

Bash's brows pinched together as he sought her out, holding onto her wide-eyed gaze like a lifeline. Neither had expected this, and the Azantian king clenched his teeth as he returned his attention to the count.

Was the count here to do Wood's dirty work? Or simply collect his bride? Margrete scowled.

Bash righted himself, steeling his spine as he assessed his new foe. "Only you."

He loomed before the plank, guarding access to the *Phaedra*. A couple of the count's men started forward, chests puffing and biceps bulging. Sailors such as these craved the fight, chased the high of a brawl.

"It's fine," Casbian said, ordering them down by holding up his hand held in warning. While he wasn't as seasoned as the men he employed, he was nevertheless well-built and commanding. "Just me."

Bash nodded, scanning the sailors for a threat. No one spoke up in disagreement. Margrete was thankful.

Bash cut an imposing figure—all broad shoulders and sculpted arms. The way his men surrounded him, their hands on the hilts of their swords, eyes gleaming with respect, told Margrete more about him as a leader than anything else. His crew would follow him beyond the shores of death.

Casbian stumbled on the wooden board. He stiffened, though his wounded pride shone clear, even as he raised his chin and tugged the cuffs of his finely embroidered tunic in a sophisticated manner. He was trying to present himself as formidable, but it was more than apparent that he wasn't accustomed to life on the seas, unlike the weathered men at his back. He also wasn't used to dealing with anyone like Bash of Azantian.

He continued marching confidently across and hopped nimbly onto the main deck, his eyes on Margrete. The intensity of his icy blue stare seared her flesh, but she held his gaze.

Something was off.

Margrete's fingers reached for the stone resting against her chest, a flurry of anticipation heightening her senses.

"You have it?" Bash kept his distance from Casbian, his arms crossed and chin defiantly raised.

"No. I have something else," the count offered, his voice wavering. "I have gold, lots of gold." He fumbled into his pockets to retrieve a scrap of paper. He handed it over to Bash, who snatched it up quickly, and Casbian fell back into place. His gaze flickered to Margrete warily.

Bash glanced at the scrap of paper for only a moment. Laughing, he crumpled the note and tossed it overboard without a second thought.

"I don't want your petty mortal riches. I want what Captain Wood stole from my people." Bash's voice rose above the whooshing wind and the natural hum of the sea. "Where is the Heart?"

To his immense credit, Casbian didn't flinch. "I—I came alone," he said, now avoiding Margrete's gaze entirely. "The...Captain Wood wasn't—"

"He was never going to come," she said. How many times had she told Bash the very same thing?

The count sadly shook his head. "No, Margrete. He wasn't."

Bash turned to her for a heartbeat, but she caught the shock flashing across his eyes. The king truly believed her father would come for her, if not for love, then for his own pride.

"I came instead." Casbian squared his shoulders, determination settling in. "I came for Margrete." He jerked his head her way. "I want to pay what is owed."

It was a noble attempt on behalf of a clueless count, but Bash didn't take kindly to the offer.

"What are *you* to Captain Wood?" he asked, evenly and without inflection.

Margrete wasn't sure where he was going with his questioning, but something told her to stay alert.

Casbian scrunched his brow. "I'm his daughter's fiancé," he replied, as if it were obvious.

"What *else* are you?" Bash shot back, cocking his head to the side, features shrewd.

Margrete could *feel* him forming a plan—one she wasn't sure she'd approve of.

"I—I'm soon to be in business with him." Casbian faltered, shifting on his feet.

Ah. That was what Bash desired to know—Casbian's worth to her father. It was so subtle that Margrete hardly took notice, but Bash's chin dipped ever so slightly, a quick nod directed at the quartermaster.

Something passed between them—

And the quartermaster gave the signal.

Men in cobalt blue leapt into position, tossing the wooden plank overboard and leaving the count stranded. Casbian's men shouted in protest, scrambling to retrieve their weapons.

They had no idea what they were up against. The *Phaedra* was no mere vessel. If what Bash had told her about the Soliana Forest was true, then its very wood carried traces of divinity.

If the count's men ignited their cannons, they risked killing their master along with the enemy. A few foolish soldiers attempted to swing from one deck to the other instead, swords at the ready, but the *Phaedra* had already begun to move.

Margrete stumbled as they lurched forward, moving impossibly fast across the waters. She steadied herself against the railing, watching the count's vessel grow smaller and smaller. They would attempt to follow, but they didn't stand a chance.

Not against a vessel crafted by sacred wood.

A shout rang in Margrete's ears. It was Casbian, calling her name as Bash's men yanked his arms behind his back. Stunned, she watched them drag the count below deck until his pleas for help became a haunting echo.

He'd braved the sea to come for her, to rescue her, and now he was a captive. The day of her wedding, she'd assumed he wanted to use her like her father, but perhaps there was more to the man than she gave him credit for.

And now, his capture was all her fault.

Guilt washed through her chest and squeezed painfully.

She turned her sights on Bash, and strode over to where he was conversing with a woman she recognized from the attack on her wedding. The muscled blonde was a warrior, not merely a sailor. There were daggers strapped to her hips, thighs, and ankles.

Margrete paused a few feet back, listening in on what appeared to be a heated debate.

"Why on earth would we take him?" the blonde snapped, uncaring that she spoke to her king with such a cutting tone. "What if we missed a tail on the way here, and Wood is following us now? What if that was all part of the captain's plan? For us to take the spineless bastard? He could very well be bait."

Bash's nostrils flared. "Atlas. No mortal-crafted ship can match our speed." He spoke through clenched teeth. "Besides, this was always the plan, remember? We figured there was a small chance the correspondence didn't come from him. That it might be some sort of ruse. But we do know one thing..." He took a step closer to the seething warrior, his voice lowering into something dangerous. "Casbian, if he is indeed bait, will know something. We can get that information out of him. In any way necessary."

At that, Margrete found her voice. "The hell you will."

Bash turned on a heel, his eyes widening. She wasn't meant to hear that last part.

"Princess." He abandoned the woman—Atlas—who eyed Margrete with keen interest, a spark of surprise flashing across her deep blue irises. "We'll talk about this when we're safely out of range. I promise." He reached for Margrete's hand, but she stepped away.

She knew very well what he planned for the count, and it made her stomach roil. The man she'd gotten to know, to trust, wouldn't harm an innocent person, and Margrete wouldn't allow him to touch the count until she knew with certainty that he was working with her father.

"Yes, we *will* talk later," she vowed, holding his gaze.

One side of Atlas's lips twitched before she slunk off into the frenzy of workers, but the look of respect she directed at Margrete wasn't missed.

Bash's handsome features twisted. He opened his mouth to say something, but Gius approached, stopping him with a hand on his shoulder.

"Sir. Your presence is requested on the quarter deck."

Margrete glanced around at Bash's crew. Now was not the time to argue. Not with his men looking on.

Bash spoke in hushed tones to his quartermaster before directing his attention back to her.

He leaned in to whisper in her ear. "Remember when I asked you to trust me? Now I truly need you to try. You *know* me."

It was those final words that weakened her rising anger, the desperate tone of them that had her nodding her head in agreement. She watched as he struggled to turn away from her, though his steps faltered as he trailed after Gius.

Margrete wanted to trust him. After everything they'd been through, he deserved the chance to explain his actions.

She only hoped she hadn't signed Casbian's death warrant in the process.

CHAPTER THIRTY-ONE

BASH

Bash couldn't get Margrete's face out of his mind. The way she'd looked upon the count as he was dragged below deck. She'd nearly married the man, though she claimed she hardly knew him. And yet the sight of her face as Casbian was hauled away had Bash's heart thumping wildly in his chest. Did she regret not marrying him? Did a part of her wish she'd gone through with the ceremony? That she was far from Azantian and Bash and danger?

Danger *he* had put her in.

Bash slumped in his chair; the captain's quarters was finally empty of bodies. Atlas had just left, likely still bristling from their argument. While the warrior was likely too headstrong for her own good, she was a fine soldier. Bash respected the hell out of her, even if she constantly questioned him.

He had to get his head on straight, to focus on the larger picture. Perhaps deep down, they always knew the captain wouldn't come, even if they skirted around the possibility. However, his absence coming to fruition had Bash feeling all sorts of hopeless.

A failure.

Hours had passed. He needed to speak with Margrete, as he'd

promised, but the thought of her looking at him with disappointment was nearly worse than letting down his island.

Bash wasn't a monster. He wouldn't torture an innocent man, especially if it was a man Margrete had...feelings for. A man who might be better for her in the long run than Bash would ever be.

He swiped his hands across his desk, sending papers flying to the floor. His stomach twisted into knots as he stood, running his fingers through his hair in an effort to rein in his overwhelming regret.

Bash marched toward her cabin, ignoring how the weight of his emotions, his own damn insecurities, suffocated him. How his chest grew taut with doubt and heavy with fear. Fear that he was right, and that Margrete would be better off without him. It was selfish to wish for anything else.

At her door, he knocked hesitantly.

"Come in." Bash sensed her frustration, and it caused his steps to falter as he went inside. His eyes drifted immediately to the woman who'd stolen something irreplaceable from him. Something he'd never get back, even if he wanted to.

Not that he did.

He approached slowly. "Princess."

She sat perched on the side of her cot, her hands placed delicately on her lap, but her eyes were fierce, brimming with distress.

Bash ignored the pang of hurt in his chest and took a seat beside her, his thigh brushing against her warmth. He could smell the lavender in the air, a scent that followed her like a summer breeze. If he could breathe nothing else but her, he gladly would.

"Tell me why you took him."

He shifted to face her. She didn't recoil from his nearness, but her features were tight.

"If Casbian is working with your father, then I couldn't let him go. You know that."

"But if he isn't?" she pressed.

"Then I will set him free."

"You promise?" Her eyes softened.

He had the urge to cup her cheek, to feel the softness of her skin and pull her into his embrace.

He resisted. Bash had to know where her heart lay.

"Yes. I vow it to you."

She nodded. "I do understand, you know. Why you took him. Just promise me you won't...torture him. He came for me when no one else did. I couldn't live with myself should I be the cause of his pain."

Once again, her goodness floored Bash.

"I would never allow you to carry such a burden." Bash glanced at his boots. "If his intentions are indeed honorable, then I won't harm him." He flinched when she entwined her fingers with his, squeezing tightly.

"Thank you, Bash. I know this wasn't what you planned, but we *will* find the Heart and right this wrong. I won't rest until my father's crimes have met justice."

Bash wanted to laugh. What chance did they have now? Even if they managed to locate her father, it was likely too late. Ortum's time and magic were running out. He wouldn't be able to hold the gates any longer, and his once vivid coral eyes were clouded with dusk, the exertion taking its toll.

Margrete scooted closer, shifting so her head rested against his shoulder. Without her eyes on him, he had the courage to ask what had plagued his thoughts for hours.

"Is there more to your relationship with Casbian? Do you care for him?" The question came out in a voice he didn't recognize. It was deep and full of glass.

Margrete craned her head to look at him, eyes narrowed into slits. "If you're asking me what I think you are, then you're a fool."

A rush of relief coursed through him. He tugged her against him and ran his fingers through her hair. "I had to know. Had to hear it from your lips."

Margrete bristled, but she lifted her palm to his chest and rested it above his heart. "After all we shared, I shouldn't have to speak the words for you to know," she said, a hint of hurt in her tone.

But Bash had to make sure. He'd never been in such a predicament.

He pressed a gentle kiss to her forehead and then forced himself to stand.

"I need to head up and meet with the crew, but try to get some rest. I'll see you tonight?"

Because he knew he'd be back once night fell, eager to wrap himself in her warmth where his nightmares couldn't reach him.

"I'll be here." She gave him a wry grin.

It was the sight of that, how her face lit up at his promise of returning, that had Bash believing that the gods weren't as cruel as he'd believed.

Even with hope in his heart, Bash couldn't seem to rid himself of the foreboding he felt deep in his marrow.

He knew all too well that hope was a dangerous thing to have.

CHAPTER THIRTY-TWO

MARGRETE

ADRIAN WAS WAITING FOR MARGRETE WHEN THEY DOCKED.

He was tense, jaw clenched, his hands grasped behind his back.

"Adrian," she greeted when she reached him, her legs wobbling as she adjusted to solid land.

"My Gods, Margrete, your eyes."

She'd nearly forgotten. How the hell would she explain this to him?

"Honestly, I have no idea what happened. I fell overboard during the storm that hit us, and after Bash dove in and saved me, they were...different."

That was putting it mildly.

Adrian lifted his head, finally noticing the many wary stares directed at Margrete's back. She'd felt those stares since she emerged from below deck. The crew likely wondered if she was blessed or cursed.

"We can talk about this later." Adrian dipped his chin and held her newly fashioned eyes. "I imagine you need your rest."

She wanted to be as far away from people as possible. The scrutiny was unbearable.

Adrian placed an arm around her shoulder, and, thankfully, didn't ask more questions about the storm or her eyes. As they walked away from the docks, thunderous shouts pierced the air, and without even looking behind her, Margrete knew whose voice rose above all others.

"I had already guessed that the trade didn't go according to plan when I saw you on deck." Adrian sighed, drawing them closer to the bridge. "But that"—he jerked his head back to the *Phaedra*—"just confirmed any doubts I may have had."

Margrete shook her head. "It all went terribly wrong, Adrian. The count was the one to meet us, not my father, and Bash took him captive."

Adrian glanced away as they continued their trek across the bridge. They were nearly to the other side. "Yes, the men took him off the *Phaedra* first. I have yet to speak with Bash and receive a debriefing."

Margrete pulled him off to the side. "I'd like to see him," she said. "Please, Adrian. Let me talk to him. Maybe I can get more information before Bash questions him."

He'd mentioned getting answers in *any* way necessary.

Adrian pinched the bridge of his nose with his thumb and forefinger, releasing a disgruntled groan.

"Please, Adrian," she said again.

He must've seen the distress brimming in her eyes, because he relented. "Fine, but no more than a few minutes." His shoulders slumped in defeat. "Bash isn't going to be happy, though."

"Thank you!" Margrete wrapped her arms around his waist. "I promise I'll be quick, and Bash doesn't have to know."

They reached the other side of the bridge and passed through the palace's grand archway. Adrian led her to a winding corridor she'd never seen where a silver door waited at the end of the hall. A rugged stone staircase lay just beyond, and they walked in silence until they arrived at the entrance of a rank dungeon.

Two soldiers stood guard before the entry, their backs rigid as they bowed their heads to Adrian. Margrete noticed wisps of heavy leaden clouds whirling inside the doorway, trapped inside the steel frame. It was the same type of mystical barrier that had secured her own chambers.

"You have five minutes." Adrian ushered Margrete forward and nodded to the two soldiers before lifting his hand to the cloudy doorway.

The portal lightened in color, and one of the men grumbled his disapproval as she passed, clearly finding issue with her presence. Margrete grumbled right back, blustering past the sullen guard and down the rocky steps alone. If he had an issue, he could take it up with Adrian.

"Casbian," she called out to the nothingness.

A hushed groan filled her ears, followed by the whimper of her name. "Margrete?"

"Here!" She picked up her pace, racing to the sound of his voice. He was being kept in the farthest corner, in a cell of iron and rust. Margrete saw the outline of a man on the floor, rising slowly as if it cost him great energy to do so.

"How are you?" She stepped close to the bars and rested her forehead against the iron. "Have they been decent?"

"They've been fine." Casbian grunted, righting himself and standing tall before he ambled closer to the bars. A single sconce flickered weakly on the wall behind her, and as he stepped into the light, it exposed his handsome face.

"How have they treated *you*?" He scanned her body for any sign of abuse. When his gaze landed on her face, his brow scrunched in confusion. "Have your eyes always been blue?" he asked. "I could've sworn they were hazel."

She sighed, shaking her head. Clearly, there'd be many questions about her recent change in appearance.

"It's a long story," she said, "but yes, they used to be hazel. You didn't imagine it." She rushed on before he could inquire further. Her eyes were not the greatest issue they had to face. "But don't worry. I plan on getting you out soon," she assured him, lifting her hand to his face. A small cut, dried with blood, decorated his chin. It wasn't deep and had perhaps been inflicted when they threw him down here. "But first, I have to know. Did my father have anything to do with you meeting Bash? Did he send you?"

Her father had caused this mess—*he* was the one who deserved to be behind bars.

Casbian vehemently shook his head, his dark hair tumbling into his blue eyes. "I went to your father after the attack at the keep. We waited until a scout arrived with a letter. Apparently, whatever these men wanted was more valuable than your life, and your father refused." He closed his eyes and let out a disgusted scoff. "After he tossed the letter into the fire, I intercepted the scout and sent along my own message on stationery I'd stolen from Wood's study. I figured it was money they were after, and I couldn't sit by when I was the reason they had you in the first place. Because I was too weak to defend you."

"It wasn't your fault."

"Even if it wasn't, I would've come." Casbian gripped the bars, pressing his face against the rusted metal. "My coming for you had nothing to do with your father and everything to do with honor. With doing what was right."

"I just don't understand," she pressed. "It isn't as if we married. You could've easily found another bride." She motioned to him then, to the striking spectacle that he was. Casbian was the leader of Cartus, and he certainly didn't have to go through all the trouble of bringing Margrete home.

He bristled. "What kind of man would that have made me? I made a vow, even before that day, and I'm a man of my word."

"You're a fool." She chuckled, and Casbian joined her, his laugh deep and hoarse.

Perhaps she might've found happiness with him, but the sight of Count Casbian didn't send flutters dancing in her stomach or shoot tingles down her arms. She felt nothing when she gazed upon him except appreciation.

"I'll speak with Bash," she said, "and I'll return here first thing in the morning."

"It seems I didn't make a mistake coming here," the count said, snaking a hand through the bars to cup her cheek. His touch felt cold against her skin, wrong.

A sudden pang of searing guilt had her pulling away from his touch. Guilt that didn't deserve a place in her heart.

"I'll get you out," she said again, taking a few steps back. She knew her time was up.

"I know you will," Casbian said with a sigh. "Until tomorrow."

Margrete nodded, leaving the prison and the man she'd nearly wed behind.

CHAPTER THIRTY-THREE

BASH

IT WAS JUST AFTER MIDNIGHT WHEN BASH ENTERED THE DUNGEON. Every step he took echoed against the stone walls like a hammer, driving the rodents screeching into the shadows. He breathed in a mouthful of stale air, aiming to calm his racing pulse. He'd interrogated prisoners in the past without a hint of trepidation, but then again, they also hadn't nearly married the woman he was beginning to care so deeply for. As Bash neared the last cell, Adrian's voice rang clear.

"Our spies have learned Cartus is all but bankrupt." His friend's tone held an uncharacteristic bite. "So please explain to me how you were able to procure a ship full of hired men for this rescue of yours?"

Bash stopped just short of the sconce's reach, waiting for Casbian to give the same response he'd offered earlier when Adrian first interrogated him.

There was a weak cough, and then, "Like I told you before. I used the last of our treasury. I refused to sit by while Margrete's father left her to rot." The count's words were impassioned, and Bash almost believed him.

Seconds ticked by.

"Nothing new, my king," Adrian said, not turning around. His commander had the uncanny ability to sense Bash's presence. Always had, even as children.

Bash stepped fully into the light and took in the humbling sight of Casbian shackled to the wall, the heavy chains lifting his arms above his head. The door to the cell was wide open. Adrian loomed before the count with his broad arms crossed.

"Same story as before, eh?" Bash sauntered into the space, brushing off an invisible speck of dust on his jacket. He eyed the count with obvious disdain, twisting his features into a smile Adrian often referred to as sinister.

Bash didn't believe a single word that came out of the bastard's mouth. Even shackled, Casbian held himself regally, his blue eyes haughty and upper lip curled. Then again, maybe Bash disliked the man for other reasons entirely. But he couldn't allow his irrational jealousy to cloud his judgment.

"As I've told your *friend* here, I've been telling nothing but the truth. I came to rescue Margrete. I made a vow to her, and I am a man of honor. A man of my word."

Bash swallowed the laughter that bubbled up in his throat. "Not according to the rumors my spies brought back to me." He took a step closer, shifting his shoulders back and rising to his full height, forcing Casbian to crane his neck to look him in the eye. "No, according to my spies, you're quite the ladies' man—even days before your wedding. So that little argument of yours doesn't seem to hold up so well."

Casbian scoffed. "You should know not all rumors are true." He eyed the cell that held him as if to make a point. "Here I am, on an island that shouldn't exist. I believed it didn't exist merely because I was *told* it wasn't possible." He shook his head, his dark hair falling across his eyes. "I've been called many things in my life, Bash. Any ruler or king, even a count, is often the talk of idle minds. Perhaps when I was younger, I engaged in activities I shouldn't have, but that was many, *many* years ago. I am certainly not the same boy I was."

Bash ground his teeth, taking in every quivering breath the count took. "Why did you want to marry her to begin with?"

The question came out before he could stop himself.

Casbian's gaze grew fierce. "Our letters. The ones we'd been exchanging for *months* before our wedding." His head slumped as he continued, the chains rattling. "She was funny and bright. Clever. She made me laugh at the simplest of things." The corners of his lips quirked. "When I saw her for the first time..." His smile flourished. "I knew she was something to cherish, and I'd be lucky to marry a woman that smart, cunning, and incredibly beautiful."

Bash's stomach churned as he took in the way the count's eyes creased with wonder when he spoke of Margrete. How he couldn't help but smile when he brought up their letters. It made him nauseous.

There was a moment of silence, and then Adrian cleared his throat, stepping in when Bash remained silent.

"He claims that when the captain turned down the offer for a trade, he stole his stationery. He then wrote the letter agreeing to meet and delivered it to our scout with Wood's seal. He is adamant that the captain had no idea of his plan. That he acted alone."

No, that couldn't possibly be right.

"What did you get out of marrying Wood's daughter? You can't have me truly believing you fell in love with her based on a couple of letters and a few minutes in her presence?"

Even as Bash said the words, he realized his mistake.

He was guilty of nearly the same thing. While they hadn't written one another sentimental love notes, and their time together had been limited, Bash had been under her spell since the moment she opened that wicked mouth of hers and cursed him.

Casbian's eyes shone as he drank Bash in, a knowing look twisting his features. "I see what's happening here," he said, straightening as much as he could. "You care for her, too. That's why you don't believe me. Or don't *want* to believe me. I'm not the villain she would spurn."

Bash clenched his fists, attempting to regain his composure.

"That has nothing to do with it," he snapped. "I don't trust you, and I will find out why you are truly here."

Bash made to leave. He didn't have time for this.

"Wait!" Casbian shouted, and Bash begrudgingly turned. "I see it in your eyes. That you *do* care. But if that were actually the case, you'd let her leave with me and get as far away from this place as possible."

"And why is that?" Bash asked, jaw clenched. His patience was running thin.

"You took her as a prisoner for fuck's sake. *Used* her." Casbian shook his head. "You haven't thought about what's good for *her* since you met. You still don't, and you never will. Not when you wear that crown on your head."

Bash's breath caught in his chest. A lump was forming in his throat, and Casbian's accusations wound around his neck and squeezed—an invisible noose.

"That's not true at all—"

"Oh, but it is!" Casbian hissed, eyes growing wide. "You will never deserve a woman like that. Not when you will always choose your people over her. Your kingdom. You're selfish and delusional to think otherwise."

The noose around his throat tightened. He opened his mouth to argue, to claim he *was* deserving, but nothing came out. The words simply froze on the tip of his tongue.

Bash was the king of Azantian, protector of its seas. It was his birthright. His life's mission. He knew then, with a sickening realization, that Casbian was right.

He *couldn't* put her first.

"Finish questioning him," he barked at Adrian in a rush, then twisted on a heel and strode away from the count and away from the truth that fell from his lips. He needed to run, to get as far from that dungeon as possible.

As Bash walked the corridors of the palace, his heart raced and his palms were slick with nerves. Those poisonous words kept looping around his mind. Taunting him.

The more he repeated them, the more he understood what he had to do. What he had to do *for* her. He may never be able to put her first, but, maybe, if Casbian *was* truly innocent, Margrete could be someone else's entire world. When all was said and done, they would survive this disaster with the sea's children, he would see to it, and Margrete would get her happy ending. She might very well find happiness with Casbian, a man who spoke of her like a treasured gift.

Bash had treated her like a ransom and only recently saw the errors of his ways.

He was at Margrete's chambers before he realized where his legs had carried him. Where his heart had carried him.

The guard standing outside her rooms eyed him curiously but stayed silent. Bash raised his hand, about to open her portal, when something stopped him. Guilt or shame or some unnamable emotion. He lowered his hand back to his side.

He turned around, the count's words growing into a sickening chorus. When he entered the privacy of his own chambers, he allowed himself to slide down the back of his door, his body crumbling onto the stones.

Honor would always dictate that Bash should put his island above all else. He'd rather see Margrete leave with the count than be a king's second choice.

Even if it cleaved him in two.

CHAPTER THIRTY-FOUR

MARGRETE

"I NEED TO SEE BASH," MARGRETE YELLED THROUGH THE CHURNING mist of her door the following morning. There were two guards posted beyond, and she shouted her demand over and over until she got a response.

After some minutes of grating shrieking on Margarete's part, one of the guards bellowed, "Stop! I'll alert his majesty. But please, for the love of the gods, enough with the screaming."

Margrete smirked, triumphant. Now all she had to do was wait.

It was another hour before Bash emerged through the portal, dark circles bruising the skin below his eyes. Had he lost sleep over the failed trade? Of course, he had. He'd all but told her he hadn't found another plan to reinforce the gates.

Bash walked closer, and Margrete stood from her bed, a book tumbling from her lap. She'd finally given up and opened the pages of *Weaponry and Defense.*

His eyes drifted to the stone he'd gifted her, openly displayed against her breastbone. She hadn't taken it off once.

"I was told you wanted to see me, but I was stuck in a meeting for most of the morning," he said by way of greeting.

Something between them was off.

"What's wrong?" she asked, unease snaking around her heart and squeezing. He'd put his walls up again, and it was something she wouldn't stand for. Not after she'd gotten to know the man behind the mask.

Bash finally met her stare, but the spark was gone from his eyes. He clasped his hands behind his back, his towering frame rigid. "Our scouts have reported no sightings of your father. Not even in Prias. His keep has been turned upside down, and the Heart is still missing." He sighed, a muscle flickering in his jaw. "But I'm hoping to locate him soon. There are rumors that he's hiding out in Haldion. We should find him by the week's end."

"What if the captain doesn't have the Heart with him?"

"Then we torture him until he tells us," Bash replied without a hint of emotion.

Margrete nodded. Unlike with Casbian, she felt nothing at the thought of her father enduring pain.

"Do what you must," she said, knowing what was at stake. "And please, ask him about Birdie. If he knows she's safe."

"I will," Bash promised.

Hopefully, her sister was under her governess's watchful eye back at the keep. Margrete couldn't afford to think otherwise.

"But tell me—" She dared a step forward. "What is it you're not saying? I know the trade didn't go according to plan, but something else is bothering you. I know it."

She stood her ground, crossing her arms.

"I'm worried about the Heart, nothing more," he replied, inching back toward the portal and away from her.

Margrete wouldn't let him retreat that easily.

"I recognize a lie when I see one," she snapped, closing the distance between them and grabbing his arm, forcing him to look at her. His muscles tensed beneath her fingers. "Bash, what is it?"

A flash of doubt crossed his features, his lips parting, but nothing came out. Even the sea star tattoo on his arm curled in on itself, once again hiding from Margrete's eyes.

"I see." She dropped her hand. "Well, at least let me ask about Casbian."

Bash's nostrils flared at her ex-fiancé's name.

"I spoke with him yesterday, and—"

"You *spoke* with him?" His hands fell to his sides, fists clenching and releasing. "When?"

Her spine stiffened, and she lifted her chin, fighting a grimace of regret. Damn it, she hadn't meant for that to slip.

"Shortly after we arrived. I needed to question him myself. He seems...sincere."

Bash let out a mirthless laugh. "And what do you know about *honorable* men?" The moment the words left his lips, shame twisted his features. He ran a hand through his hair. "Shit, I didn't mean that."

"Maybe you did," she muttered, but he shook his head in response.

"He may very well be honorable, but we need to make sure. If he's working with the captain, then Adrian will know soon enough. He's nearly done questioning him."

"What does that mean?" She already suspected the answer, but she had to ask. As she so often did as of late, she reached for Bash's necklace, the weight of it comforting.

He looked at her from beneath a heavy brow. "If Casbian is telling the truth, then there's nothing to worry about. Once we locate the Heart, he'll be free to do as he wishes, and...so will you."

Margrete took a step back, reading the implication shining in his tone and in his eyes. "Bash. I have no plans on seeing the count after his release, let alone marrying him. Is that what you think I want? Gods, I thought we talked about this yesterday. I made myself rather clear on the subject."

Bash shook his head, his shoulders slumping in defeat. "Margrete, if Casbian is an honest man who dared defy your father and ventured across the sea to find you, then he is a worthy man. Worthy of you. And I believe..." He took a ragged breath. "If he truly is all you claim him to be, then you should go with him when he leaves. There's nothing I can offer you here."

An invisible band wrapped around her throat, cutting off her air as she processed his words. "Y-you *want* me to leave with him?" Her hand fell from her necklace. "I thought..."

What *did* she think? That the king of a mystical island would fall in love with her? A man who had the essence of a sea god coursing through his veins? She was a mortal, a human who wasn't even of noble birth, and he was a damned *king*.

It was laughable. Truly.

Margrete's cheeks heated with embarrassment. She turned, giving him her back as she hid her shame. She knew what they shared had been real, but she hadn't thought about what would happen *after* they defeated her father and found the Heart.

A chill chased across her skin as he moved closer, until his heat was only inches away.

"Princess," Bash whispered, his voice cracking.

She squeezed her eyes shut. "Don't. I understand." After a long moment, she opened her eyes but didn't dare turn and look at him. Instead, she spoke over her shoulder. "There's nothing more to say other than to profess my wishes for Casbian to be moved to more appropriate quarters until he can be deemed innocent."

Silence followed, the air saturated with tension.

Tears welled in her eyes, but she refused to let them fall. Bash had made his intentions clear. He didn't want her. Or, he *did*, but he couldn't.

"Please leave," she asked when Bash didn't utter a word. She needed him gone before the tears inevitably fell.

"Margrete—"

He was so close that she bunched her shoulders, trying to avoid the way his voice caressed her neck.

"Please," she implored. "I need to be alone."

Seconds later, his boots thudded against the stone floor. Margrete waited for the door to shut before she turned around. A foolish part of her expected to see him still standing there, an apology poised on his tongue.

But she was alone.

And Bash had made his decision.

CHAPTER THIRTY-FIVE

BASH

Bash wanted nothing more than to take back every word he'd spoken. He didn't want Margrete to leave, and he certainly didn't want her to leave with the *Count*.

Hours after he'd left Margrete's chambers, Bash rounded the corridor leading to the Adiria Cavern. The soldiers he passed avoided his stare. Adrian planned to meet him below the palace soon, but until his friend arrived, Bash would be free to dwell in the darkness and clear his head.

Bash unlocked the door to the cavern, grabbed a torch, and began his descent, the air growing colder with every step he ventured. The light of his flame ate away at the shadows surrounding him, but he didn't feel an ounce of dread.

There were far worse things to fear than the dark.

He halted right beneath the apex of the vast cavern. A trickle of sunlight filtered through the small chasm in the ceiling but was devoured by the eternal night that thrived in this place. Since he was a child, Bash would come here when he needed to be alone and think. The Soul of Azantian spoke to him, welcomed him into its numbing obscurity with open arms. Here, his mind would go blissfully quiet.

But not even the Adiria Cavern could still his thoughts now.

Bash sat on a stone, his torch flickering as it fought with a gust of cold air. The chilled breeze grew stronger, and his meager flame sparked and popped in response, struggling to reignite.

It lost its battle.

Bash was left alone in utter darkness as his torch fizzled to nothing.

"Of course," he muttered, cursing, though he wasn't worried. He knew this place like the back of his hand. Instead of hastening to find his way out, Bash tucked his knees to his chest and breathed in the nothingness that enveloped him. There was the comforting staccato of water as it dripped from the rocky walls. The faint murmur of wind. The smell of salt and the sea.

The smell of home.

Bash shut his eyes, though it hardly mattered, and dropped the useless torch to the ground. His heartbeat, which had thudded in his ears seconds before, quieted to a gentle drumming. Without his sight, Bash was forced to delve within himself, to glimpse a mind that was anything but collected and calm. He certainly wasn't a man who had control over himself, let alone a kingdom.

A hiss of vicious energy sliced across the rugged stones.

Bash opened his eyes with a start. The flare of violet crashed into the sides of the cavern with the fierceness and strength of lightning, brightening the space with an unnatural glow. Bash sucked in a mouthful of air.

The cavern only came alive two hours before midnight. It had been that way since the beginning of Azantian.

And yet—

Another bolt, this one brighter than the last, fanned across the rock until it collided with the dead center of the cavern floor and crashed into the stone with a fizzle of electricity.

Bash jumped to his feet as chunks of rock loosened, his hand rising protectively to his face. Ignoring his instincts that screamed at him to *run*, he rose instead and walked toward the center, drawn by the remnants of light that still simmered.

He dropped to a crouch and trailed his fingers across the stone, the ground still warm. Flattening his palm, he pressed it against the hard earth, shivering as tingles raced across his skin. His body seemed to sigh in relief, almost as if the current of energy invigorated him. He couldn't explain it, not even to himself, but it felt familiar in a way he couldn't describe.

Bash jerked away with a start, seconds before another round of lightning crashed mere inches from where his hand had rested.

Gods, what was that?

"Bash?"

He twisted his head around at the sound of his name, which seemed to come from everywhere as it echoed off the stones. The voice called his name again, though this time, Bash recognized who it belonged to.

The soft glow of a torch came into view, and Adrian's footsteps were heavy as he exited from the tunnel.

"What are you doing under here without a damned torch?"

Bash was nearly too stunned to reply, but he pushed up from the ground, finding his voice.

"It went out," he said, warily scanning the walls of the cave as though expecting the shadows to reach out and grab him.

Adrian's face contorted with concern. "I suspected things were dire when you asked to meet here."

Those closest to Bash knew he sought out the Adiria Cavern whenever the weight of his crown was too much to bear. Whenever he missed his father or thought of the mother he'd never known. She'd died giving birth to him, but it didn't stop him from conjuring a vision of what she might have been like.

"I needed the quiet," he admitted. "I hate waiting for the scouts to return. You know I get restless."

His friend rubbed a hand across his tight black curls. "They should be back soon, and once we know where Wood is, we can proceed."

"Let's just pray the gods have mercy on us, and the scouts deliver good news," he said, though he didn't believe it for a second. Mercy wasn't something the gods bestowed.

Adrian sighed, clearly exhausted from the past few days. "In the meantime, we should continue with the feast this evening. People might suspect the worst should we cancel, and it would be the first time in a thousand years it wasn't held to honor the moon goddess."

Adrian was right. If they called the feast off, then his people would worry Bash had already failed. It didn't help that they were superstitious and feared displeasing any of the gods, especially Selene, who commanded the tides.

"Will you be escorting Margrete?" Adrian asked. The mere sound of her name was devastating.

"I don't think I should."

"And why the hell not?" Adrian scoffed. "I'm not blind. I've never seen you look at another living soul that way before. Even when you look in a mirror."

Bash shoved Adrian's shoulder, though his friend's jibe did little to lift his spirits. "She's been through a lot. Once this is all over, she should find happiness with someone who can put her first. And that's something I can never do."

"You're a fool." Adrian shook his head. "That woman cares about you. You're only protecting yourself by pushing her away. You're using what the count said as an excuse, and you know it."

He wasn't doing that. Bash was being selfless.

"No, if the count is telling the truth, then he's a decent man. He didn't have to come for her, and he did. She belongs with someone who'd risk it all to be with her."

Adrian bristled. "No, Bash. She *belongs* with whomever she damn well chooses. She's well aware of what she'll get when it comes to you and your crown. You'd be a spineless fool if you take that choice away simply because you're too afraid of getting hurt."

Bash cocked his head. He'd never heard Adrian raise his voice. Margrete had not only found a place in his heart, but in his friend's as well.

"She's had enough of her life decided for her, don't you think?" Adrian continued, undeterred by his king's silence. "And you—" He raised his finger, shoving it into Bash's chest. "You are the most decent man I know, king or not." In a whisper, he added, "You've never given yourself enough credit."

"I'm hardly a good man." He tried to shake off Adrian's hand, but his fingers only bit harder into the muscle of his shoulder.

"You're a good man because you care about doing what's right, even if it has cost you your own chance at finding happiness."

"You're just fishing for a raise." Bash attempted to joke, but Adrian wasn't having it.

"You're my brother, Bash. Always have been, regardless of blood. I love you." Adrian glanced at his boots. "I only wish you carried that same love for yourself."

Bash didn't know what to say. Adrian's passionate words struck a chord deep within him. There'd never been the time to focus on himself, not when he had a kingdom to run, but when the nights grew long and sleep wouldn't come, loneliness crept up, and that was when he turned to the bottle, drowning out his doubts with drink.

An image flashed across his mind. One of her...on his arm. At his side. His partner.

Them. Together.

As usual, his commander had made a fair point—it was Margrete's choice what kind of life she wished to lead. Him making that decision for her only made him the coward Adrian likened him to.

"Tell her how you feel at the feast." Adrian jolted him from his thoughts of the life he could have, a life he hadn't dared envision before. "We may not be able to save the island, or the world, in time, but you do have control over what you say and do before it all goes up in flames."

The night she drugged him, she spoke of sharing the burden, the weight crushing him, but he never believed that she might actually wish to endure the responsibility alongside him. *He* barely desired to carry it. But Adrian was right. Margrete should decide her own fate. And tonight, Bash would give her the chance.

Him or Count Casbian of Cartus.

He always did love a challenge.

CHAPTER THIRTY-SIX

MARGRETE

MARGRETE WATCHED AS THE ISLAND'S CITIZENS CAME TOGETHER. Every person that lived and breathed for Azantian had been welcomed into the palace's main hall, from the lowly peddlers to the fishermen.

Bash wasn't the kind of ruler to sit above them all or separate himself on some raised throne. He immersed himself in the sea of his people, a graceful shark that swam through the current of souls. People bowed and clapped as he strolled among them, for even if nothing had changed— even if the Heart was still missing—he was the man they placed their faith in.

Beside Margrete, Nerissa chatted merrily with Bay. While he occasionally nodded to whatever she said, his gaze never strayed from Adrian, eyeing his boyfriend as if he were the only person in the room.

A cool breeze drifted past the courtyard's doors, caressing Margrete's gauzy skirts of crimson. Shade had sent the garment to her chambers just hours before the start of the festivities with a note that simply said, 'Red would look good on you.'

The gesture had taken Margrete by surprise, only because the gown was the exact color as her wedding dress. But Shade couldn't have known that, and the daring neckline was a far cry from the uptight lace dress she'd been forced to wear.

Margrete found Shade across the room, busy mingling with laughing partygoers. Her red hair was down, curled to her waist, and a body-hugging green dress clung to her curves. She looked sinfully stunning.

Margrete was about to glance away when Shade dipped her head back in laughter, her hair falling aside to reveal an angry slash of red marring the skin behind her right ear.

A shiver of unease raced down Margrete's spine at the sight of it. Before she could examine the mark further, the alluring treasurer dashed out of sight, aiming for another waiting party of revelers. Absentmindedly, Margrete went to grasp the gem Bash had given her, but her neck was bare, the soothing weight of the stone absent. She'd opted not to wear it this evening.

It was just another painful reminder of what she couldn't have.

In spite of her melancholy mood, the band struck up a merry tune, the crowd bellowing in esteem. Margrete looked up. Floating orbs hovered above them in the rafters like giant raindrops filled with tiny swimming creatures. She stared, captivated by a rainbow fish splashing from one suspended pool to another, frolicking with a pair of animated clownfish.

"Margrete."

She lowered her eyes, the magic of the room forgotten. Count Casbian stood before her, adorned in fine onyx trousers and a luminous ivory shirt buttoned with pearls.

Bowing, he gently grasped her hand, placing a chaste kiss on her knuckles. "You look radiant."

"What are you doing here?" she asked, stunned by his presence.

"Bash has graciously permitted me a personal escort." The count jerked his head to the stout soldier leaning stiffly against the wall behind them. "He follows me everywhere—and I mean *everywhere*," Casbian whispered.

Margrete couldn't help but chuckle, elated to see the count unharmed and amongst such finery.

"Since it's been a rather unusual past few days, would you care for a dance?" He slid his hand to the small of her back, and Margrete exhaled sharply. "I *did* come all this way to see you," he added with a crooked smile, which made her reluctant heart flutter.

While she knew Bash was a man of his word, his actions still surprised her, especially that he allowed Casbian to walk among his people on such a sacred night.

"Of course," she finally replied. "I'd love to dance." She bit back her hesitation and placed her hand in his. One side of the count's mouth curled up delightfully, his handsome face beaming, but Margrete saw the act as too perfect, too rehearsed. The smile felt hollow.

"Count Casbian," she began, but he stopped her.

"Cas. Please, just call me Cas. Count Casbian is quite the mouthful, don't you think?"

She nodded in polite agreement. "I'm glad you're all right...Cas."

The name didn't feel right on her tongue.

He drew her in, one hand on her waist, the other clutching her hand. He smelled of deep woods and exotic spices, his eyes wide and blindly open to the future. Apparently, a future that still involved her.

Icy dread pooled in her belly. They'd be lucky if they had a future to worry about at all.

Casbian released Margrete into a graceful spin. His arm gently tugged her back to him a moment later, but she'd already spotted the man she couldn't stop thinking about.

Amidst an adoring crowd of revelers, their eyes locked. Bash's stare brimmed with fire and intensity even as people spoke into his ear, trying to gain their king's attention. Margrete's heart thundered, and not because of the count's hands on her body. Bash hadn't stopped staring, never once losing sight of her as Casbian twirled her around the room.

When the song ended, guests applauded and praised the musicians on the marble dais. They bowed in reply, instantly slowing the music into something hauntingly wistful.

The revelers parted as Bash glided past them, his steps determined as he moved through a sea of color and laughter and light.

The sight of him approaching sent Margrete stumbling, but the count didn't let her fumble. Casbian merely transformed her misstep into a sweeping spin.

She'd barely righted herself in the count's arms when Bash's voice—low and deep and impossibly gut-wrenching—pierced the air.

"Miss Wood, would you honor me with a dance?"

Bash's steely gaze cut into Casbian, his broad shoulders tense. Margrete looked at them, two men who couldn't be more unlike the other.

"Of course." Casbian shot Bash a chilling look, one that relayed how he *truly* felt about Azantian's king. If Bash was bothered, he didn't let on.

"I believe I asked Margrete," Bash corrected, turning to face her.

"Y-yes," she managed, watching as Casbian stepped aside, a scowl contorting his features.

Bash was thoroughly confusing her. He'd practically shoved the count on her, and now he was interrupting their dance. She eyed him warily before taking his offered hand.

"Bash," she greeted, swallowing hard when his gaze traveled the length of her body. His eyes sparkled with longing.

"Margrete," he said her name slowly, seeming to savor every syllable. The sides of his mouth lifted into a sinful smile. When he dipped his hand to her lower back, she let out a gasp, and he curled his fingers against her possessively.

She raised a brow. He was touching her like a lover. Not like a man who'd rejected her and left her in tears.

She cocked a brow at him. "What exactly are you doing?"

"I'm dancing with you, princess," he replied, pulling her against him. She gasped again and clutched the lapel of his jacket, a gilded affair with metal sea stars embroidered along the collar and cuffs.

"Then why does this feel like more than dancing?" she asked when his head dipped closer, his mouth inches away. His warm breath tickled her lips, and she let out a quivering exhale.

"Because it is," he replied, a seductive whisper.

Margrete hardly felt her feet move as they glided across the floor. She was trapped in his gaze, his words echoing in her mind, but it was her dignity that had her pushing gently against his broad chest.

"No," she said, growing angry. Her feet stopped moving, compelling him to still. "I'm not doing this with you again. You can't spurn me one moment and expect me to fall into your arms the next."

"I never should've said those things to you."

"But you did," she argued. "You said them, and surely a part of you must've meant them."

He tightened his grip on her waist. "I thought...I thought you'd be happier. Happier with *him*." He sighed, swallowing hard. "I saw the way you looked at him on the *Phaedra*. And I thought perhaps you might be better off with someone who was free to put you first. A man who wouldn't place his duty above the woman he cared for."

All around them, dancers spun and twirled, their smiling faces a blur.

He must've read the hesitation in her eyes, saw the question her lips didn't dare ask, because he continued, though his voice was strained.

"My responsibility is to protect this island first, and it killed me to think of placing you behind such an overwhelming burden. The only difference between this morning and now is that I realize the choice is yours to make. You know who I am, what the price of being with me might cost, but it doesn't mean I wouldn't go to the ends of the world for you. That I wouldn't do everything in my power to see you happy. Because when you laugh, when you smile..." His hand trembled against her exposed back, his eyes flush with the kind of raw vulnerability that made her head swim. "When you smile, I feel as if I'm being called home."

Margrete faltered at his declaration, her knees weakening.

Home.

Bash likened her to a place she'd never known. A *feeling* she'd longed to experience. But now, looking into eyes that beamed with adoration, affection, and tender yearning, she realized the home she sought could be found in those pools of green.

"I made a vow to you on the *Phaedra* that my sword was yours..." He guided her hand to rest above his beating heart. "But it isn't the only thing I wish to belong to you."

Beneath her palm, she felt the wild beating in his chest, his pulse a hopeful melody. Margrete lowered her eyes to where they connected, where his fingers moved to entwine with her own. Seconds passed before she raised her gaze to his, drinking in the fear and longing in his eyes. The flecks of gold dotting his irises sparked with tentative hope, and she knew then what her answer would be. What it always had been.

It didn't mean she would let him off the hook that easily.

"I don't plan on leaving with the count when this is all over." Below her palm, his heartbeat fluttered. She didn't think he was breathing. "Perhaps I would like to stay, if only to discover my connection to this place."

"I see," he said, though she noted how one corner of his mouth twitched. "I do know more about Azantian than anyone else. Well, besides Ortum, that is. Maybe I could be of assistance."

The orchestra began to play something lively and fast-paced, and laughter filled the air. The melody seeped through her skin and lifted her spirit.

She smiled, and Bash mirrored her, his grin brightening his entire face.

Bash leaned in, his scruff tickling her cheek as he whispered in her ear. "Meet me in the throne room in ten minutes," he said, his voice a desperate rasp. "Please, princess."

She was nodding before she realized she was doing so.

Bash chuckled against her neck, the sound brimming with joy. She wanted to bottle it up and keep it forever.

Reluctantly, he pulled away, but before he left her on the dance floor, Bash slipped his hand across the back of her neck and kissed her forehead. She closed her eyes as he lingered, savoring the unspoken promise they made to one another.

"Until then," he murmured against her skin.

When he finally walked away, Margrete couldn't help but feel like he'd taken a piece of her with him.

CHAPTER THIRTY-SEVEN

MARGRETE

Margrete floated beneath the swooping arches and beyond the perimeter of the grand hall where the feast was held. Picking up her skirts, she abandoned the festivities and dashed down the hall to the throne room.

Bash had yet to arrive, the chamber devoid of revelers. The place still unnerved her, though she didn't understand why. Whenever she drew near the dais, her skin prickled, and the heavy sensation of foreboding wrapped around her throat and squeezed.

Gritting her teeth, she ambled over to the steps leading up the dais, determined to squash her nonsensical trepidation. The silver netting shone brilliantly beneath the sconces, and the throne appeared otherworldly beneath the intricate lattices. Having never been this close, she was only now noticing the carved symbols of convoluted design encircling the empty bezel of silver. It looked as if a jewel would rest there, and then she remembered—

The empty bezel used to hold Malum's heart.

With a hasty glance behind her, Margrete touched the foreign yet familiar figures, tracing each swirl and line. The silver marks roused a distant sort of memory, one that didn't belong *only* to her.

As her finger outlined the final marking, completing the circle, something ached inside of her, an old and obscure yearning that exposed itself in the form of fluttering nerves. These nerves tickled her stomach, spinning in her gut and rising up her throat. It was a strange sensation.

Margrete wondered if it was nerves at all.

Cautiously, she turned and lowered herself onto the throne. It was more than harmless curiosity that had driven her to sit, to rest her hands on the carved arms and caress the delicate designs the God of the Sea had supposedly crafted himself.

Sit. Watch, a voice whispered in her ear—the voice she knew in her soul didn't belong to Malum. It belonged to *him.* Darius.

Margrete closed her eyes and a surge of adrenaline swept through her veins. It was heady and addicting, and her body buzzed with it.

When she opened her eyes, she realized she'd been tricked.

MARGRETE COULDN'T MOVE FROM THE THRONE.

With a grunt, she tried in vain to pry her arms free, but invisible shackles held her wrists in place, imprisoning her in the ancient chair.

She heard the distant screams, but they faded as the world shifted and blurred. The scent of copper filled the air, clogging her nostrils.

She blinked, squeezing her lids closed in the hope that this was merely some nightmare, but when she opened them once more, she knew the scene before her was anything but a dream.

Watch, said the same sensuous voice she'd come to know. Its rich timbre was a far cry from Malum's gentle caress, passion and hunger embodying the deep growl of his command.

Margrete gripped the armrests as a milky haze wafted into the opulent chamber, the scent of metal and rust potent in the air. Blood.

It was everywhere, painting the throne room floor and speckling the grim statues lining the chamber. It coated the intricate tapestries and azure drapes, and crimson splatters stretched up to mark the arched windowpanes that let in the moon's hazy glow.

What is this? she asked, hoping the voice would answer. She needed to be reminded that this wasn't real. That there was an explanation for why she was being forced to see this.

A stuttering heartbeat later, the voice answered.

This is your beginning.

She was about to scream, to yell out to the supernatural entity haunting her, when a new voice—one she didn't recognize—broke through the air. She squinted as the churning fog cleared, revealing a man on his knees, gazing up at a cloaked figure cast in shadows.

"I trusted you." The wounded man spoke, his voice cracking. He clutched his stomach with both hands, crimson saturating his cerulean robes. "Why? After everything we have been through, my friend?"

Margrete tasted the anguish in the man's voice—the betrayal—but she was anchored in place. Even without the invisible bonds, she couldn't have looked away if she wanted to.

Ten soldiers wearing thick leather and carrying broadswords swept into the room as the hooded man chuckled, the sound one of twisted triumph.

Gods. His was a voice she knew all too well.

Margrete gasped as the men formed a circle around their leader who now lowered himself to his knees and reached out to grasp the dying man's chin.

"Oh, Eldoris. This is all your fault, really. You were the one who showed me what could be achieved. What I could do with the magic you were too weak to utilize." The captain gave a humorless laugh. "The world could've been yours to rule. Not just this small island." His hand dropped from the man's chin. "You settled for a crown when you could've been a god."

Margrete twisted in the seat. She wanted to go to the man on his knees, to save him. But through his pain, the man, who wore a thin circlet of gold, lifted his head.

At that moment, she knew who he was.

Bash's father.

The hood fell from the captain's head. He turned his steely gaze to the throne, seeming to look directly into his future daughter's eyes. Her breath hitched, and with one simple glance, every act of cruelty he'd inflicted on her over the years hurtled into her rapidly beating heart.

The captain looked away and returned his focus to the King of Azantian. "You lost, *friend*," he hissed, his lips twisted at the corners. Her father went to say more, but fresh footsteps sounded from behind the line of soldiers, interrupting whatever cruel words he planned to deliver.

The muscled warriors parted, revealing a beautiful dark-haired woman with red lips and the deepest hazel eyes Margrete had ever seen. With a hand clutched to her protruding belly, she approached the captain, who bestowed her with a smile borne of deep affection. It was a look Margrete had never seen him wear. The sight of it was nearly as shocking as the scene playing out before her.

"Arlin, my darling." He took her delicate hands within his and pulled her to his side. "I was wondering where you ran off to."

The woman—Arlin—beamed at the captain, her eyes twinkling beneath his adoration. "I had some loose ends to see to," she said, her voice a delicately cruel thing, "but I wouldn't have missed this for all the world, my love."

The king sputtered blood, barely able to keep his head lifted, though he managed to speak, hatred lining every syllable he forced out. "You're a traitor, Arlin." He fumbled to stand but slipped in his own blood, his hands splayed out flat upon the throne room's floor. "How could you do this to your people?"

Arlin scoffed, rubbing her belly. "You know why better than most why, my *king*," she spat the last word. "You always overlooked my talents. My intelligence. When I asked for a larger role, you surpassed me in place of half-witted men who didn't have the sense to see what Azantian could become."

"I overlooked you because you are short-tempered and—"

"Enough," Arlin thundered. "I don't want to hear any more of your lies. You are weak. *Soft*. And you never deserved the crown you wear."

Margrete's lips parted in a soundless shout as a soldier kicked the king in the gut. His grunts of pain echoed throughout the room. More mercenaries rushed to attack the old king, but her attention drifted, captured by another sight she questioned was real at all.

There, tucked away in the corner, well behind the captain and his men, was a whirling of dark shadows. The dancing haze morphed and settled until the faint outline of a man took form.

The captain was speaking now, but she couldn't take her eyes away from the intruder, from the magic that he possessed as he took shape.

Ortum.

Margrete gripped the throne as Ortum's lips moved without a sound. He lifted his hands in the air, his fingers curled like talons. Time froze as a rush of wind blew through the hall, and the captain slowly lifted his face from the dying king to scan the room.

Her heart thundered when his eyes landed on Ortum, but her father's gaze moved on, clearly unable to see the advisor or the power Malum's descendant wielded. He returned his attention to Arlin.

A woman who wore Margrete's every feature.

She knew then, with a sickening realization, who Arlin truly was. Perhaps she'd known since the moment she saw her walk through the throne room doors.

"It's time we end this," the captain grumbled to the king, reaching for his sword. "I'll do you the favor of putting you out of your misery before I kill your son. Consider it my final act of *friendship*."

At the mention of Bash, Margrete's heart ached. Her skin burned as she twisted to free herself from the throne. Never before had she desired to kill her father as much as she did now. The phantom bonds around her wrists slackened before pinning her back in place.

"May the sea god embrace you," Arlin said, grinning.

As the captain lifted his weapon, ready to bring it down up the old king's neck, the shadows that cloaked Ortum whirled once more. With his hands raised high above his head, Ortum mouthed a final word. A flash of iridescent blue light flared across the expanse of Arlin's belly, there and gone before anyone noticed.

A wave of adrenaline shot through Margrete as the light faded, and a deep knowing settled into place—Ortum had transferred the Heart's power.

Into Arlin herself.

The figure of smoke that was Ortum wavered, but before he vanished, Margrete made out the way his mouth gaped, his coral eyes wide with shock.

He hadn't meant to transfer the Heart to Arlin. He'd made a mistake, and a dire one at that.

Margrete's thoughts were cut off as the captain's sword fell. It sliced through bone, severing the king's neck. She screamed as blood splattered her father's face, which blazed with triumph.

"Now, the Heart." The captain stepped over the king's dismembered body, his boots leaving bloody footprints across the floor as he strode for the dais.

Margrete thrashed in her restraints. Every step her father took, each inch closer he came to her trembling form, sent wave after wave of pure, unbridled panic surging through her veins.

Just as the captain reached the steps leading to the throne, mere feet before the daughter he couldn't see, he lifted his gaze.

His eyes seemed to find hers in the space across time, the icy blue searing into her flesh. Margrete saw hatred and greed trapped in his irises, but there was also a sliver of what appeared to be a feral sadness, the kind that eats away at a person until there is nothing left.

Margrete wouldn't let him do that to her. Not anymore.

Her father took a step up, then another, and Margrete clenched her fists and roared. It was a savage sound, one mixed with fear and cutting rage. It held all of the venomous hatred she'd been forced to suppress. The resentment. The fear. The helplessness.

Margrete erupted.

The shackles holding her to the throne burned her skin, and flames coiled around her insides. This fire flared within her chest until there was nothing but a fine red mist of rage and a pounding heartbeat in the air. Her body shook from the sheer intensity of foreign power, but the shackles around her wrists continued to hold her down.

Margrete let loose a screech of frustration as white fog curled around the edges of the room, dancing up the pillars and statues. Her father's face blurred, but the malice that contorted his features could never be washed away.

That cursed voice returned to her ears, echoing in the chambers. That damned voice that refused to leave her alone.

You're the one I've been searching for.

CHAPTER THIRTY-EIGHT

BASH

"Where the fuck is Ortum?" Bash screamed, attempting to shake Margrete free from whatever trance she was under. But she was glued to the damned throne, held down by some kind of dark magic.

Bash didn't know much about the dark arts, which his father had banned decades prior, but he surmised only a potent spell could be used to paralyze a person, to still their body as their mind drifted someplace else. At least, that was what he assumed to be happening, if her clouded eyes were any indication.

He was late coming to meet her, stopped by too many doting courtiers, and when he walked into the throne room, he found her perched on the dais, eyes glazed and unseeing.

His panicked shouts must've been heard, for Adrian appeared at his side minutes later, and his friend ordered guards to search for Ortum. The advisor may not be as powerful as he once was, drained from decades of holding the sea's children back, but as Malum's descendant, he knew more about magic than anyone on the island.

A guard raced over to whisper into Adrian's ear, and his commander's features fell. "No one can find him, Bash," he said in a frantic rush.

Adrian rarely lost control, but his breathing hitched, and panic shone clearly in his eyes.

"Well, search harder!" Bash grabbed at Margrete's arm, attempting to pry her free, but just as before, she couldn't be moved.

A sharp ache throbbed in his chest, intensifying the longer she remained under her spell, his desperation causing his hands to tremble. Sweat lined his brow, and he let out a guttural curse.

Bash rested both hands on the high back of the throne as he hovered over Margrete. He'd never felt so powerless.

"This is dark magic, Bash," Adrian murmured behind him. "The air reeks of it."

Indeed, the room smelled of rust and smoke, and a scent he didn't recognize. Only once before had he witnessed dark magic with his own eyes. He was five at the time, and a disgruntled council member of his father's had turned the fresh water supply into blood using an ancient spell book he had salvaged. Bash could still recall the scent of darkness, of the lethal enchantment the man had used. The spell was broken the moment his head tumbled from his traitorous shoulders, the old king delivering the fatal blow himself.

Only those willing to sacrifice a piece of their souls used such magic. Their power was supposedly granted by Charion, God of War and Vengeance, but only once they relinquished all the good within their hearts, turning them into a husk of the person they'd once been.

Now someone was practicing the forbidden magic again, but *who* would target Margrete? And why?

After the council member's death, his father destroyed all texts and lore devoted to the subject. He sent guards from home to home, sweeping the island for practitioners, and there had been no signs of it since. Until now.

"Margrete," Bash whispered, reaching out a shaking hand to cup her cheek. "Wake up, princess." Her skin was like ice, and he flinched at the contact. "*Please.*"

Bash was aware of the shuffling footsteps behind him, of the courtiers' hushed murmurs as they wandered into the room. His people were watching as he leaned over Margrete, his emotions on display for all to see.

Bash didn't fucking care.

"Princess." He trailed a finger down her cheek, gently clutching her chin with his thumb and forefinger. "I'm so sorry."

Sorry for bringing her here. For initially hating her because of the blood running through her veins. Sorry he hadn't shown his true face to her when he had the chance. Because her pulse was slowing, her skin growing even more pallid, and Bash feared—

He feared so very much.

"Bash." A heavy hand fell onto his shoulder. "People are watching, and as much as I hate to say this, it probably isn't for the best that you—"

"Wait." Bash cut Adrian off as his eyes landed on a hint of red. He twisted around to the side of the throne and crouched, bringing himself closer to inspect what appeared to be two interwoven circles.

Painted in blood.

"I need a cloth. Water!" he barked. A minute later, someone sat a pitcher of water and a clean cloth at his feet.

Adrian wordlessly hovered above him, but Bash ignored his friend and instead swiftly dipped the cloth into the warm water and scrubbed at the throne, where the circles—no more than two inches in size—had been drawn. When the metal shone clean, he dropped the cloth, red streaks staining the pristine white linen.

"Was that what I think it was—"

A loud gasp silenced Adrian.

Margrete's lids flew open as she sucked in air, her eyes wide with terror.

"Margrete!" Bash grasped both her arms, helping her rise before clutching her trembling frame to his chest. He didn't give a damn if everyone on this island witnessed him now, because she was alive, and he hadn't lost another person he...Well, another person he cared about.

And he did care about her. More than he thought possible.

"Are you all right?" He supported her head as she leaned back to meet his worried gaze. "What the hell happened?"

He wondered what could have possessed her to sit on the throne, but the blood he found painted on its side was evidence enough that someone planned this.

Margrete caught her breath, her cheeks regaining color, but the fear remained in her eyes.

She met his stare, opened her mouth, and spoke the words that would shatter his world.

"Bash. I know where the Heart's power went."

CHAPTER THIRTY-NINE

MARGRETE

Bash scooped Margrete in his arms and carried her from the throne room, past the gossiping onlookers. Margrete felt safe against his warm body, her face tucked into the crook of his neck. They didn't speak as he carried her up the staircase, where he paused only long enough to shift her in his arms and open the door to his rooms.

He kicked it closed behind them with his boot and gazed down at her, his eyes shadowed and full of worry. She could tell it had taken him great effort to keep his emotions in check before his people, but his facade was crumbling. She'd never seen him so pale.

Without a word, he brought her over to the bed and gently lowered her onto the plush bedding. Taking great care, he climbed in beside her and pulled the blanket over them both. He held her close, his muscled arms winding around her, one hand pressed into the small of her back.

Would she ever be able to get the image of his father bleeding out on the throne room floor out of her mind? Or the captain and Arlin's cold, cruel gazes as they watched the king die? Margrete already had enough nightmares to contend with.

"Feeling better?" he asked.

"Yes. A little." She couldn't help but hold onto him. He felt like an anchor tethering her to reality.

Bash watched her, one hand propping his head and the other resting on her waist, his thumb rubbing circles. "Can you tell me what you meant when you said you knew where the Heart's power went?"

Margrete could still see the stunned look on the faces of the onlookers. Their whispers echoed in her mind.

Unnatural.

Blessed.

Divine.

She let out an involuntary shiver.

"I was early meeting you," she began, her throat painfully hoarse, "and there was this urge, this *voice*, compelling me to sit on the throne." It was well past time she told Bash of the two entities, the two otherworldly voices that whispered secrets into her ears. He deserved to know, especially after what her vision had shown.

"A voice?"

"Yes. I've been hearing it since I came to Azantian," she confessed, and the weight fell from her shoulders. "I should've told you sooner, but I thought I was imagining it. Or maybe I just *hoped* I was."

Bash drew her further into his embrace. Her nerves lessened, even if she dreaded speaking the next words.

"When I fell into the sea during the storm, I heard Malum. I understand how absurd that sounds, but I know it was him. He told me he was trapped but working to free himself." She squeezed her eyes shut at the memory of drowning. When she opened them, Bash was staring at her in awe. "But tonight...Tonight, I heard another voice, one that I recognized, and I believe I understand who it may belong to."

Darius. Malum's brother. The other god of the sea. It had to be.

She didn't know why she felt so certain, but she couldn't deny the truth that reverberated inside of her like the drums of war.

"He told me to sit on the throne, and I foolishly heeded his request. The next thing I knew, I was no longer...I was somewhere else. Still in the throne room but trapped in a different *time*."

She expected Bash to look at her like she'd lost her mind, but instead, he took in a steadying breath and asked, "And what did you see?"

"The night your father was murdered. The night my own father attacked Azantian." She cleared her throat, preparing for the next part. The hardest part. "As the captain killed your father, I spotted Ortum. He was hidden in the shadows, murmuring something beneath his breath. Performing some kind of enchantment, I assume."

Bash's breath hitched, but she continued.

"And then there was a small flash of blue light, and it sparked across the pregnant belly of the woman who stood at my father's side. They were...together, it seemed." Her eyes held Bash's, focusing on those endless green pools and the gold dusting his irises. "Bash. She looked like me. She had my nose, my chin, my hair. My hazel eyes, before I drowned, were *her* eyes."

He stiffened, seeming to grasp what she was trying to say. Bash had asked her once about her mother and where she might have hailed from, but when she told him, she could tell he didn't believe her.

"No one in that room seemed to notice when that light flashed across her pregnant belly at the same time Ortum performed his enchantment. I think..."

"That the Heart's power went into her. Into the child she carried." Bash gave her a pointed look, and his hold on her hand tightened. He had put it together—what it would mean if Arlin was indeed her mother. "Before the captain attacked him, my father asked Ortum to attempt the ritual, even if it carried unforeseen risks."

Bash clenched his jaw, eyes flitting to the shadows that clung to the corners of the room.

"What is it?" she asked, pulling her hand from beneath the covers and placing it on his shoulder.

"Ortum is missing," Bash whispered, his chin dipping. "We sent for him when you were on the throne, but no one has been able to locate him."

"I don't understand," she said. "I could have sworn I spotted him in the hall on the way to the feast."

Bash nodded. "I know. It doesn't make sense, and I know he wouldn't just leave. That's why I think something else, something we don't yet understand, is at play. And then there was the blood on the throne."

Her brows scrunched together. "What blood?"

He heaved a sigh. "I found evidence of dark magic, blood magic, being used on you tonight. Two intertwined circles were painted on the side of the throne, and when I rubbed it away, the enchantment finally released you. My father outlawed the practice decades ago, but I'd recognize it anywhere. It leaves a distinct smell." His nose wrinkled in disgust.

Margrete had heard stories of blood magic, of how the practitioner would sacrifice a piece of their soul in order to gain access to power no mortal should own. But that's all they had ever been—*stories*.

"Are you sure?" she asked. Bash nodded without hesitation.

"Someone wanted you to sit on the throne, and they wanted you to have that vision. I just don't know *who*."

If what she suspected was true, if Arlin was her mother and Ortum had mistakenly transferred the power of the Heart into her pregnant belly, then did that mean—

"I think you were always meant to come here," Bash murmured, his thumb still rubbing circles on her hip. "Ortum said the blood of my enemy would bring me salvation, and I think he knew what he'd done that night. I just wish he was here so I could ask him." Margrete grimaced, her heart aching for him. "But Ortum hasn't been himself for the last few weeks. I noticed the change, the way he kept to himself, how he seemed withdrawn and guarded, like there was something he was hiding. I could see it plainly in his eyes, but I kept quiet, trusting that if it was important, he would come to me. It got worse when you arrived, and I suspect I now know the reason why. He knew what he'd done."

Margrete grasped his chin, forcing him to look at her. "Is it truly possible?"

For her to be carrying Malum's essence? The very power that had filled his heart?

Bash's eyes grew dark, the flecks of gold dimming. She knew his answer before he spoke.

"I-I never did believe in chance, Margrete Wood." He gave her a grim smile, and her chest ached at the sight.

Bash brought her to lay against his chest, and her cheek pressed against the silken material of his fine jacket. They didn't speak, didn't move. The answers they needed may very well destroy them, but right now, they merely held one another.

It was an hour later, when Margrete's eyes fluttered open, that she realized she'd drifted to sleep.

Bash was not beside her.

She shot up in his bed and scanned the room until her eyes landed on his pillow. A folded note was placed on top.

I need to speak with Adrian.
Sleep, princess. I won't be gone long
-B

She dropped the note and slumped against the headboard. Without a doubt, he was discussing what was to be done. Done about her.

Margrete didn't find sleep again until the first rays of light peeked across the horizon.

Bash never returned.

CHAPTER FORTY

MARGRETE

The next day, Margrete drifted back to her own chambers, tired of waiting on the king. She was stuck between uncertainty and hopelessness, and she wasn't sure which was worse.

An hour after she'd bathed and dressed, Casbian arrived at her chambers with two armed guards at his back. Still reeling from the monstrous vision, Margrete couldn't seem to summon anything other than a polite smile.

"Morning," she greeted weakly.

"I was hoping I could escort you to the gardens?" Casbian snuck a quick peek over his shoulder, the soldiers glaring daggers at his back.

"Fresh air might be nice," she replied, heaving a sigh. Staying cooped up with her thoughts wouldn't do her any good. They trekked down the staircase and through a winding corridor leading to the western side of the palace, where the guards motioned them to a set of stained-glass doors.

Casbian pulled on the handle to reveal lush green plants and overflowing buds. There was a gravel path at her feet, and Margrete stepped out into the untamed oasis.

"I overheard what transpired at the feast," he said from behind her. She stopped beside a palm and faced him. "You had some sort of vision?

Margrete hardly wished to discuss that with him. So instead, she lied. "I must have had too much to drink. You know how gossip starts." She continued down the path, Casbian rushing to keep up. Maybe a walk was a bad idea.

"Well, I was hoping to speak with you. About what happens after we leave...together, I hope," he began, unwavering.

She stopped short.

"I don't want to be married." The words were harsh but true, every syllable heavy with conviction.

The count's eyes darkened.

"Listen, we have much bigger things to worry about than marriage. Believe me when I tell you, we will be lucky if we see tomorrow."

Casbian's jaw clenched, and his eyes flashed with what she believed to be anger. "I see," he said. "Well, perhaps we can speak of this at a better time. You don't seem like yourself."

As if he knew her at all.

"You know, I think I was too quick to agree to a walk. I'm still feeling out of sorts," she said. The second lie came easily. It had been a bad idea to see Casbian, especially since she couldn't even fake a decent nicety.

"We should get you back to bed then," he gritted out, clearly eager to relieve himself of the unpleasant situation.

Margrete accepted Casbian's arm as they made the quick trek back through the palace. It was an uncomfortable walk, and the count had yet to meet her eyes.

They'd just entered the main hall of the palace when she saw a familiar head of auburn hair. She froze, watching as robed figures in blue emerged from a set of double doors, their eyes downcast as they avoided their seething king.

Bash rubbed at his temples, his eyes shutting. He only opened them when a robed man with greying hair approached, his thin lips moving inaudibly.

"There's no gods' damned way I'm allowing that!" Bash roared a moment later, his upper lip curled in anger. The man before him flinched, but he continued, speaking too low for Margrete to hear.

Whatever he said only worked to enrage Bash more.

In a flash, the king gripped the collar of the man's robe and lifted him up into the air. His sandaled feet dangled as he sputtered.

Beside her, the count let out a soft gasp.

"Find. Another. Way," Bash snarled, every word meant to wound. "That's your job, isn't it? Think of something else!"

He dropped the man's robe, ignoring him as he tumbled to the stones. Turning around, Bash grasped the arm of a passing guard.

"The advisor?"

"N-nothing, my king," the young guard sputtered, clearly fearful of Bash's wrath.

"Fuck!"

Bash spun around, stilling when he locked eyes with Margrete across the hall. She'd never seen him look so angry, and the sight of him unsettled her. Something dire had occurred, something bad enough for Bash to lash out in such a way.

He cursed again, this time softly, and began slowly walking in her direction. His fists were clenched at his sides, but he forced his features to soften. Still, Margrete could taste the anger that rolled off him in waves.

"I'm glad to see you up and about." His eyes remained on her, ignoring the count entirely. He might as well have not even been there. "I meant to come back this morning, but I got delayed..." He glanced at the open double doors, to what appeared to be some sort of meeting room. "I should have more answers tonight. Perhaps we can talk then?"

"Yes, please let me know what you find," she replied. Her brow scrunched as she took in the disheveled sight of him. Bash nodded stiffly and finally turned to acknowledge Casbian, though he only gave him a disapproving glance.

"Tonight, then," he promised, before taking off in the opposite direction, his steps heavy. Before he vanished into the corridor, he paused and twisted back to look at her. In that brief exchange, Margrete saw all the shadows of conflict...and a hint of regret.

WHEN SHE RETURNED TO HER STRETCHING HALLWAY, MARGRETE found the oddest sight: there was a solid wooden door at the end of it.

"What is that?" she asked of the lone guard posted beside it.

He eyed her as if she were a simpleton. "That's a door."

Margrete scoffed. "Yes, I'm fully aware of what a door is, but what happened to all the..." She waved her hands about. "The mist and clouds and such?"

"King's orders," he replied. The guard opened the door for her politely, and she drifted into the familiar space. While nothing had changed, it seemed as if *everything* was different.

Margrete was thankful for the time alone, however, and was glad that Casbian had left her to her thoughts for the remainder of the afternoon. She was sure he wanted time to lick his wounds, though his ego was far from her concern.

Out on the balcony, Margrete took in the view of the city and the waves surrounding them. The seas were tranquil, unnaturally serene. Numb.

An hour passed before a lilting voice greeted her.

"I hope I'm not disturbing you." Adrian crossed through her chambers and joined her on the balcony.

"Not at all," she replied, refusing to peel herself away from the view. The sea didn't own a pair of pitying or sympathetic eyes. Ones that would inadvertently make her soul weep even more than it already was.

Adrian settled at her side, resting his elbows on the railing.

Margrete got directly to the point.

"So he thinks it's true. That Ortum placed the power inside my mother, in *me,* the night my father attacked."

"Yes." Adrian didn't hesitate. "Since day one, you've held an unnatural connection to the island. Your vision simply confirms the reason as to why."

"And do *you* believe my vision holds truth?"

"Bash may be more superstitious than I am, but I find I agree. It can't be argued that the events of that night don't correlate perfectly with the timing of your birth." Adrian gave her a pointed look.

She swallowed down the rising anger she felt at the mother she'd never known and asked Adrian about what she'd seen transpire this morning.

"Why was Bash...Why was he so furious when I saw him?"

Adrian's hands slipped from the railing and came up to grasp both of her arms. "The council members want to...They want to test you. Bring you to the Kardias Cave, to the gates themselves, and try to attempt the transference into a temporary vessel until we find the original Heart. They've secured a jewel that belonged to Malum's lover, an onyx stone the god created just for her. They hope it will be enough to hold the god's power, seeing as he forged it himself."

"But what if it doesn't work?" she asked, fear making her voice small. She didn't want to be afraid, but unknowns of this magnitude would frighten any sane individual.

"It could very well kill you."

Margrete's heart stilled at that.

"You don't shy from the truth." She let out a humorless scoff. Adrian glanced at the waves over her shoulder, frowning.

"If this new stone, however sacred it might be, rejects the power, then we cannot say what might happen to your mortal body. That's why Bash is having such a difficult time. He knows what he *should* do as king, but as a man? That's where he's at war with himself."

"Well, I don't really see another option. He needs to at least try. Everyone is counting on him, and, if it works, then that means we keep the world safe from the sea's children. Especially with Ortum missing, it'll be worth the risk." Even before the final word slipped past her lips, she knew it was true.

Adrian nodded in somber agreement. "We're hoping to find out what happened to Ortum soon, but I'm losing hope."

Margrete didn't know the advisor well, but she grasped how much he meant to Bash. A hushed quiet fell over them as they gazed out at the horizon, both likely wondering what the next few days would bring. What terrors they'd encounter.

Margrete felt the foreboding in the air, and it weighed her every exhale.

"I've given up so much in my life," she began after some time passed, breaking their uneasy silence. "But the reason for doing so has always been the same."

She thought of Birdie. Of the nights she put herself in their father's path so her younger sister might avoid his wrath. She imagined her sister's sweet face and hopeful smile, and her heart lifted, knowing her years of suffering had all been worth it.

Margrete grasped Adrian's hand and squeezed. "I've never feared death, or what might come after I take my final breath. I've only ever feared regret. And I will not sit by when I could save this island. The very sea itself. The *world*. The council has to try whatever they can. It must be done."

Adrian's fingers tightened around hers, his eyes welling with unshed tears.

"Don't worry, my friend. Perhaps the gods will have mercy on me," she said, though this time, she knew it was a lie.

The gods were never merciful.

CHAPTER FORTY-ONE

MARGRETE

It was nearly eight in the evening when a knock sounded.

"Come in," she called out, placing the book of poetry Bash had given her on the bed. She sat up and moved to the far edge of the mattress as the door swung open on its hinges. The sight of it was going to take some getting used to.

Bash shut the door behind him, his lips pursed as he strolled inside. Margrete noted how his jaw clenched, as if each step forward was physically painful.

"Good evening," he offered, avoiding her eyes. Margrete's aching heart throbbed against her ribs.

"Bash," she replied. He shifted on his feet before running his hands through his disorderly strands. The subtle trembling of his fingers didn't escape her.

Bash opened his mouth as if to speak but promptly shut it, glaring daggers into the wall instead. Margarete filled the uneasy silence.

"Adrian told me about what the council wants to attempt, and I have to say I agree with them."

Bash's eyes darted to her, his lips parting as if he wanted to argue.

"This is your last chance, Bash. If they can make this work, tie what remains of Malum's Heart to another vessel and reinforce the gates, then they should." She rose from the bed. She'd made up her mind.

"I..." he began as she slowly approached him. "I'm sorry I didn't tell you of the council meeting right away. Of what was said. I should have, but I—I simply *couldn't*."

"Why?" Margrete knew the answer, but she selfishly wanted to hear it from his lips.

His breathing hitched. "You know why, princess," he said, voice cracking. "Are you really going to make me say it?"

"I didn't take you as a coward, Bash," she teased, but it was strained.

Bash breathed in sharply and strode toward her, closing the distance. With fierce eyes brimming with anguish, he took hold of her arms. "You could die. You probably *will* die, even if they are successful."

"It needs to be done, Bash." She shook her head, tears prickling the back of her eyes. "It may be a long shot, but we need to do anything we can, no matter the risk. If we run out of time to procure the Heart, nothing will hold the beasts back. Especially with Ortum missing."

If she died, then so be it. At least her sister and other innocents would be spared. She'd been making sacrifices her entire life, so what was one more?

Bash dropped his hands and turned, giving her his back. She could see how his frame shook.

"There has to be something else we can try," he murmured, beginning to pace. "I wish Ortum was here to help guide us." His voice broke on the name of his advisor and friend. "I've lost too much, Margrete, and for years I made it my life's mission to protect this island and its people. To put everyone else before myself, and just when I find—just when I find something that could bring me joy, the gods decide to take that away, too." He stilled and twisted around to face her. His admission warmed her soul. "None of this is fair."

She sighed. "I don't think it's supposed to be."

It felt decided at that moment, her fate cemented. Death hovered on the horizon—ready to finally devour her—and all she wanted was one more night with him. To act as if they had all the tomorrows to explore what could have been.

She boldly took his hand in hers. "It's all right, truly," she promised, praying he believed her even as her voice wavered. "It has to be done."

Bash wrapped his warmth around her, the raging storm in his eyes beginning to settle. Outside, beyond the balcony, the air sizzled with electricity. Margrete smelled the promise of rain, and she welcomed it.

"I will always cherish our beginning, Bash," she whispered. "Not many are lucky enough to even have that."

He didn't speak, but his nostrils flared slightly as he processed the meaning behind her words: that this could be the end of their story. A story that fate cut short.

She thought he planned to release her when his grip on her hand loosened, but then Bash did the unexpected.

"No," he hissed. "I'm not chancing your death. Not on some last-minute plan that may or may not work." That spark she loved returned to his eyes, the golden flecks igniting. "And no one but me is going to touch you," he vowed, right before pulling her into his arms.

Bash tucked her against his heaving chest and his velvety mouth fell to her lips. His fingers were in her hair, grabbing at the back of her neck, keeping her in place as his tongue traced the seam of her lips and explored. His movements were savage, and she tasted his passion with every bruising kiss. Kisses she was helpless but to return with a fervor of her own.

He moved his free hand to cup her cheek, his fingers pressing into her smooth skin, and Margrete leaned into his demanding touch as she kissed him back. Their desperation grew into something beautifully wild, and she could feel his need for her push against her stomach, her hips arching in response.

Bash let out a deep groan as she glided her body up and down his length, her nails digging into his muscled back as she held him in place. When he bit her bottom lip, she released a soft moan, the noise seeming to drive him mad.

With an eager touch, Bash trailed his hands over her body, and a barely audible hiss left her when he traced the swell of her breast. His mouth devoured the sound as though he couldn't bear not savoring it.

"Bash," Margrete murmured when he abandoned her lips to plant kisses up and down the length of her neck.

"Yes, princess?" He spoke against her skin, which burned and tingled everywhere he touched.

"We shouldn't be doing this. It'll only make things harder," she whispered, trying to remember why that was so. It was impossible to think clearly with his body against hers.

His fingers pressed into her hips, and his voice was rough when he spoke. "I told you, I won't allow the council members to touch you, and I damn well meant it."

Shivers danced down her back. Such conviction laced his voice, hardening his words. Yet beneath the boldness of his tone, she sensed something else, something deeper—a trace of anguished sorrow.

"We *will* find another option," he continued. "I would rather drive a sword through my heart than hand you over as a sacrifice. You've done enough of that for one lifetime." Bash's grip tightened on her waist. "And now..." He pressed his lips along the curve of her throat. "I want to give you what you deserve." He nipped at the sensitive skin behind her ear as he whispered, "I want to give you everything."

Margrete groaned in response to his sinful promise, her eyelids fluttering shut as he moved to kiss her breasts through the thin barrier of her shirt. He closed his talented mouth around her peaked nipple, and she reveled in the subtle sting of his teeth.

"I don't want to be the reason Azantian falls," she managed to whisper, though it was difficult to sound convincing when he began to suck on the sensitive bud. "Gods, we should never have crossed this line."

Bash lifted his head, his gaze saturated with desire. "We crossed that line the moment you stumbled into my rooms and held a blade to my throat." Bash peered into her eyes, a devilish gleam igniting the gold in them. "I saw how your body trembled." He laid a gentle kiss upon her chest. "How your eyes darkened." His mouth drifted higher, those luscious lips caressing her collarbone. "I knew then that while you told yourself you hated me, you still wanted me."

She fisted his shirt, overwhelmed by the foreign sensations he brought to the surface.

His eyes found hers and held them. "But now...Now that I know you, *see* you, I want you all the more. Your body. Your mind..." He trailed off, nipping at her ear. "Your heart." His hot breath sent tingles racing down her spine, his confession undoing her entirely. "I want all of you."

Margrete shuddered, and her eyes closed as he kissed her neck, biting and sucking the tender flesh.

She couldn't form the words to argue, not when he was doing *this* to her. When Bash pulled away, Margrete nearly whined in protest. "Tell me, princess...What is it that *you* want?"

She peered into those emerald eyes, full of desperation and desire. Hope. Bash stared at her as if her answer would be his salvation. Or his destruction.

"I want..." Margrete exhaled slowly, and Bash's fingers bit into her waist as he awaited her reply. "I want you, Bash. Not the pirate. Not the king. The man."

And Gods, did she mean it. In his presence, Margrete had never felt more alive, more truly herself. It was both frightening and wholly freeing, and she no longer saw the need to hold herself back from what she wanted.

Margrete knew all too well that a life of regret was not how she wanted to live, and she wasn't sure how much time she had left.

"You are going to be the end of me," Bash murmured in a rush. His eyes were alight with pure flame, and he kissed the tip of her nose sweetly, the tenderness surprising her.

"And you were my beginning," she whispered, her nose pressed against his. From the moment she saw him, she knew he would be her ruin. What she hadn't known was that he would also be her rebirth.

Sliding his hands into her hair, Bash kissed her again, his mouth pressing against hers as he breathed life and possibility and exhilaration into her lungs.

Bash untied the neck of her tunic and pulled it over her head. He palmed her breast through her silken undergarment, his thumb and forefinger squeezing her peaked bud as his gaze dripped with desire.

This time, she didn't wait for him.

Margrete tugged off her camisole and tossed it to the floor, leaving her upper body bare for his heated perusal. His eyes flared as he raised his hands to either side of her, grazing her ribcage before he worked his way up to cup both breasts, his calloused fingers rough against her smooth skin.

"Margrete." Her name was a request, a demand. Slowly, painfully so, Margrete exhaled a trembling breath, dizzy with a combination of fear and excitement.

His head dipped as he took one of her nipples in his mouth, the subtle sting of his teeth causing a shiver to wreck her. Taking his time, he lavished each bud, his wicked tongue worshipping her curves. Margrete released a moan when he bit down on the aching peak, only to quickly kiss away the delicious hurt.

As her hands twisted in his hair, his mouth still adoring her every inch, Margrete decided that if she was going to do what she planned the following morning, what she knew to be *right,* she wished to at least experience this. *Him.*

He would be furious with her later, angry she went behind his back, but she knew that, in the end, it would all be for the best. She would find a way to get to the council members herself, and if they had to disobey their king for the greater good of Azantian, she had no doubt that they would.

With her mind made up, Margrete's hands dropped from his silken curls and flew to undo the belt securing her trousers. When she tossed it to the side, strong hands grasped her wrists.

"Are you sure you want this, Margrete?" Bash's chest rose and fell rapidly, a look of uncertainty flashing across his eyes. "We can stop—"

"If we stop, then I might actually kill you," she threatened.

Bash's hold on her loosened. "Well, we wouldn't want that." He chuckled, the sound so joyous and pure that it nearly broke her heart.

He moved to his own trousers and discarded them with a skill she found impressive. His shirt was next, the buttons ripping free as he tore it from his muscled body.

Seeing him bare and standing before her sent a fire through her blood and a deep, raw ache between her legs. An ache only he could satisfy.

Bash didn't utter a word as he scanned her from head to toe, taking in every dip and swell, eyes pausing briefly at her chest before he continued his roving. The edges of the room blurred until she only saw him and the hunger darkening his gaze.

"You're so gods damned beautiful," he said, his voice a low growl.

In a move that stunned them both, Margrete curled her fingers around the back of his neck and yanked him to her, shoving her lips against his as she let herself go. Nothing else mattered except the need to be close, to breathe him in.

His hands roamed up and down her spine, settling on her backside right before lifting her up and forcing her legs to wind around his broad torso. He carried her to the bed and gently lay her down upon the cool satin sheets.

Bash leaned down, ready to crawl over her, but she pressed a hand to his chest. "Wait. I haven't gotten my fill of you yet."

His eyes shuttered at her words, but he straightened obediently, letting her gaze rove over him. She studied his broad shoulders and sinewy arms, the many tattoos painted across his skin, and then she let her stare drift down to his thick chest and muscled stomach.

Finally, she took a breath and dropped her attention even lower, following the dusting of dark, burnished hair trailing to a part of him she'd touched but never seen.

Gods and stars, he was beautiful. Long and hard and so swollen with need.

Margrete wrapped her fingers around him, her thumb brushing against the sensitive tip. His stomach rippled as he flinched, eyes fluttering and lips parting.

"You do so love to torture me," he murmured, letting out a groan when she released him.

"Don't worry. I plan on torturing you all night." Margrete moved her hands to his shoulders and wrenched him impossibly close.

She lifted her mouth to his and kissed him with an animalistic need, the feel of his bare skin on hers driving her to the edge of sanity. It was her turn to groan when Bash slowed his movements, drawing away to lift her hands above her head and forcing her to still.

Margrete arched her hips and pressed against his hold on her wrists. She urged him to continue, to ease the delicious throbbing he'd caused.

Trapping both of her wrists with one hand, Bash moved the other between her thighs, leisurely gliding a finger into her wetness, the friction eliciting a whimper. When he added a second finger, Margrete nearly broke.

He moved in and out of her in lazy thrusts, drawing almost all the way back, only to drive into her again. Just as her body tensed, preparing for release, Bash pulled out.

"Don't stop," she whined, not caring how desperate she sounded.

Bash shook his head as a smirk played across his lips. He brought his fingers—the same ones that were just inside her—to his lips and sucked them into his mouth.

Margrete panted as she watched him. The lewd act only made her ache more.

"I've dreamt about your taste on my tongue. Fantasized about it." His body shook as he growled his approval. "It's so much better than I could have ever imagined."

He wrapped his powerful hands around her thighs and gripped them tightly. Then, he lowered his head between them, and Margrete's thoughts scattered.

Warmth fanned across her exposed flesh as he gazed at her body, his eyes wild with desire and something akin to awe. Slowly, he placed a featherlight kiss on each hip, his warm breath trailing down, down, down—

He paused just above her entrance, and it took everything in her not to arch her hips. To feel his mouth on her most sensitive place. She craved it, needing to feel him more than she needed air.

"Tell me you want this," he rumbled against her, sending vibrations dancing up and down her hypersensitive skin. "Tell me you want me just as badly as I want you." He kissed one thigh, then the other, and then lifted his eyes. "I need your words, princess."

She opened her mouth, but only a strangled whimper escaped.

Gods, this man.

One side of his lips quirked as if he knew exactly what he was doing to her. "That wasn't quite the answer I was looking for." She groaned when his tongue flicked out, and he traced the seam between her thighs.

"Yes." She panted, flinching as his tongue glided back up. "I want this, Bash, I want *you*. I just..."

"Just what?" he asked, raising his head when he heard the apprehension in her tone.

Margrete's cheeks heated. "I've never...I mean, no one has ever..."

Possessive desire hardened his features, and then he brought those sinful lips back to her center. "Oh, I'm going to enjoy this."

A violent tremor wrecked her as his mouth closed around her bundle of nerves. There was no hesitation now, no teasing. Bash devoured her, sucking and biting, his movements eager and full of desperation. Warmth pooled between her legs, and Bash groaned.

"Gods." Margrete dug her fingers into his scalp, and her body bowed from sheer pleasure. She was so damned close—

"The gods won't help you now," Bash said as he drew back, his eyes molten fire. "And they certainly aren't going to be the ones to make you come."

Margrete lost control.

Bash's words set fire to her core, and she thrust her hips up, meeting his lips. His fingers bruised her thighs as he held them open, his talented tongue toying with her, bringing her closer and closer to sweet release. She almost shattered—she felt so much all at once.

Too much.

Instinctively, she pushed against his head. Her need for him had turned her into nothing more than a quivering mess.

Bash growled against her flesh.

"No. I'm not done with you yet," Bash warned. His hands grasped both of her wrists and moved them to her sides. "You taste too fucking delicious for me to stop now."

He lowered his head once more and dipped his tongue inside her. It took everything in Margrete to breathe. To simply *take* the ecstasy that he gave her.

When his tongue thrust deep inside of her and his finger thrummed her bundle of nerves, Margrete broke, her mouth opening in a soundless scream.

"Yes," Bash praised, still moving forcefully against her, wringing out every ounce of pleasure. Only when she stilled, her core throbbing, did he release her wrists and crawl up her body.

"Beautiful." He placed a single kiss on the corner of her mouth and cupped her cheek. "Fucking beautiful. Every damn inch of you."

The reverence he radiated as he took her in only made her want more of him.

"I want you," she whispered against his lips. "Bash, please."

He shivered and pressed against her, his hardness molding perfectly to her softness. He taunted her, sliding his throbbing tip up and down, teasing, not *taking* her the way she craved.

She gripped his shoulders, but he ignored her soundless plea. Margrete was about to protest when his lips drifted to the shell of her ear. He wrapped his fingers around the nape of her neck. "I'm going to savor this. Every. Second. Of it."

In the next heartbeat, he thrust into her, pressing so deep, *impossibly* deep.

"Bash," she whimpered, stretched so full of him, filled so completely. She tightened around him and arched her hips, trying to draw him even deeper, even closer.

A guttural curse, low and raw, roared out of his chest. He pulled back, only to drive all of that glorious hardness into her heat once again. Margrete couldn't hold back the moan that left her, and Bash swallowed the sound, his lips molding to hers.

He kissed her like a man starved—like he lived for the sole purpose of tasting her lips and feeling her shatter around him.

Margrete's heels pressed into his backside as she urged him on, frantic with a desire that consumed all else. Her eyes peered between their bodies, watching where they joined. The tension grew as she took in the sight of him entering her, of him claiming not only her body, but her soul.

She became drunk off his kisses, how his every forceful movement made her dizzy with pleasure. His essence enveloped her until all she could taste was him—freedom and power and dominance. Everything that Bash was and ever would be.

When his teeth gently grazed her neck, Margrete dug her nails into his back. She was likely leaving little crescent moons on his tanned skin, marking him as hers—just as she was now his.

"Your body was made for me, Margrete. In every way."

Her eyes fluttered open, half-hooded as she lay caught beneath his penetrating gaze.

Margrete kissed him hard, biting his bottom lip and eliciting another groan. "Show me," she whispered.

Holding her stare, he gripped her knees and opened her to him more fully, and then he drove into her with a thrust that pushed her body farther up the bed. She whimpered when he took one of her nipples between his lips, making pleasure strike everywhere at once.

Tingling heat swelled in her core, and with every savage advance, Margrete climbed higher and higher, chasing after sweet relief.

"Come for me, princess," he commanded. "I need to feel you."

Her body tensed, preparing for the inevitable fall.

Bash groaned as her eyes rolled into the back of her head. Sparks flashed behind her closed lids, every nerve electrified. It was a moment of freefall, one where she couldn't breathe or think or move.

"Fuck," Bash cried, beginning to chase after his own release. He moved harder, faster, his length thickening, throbbing.

She gripped his arms, desire coiling tight inside her again. His eyes were so dark, and his body glistened under a fine sheen of sweat.

"Margrete," he whispered.

Her name was a plea, and she wrapped her legs around his waist in reply, holding him secure as his brow furrowed in pleasure. The muscles in his abdomen tensed as he rode out his own euphoria with a rumbling groan that made her body clench.

Watching *him* fall apart nearly set her off again.

When it was over, his chest rising and falling in uneven movements, he propped himself up on his elbows, thoroughly caging her in.

"Margrete." He said her name over and over again, resting his forehead against hers. "That was..."

"Amazing," she finished for him, a satiated smile tugging at her lips.

Bash smiled. "Now that I know what you feel like"—he kissed her jaw—"I don't think I can ever stop." More kisses landed on her cheeks, her nose, her lips. "And I don't plan to."

Margrete touched his cheek, and he leaned into her embrace, eyes fluttering shut. Although she'd never been happier than at this moment, inside a battle still raged. She was falling for this man, so hard and so fast. What they'd done went beyond sex. It was a molding of two souls that called out for the other.

She felt a complete sense of peace and adoration, and, because of that, she refused to think about what she had to do when the sun rose in the morning. Rather than ruining this moment with the truth, Margrete chose to say words that were equally as true.

"You are the freedom I've been searching for, Bash."

He was what she'd sought whenever she hid away in her tower to watch the wild waves play with the sands, dreaming of a life she never thought she'd have. This was it. Bash was *her* choice.

"Mon shana leandri le voux," he whispered against her lips. His smile was radiant.

"What does that mean?" she asked.

One word stood out amongst the rest. *Shana.* The name Malum used for her.

Bash's smile blossomed. "It means, my heart beats with yours." He kissed her as deeply and fervently as before.

Margrete felt his smile with every kiss, sensed his unbridled joy with every lash of his tongue. He was hopeful; it was a side of him she'd not seen before.

She shut her eyes as his tender words repeated in her mind. *Shana. Heart.* It confirmed everything she already knew.

"Where did you just go?" Bash asked, and she willed her eyes open.

"Nowhere." She flipped Bash onto his back and straddled him. "There's nowhere else I'd rather be."

CHAPTER FORTY-TWO

MARGRETE

MARGRETE DIDN'T SLEEP, NOT EVEN AS BASH RESTED PEACEFULLY beside her. She merely stared up at the ornate silver ceiling, exploring the fine details and depictions of nymeras and legends.

Her body felt deliciously sore from what they'd done—from what they shared—and while their time together was to come to an end, Margrete would carry this night with her, a final gift before it all came crashing down.

Bash made his choice, too. She knew this the instant he grasped her face and commanded her lips. The King of Azantian knew the dangers they would face should she not relinquish the Heart's essence, should the beasts straining against their prisons finally burst free.

It would cost lives. Innocent lives. And Margrete simply wouldn't allow this.

Her mind had been made, but staring at the king, his thick lashes dusting his cheeks and a hint of a smile on his lips, she felt her resolve waver.

Was she not courageous enough to sacrifice herself for so many? Margrete had always believed herself to be a good and decent person with an honest heart—but now, she wasn't sure at all. She could only see a girl eager to taste her own happily ever after, like some lost princess in a fairy tale from one of her childhood books.

Though she'd found a semblance of a happy ending tonight, it would be as close to it she would allow. How could she hold her head high when her joy cost others their lives?

She ran her hand against Bash's stubbled cheek, careful not to wake him as she committed his handsome face to memory. Her fingers paused on the curve of his jaw when she heard it.

Margrete.

She flinched, her fingers jerking from Bash's heated skin.

Come find me, little one, it demanded. The usually deep timbre turned into a near growl.

Darius.

He sounded angry tonight, and, if she wasn't mistaken, he'd directed his rage at her. She just didn't know why.

Couldn't she enjoy her last night a little bit longer? She squeezed her eyes shut, willing the voice and its commands to leave her alone, to allow her to spend just a little more time in Bash's arms. But he was persistent, and the next time he spoke, there was no mistaking that it wasn't a request.

Go to where I showed you the truth. To where it all began. Now.

Margrete shuddered at the thought of returning to the cursed throne room. She could still see the blood painting the floor. Because she faltered, the voice—Darius's voice—delivered one final warning. One she couldn't ignore.

I will not hesitate to end him.

Margrete's heart thrummed as dread pooled in her stomach. She didn't know Darius, not that she claimed to know his twin. Still, whenever Malum spoke to her, she felt only peace.

Now, she felt fear and the poisonous weight of his promise.

Margrete slipped from bed and pulled on her discarded trousers and shirt. Her pulse thundered in her ears, the threat on Bash's life causing her fingers to tremble.

Good girl, the voice praised, and Margrete grimaced.

She yanked on her boots and took one last look at her slumbering king, then tiptoed to the door. Only one guard had been posted outside, and he was fast asleep. A mug—which no doubt contained wine or ale— sat at a precarious tilt in his hand.

Sneaking past the slumbering soldier, she dashed along the corridor. Her feet were light and nimble as she flew down the staircase.

Soon, the main floor approached. She stepped out, and her boot landed resoundingly on the stone. Tomorrow she would sacrifice herself for an island she'd grown to care about, but tonight, the voice that haunted her demanded an audience.

Padding down the corridor, Margrete kept close to the walls, on alert should one of the midnight patrolmen come near. There was only one close call on her way through the palace. When she heard the sound of heavy boots, Margrete dashed into a shadowy alcove and held her breath as two men marched past. They didn't spare a look back.

The throne room was coming up on her left. Margrete was about to take that last corner when her feet stilled.

Someone was approaching, frantic footfalls pounding the stones. She sucked in a breath, searching for a place to hide, but there weren't any alcoves or doors she could slip inside. She twisted around, ready to race back down the hall, when someone called her name.

"Margrete?"

She froze. Turning, she found the last person she'd expected.

"What are you doing here?" she hissed at Casbian.

The count stood before her, his raven hair sticking to his sweat-lined brow, a crazed look widening his blue eyes.

"We don't have much time, Margrete." Casbian closed the gap between them and grasped her hands in his. "I was just coming for you. I have a plan to get us out of here tonight, but you have to follow my lead and hurry."

She resisted the urge to yank her hands out of his grasp. "What do you mean you have a plan? How did you escape your guards?" Bash had him heavily secured. If he'd managed to evade them, he must have had help. Something didn't feel right.

"I was able to persuade one of the guards to look the other way. I promised he'd be well compensated shortly."

"I still don't understand," she murmured, warning bells ringing in her head. He knew nothing about the Heart or Malum or the transference.

"Your father is coming." Casbian grinned. "He'll be here soon, and then you won't be a prisoner anymore. He's told me all about the Heart, how it's trapped inside of you, but he has a plan to free you of that burden. You'll be able to come back to Cartus with me once this mess is all over." Casbian's eyes flashed with a nearly manic delight. He appeared unhinged.

"My father...He's coming?" She could barely get the words out. They weighed on her tongue as her throat constricted.

"You have to come with me." Casbian yanked on her hand. "*Now.*"

Margrete fell forward, unable to free herself of his ironclad grip.

"You...you lied," she murmured, almost to herself. "I believed you when you said you weren't working with my father." He'd appeared so sincere, so raw, when he promised he came for her with honor in his heart.

All lies.

"I had to lie to you in case someone was listening," he snapped, his patience growing thin. "Come on, we have to run." Casbian pulled on her again, but she dug in her heels, putting all of her weight against him.

"I'm not coming with you! Don't you understand what's at stake? Whatever my father has told you is a lie. If Bash doesn't get the Heart back and call forth its missing essence trapped inside of me, then the gates will unleash the sea's children, and they will be set upon the world. Thousands will die!" She was screaming now, uncaring if they were over-heard. In fact, she hoped they were. There was no way she'd be able to fight him off herself.

Margrete hissed as Casbian tightened his hand around her wrist, and pain lanced up her arm. "I told you I'm not coming!" She jerked backward again, but he didn't release her. "Please, Casbian, you have no idea what my father is capable of, and if you take me to him, you're just as evil as he is."

Tears welled in her eyes as she pleaded with the man she almost married. A man she'd been foolish enough to trust. How wrong she'd been.

Casbian's upper lip curled, and he leaned down to whisper in her ear. His tone was lined with gravel. "This. Is. Happening." He bit out every word. "Now, shut your mouth and come with me before you make me do something I'll regret."

Margrete acted without thought, only instinct.

Fashioning her hand into a fist, just as Adrian taught her, she struck him, using all of the force she possessed to punch him square in that perfect jaw of his.

Casbian bellowed, clasping his hands over his wounded face as shock twisted his features.

Margrete didn't hesitate.

She took off in a sprint, racing down the corridor for the spiral staircase that would lead her back to Bash. She'd warn him, and, hopefully, it would give him enough time to prepare his men for when her father arrived at their shores.

Her legs pumped, burning from the exertion, and sweat pooled down her back, but she didn't stop. Not when she knew what would happen if she failed to evade Casbian. He'd take her back to the captain, where he would possess both the physical Heart *and* the magic she carried inside of her. Then, he might be able to reunite the pieces and make Malum's heart whole again.

Boots sounded behind her, her name a snarled word on Casbian's lips. He was gaining ground—

One moment she was running and the next, a heavy body pummeled into her, sending her flying through the air. Her hands shot out instinctively to protect her face from colliding with the stones.

Casbian pushed into her back, using his full weight to hold her still. She opened her mouth to scream, but before any sound escaped, a foul-smelling handkerchief was pressed to her lips.

"You shouldn't have run," Casbian panted. The weight of his body stole the air from her lungs.

Margrete tried to hold her breath, to not take in whatever poison drenched the handkerchief, but she failed. Her head grew dizzy as she gasped for air.

She was losing consciousness. Drifting away.

The last thing she remembered was being rolled onto her back and the count's face looming in her vision, a cruel smile on his lips.

Then the world cut to black.

CHAPTER FORTY-THREE

BASH

Bash woke with a start. He felt cold; the heat of Margrete's body was absent. He reached into the darkness to tuck her back where she belonged, but his hands found nothing but empty sheets.

"Princess?" Perhaps she was in the bathing suite.

Bash shifted in bed, trying to find a comfortable position until her return, but as the minutes ticked by, knots formed began forming in his stomach.

Something didn't feel right.

Had their night together been a dream? It couldn't have been. The scent of her still clung to his skin, and he inhaled it deeply, assuring himself that he indeed made love to Margrete Wood last night. But the knots in his stomach remained and grew in might, and eventually forced him to leave the comfort of the bed.

He searched the bathing suite first but found it empty.

Racing to the balcony and tossing the gauzy curtains aside, he found nothing but the moon and mocking stars staring back at him.

Bash cursed, swiveling about the room, searching for a clue as to Margrete's whereabouts. Something deep within urged him to hurry. She wouldn't have abandoned him after their night together.

Tonight had been about more than sex, at least to him. It felt like coming home after years at sea, like he'd found a worthy partner who saw past his crown. Who saw the broken man he was and discovered beauty in the flaws he'd tried so hard to disguise.

And she was gone.

Bash made quick work of dressing, yanking on his discarded trousers. He didn't brush his hair in place, and the long strands stuck up in every direction.

He marched to the corridor, where he came across the lone guard stationed outside of her room. His mouth was open, and guttural snores escaped from his lips. Kicking at the soldier's foot, Bash had to remind himself to hold back his simmering anger. The boy snorted, drowsy eyes widening upon finding his king glaring down at him.

"Sir!" He bolted to his feet, a deep red blush painting his cheeks and ears.

"Where is she?" he asked, his tone menacing in its timber. The guard shook his head, clearly uncertain Margrete was missing in the first place. "I—I don't kn—"

"Alert the others," Bash barked. "Find her." The pounding in his chest amplified as he dashed down the stairs. The clatter of waking guards filled the midnight halls. "Check on the count," Bash snapped at a passing soldier. The man nodded and raced off to fulfill his task.

He didn't particularly enjoy this new sensation of crushing concern, of overwhelming alarm. It tugged at his heart in ways that caused his breaths to turn ragged. He knew Casbian had to be involved with her disappearance. Bash didn't believe for one second that Margrete would have left him willingly.

She'd made her choice, as surely as Bash made his.

His men were halfway through their search of the palace when sirens rang out in the early morning light. Three sharp pangs of warning.

The tolling bells of an impending attack.

Bash cursed beneath his breath as he raced to an open balcony overlooking the southern side of the island.

Adrian marched over to his leader and grabbed the railing at his king's side. It appeared as if the commander had yet to sleep, and dark circles painted below his eyes.

"Margrete's missing," Bash said in a rush.

"What about the count—"

"He's gone!" A guard raced over, interrupting Adrian. "Casbian's room is empty as well, and his guards are unconscious."

"Search the grounds!" Adrian barked commands to his men, his voice uncharacteristically severe.

"Here." Adrian handed over a silver spyglass. Bash nodded his thanks and brought the glass to his eye to scan the horizon.

The sky lit up before Bash's eyes. The apparatus was one of Azantian's greatest feats of machinery. Instead of endless black, the instrument painted the world in an amber glow, just bright enough to clearly make out the reason for the alarm bells.

Black sails fluttered in the wind, a red and onyx flag soaring above the crow's nest, the mighty hawk sigil flying through the skies.

Captain Wood's flag.

Wood's grand vessel, the *Iron Mast,* was anchored about one hundred yards beyond the outer band surrounding the island. The steel barrier would do well to hinder his advance, but Bash knew it wouldn't stop him for long.

"Are all the bridges drawn up?" Bash asked in a low voice, his rage barely concealed.

"Yes. My men raised them when he was first sighted," Adrian replied, "but they've brought longboats with them. They're making their way across now."

Bash let loose a string of colorful curses.

"Is everyone at their stations?" he asked, though his mind was elsewhere. He felt the rush of adrenaline only an impending battle could ignite, and the surge of icy fear brought back the painful memories of the night he'd lost his father. The first night the captain raided his home.

He refused to let Wood attack Azantian a second time.

"Yes, we have initiated our contingency plan. Five hundred armed soldiers are manning the southern banks, and the remaining men are preparing the city for a possible ambush should they breach the perimeter."

There couldn't be a way for a ship of that size—perhaps carrying two hundred men—to breach their defenses and defeat five hundred Azantian trained soldiers. This was the thought that Bash repeated over and over again until he believed it to be true.

"Good. Bring me updates." Bash lowered the telescope. "Everyone needs to be on guard." Captain Wood might very well have something up his sleeve. He'd already proven that he would commit any crime—no matter how heinous—to further his own agenda.

Nothing was out of the question.

He also knew it was no mere coincidence that Margrete vanished just as the captain readied to storm Azantian. Somehow, he'd gotten ahold of her, right out from under Bash's nose. It was his fault that she was gone, back in the clutches of her despicable father.

"Sire!"

Bash reluctantly turned to find a young soldier sprint into the room, sweat dampening his dark brow. "The advisor..." He panted, trying to catch his breath. "We found him on the beach. His throat—his throat had been cut."

"What?" Bash shook his head, disbelieving. Black spots fluttered across his vision as his heart squeezed painfully.

"That's not the most unsettling part, my king." The young guard swallowed hard. "It appears as though he's been dead for some time. At least a few weeks. The body shows disturbing signs of decay, and the stench—"

"We'll discuss this later." Adrian dismissed the man with a nod and turned to Bash. Their eyes locked.

Bash felt his entire world shift. How could Ortum's body show signs of decay? It was impossible. He'd only *just* gone missing, and the gates still held, even if just barely. If Ortum had been dead for so long, the whole island would have known it by now.

"We'll find out what happened," Adrian vowed, squeezing Bash's shoulder. "Right now, we need to hold off Wood's mercenaries."

Sensing the impending threat, the shark on his forearm lurched to life, its pectoral fins twitching in warning. The beast unhinged its mighty jaw to reveal rows of razor-sharp teeth ready to clamp down on its prey.

Soon, there would be blood in the waters.

CHAPTER FORTY-FOUR

MARGRETE

MARGRETE'S EYES FLUTTERED OPEN AS A POINTED BOOT POKED HER in the ribs.

The world was awash in shades of yellow and burnt orange, the taste of wood and salt heavy in the air. As her vision cleared, the blurred shadows grew sharp.

She was once again in a cabin aboard a ship.

Although, this time, it wasn't the *Phaedra*, and the man looming above her was not a handsome king set on saving his island home.

The man's polished boot lowered back to the planks with a thud.

"Good. You're up." Her father's voice was just as she remembered it: hard, cold, and all things grating. Its jilting melody was like sandpaper to exposed flesh.

Margrete pushed up onto her elbows, her head swimming from whatever Casbian dosed her with.

"You."

There was malice and anger and years of heartache directed into that one syllable. She hoped her father choked on its venom.

"Did you miss me, dear daughter?" The captain hooked his thumb through his belt loop, a triumphant sneer curling his thin lips.

"Go to hell," Margrete snarled, her teeth bared.

"Oh, not even the underworld could hold me for long." Her father chuckled, his eyes crinkling. "It seems you've found yourself a spine during your stay here. Not that it will matter."

The captain took a few steps closer to the cot, hovering like a gray rain cloud. Margrete twisted the sheets, her fingers twitching. She wanted nothing more than to curl her hand into a fist and attack him the way she had Casbian.

"All of this mess"—he waved his hand to her trembling frame—"could have been avoided if you'd just given me what I wanted. But no, not even hours spent inside the box confined with the Heart could persuade you." He laughed harshly. "I always knew it would take something more drastic to make you cooperate."

Margrete flinched.

All those many years of her father shoving her inside the iron contraption. He hadn't just been punishing her—

"You locked me in the box with the Heart." It wasn't a question. "What did you expect would happen, hmm? That the pieces would reunite simply because you placed us close together? How did you even know what I was?"

The captain went rigid. "It was obvious to me that day in my study all those many years ago. The Heart hadn't pulsed with life for years, but the second you entered the room where I'd kept it safely hidden, it came alive again. I thought Malum's magic had returned, that his power would be mine, but the stone was merely reacting to your presence. Nothing more." He scowled.

That day in his study came back to her like a violent surge. She'd been so young, but she remembered him holding something in the palm of his hand, and, for once, when she came to him, he didn't send her away. It was the very next day that he began locking her in the box.

"If it didn't work for all these years, then how the hell do you plan on joining the Heart and the magic inside of me?"

"Ah, yes." He lifted his shoulders, a cruel confidence sparking in his eyes. "I was rather fortunate when Casbian came to me in hopes of forming a business partnership. When I paid him a visit on Cartus, he was kind enough to show me his extensive library." Her father turned to his desk and grabbed a simple, leatherbound book. He held it in the air for her to see. "This is what I've been searching for all these many years. A back-up plan should the pieces not come together...naturally."

He took a step closer to the bed, causing her to flinch.

"What is that?" She despised how her voice cracked.

"A book that contains outlawed magic. I thought all traces of the practice had been wiped from the earth, but Casbian possessed a single volume, and, within these pages, I discovered everything I need to complete the transference. In return, all Casbian requested was to marry *you*." He scoffed as though the thought were truly laughable. "Well, he was aiming to gain the hefty dowry that would come along with you, I suppose, seeing as his treasury is all but empty. Either way, it was an easy trade to make."

Margrete wished she was still capable of being shocked by such an admission, but his words washed across her without provoking an ounce of emotion. Nothing he could do would surprise her.

"You have no idea how long I've waited for this moment," her father continued. Margrete pressed her lips together, refusing to indulge him with her words. "When I returned home from Azantian, the Heart had turned dull and gray, barely pulsing with life. I knew something transpired on that island, and Arlin had her suspicions, too. Especially when you were born. That was the day the seas ravished Prias, and a great storm assaulted the city. She held you in her arms just before she died, and do you know what her final words were?" He paused, nostrils flaring slightly. "Arlin looked me in the eyes and told me, 'I can feel it in her. We always had it.' Though I was never awarded the time to ask what she meant, it was made clear years later. Somehow, while you were still in her womb, you were given the magic that should've been mine."

Margrete wondered if her father knew about Ortum's role the night he attacked Azantian. Then again, in her vision, when the advisor drained the Heart, he'd been cloaked in shadows.

"What are you planning?" she asked, her breathing growing uneven.

With the heart of a god, he would be unstoppable.

"I will command the sea's children, of course." He answered like it was obvious. "And the tides themselves, I suppose. Though one would imagine an army of monsters at my disposal will convince my adversaries of my right to the throne of Marionette. Finally, the Heart will thrive, and the beasts will be forced to listen. They were created from its power and will follow its command."

Gods. She prayed Bash discovered her missing, that he'd look to the waters and see the captain's ship on the horizon.

"While it's been fun catching up, I've waited too many years for this moment," her father said as he yanked on her arm and lifted her from the bed without care. He forced her above deck, where the moon shone with ominous brilliance. Men scurried all around the *Iron Mast*, their boots pounding on the wooden planks, weapons in hand.

They were already moored at the southern arch, held back by the steel outer band. She noted the remaining crew was busy lowering thin longboats onto the waves.

"Hello, Margrete."

Casbian emerged from below deck, his hands tucked into his trousers. "Sorry about earlier, but we had a schedule to keep."

Margrete snarled at him. "You idiot!" She seethed. "He's just going to use you like he does everyone else!"

Casbian shrugged. "Not when my influence with the nobles will help ease the transition of power. As you've been told, I hold a decent amount of sway." He smirked, clearly pleased with himself.

He had no sense, no idea of who he was dealing with if he believed the captain would honor their deal. Margrete watched as he sauntered over to the vessel's railing, leaned against it, and crossed his arms. Not once did his confident smile falter.

"Alright, daughter." The captain shoved her in front of him. "You'll have enough time later to talk with your fiancé, but now we must prepare."

A snicker left Casbian, and she wished she had inflicted more damage on that pretty face.

Craning his neck, her father snapped an order, and a lanky guard fell into place.

"Bring her up. We're ready to begin."

Her?

Two dim figures emerged from below, one clearly a woman, and the other—

"No!" she shouted, a wild scream that came from the deepest parts of her soul. She thrashed in her father's grip as her little sister was ushered forward by her governess. The older woman's face was pinched in remorse.

"Margrete?" Birdie took a hesitant forward, her crystal blue eyes wide with fear.

"I'm here, Birdie," she cried, tears welling up in her eyes. "I won't let anything happen to you." Even as she made the promise, Margrete knew it might not be one she could keep.

"What's going on?" Birdie turned her head toward their father, who heartlessly avoided her gaze.

"What is she doing here?" Margrete asked the captain, twisting her head to snarl in his ear. "If you hurt her, so help me—"

"You'll what?" He jerked her against him and lowered his voice so only she would hear. "There is nothing that can be done. I need her in order to complete the transfer. Believe me, if I could use you, I would. But I need you alive for the process. Unfortunately."

Alive. He needed Margrete alive, which meant—

"This is too far, even for you!" He was a monster. Worse than anything she could've ever imagined.

The captain used his free hand to reach into the pocket of his jacket, and Margrete *felt* the power before she saw it. Her skin buzzed almost violently.

Within his palm was a pale, gray-blue gem. At the sight of it, her stomach plummeted.

Malum's Heart. It had to be.

Margrete peered down, watching in amazement as a gentle light pulsed at the core of the gem. It was weak, the light, but it throbbed like that of a beating heart.

"Take her," the captain commanded, and Margrete was suddenly thrust in the direction of one of his men, whose thick arms banded around her torso and rendered her immobile. From beyond the dim light of the lanterns, she heard Casbian chuckle.

She tore her eyes from the Heart as her father was handed a wrinkled piece of parchment. With the sacred gem resting in his palm, he unfurled the paper, revealing words belonging to an ancient tongue scrawled in red ink on the page.

No. Not ink. *Blood.*

She scanned the paper, hoping against hope that she was wrong and that this was a nightmare she'd wake from.

There, at the bottom right-hand corner of the page, was a symbol etched in red—

Two-interwoven circles.

And now her father held a parchment—written in blood—with the same emblem that had tied her to the throne the night of her vision.

Blood magic.

"What is that?" she asked. Tears burned her cheeks as they slipped free, sliding down her face in tiny rivulets.

"It's a sacrifice, Margrete." He brought the page closer. "Birdie's blood must be spilled before I can transfer Malum's power to its original vessel." The gem pulsed in his hand, seeming to sense its missing power nearby.

Margrete fought against the arms that held her, kicking out her legs in a futile attempt to escape. "Why *her*?" she roared. "Why?!"

He sighed, seemingly bored. "Because this enchantment requires the blood of your kin, and Birdie is my only option."

"It won't even work!" Margrete bared her teeth. "If one of Malum's own descendants couldn't figure it out, then what makes you think you can? You're risking your own child's life, and for nothing!"

"It is a chance I'm willing to take," her father gritted out, jaw impossibly taut.

"I'll kill you!" Margrete vowed. She stomped on the boot of the guard holding her back. He grunted, then jabbed her in the ribs. Pain radiated up her torso, but she hardly cared. She could only feel Birdie's fear and hear her tiny sobs.

"Hold her steady." The captain jerked his head to his youngest daughter, who let out a startled scream as two guards swarmed her on either side.

He transferred the paper to the same hand as the Heart and reached for a gilded dagger. A blood-red ruby decorated the hilt.

Birdie cried into the night, her whimpers cleaving Margrete in two.

"It's all right, Birdie, it's going to be all right," Margrete whispered, her face a mess of tears and anguish.

But nothing was all right.

Margrete focused her gaze upon her father. He turned the knife over in the moonlight and lifted the parchment, beginning to read the guttural words that were meant for no mortal.

A tortured scream pierced the air before Margrete realized it belonged to her. "I'll kill you!" she repeated, shouting over the captain. Her blood boiled, and the guard who restrained her struggled to keep her still. Margrete was the embodiment of rage.

Ice snaked its way into her core, traveling up to encircle her pounding heart where it squeezed. Her body buzzed, and suddenly Margrete felt nothing but the chill, which stung her skin and awakened something deep within her soul.

She felt weightless. A wraith without a body.

And it felt good.

Margrete welcomed the foreign sensation, allowing it to blossom and ignite, to wash across her vision until all she saw was red. Just as she shuddered from the intensity of its grip, just as it was about to consume her whole, a wave crashed into the hull of the *Iron Mast*.

The arms around her loosened for only a second, but a second was all she needed.

Thanking Adrian for his lessons once more, she jabbed her elbow into the soldier's ribs and knocked the air from his lungs.

Another wave shattered against the ship as Margrete lunged toward her little sister and swaddled her in her arms.

"I've got you, I—"

The island trembled. A violent roar reached out into the waters, and the planks of the ship vibrated beneath her boots. Birdie gripped Margrete, her soft cries muffled as the winds picked up. Behind them was the shuffling of feet, and then her father roared above the chaos.

"The gates are opening! Ready the men!"

Margrete rocked Birdie gently back and forth, shushing softly into her ear. If the gates were opening, then death was coming for them all.

CHAPTER FORTY-FIVE

BASH

THE SPYGLASS TREMBLED IN BASH'S GRIP, HIS CLAMMY HANDS slicking his hold. "Tell me I'm not seeing this." Adrian's heavy breaths sounded in his ears, a wheezing rattle emanating from his chest.

That wasn't a good sign.

Knots formed in Bash's stomach as he lowered the spyglass from the Kardias Cave. From where the waves pushed out from the rocks.

Something was emerging. Something large.

"Shit." Bash tightened his grip on the scope, his breath stilling.

Silvered scales rose from the charcoal waters, the moonlight illuminating a single jagged fin. The swells parted as a beast thrust beyond the cave's opening, its massive body launching forward to freedom.

"The gates are open." Bash's heart crumbled as he spoke the words aloud.

"Look to the *Iron Mast*, my king," Adrian urged, trepidation heavy in his voice.

Slowly, Bash turned where his commander instructed.

"Fuck," Bash hissed, biting his lower lip hard enough to draw blood. "I'm going to kill him."

Just behind the obsidian figurehead of a soaring hawk was Margrete.

He could hardly keep the spyglass steady as he took her in, those wide eyes of hers glinting in the amber light. The captain stood at the railing, his back to his daughter, but she never once took her heated gaze from him.

Bash inhaled sharply through his nose, swallowing down the rage that had him clenching his fists in a promise of what was to come. The blood he would soon spill.

He was about to bark orders at Adrian, alert his men that Margrete was onboard the enemy's ship, when a head of blonde curls appeared at the end of the lens. The little girl peered up at Margrete, tears streaming down her ruddy cheeks.

That had to be her sister. Birdie.

Why would the captain bring his younger daughter here? Even if he didn't care for his daughters' lives, he wouldn't wish for a child to get in the way of his invasion. It didn't make sense.

Bash lowered the spyglass.

"He's got them both. Margrete and her sister," he told Adrian, who laid a comforting hand on his shoulder. Bash couldn't look at him, couldn't handle seeing the look of disappointment that would surely line his eyes.

"Stop," Adrian commanded. "This isn't your fault. It is *him* who is guilty. Not you." He gave Bash's shoulder a quick squeeze.

Bash took in a strained breath, but the steadiness of Adrian's hands wasn't enough to ease the grief that bled from a wound opened long ago.

"What do we do, sire?" Adrian rarely addressed him in such a way, but Bash wasn't his friend right now. He was his king.

There were the obvious answers: send his men barreling for the *Iron Mast*, wipe out all of the mercenaries, or employ the cannons and simply sink the vessel entirely.

But then Margrete and her sister would be caught in the crosshairs, and none of those plans stopped what had been done. The gates were open, and the monsters were slowly creeping their way out of their rocky prison.

Bash could almost feel the ocean shift as the beasts slithered below its surface, as bubbles rose to touch the crests surrounding the Kardias Cave. Only the fiercest of Malum's children, the lethal sea serpent, dared show itself above.

Without an answer to give his commander, Bash turned to his oldest friend, his hands curled into fists. "Ready the men and prepare the cannons."

Adrian's mouth fell open. His eyes darted to the ship Margrete stood aboard.

"*But*," Bash emphasized, his eyes hard, "do not fire without my command."

Adrian solemnly nodded and raced off to alert his men.

As Bash watched the murderous beast glide through the waves, as he considered the *Iron Mast* within reach, he knew what he had to do.

It likely wouldn't end well for him.

CHAPTER FORTY-SIX

MARGRETE

TIME WAS A FUNNY THING. ONE MOMENT MARGRETE WISHED FOR it to speed up and to never stop. The next, it moved at the pace of a sailless vessel on a windless day at sea.

Right now, it stood still.

Still enough for Margrete to make out every detail—each silver scale and jagged tooth—of the monster freed from its cage. It was horrendous to look at, its sheer size overwhelming, and its soulless eyes were cruel and calculating.

The infamous sea serpent—a creature rumored to have once taken out an entire fleet of ships in one attack. Margrete shivered, holding Birdie to her side. Her sister had ceased her gut-wrenching sobs, though her silence was somehow worse.

With wide eyes, Margrete watched helplessly as the serpent headed for the shores of the island. An island full of innocents. It would devastate a place of beauty for the pleasure of watching it fall.

Her father took in the scene before him with delight, and a rare, genuine smile curled his lips. He thought the serpent, as well as the other monsters hiding beneath the swells, would be his to command soon. Once the transfer of power occurred, once Margrete was drained of the divinity in her soul, he'd have the greatest arsenal known to man at his disposal.

Margrete would throw herself overboard before she ever let that happen.

In the distance, the serpent slowed, its elongated body stilling five hundred feet from shore. The fool she was, Margrete hoped, for but a second, that her prayers wouldn't be ignored. That it would turn and abandon Azantian and the promise of bloodshed.

That hope quickly dissipated.

With a guttural roar, one that shook Azantian and all of its people, the creature lurched high into the air. It plummeted back to the waters with a resounding splash that turned into a massive hundred-foot wave— one that barreled toward the southern side of the island. Even in the dark, Margrete saw its hasty rise, how the waves crested and glimmered with deadly passion.

In the span of a blink, the colossal wave fell, crashing past the golden beaches and colliding against the sea glass homes and colorful markets of Azantian. She could hear the screams from across the waters, though the sounds were distant and masked by the thick evening air. Nevertheless, Margrete made them out, and more and more cries pierced the night until the panicked noises became one eerie sound of all-encompassing fear.

Something about watching the wave strike Azantian roused her courage.

On those very shores, Margrete had shucked the mask of a lost girl who cowered before her father. It was on Azantian, that she rediscovered her will to fight, a will long since buried beneath years of trauma.

Twisting to the rail, she peered into the obscurity, to where the serpent headed for shore once again. This time, it swam faster and with a dogged purpose. She could hardly focus on anything other than the threat before her, the serpent's spiked tail whipping out from the waters as its body flew into the air.

Margrete felt the first rush of searing ire pulse into her being. It was lava and deadly crimson that heated her blood. When the serpent eventually fell—splashing into the waters and launching another wave at Azantian—something shifted within her.

The song of the sea mingled with the smoldering heat of pure rage. She prickled all over, the pins and needles of wrath as sharp as any blade.

She watched as mighty vessels splintered, as sea glass homes toppled and collapsed on the sands. The screams of women and children and soldiers made their way to her ears, and her heart dropped into her stomach as bile rose in her throat.

Margrete was gazing at her father—the man at whom all her rage was directed—when he raced over to the railing, his men following his lead. The sheer ruin entranced them, and their twisted shouts filled the air.

"Look!" someone called out. "There's a vessel out there!"

More boots pounded the decks until even Casbian leaned was leaning over the side and staring into the abyss. The creature didn't pause as it thrust forward, its long tail swaying back and forth, causing massive wakes to rise in its path of destruction.

Margrete cursed, sparing a glance behind her. The crew left onboard the *Iron Mast* was bewitched. They ignored the prisoners they'd been instructed to guard, too taken by the living myth before their eyes.

This moment was her only chance.

Margrete held her breath as she inched back, away from her father and his gaping men, away from the governess. With their attention secured ahead, Margrete turned to where Birdie sat huddled beside a barrel, her knees pulled up to her chest. Now was the time to get her out, to save her before her father's focus returned to his daughters.

Before he spilled blood.

"Birdie," she whispered, crouching. "You need to follow me. Now." Margrete held out her hand, which remained surprisingly steady. She couldn't afford to be frightened, not when Birdie was near tears.

Birdie lifted her grimy, tear-stained face. Without a word, she placed her tiny hand in Margrete's, trusting her to deliver her from danger. As she always had before, Margrete would make sure she didn't betray that trust.

Margrete pulled on Birdie's hand and led her to the ladder. A long-boat was already rocking against the ship below.

Margrete went down the ladder first, ready to catch her sister should she stumble. She was proud when Birdie's grip held fast, her small shoulders squared with determination.

When they reached the bottom, Margrete helped her settle. She untied the ropes and grabbed the oars.

As they pushed off, a shriek rang through the air, a tormented sound of anguish.

Her arms shook violently, but she rowed the longboat around the side of the *Iron Mast*, bringing them closer to the outer bands.

Margrete didn't have much of a plan other than to get to the docks, where several small longboats were secured beside the larger ships. Being in the water with the sea's children wasn't an option, especially with her sister in tow, but neither was staying on her father's ship.

So far, the serpent was the only beast to show itself, but Margrete surmised that might soon change. If they fled their prison and headed to the mortal realm, then she knew Bash wouldn't stop until he had hunted them all down.

And she'd be right there beside him.

Margrete's every muscle strained as she pushed them closer to the ring, to the southern docks, but even just a few grueling training sessions with Adrian had helped prepare her for such a moment.

"Margrete," Birdie hissed, speaking for the first time. She pointed out to the expanse of black, to where the serpent slithered, readying itself for another assault.

"What? What do you see?" Margrete gasped, out of breath from the exertion.

"A boat," her sister replied. "Someone is out there on a boat."

All the air rushed from her lungs as her gaze followed the path of Birdie's finger.

There. A flash of silver. The glint of metal bobbing on the waves. The blaze of a white sail whipping against the wind.

A part of her already suspected who manned the vessel. It was the only person who was brave—and stupid—enough to face one of the sea's children head-on.

Gods, she wanted to throttle him.

Bash. She murmured his name under her breath as her heart raced savagely in her chest. It pounded and thrummed against her skin, begging to be released, to somehow find its way to where the King of Azantian decided to challenge an undefeatable opponent.

"W-who is that?" came Birdie's muffled voice.

Margrete didn't answer. The serpent rushed past Bash's vessel, its wake nearly turning it on its side. The figure, cloaked in shadows, moved, adjusted the sail, and maneuvered the ship to turn back to the creature.

"You need to listen to me again, little bird," Margrete murmured, her eyes never once leaving Bash. The outer band was nearing. "You're going to stay here, on those docks"—she tilted her head back—"unless Father or his men come for you. Then use one of the longboats and get to shore."

"What do you mean?" Birdie protested, scrambling from her position and into Margrete's lap. "You can't leave me!"

"Shhh," she soothed, gently lifting her sister in her arms and turning to where the polished metal met the water. Leaning over, she grabbed a rope and tugged their longboat against its side.

"I need to make sure he's safe. He's the king, Birdie, and if I don't save him, if the serpent kills him—" She swallowed back tears. "If I can't help him, and he fails, then more of those monsters will come, and the seas will no longer be safe."

Of course, it was more than that. If she didn't get to him—get him away from the beast and back to land—she'd lose a part of herself that she had only just begun to explore. The part that loved and was loved so fiercely in return.

The part made only for him.

Margrete lifted her sister onto the dock. The *Iron Mast* was still far enough away that Birdie could run should they venture near. "Now, please, stay here. I promise you, I will return." She held Birdie's blue eyes, which brimmed with tears. "I'll never leave you. Ever."

Not even death could sever their bond.

With a weak nod, Birdie backed away, and Margrete gave her a final look before she pushed back into the thrashing waters.

Waters that now belonged to the god's children.

With the *Iron Mast* to her left, Azantian straight ahead, and Bash and the serpent nearing on her right, Margrete steeled her spine and rowed as fast and as hard as her body would allow.

Another screech rang out, followed by the roar of a man. Bash leaped off the side of his vessel—

Directly onto the serpent's back.

He paused, gathering his footing, and then ambled closer to the serpent's head. Bash planned on attacking where it would hurt, where he would have the greatest chance of killing the beast.

He was nearly there when a wave crashed against the side of the serpent, sending Bash careening forward. Time slowed as he raised his dagger, the metal flashing in the moonlight. He let out a cry of war as he thrust the metal into the creature's back, near its neck.

The serpent released an ear-piercing squeal, its mighty tail beating the waters as it screeched in outrage. Bash hugged its back, somehow able to lift his weapon again and bring it back down, slicing between the serrated scales.

While the serpent thrashed, bucking in an attempt to throw Bash off, a rumble of thunder shook both land and sea. As if in response, the animal stilled its jerky movements, its giant maw rising out of the waves and into the night, searching.

Bash held on, gripping the pommel of the knife still embedded in the animal's back, but he, too, followed the direction the serpent looked.

The island gave an enraged shudder, and jagged streaks of lightning traversed across the clouded sky. Thick raindrops pelted Margrete's skin and sliced at her cheeks, but each swell brought her closer to Bash, and she refused to stop.

The serpent slowed, allowing her the chance to catch up to its lithe body, though she remained wary of its deadly tail. This close, Margrete could make out its spikes, which glinted in the moonlight.

Only thirty feet now separated her from the man she cared for. The man she was going to rescue. Bash had saved her more times than he realized—and not just from death.

Before the sky erupted, the waters surrounding the serpent rippled. Margrete clutched her ears as a deafening boom pierced the air. In the center of the foaming waves, water began to rise, and a silhouette of a man climbed from a whirlpool of foam and charcoal. Margrete's eyes widened as the brutal winds whipped painfully at her face.

She had to get to Bash. *Now.* Before whatever that was came for them both.

"Bash!" she screamed into the chaos and wind. The king, barely holding on to the serpent, turned at the sound of her voice. His emerald eyes were a spark of color amongst the darkness.

"Margrete!" he called back, voice pained. "Get away! Don't come any closer."

Her hands tightened on the oars. She kept rowing against the roiling waters, ignoring his pleas and desperate shouts for her to turn away. Bash should know her better by now.

Only when the figure's image sharpened did her resolve waver. From the sea spray, he ascended. His bare body was slick and covered in kelp, and a mass of tangled black strands crowned his head. He had a straight, thin nose, hair the darkest shade of midnight, and a square jaw. Margrete stared on in shock as she took in his eyes, which were the color of the clearest sapphires. Chains hung from around his throat, thick iron that wrapped around him and rattled when his ethereal form advanced toward the serpent. Toward Bash.

The man didn't walk across the waters he commanded, he *glided*, the current driving him forward.

Margrete had never seen a god before, but she knew, without a doubt, one stood before them now. The power within her sung as though recognizing its true owner.

Malum.

The sky erupted, silvery streaks of fire spiderwebbing across the black storm clouds. As the world ignited, Margrete caught sight of Bash struggling to stay on top of the serpent. He'd never stood a chance against the beast, and his dagger had done nothing but irritate the creature. He wasn't one to stand by and watch his home be destroyed, even if he all but ensured his own death.

When the serpent slowed, almost as though it sensed its creator, Margrete shouted Bash's name, a frenzied screech that matched the roar of the ensuing thunder. The king lifted his head in her direction, and the whites of his eyes flashed in the dark.

"Margrete!" Bash screamed, his voice cracking. Their eyes locked, even from a distance, even as she sensed Malum nearing. Power rippled off his immortal body, the air ripe with tension.

The swells surrounding the serpent began to rise, but Bash wasn't paying attention. His focus remained solely on Margrete, and he didn't even flinch when the God of the Sea roared, the noise shaking the very waves they rocked upon.

One moment, Bash was in her sights, alive and fighting to survive, and the next, the sea he loved crashed down upon him and stole his body below.

He didn't rise.

CHAPTER FORTY-SEVEN

MARGRETE

Margrete screamed into the night, the sound coarse and broken and full of rage.

Rage at Malum.

A boiling anger that simmered in her blood and set her vision red.

The serpent had been pummeled below the waters, Bash along with it. Neither had resurfaced.

She lifted her gaze to Malum's.

His eyes were blue, clearer than any precious gem. Otherworldly.

"Save him!" she roared, teeth bared and hands clenched. She dropped the oars, and the wood thudded to the bottom of the boat. Her arms were sore from her strenuous rowing, and blisters opened her palms. Rain drenched her from head to toe, her long hair a tangled crown around her head. She'd pushed her body to the brink, both mentally and physically, and now she was teetering on the edge, one foot hanging over the side of the cliff.

She dared call his name. "Malum!"

The winds devoured the sound of her voice, but she knew he heard her, knew he could taste her bitter anguish.

The God of the Sea towered over her—well over ten feet tall—and water danced along his massive calves. He glanced down to where Bash had been hauled under, and a thoughtful look washed across his slick face. Then he lifted his head.

Their eyes locked, the world around them forgotten.

She whispered now. "Please." A single tear glided down her cheek, mingling with the rain.

A heart for a heart, was all he said, his voice soft against the edges of her mind.

Margrete nodded, choking on a sob.

He was going to save him. He would rescue Bash, and all it would require was something she didn't even want—the heart of a god.

Malum cupped his palms and lifted them to his chest. His full lips moved soundlessly as he spoke, uttering words she knew didn't belong to mortals.

Margrete gripped the longboat. The waters were parting, moving, whirling. They spun and roiled and swayed...

After what seemed like an eternity, a head of auburn emerged from the depths, and the king of Azantian's body was lifted above the sea, his legs dangling.

His eyes were wide.

Margrete released the air in her lungs in a painful rush as more tears fell, though these were borne of joy. He hadn't drowned. Malum saved him before he'd been taken from her.

He lives, little one, Malum said. *Now I need what I am owed. I will destroy—*

Bash was knocked from the air, tossed back into the waves like a rag doll. Margrete cried out, flinging herself precariously close to the waters that splashed over the sides of her vessel. She searched for the top of his head, for the deep russet of his hair, not even sparing the God of the Sea a glance.

"Margrete!"

She turned, chasing the voice that would forever find her. *There.* Bash was floating, rocking on the waters to her left, treading water.

Margrete turned back to Malum.

The god was no longer there.

She skimmed the surface of the waves for any sign of him, but only the rippling blue and black stared back. She settled into position and swiftly picked up the oars, dipping the paddles and rowing toward Bash.

She couldn't think of where Malum had gone. It was taking everything she had to get to Bash.

Margrete was nearly upon her king when a great wave pummeled her boat. It came out of nowhere, so fierce, so impossibly strong, that it shattered the wood and broke the vessel in half with a sickening crack.

She was flying...and then, just as suddenly, she was falling, plummeting. Margrete struck the water with enough force to steal her breath, and her arms flailed as she clawed at the water. Panic robbed all else, and there was only the need to stay above, to not succumb to the depths that would end her life.

Margrete's hand landed on one half of the broken boat, her chest heaving as she pulled herself over the side. The wood dug into her stomach, and she gasped, sucking in air, cursing herself for never learning how to swim. It would be her ruin.

Wiping hair from her eyes, she turned her attention ahead, to where two immortal bodies collided like thunder.

A mass of black and gray crashed into the figure she knew to be Malum.

The clouds of gray morphed, turning into arms and legs. Margrete watched as the other entity, Darius, made himself whole. Golden hair, a compliment to his tanned body, crowned his head, the strands appearing to be spun of pure sunlight and silk. She could feel him, *hear* his velvety voice even now, as he turned her way. A silver mask embedded with crushed opals covered the upper half of his face, though she glimpsed a pair of eyes that were the color of the clearest seas.

Darius broke contact and twisted back to face his foe. He wound his arms around Malum's neck, his brother's movements sluggish as he struggled.

Margrete imagined that the centuries trapped in the ravine had weakened him and that the chains around his neck weighed him down. She understood what he'd given away when he gifted Azantian with his heart.

His recklessness would be the reason for his death.

Darius grasped the ends of a thick chain, and a bolt of lightning struck as he released a growl. His hold tightened, and the metal dug viciously into Malum's throat.

Thunder shook the world hard enough for Margrete's bones to rattle, and the skies opened to allow violent rain to fall, the drops forceful enough to bruise.

This was no ordinary storm.

"Give in!" Darius bellowed, forcing the chains deeper into his brother's throat. They were both suspended in the air, the rushing waters reaching up to graze their divine forms.

Malum shook his head, and his hands went to his neck to tug on his shackles. He hissed just before Darius drove them under the water, moving as swiftly as the lightning that broke the night.

"Margrete!"

She turned at the sound of her name to find Bash swimming over to her, his arms threading through the water with power and ease. "Stay where you are!"

As if she could move if she wanted to.

Bash closed the distance between them, panting as he struggled to stay afloat. He was alive, but staying underwater for so long had clearly cost him.

"Are you all right?" he asked, his voice a thing of misery. "Why did you come here?"

Margrete would have laughed at the anger in his tone if they weren't on the precipice of death.

He grabbed for her hand, steadying her trembling fingers. The air was unusually cold, and she realized then that she was shaking.

"I-I had to get y-you," she stuttered, her lips quivering. "So that I could k-kill you myself, you fool." She let out a choking laugh, and her insides warmed when a smile graced his face.

The hand around hers tightened. "I couldn't let you stay on that ship, and I had to slay the serpent before it devoured everything in its path. I couldn't watch...I couldn't watch you die."

Margrete swallowed hard, ready to berate him for risking his life, when a resounding boom drowned out all sound.

The brothers shot through the air, straight up from the waves, their muscled arms and legs a blur as they fought. Darius still maintained the upper hand, but Malum wasn't giving up.

When Malum delivered a punch that sent his brother flying, Margrete's lips twitched into a hopeful smile.

But Darius was already back on his feet, floating across the waves toward his brother.

He paused halfway to peer over his shoulder, and those piercing blue eyes caught hers even as she bobbed up and down on the ocean. Margrete gasped as he smiled, his lips curling into something wicked. The mask shielded the rest of his face, but she could see his sinful delight well enough.

I'm coming for you next, darling.

The words whispered across her thoughts, phantom hands seeming to reach out and graze her mind. She could sense him everywhere—Darius breaking through her mortal barriers with ease. That smile of his flourished, and then he was turning back to his brother.

"This is madness," Malum roared. "Haven't you had enough after a thousand years? Isn't it time we end this?"

Darius laughed, the sound like a purr. "Oh, yes. I do believe it is time we end this once and for all, dear brother."

One moment Darius was fifty feet away from Malum, and in the next, his muscled frame was colliding against his twin's. The two immortals crashed together and erupted in an explosion of devastating light.

Margrete gripped Bash's hand as the gods drew closer. Darius held Malum's chains, though this time, he twisted his brother to face Margrete and Bash. A devilish gleam sparked in his inhuman eyes as he pulled the shackles taut. Malum's face contorted as his skin turned a sickly shade of blue, and then Darius let go—

His twin's body plummeted to the water, shattering into wisps of light and sea foam.

Darius turned once more to where Margrete clutched Bash. His sights were now set on the king, and his eyes glowed silver, fizzling with sparks of electricity. He smiled.

And then Darius released the remainder of his power.

Directly onto Bash.

CHAPTER FORTY-EIGHT

MARGRETE

Bash's hand slipped from hers before Margrete could react, and his body was dragged beneath the churning waters. The only god here was the one who would do nothing to save him.

Margrete's heart stopped.

Broke.

Shattered.

She couldn't even scream, couldn't beg Darius to spare him, for she knew he had no intention of heeding her request. With his brother's effervescent remains at his feet and nothing but foam rising and falling on the crests of blue, Darius trained his gaze onto her.

Now, everything is as it should be.

Margrete took him in, stared down the vengeful god who seemed determined that she suffer, and then she released a deafening shriek of rage.

Her body burned, and the essence within seared, coiling like a snake preparing to strike. When Margrete lifted her hand from the broken boat, a flare of blue kindled in her palm like a wrathful fire.

Darius's eyes narrowed, frowning at the sight.

I'm coming for you next, she thought, sending her lethal vow out into the world. She shot him one final look of blistering hot rage before she let go of the wood completely and dove into the waters that once would have drowned her.

Her body was alight with a foreign energy, a buzzing that propelled her legs to move and her lungs to swell with water. She inhaled the water and released it as though it were air. The sight of Bash, driven into the sea, had killed the girl she'd once been. Destroyed her.

In her place was a woman who would tear apart the seas to find him.

Margrete thrust forward, kicking her legs, deeper into the eternal black as the water aided her plight. She called out to the sea itself, the many parts that made it whole. She spoke to it. *Commanded* it.

The sea listened.

It grew dark, darker than even the blackest of nights, but Margrete willed herself to see, to adopt the vision of a deep-sea creature. Little by little, the dim became a hazy, cloudy blue, well-lit enough to make out the drowning figure not more than ten feet away.

With only Bash occupying the space of her mind, Margrete swam with ferocious speed to him. Wisps of his auburn hair floated about his lifeless face.

A battle cry escaped into the bubbling depths, one of promised vengeance and desperate love. It wasn't muffled like most sounds this deep, but instead was as crystal clear as the northern star on a cloudless night. She reached out, her hand seeking to grasp the tips of his fingers.

He was sinking. Fast.

While adrenaline flamed within her, Margrete knew that she was losing energy, even with the ancient magic of a god coursing in her veins.

A power she had no idea how to use.

His emerald eyes were closed, skin pallid, but she was resolved to see those green eyes again. That taunting smirk, and the rare, genuine smile that stopped her heart when it appeared. Bash would open his eyes and kiss her lips, and she would scold him for being foolish enough to attack the serpent on his own.

Bash wasn't about to die. Not when she had just only experienced him.

With a crushing rush of purpose, Margrete kicked her searing limbs, and her fingers finally grazed the linen of his shirt. She yanked him upward, wrapping her hand tightly around his arm, and hauled his weightless body to her own.

Margrete held her pirate to her chest, panic surging as she set her sights on the surface. She ground her teeth as she pushed herself to keep swimming. Even though her limbs trembled and her vision flickered with black pinpricks, she kicked and thrashed as an unnatural current lifted them higher. The fight had not left her yet. Bash had saved her once when the very waters wished to claim her life, and she meant to return the favor.

She wouldn't let go.

Ever.

CHAPTER FORTY-NINE

MARGRETE

THE NEXT TIME LIGHT STRUCK THE TUMULTUOUS WAVES, IT WASN'T borne of electricity. It was a cataclysmic collision of transcendent rebirth and the commanding force of pulsating love.

Margrete choked as she breached the surface. Unused to lungs that could breathe water, she coughed out the salty liquid and greedily gasped for air.

In her trembling arms was a body belonging to a king. His muscled form weighed her down, but Margrete fought against the current. She screamed his name, over and over again, as one might say a prayer.

Or a curse.

The smoldering heat within her swelled with each passing moment that Bash didn't gasp for air. With every second he didn't open those eyes and smile.

Her arms tightened around him protectively, and that mystical fire within her blossomed. It erupted and shattered. Broke her and put her back together again. Margrete felt like she was being remade from the inside out.

The waters, as if sensing the divinity flowing through her blood, responded, lifting her and Bash above the crests. They were pushed to the western shores. To land. To safety.

The sound of the sea was all she could hear—the melody comprised of both tender and vicious notes. Margrete cradled Bash as the celestial aria lulled to a soft whisper, and the tide delivered them at last to the sands.

Without the aid of the waters at her back, Margrete struggled to lift the king, to haul his limp frame farther up the beach. But something just as potent as the Heart's power gave her the strength to carry him, to gently lower him to the fine golden grains.

"Bash!" she screamed. There was no response other than the crashing waves.

Placing her head to his chest, she listened for a heartbeat, a sign of life.

She heard nothing but the empty silence of death.

Margrete cursed and took him by the shoulders, shaking him. When he didn't rouse, she pounded her fists against his chest.

Nothing—his chest remained unmoving.

The war raged all around her, but she paid no mind to the distant cries of battle. She couldn't breathe, not when Bash couldn't.

In a fit of panic, she pummeled his chest with her hands, struggling to restart the heart she knew had ceased to beat. Time passed in a blur, but still she worked, her voice hoarse from shrieking into the night. It might have been his name she called, but it was guttural and raw and altogether animalistic.

It was the sound of anguished defeat.

"No." She sniffled, her hand quivering as it reached to cup his cheek. He looked so pale, so frozen. "Wake up!"

Her tiny fists banged against him once more, bruising and violent in their descent. She cared for nothing but the rise and fall of life—of air filling his lungs.

He remained so very still.

"You can't die," she whispered under her breath. "Your people need you."

She needed him.

"Don't you dare," she threatened, swallowing painfully. Every inhale was excruciating. Every minute he didn't stir roused a new wave of agony inside of her. "You—"

Margrete stopped.

She lifted her hands from his unmoving chest. The moon shone on his handsome face, and he appeared to be sleeping. Peaceful. This sickened her all the more.

He was but another soul that the sea—no, *Darius*—had taken, and for reasons she didn't yet understand.

It was then that the most astonishing thought occurred to Margrete.

The sea was where he lost his life.

The sea had nearly taken *her* life.

Margrete held some of the sea's powers. Malum's powers.

With renewed purpose, Margrete inhaled sharply and placed one hand on either side of his face. She gripped him tightly enough to bruise, but her mind had already begun to drift into a realm beyond the physical: into the place where the sea and her own life mingled.

Where Malum's sacred essence dwelled.

"Bash, come back to me," she ordered, her heated breath tickling his pallid flesh. The wind picked up in response, and a ghostly breeze stroked her cheeks and tousled her curls. "I demand it."

As the words fell from her tear-stained lips, her body shook, and the sacred warmth of a god's stolen heart seared her insides.

Margrete screamed as a thousand images flashed through her mind.

Cruel gales and beautiful sunrises. Gulls with spread wings gliding across the vast sky. The full moon grazing the top of seafoam waves, its light filtering to paint the depths with magic.

Margrete sensed a pack of wild dolphins beyond the breaks. Great whites hunting for their meal. She glimpsed the vibrant coral reefs and spotted an orange starfish on the sandy floor. Freshly hatched sea turtles swam for the first time in the blue deep, and rosy jellyfish whirled above their green shells. There was an entire world beyond the shores, full of striking beasts and achingly beautiful creatures of color.

She sang to them all, called to them as she pleaded for a single soul to be returned to her. The dolphins gave a high-pitched whistle, and the sharks slowed their pace and ignored their bloodlust to listen. The jellyfish glowed with foreign light, and the sea turtles flapped their flippers. Farther away, a pod of blue whales emitted a reverberating reply of their own.

Stingrays, seahorses, octopi, squids, crabs, clams, eels—

The entire ocean answered in a jumbled chorus of abundant life.

"Come back to me, Bash."

A sharp pang struck her chest, lasting but a heartbeat. It pierced her heart, and an exquisite light blinded her vision.

And then she heard it—

His inhale.

"Bash!" she shrieked. She helped him turn onto his side as he retched saltwater and the remnants of death.

Minutes passed before he turned to face her, and the sight of him, alive and breathing, was the most beautiful thing she'd ever witnessed. But the handsome face she'd grown to love had changed.

His eyes...They were no longer the shade of emeralds, and no golden flecks dotted his irises. The sea had taken his life and returned his soul after death. Because of this, he would be forever changed.

Bash met her gaze with adoration and tender affection—with irises of silky midnight and ashen smoke.

"P-princess," he sputtered, coughing.

Through her own altered blue eyes, Margrete drank in the darkness of his murky pools and glimpsed the beauty of their eternal night.

"Y-you were n-nearly lost to me," she stammered, disbelieving that he was here in her arms, color slowly returning to his cheeks. "Darius. H-he used his power on you, looked right at you as he slayed his brother. As he killed Malum. He wanted to kill you, too, and I think he...I think he succeeded."

And with Malum's powers, she had brought him back.

"Malum is dead?" Bash fought to raise himself onto his elbows, alarm twisting his features. Margrete snaked her arms around his torso and held him upright.

"He turned to sea foam before my eyes," she said, her chest tight. She didn't know Malum, but a piece of him had resided inside of her all her life, and in that way, she felt the loss of him.

"What happened to Darius?" Bash asked, his eyes growing sharper, his body tensed as if preparing for the fight to come. And there would be a fight. Darius had all but promised he'd come back for her.

That she was next.

"I'm not sure what happened to him," she admitted. "I dove in after you."

Bash shook his head. "You can't swim. I don't understand."

"I don't either, Bash, but when Darius sent you below the waves, I experienced this...*heat*. This strength. I can't explain it, but I feel *him*. Malum."

Bash placed a gentle hand on her shoulder, his fingers shaking. "Whatever it is, we will find out together. Remember, you're no longer alone."

She smiled. "And neither are you."

Bash squeezed his eyes shut before opening them to gaze upon her, his stare brimming with a thousand unspoken words.

Words he would never need to speak for her to understand.

So instead of answering him with her voice, she lowered her lips to his, tasting the sweetness of rebirth.

The kiss was a gentle caress. A reminder that life flowed through their veins, air filled their lungs, and, for the moment, they were not defeated. They were whole.

Bash pulled away first, just enough to peer into her eyes, which were full of unshed tears. He looked at her as if she were the most beautiful and enchanting being he'd ever glimpsed.

But it was time for her to release him—

Time to face Darius and her father.

Margrete knew what she had to do, and she implored Bash to trust her.

"I have to do this." She cupped his stubbled cheeks before helping him stand. "*Alone*," she added when he raised a brow. "This isn't only between my father and me, but between me and Darius. That strength I told you about? I feel it now. And I know I can face whatever is out there."

"I don't like this." Bash sighed, his Adam's apple bobbing with emotion. He placed both hands on either side of her face, his touch freezing against her heated skin. "I can't lose you, Margrete. I *won't*."

Fear rang clearly in his voice, and Margrete gave him a grim smile. "Bash, this *thing* inside of me...I *have* to do this." She tilted her head to the south side of the island, to where the *Iron Mast* was moored. To where two gods had battled. "You have to trust me, as I've trusted you. What I need is for you to make sure Birdie is safe. *Please*."

A war raged in his eyes, but Bash nodded, his jaw clenching. "I'll find her," he vowed. "And I do trust you, but if something happens to you—"

"It won't," she promised, but they both knew she couldn't promise such a thing.

"Then go," he said, reaching for her hands. "But come back to me, princess."

"Always, Bash." Margrete dropped his hands and stepped back to the waves. She held his eyes until the waters grazed her calves, and then, with one final look, she turned and faced the sea that called to her.

She closed her eyes and listened to the ethereal whispers that danced across her mind, her lips moving, echoing the voices of the ancients.

And then Margrete Wood was rising, the waters at her feet lifting her above the swells.

She took her first step forward.

The waves followed.

CHAPTER FIFTY

MARGRETE

THE WINDS WHIPPED MERCILESSLY AT MARGRETE'S FACE AS THE mighty wave she commanded brought her closer to where the battle endured.

Now, she tethered her thoughts to a single word—

Rise.

The magic within her soul flared to life as her skin caught fire. The sting of it centered her, and an eerie peace encircled her form.

She was always meant to be here, always meant to endure the captain and his heartlessness, because she was destined to destroy the darkness within him.

It didn't matter if gods had guided her to this very spot. Margrete would take back control, and she certainly wouldn't be a pawn.

Not even one belonging to a god.

On instinct, her arms shot out to the brightening skies, dawn but hours away.

"*Arias moriad!*" The command tumbled from her lips without thought. The words were as ancient and as magical as the blood flowing through her own veins. A great surge of energy shook her bones as the furious waters mounted, ready to do her bidding.

Nestled deep within her core rested a well of iris blue light. Tendrils of it tickled the inside of her mortal form, reaching out to cloak every inch of vulnerable flesh. Stardust yellow bloomed from the center of her smoky soul, a force of ancient enchantment that slowly took shape. Margrete delved deeper, whispering to the sheer force she contained, demanding the strength of a foreign magic.

Margrete's shut lids trembled, and her body swayed. Back and forth, the waves rocked, until a violent wind guided the waters and shaped them into the wall of liquid stone before her—one that promised devastation. This colossal wave rushed past the southern side of the island, Margrete floating like a wrathful god at its back.

There. Just a blemish on the waves was the *Iron Mast.*

Margrete glimpsed its red and black sails. She recalled her youth, a time when the ship seemed to be the mightiest and most formidable vessel known to man. Now, it looked no more than a toy.

Easily breakable.

Margrete flew behind her wall of water, the ruthless winds propelling her closer. There was only forward. Only her target.

Margrete's rage swelled as she scanned the waves for Darius, for his ethereal form of smoke and silver, but there was nothing but the *Iron Mast* and the mercenaries battling on shore.

She turned her full attention to the captain's vessel. She'd worry about the God of the Sea later. Now, she demanded the blood of the man who had tried to ruin her. The man who'd been adamant about extinguishing her fight. He had failed, and she was going to make sure his darkness never tainted another living soul again.

Taking in the black sails that inspired fear in the hearts of so many, Margrete made out a small figure on the deck, his graying blonde hair flying in the breeze. Beside him stood the count, his face turned toward her, mouth agape with panic.

As Casbian screamed and pleaded, her father remained still, the gray-blue stone that once belonged to a god clutched in his hand. Somehow, even in such a powerful state, Margrete felt the captain stir her fears, rouse her unrest. This time, Margrete *used* that terror to aim the wall of water at his vessel of sin.

As the wave approached—Margrete floating like a vengeful angel behind the colossal swell—the captain smiled up at her. His grin seemed to glow with a cruel pride.

Margrete didn't smile back. Not as the barricade she'd crafted slammed mercilessly into his ship, devouring all of the men onboard. The wooden planks shattered and split, and the deafening screeches of the crew filled the air.

She took no pleasure in destruction. Not even his.

The last thing Margrete saw of her father—of the man who had failed to break her—was the gleam of steel in his eyes. It remained, even as the leaden waters swept him from the deck and hauled him down into the chaos of the waves, devouring him in one crushing blow.

He would perish...and so would the Heart. It would be dragged beneath the swells and carried away by the current.

What little power remained in the gem would be lost—

For now.

Margrete raised her arms, and the waters she commanded spun into a frenzied whirlpool. Escape from a watery death would be beyond possible.

The roiling waves eased their furious dance and soothed themselves into a calming sway. Only when the captain was no more, once his wicked ship had been destroyed, did Margrete rest. The weight of her years beneath his watchful eyes of stone lifted. The air was sweeter, and honeysuckle mingled with the natural saltiness of the ocean breeze.

When she turned her eyes away from the ruin of her past life, Margrete Wood aimed her sights on the island of Azantian. A place of magic and myth.

A place she would now call home.

A destiny she had chosen.

CHAPTER FIFTY-ONE

MARGRETE

Margrete's lids fluttered open to a room full of shadows. Her head was a pounding mess and every muscle ached and throbbed. She cursed, blinking until her vision cleared, though pinpricks of black continued to dance across her sight.

She scanned her surroundings.

Heavy black covers were draped across her body, and she was carefully positioned in the middle of the softest bed she could imagine. Close by, a weak fire blossomed in a hearth before two high-backed velvet chairs. Smoke and wood and another familiar scent filled her senses.

Bash's chambers.

With a groan, Margrete propped herself onto her elbows and squinted in the dim light for a sign of the king. The last time she'd seen him was just before she destroyed her father's ship. After that...

Margrete had no idea how she wound up here.

She was about to open her mouth and call his name when a broad figure emerged from the shadows of the room. Instinctively, she jolted at the sight. Her mind went to Darius, to the god who vowed he'd come for her next, but then the man stepped closer to the fire, revealing the concerned face of her king.

"Bash," she said, her voice hoarse. "What the hell happened?" She squeezed her eyes shut, her fingers going to her temple.

"Hey, it's all right, princess. You're all right." She opened her eyes to find him already at her side.

She realized then that, even with the covers, she was shivering. Her entire body felt like it had been dipped in icy water.

Bash perched beside her and grasped both her hands. The meager flames from the hearth highlighted every twist of emotion he couldn't mask.

"Everything is fine," he said, before she could ask. "The captain is gone, and Adrian and Bay took out his mercenaries."

She relaxed, if only slightly. Adrian and Bay were alive.

"And Birdie? Where's my sister?" Fear laced her words. She'd left her on the docks, where the serpent—

"She's safe, I promise," Bash rushed on to say. "Shade found her hiding beneath a longboat after...after Wood's ship went down."

He meant after Margrete *killed* him.

Her chest squeezed painfully.

A memory of Shade at the feast came back to her, of the jagged burn mark concealed by her hair. Margrete shook off the unease the image conjured. She was being paranoid, but after everything she'd experienced, there was every reason to be.

"Where is Birdie now?"

"Sleeping safely down the hall," Bash said, cupping her cheek tenderly. "I'm sure she'll want to see you when she wakes."

"Darius?" His name was a curse on her lips.

The bastard had vanished before she could face him again.

Bash sighed, moving his hand to the nape of her neck. The solidness of him soothed her frayed nerves. "No one knows. We searched the island for signs of him, but we found nothing..." His brows pinched, and he glanced away, jaw tense.

"What is it?" Sitting upright, she took his chin between her fingers and turned his head to face her. "What else aren't you saying?"

His throat bobbed. "We found Ortum's body. He was discovered right before Wood deployed his men."

"Ortum's...dead?"

Bash nodded, the movement stiff. "That's not all that was found."

Margrete wound her arms around his torso, sensing his pain, even if he tried to temper it. She would be there for him, as he'd been there for her when she needed him.

"There was a brand on his body. Two interwoven circles." Bash glanced up at that, finally meeting her eye.

The same symbol that haunted her. The one she couldn't help but believe belonged to a certain vengeful god.

"We're not sure what to make of it, but his body...Well, it appears as if he's been dead for weeks."

She swallowed hard. That was impossible.

If Ortum had been dead for weeks, then who the hell was the man she'd met? Someone pretending to be the advisor as they wore his every feature?

No one had that kind of power, only gods—

Gods.

Only a god could possess such potent magic.

The kind of god cursed to live as a mortal, to hide behind human faces.

Margrete ignored her racing pulse. Until she knew for certain, she wouldn't voice her thoughts. Bash was already suffering enough.

"We'll figure out what happened," she said, though it was a weak comfort. She was drained, both mentally and physically, her body still buzzing with that overwhelming energy she couldn't name.

Bash drew back the blankets and slipped into the bed beside her. Gently, he eased her head onto his chest and wrapped his thick arms around her. She could hear his heartbeat pounding in her ear.

She held onto that sound, the sound of life, holding its melody close to her own heart.

"You saved us all, princess," Bash said after many long moments passed. "You...you were magnificent."

"I didn't do it. Malum's heart did."

It wasn't her power. Not *really*.

She shifted to her side, and Bash mirrored her movements. They were nose to nose, his breath fanning across her lips.

Bash took her chin between his fingers. "*You* saved us. Not a god. Not the Heart. You were brave and daring and raced out to protect this island. That was all *you*."

She didn't *feel* like it was her, and she certainly didn't feel brave.

"Bash, I—"

"No doubting yourself. Not anymore," Bash said, his tone hard. "You were magnificent, princess. A goddess."

Margrete shivered beneath his piercing gaze. His eyes were full of shadows and the deepest shades of night, but within his irises, stars sparkled. Margrete could get lost in them.

She already was.

She snaked her hand out from below the covers and trailed her finger along the underside of his strong jaw. She'd almost lost him today, and she needed to *feel* him. To remind herself he was still beside her.

Alive.

"I thought I'd lost you," she choked out, biting the inside of her cheek to keep the impending tears at bay.

Bash's face softened, his dark eyes creasing at the corners. He grasped her hips and pulled her impossibly close, her breasts pressed against his muscled chest.

She shuddered at the contact.

"I told you. Not even the gods could stand in my way." Bash's hold on her waist tightened. "Not when it comes to you."

Her heart fluttered, and a single tear escaped.

"You kept your vow," she said. The one he made to her on the *Phaedra*. But now, it was so much more than a vow. So much more than a promise.

Bash's lips grazed hers in a tender caress. "And I intend to keep it." He kissed the corner of her mouth. "And I will strike down any god"—his lips moved along the curve of her jaw—"who tries to take you from me."

Margrete wanted to believe that, she did, but that maniacal look in Darius's eyes when he promised he'd come for her had been seared into her mind.

"Bash," she murmured. His mouth drifted to her throat, gently worshipping her skin. His every movement was languid, unhurried, as if they had all the time in the world to be here. Together.

"Kiss me already," she demanded, grasping his chin and bringing his face to hers. "I need to feel you."

Right here, with him, Darius wasn't out there waiting, and the heart of a god didn't rest within her soul.

It was only them.

"So demanding," he whispered, just before pressing his lips against hers. The kiss was long and deep and full of fizzling sparks that tickled the inside of her chest. Bash groaned into her mouth, the sound brimming with unspoken need.

He wasn't holding back anymore, and Margrete refused to either.

They would never pretend with one another again.

She smiled against his mouth.

"What is it?" he asked, drawing back to look at her. He didn't ease his fierce grip on her waist, though she couldn't imagine his arms anywhere but wrapped around her.

"Nothing," she said. "Even with everything we've yet to do, I'm just...happy."

Gods, was she happy.

She thought about tomorrow. About all the tomorrows they would have. How, for the first time in her life, she looked forward to the days ahead. Even with beasts loosed upon the world, and a missing god set on hunting her, Margrete knew she could face it all.

She had the King of Azantian at her side. But more than that, she was powerful in her own right, with or without the heart of a god inside her.

Margrete Wood changed her fate after all.

Gods and men be damned.

EPILOGUE
THE RETURN OF A GOD

As the stars twinkled their approval, and the red-rimmed moon cast eerie light onto the two paramours, a tremor shook the sacred cavern of Azantian.

This tremor became a humming vibration that loosened the final stone imprisoning what had been locked away for a thousand years.

Barbed tails with silvery scales swam through the shattered crevice leading out to the sea, finally released into the humid air and into the world. With torsos of mortals and spiked fins of fish, they were creatures with onyx souls and merciless hearts.

While they escaped through the rocky portal of their gloomy prison, a king and the woman he loved fell asleep in one another's arms.

Hidden in the shadows, a god who had worn many faces watched with eyes borne from sprays of sea foam and early mornings. This man drank in the woman who had stolen the heart he'd hungered to own for centuries.

The stranger observed as she shifted in the king's arms, her brows growing furrowed as a nightmare took hold. On silent feet, the man approached, reaching out to stroke her exposed shoulder. She was soft, delicate, and unlike anything the ancient god had touched before.

Beneath his fingers, dark ink sprouted, thick spirals of obsidian stretching out to form a massive tangle of whorls and ever-shifting lines. He retracted his hand, eyes narrowed on the tattoo that now marked her bronzed skin.

Malum's final gift to Margrete—

A mark of protection. A lock.

One Darius couldn't open—even to take what was meant to be his.

A growl left his lips. He expected her to wake, but she only murmured in her slumber, exhaustion painting her every lovely feature.

The god drifted back to the shadows from whence he came, unable to peel his eyes from the woman who consumed his every waking thought. He would get what he needed from her, no matter the cost. He would find a way. He always did.

Still, the god felt something other than spite or hatred or anger. A foreign sensation that caused his beating heart to flutter. He'd never felt anything like it in all his many years.

He decided it was a feeling he desired to explore.

And, soon, he would.

The god watched as the king he failed to kill nuzzled her hair, muscled arms encircling Margrete's waist as he tugged her ever closer. His tattoos were settling for the night, the ink he carried weary from the day's struggle. The sea star tattoo danced across his forearm before resting beside the timid squid. The shark swam below the cover of a sleeve.

It was the tattoo on the king's chest that roused beneath the moon, the treacherous nymera depicted across his skin opening her opaque eyes wide. She smiled, and the jagged edges of her teeth poked into her bottom lip.

As the king and Margrete slumbered peacefully, the curves and lines of ink on his chest blurred, the slithery beast of nightmares fading to a place beneath the flesh.

The Soul of Azantian had opened. A god had been reborn. And soon, the human world would know what wickedness truly was.

Thank you for reading! Did you enjoy? Please add your review because nothing helps an author more and encourages readers to take a chance on a book than a review.

And don't miss ON THESE WICKED SHORES, book two of the The Azantian Trilogy, available now. Turn the page for a sneak peek!

You can also sign up for the City Owl Press newsletter to receive notice of all book releases!

SNEAK PEEK OF ON THESE WICKED SHORES

Darius had worn many faces over the centuries of his long, *long* existence, and he'd gone by twice as many names. Yet as he hovered over a sleeping Margrete and her Azantian king, he found himself wishing his *true* name would slip past her lips, for once free of derision or scorn.

He'd forgotten what it was like to feel.

It was both a blessing and a curse that Margrete Wood helped remind him.

For months, he'd infiltrated her dreams, sneaking through the cracks of a fragile reality. Like seeds, he planted thoughts, watering them until they grew. Oftentimes, they served his purposes—to make Margrete yearn for the power she refused to express. He'd witnessed her struggle over the long weeks. She couldn't tame his brother's magic and had no idea *she* was to blame for her own failure—because she didn't remember.

Remember what she once had been to him.

But that had been another life, Darius supposed, and he couldn't fault her for her ignorance. He only recently allowed himself to get close enough to glimpse the familiar soul shining beneath. At first, he'd foolishly believed her to be some unassuming human, lucky enough to have been in the right place at the right time, gifted with the powers of a god. How very wrong he'd been. Darius saw the truth now, and it blinded him.

If only she would remember me.

But she didn't, and she wouldn't—unless he forced his hand.

So, every night he opened his soul—his own magic seeping into her veins, giving her just a taste. Eventually, she wouldn't be able to hinder herself and hide from who she was, and then, she'd take her place beside him. All would be right again.

When dawn chased away the night, Darius would melt into the shadows he commanded. But he never truly left her. Not really.

Not when this woman was the key to his salvation.

Margrete Wood carried Malum's heart, his brother's divine essence. The final boost of power he needed to reign as the sole ruler of the boundless waters. That, and she'd inadvertently stolen something else, something far more precious than his brother's magic. But that would all come to light later. He'd make sure he revealed his cards at just the right time.

Of course, Malum's final act—done just before Darius ended him once and for all—had been to place a symbol of protection upon Margrete's skin, a roiling wave grazing her collarbone. That damned mark made it impossible for Darius to steal her newfound power, but more importantly, it denied him complete access to her mind. Sure, he could slip inside for moments at a time, but he couldn't stay long, and Darius was never fond of being a bystander in a game of his own making.

He decided he'd create a new game.

One with rules *he* could control.

Darius was resourceful, and notorious for bending the rules, and something told him Margrete would be a challenge he wouldn't soon forget. If she was who he knew her to be, then he would expect nothing less.

A smile blossomed as he watched Margrete's eyes flutter in her sleep. Soon their fates would be irrevocably tied together, and he would finally, *finally,* no longer be alone. The thought made a foreign warmth settle in his chest. The sensation was a nice one.

Below his towering shadow, Margrete hooked an arm around the Azantian king's bare waist, her pert nose nuzzling his hair. So at ease, so sickeningly happy. The unconscious act of tenderness made him clench his fists.

The love Margrete possessed for her king vexed him to no end, and when Darius thought too long of it, his vision became painted in red.

That should be me.

During these long months, he longed to reach out and feel the softness of her skin. He'd held back during his nightly visits, afraid of reliving the overwhelming emotion that had assaulted him the last time he touched her. But he grew tired of his role as a silent observer.

Against his will, Darius remained at her bedside until dawn beckoned. She appeared so frail in her mortal body. Weak and easily broken. Still, he felt her spirit, her *soul*, and it sang to him until the early morning hours.

With a frustrated growl, Darius turned to leave, knowing there was much work to be done to fix a mistake committed a thousand years past, but his feet abruptly stilled as though an invisible cord snapped and grew taut. That cord pulled him back to the bed, and this time, when he reached out, he didn't stop himself. He couldn't.

Darius trailed a lone finger down her cheek, the skin just as soft as he recalled. Better, even. She felt like summer itself—warm and light and full of hope. His skin tingled, and his heart pulsed erratically, and in that captured moment in time, memories he hadn't allowed himself to hold onto rushed back to him.

He smiled. Maybe he could right the past and change his future.

Maybe he could have it all.

Don't stop now. Keep reading with your copy of ON THESE WICKED SHORES available now.

And find more from Katherine Quinn at
katherinequinnauthor.weebly.com

Don't miss ON THESE WICKED SHORES, book two of the The Azantian Trilogy, available now, and find more from Katherine Quinn at katherinequinnauthor.weebly.com

A king chased by the demons of his past. A merciless god seeking redemption through bloodshed. And the woman whose very existence defies possibility.

It's been three months since Margrete Wood defeated her depraved father and saved the mystical island of Azantian. But the monstrous creatures released that night have hidden themselves in the human realm, and Margrete and her king set sail to hunt them down.

When disaster strikes on the high seas, Margrete and the crew find themselves stranded on the shores of a new and dangerous island. It's there that they come across an ancient coin, one that legend claims belonged to a powerful goddess. It signifies the first of three deadly trials that must be completed. If they fail these tests, they forfeit their lives to the very place that traps them.

As Margrete and Bash struggle to survive gruesome horrors lurking around every turn, a mighty god watches. He's waited centuries for this moment, and in Margrete, he sees the queen he's been searching for.

Once the third and final coin is found, Margrete and Bash will discover if their love can conquer all... even death itself.

Please sign up for the City Owl Press newsletter for chances to win special subscriber-only contests and giveaways as well as receiving information on upcoming releases and special excerpts.

All reviews are **welcome** and **appreciated**. Please consider leaving one on your favorite social media and book buying sites.

Escape Your World. Get Lost in Ours! City Owl Press at www.cityowlpress.com.

ACKNOWLEDGMENTS

I'd like to first thank my husband Joshua, who made this book possible. I wrote this story when all three of our kids were under the age of three. He was the one who watched our heathens every evening and all day on the weekends, making sure I got the work in. He believed in me when I didn't believe in myself, and whenever I was close to giving up, he'd give me a pint of Ben and Jerry's and tell me to make it work. He's my best friend—even when he drives me absolutely insane—and I'm very lucky to have him in my life.

To my mother—I'd like to thank you for reading every single manuscript I sent your way. Like, all of them. And there were a lot. She's my biggest fan, always has been, and has supported my dreams since I was six and writing my stories in crayon. I love you so much.

It was my grandfather Benjamin Narodick who told me I'd be a writer one day. Well, he first told me I'd be the president, so I hope he's happy with my second choice. I think about him every day, and I miss his light. He was a father to me growing up and the greatest role model a girl could ask for.

To Charissa Weaks, an amazing writer, editor, and mentor. Without you taking a chance on me, I wouldn't be writing this. When I received your letter of representation, I cried. You took a story that needed A LOT of work and made it into something I'm proud of. For that, you will always have my immense gratitude and respect.

To Ashley R. King, a beautiful soul and an amazing writer. You were my personal cheerleader throughout this process, and your hilarious emails made me choke on my coffee every morning. Your positivity and joy are gifts, and I'm so lucky I was able to get to know you.

And to Tina Moss, Yelena Casale, and the entire City Owl team, you've changed my life forever. Words do not suffice to relay my immense thanks.

And finally, a thank you to everyone who has read Margrete and Bash's story. These pages contain my heart and soul, and I can only hope they filled you with joy. You are the reason I write, and for that, my thanks will never be enough.

ABOUT THE AUTHOR

KATHERINE QUINN is a fantasy romance author and poet. She graduated from the University of Central Florida with a degree in psychology. She resides in Houston, Texas with her husband and three children.

Her love for writing began at age nine after she read her first fantasy series, *Song of the Lioness*, by Tamora Pierce. After that, she wanted nothing more than to be a dagger-wielding heroine. Unfortunately, it's frowned upon to give a child a dagger, so she settled on writing about daring adventures instead.

Coffee is her true love, and she believes everything can be fixed with Starbucks and dark humor.

katherinequinnauthor.weebly.com

 instagram.com/Katherinequinnwrites

ABOUT THE PUBLISHER

City Owl Press is a cutting edge indie publishing company, bringing the world of romance and speculative fiction to discerning readers.

Escape Your World. Get Lost in Ours!

www.cityowlpress.com

 facebook.com/YourCityOwlPress
 twitter.com/cityowlpress
instagram.com/cityowlbooks
 pinterest.com/cityowlpress